CHASING LAZARUS

RICK LAWTON

Sasha Press
San Francisco, CA
www.sashapress.com

Published 2010

Published by Sasha Press
San Francisco, CA
www.sashapress.com

ISBN 978-0-9788862-1-9

Library of Congress Control Number: 2009941440

Printed in the United States of America

There is no death.

O'Neill
Lazarus Laughed

CHASING LAZARUS

1

Potato said, "We been out here two days. Sure must be time to go back."

Scab lifted the King Cobra forty-ounce to his lips, took a swig, and smacked his lips. Scab was an inch short of six feet, lean and knobby with lank brown hair, a dirt-streaked face, and sunken brown eyes, a street-weathered, crazy-mean drunk. He peered at Potato's glazed red eyes as if he were looking for the answer. Then he switched his gaze to Sugar's wine-puffed face. He shook his head. "It's about time. In a bit."

"A bit?" said Sugar, frowning so that puffy ridges bisected her forehead. "But it's cold and it's damp, and my butt's cold, and my stomach's rumbling like a damn volcano. We should be back on Haight where it's warm, and there's burgers from McDonalds."

"Don't backtalk," Scab said, scowling.

"Shouldda left by now," said Potato, mashing his oily hair down with a smudged nail-bitten hand.

The three were bent over in a scrape littered with crushed cans, bottles, crumpled papers, and open-mouthed red-and-white takeout cartons near the ocean in Golden Gate Park. That western tag end of San Francisco's three-mile-long park had been abandoned years ago by the crowds, tourists, and museums. Since the 60s, it had remained a spectral place, a place of gay pick-ups, trash, and homeless who burrowed in thick brush hollows.

The three huddled against the fog.

Potato grabbed for Scab's King Cobra, but his hand clutched air as Scab whipped it away. "My turn," said Potato, scowling dumbly.

"There ain't enough left for a good heat," said Scab.

"It's simple," said Potato. "We get some more."

"With whose money?" said Scab.

"Not mine," said Potato.

"Fuck, we knew that. Here."

Scab handed Potato the Cobra forty. Potato hefted it, saw it was empty, crushed it with his hand, and flipped it over his shoulder into the brush. "Thanks for shit."

Scab reached under his coat and ran his finger along the top edge of a paring knife. "So you want to..."

"Yeah, I want to," said Potato, pushing off the dirt.

Scab tried to rise but stopped. They both stopped. All three turned their heads towards the road. Through the tiny tear-drop leaves and gnarled branches, a medium-sized hatchback ground out of the fog. It pulled up in front of the windmill.

The grinding stopped. In the distance, traffic hissed along the Great Highway, and past the sea wall and beach, waves curled dead white on the black ocean.

Scab and Potato crouched down.

"First car I seen tonight," whispered Scab.

"I don't like it," whispered Sugar. "I got a bad feeling about that car. Let's go."

"Hey," said Scab, softly. "I know that car and the guy driving. Lives near the park. Seen him in Tully's. Dealer. What is—"

A man emerged from the passenger side of the hatchback. He looked towards the ocean, then towards the scrape of bushes.

Scab, Potato, and Sugar crouched.

"What's he doing?" Sugar whispered, eyes narrowed.

"Shhhh," Scab said, his finger to his lips.

The man was swarthy, bearded. Satisfied he wasn't being watched, he left the door open and crab-legged past a sign in front of the windmill up to the base. He stooped and leaned a brown valise against the windmill. He backed up a few feet, took out a camera, and a second later a flash brightened the clearing. Then he crab-walked back to the car and slammed the door shut. The hatchback did a U-turn and sped away, but screeched to a stop blocks away.

"What the fuck," said Potato.

"Wait," said Scab.

"Drop?" said Potato.

"Here?" said Scab.

"Don't like it," said Sugar. "Something bad's going to happen."

"Shut up and watch," said Scab.

8

Sugar held her breath. Potato and Scab breathed slowly, occasionally turning and squinting furtively at the hatchback. A few minutes passed, five...

Wooosh.

An intense light lit up the mill and clearing, followed by the sound of a jet engine. Wooden shards rained down. A latticed windmill blade crashed in front of their hiding place. Dust eddied slowly through the shrouded streetlight; tree limbs, shattered, swung in the wind and fell across the road.

"Jesus Christ," Scab gasped. "They just blew up the fucking windmill."

"Wow," said Potato, rubbing his eyes with a dirty fist. "Some fucking blast."

"We'd better get out of here, and now," said Sugar loudly. She started to get up.

Scab pulled her down. "Idiot! Wait till they're gone."

They all turned towards the hatchback, a ghost in the fog and haze. A window rolled down; the pale face of a woman appeared. The window closed. The Subaru sped away.

Scab got up. "My heart must be going a hundred miles an hour."

"My ears hurt," said Sugar, tilting her head right, then left.

"I can hardly see," said Potato.

"Know what?" said Scab, as he surveyed the destruction and the hole in the mill.

"What?" said Potato.

Scab waved away the dust. "I'm going to make us rich."

"Rich?" said Potato, smirking.

Scab snickered. "Not real rich, but we're gonna have lots of Cobra 40s."

Sugar shivered and wrapped her arms around her shoulders. "How so?"

"Going to have a little talk with the guy driving, the dealer, the red-haired asshole. Somebody just handed us a ticket. A ticket to ride."

9

2

Harry Mach had fallen asleep watching the fog swirl in the window. His sleep that night was not restful; he wiggled and squirmed all night, visions of the coming day peppering half-awake moments.

Up, he lurched towards the bathroom and shower. The water sluiced off his body. Steam rose up, and rivulets snaked down the sides of the shower. Harry's mind, blank before showering, became a potlatch of scenes from the previous night with his on-again, off-again girlfriend, Shelly. After orange-braised salmon and chocolate mousse at the high-windowed tony One Market and postprandial drinks at Zuni's dimpled bronzed bar, they'd ended the night in his king-size bed, orally. But his body humming with salmon and brandy, and his mood punctuated with images of Shelly's hair drifting lazily over his thighs, he thought of the Trifecta.

He kicked Shelly out at two, frowning and huffy.

He wiped off the mirror and regarded his crafty Ralph Cramden visage. He was a Jackie Gleason look-alike, but slimmer, tougher, not a down-on-his-luck apple-shaped everyman.

Harry shouted, "To the phones!"

Harry toweled, dressed, and strode down the carpeted hallway of his renovated Upper Parnassus Stick Victorian. Five minutes later, he was in Harry Mach Mode. Wall Street Journal and Times to his left, fifteen-inch Sony laptop in front, burgundy notebook to his right.

Buzzword's stock quotes flickered like a light about to burn out in a corner of the laptop screen: up a point, down a point. In the opposite corner, Coloprobe's quotes held steady at 48.

Trifecta, Leg 1.

Harry's father, Karl, genius and gambler, had his own Trifecta. Karl's Trifecta started, naturally, at the race track. He'd chosen an easy race and had won. Harry didn't expect any less with his Leg 1.

Harry set up for Buzzword, the dot-com social networking site. He'd bought at 2, and it was now up to 100. He had ten clients in it, and they kept coming. The only problem was that Buzzword didn't have a chance of being profitable in 2001. Social networking site? Website hits into digital 1s and 0s in bank accounts? Maybe 0s. The bubble was about to implode. Other dot-coms had tanked; it was only time before Buzzword would too.

Harry set up, and without waiting for the stock to swing up or down, sold it.

Leg 1: Finis.

Harry's juices started flowing. Karl must have felt the same. It wasn't just risk. Was he just a slick businessman, or was he more? Was he heroic in a modern, possibly negative, sense? Of course, once the money was made, the bank accounts full, the accountants and lawyers in place, no one could touch you. He was already a hero to his clients; somehow lately, it wasn't enough. The Trifecta had glimmered at the edge of his consciousness for months.

Trifecta, Leg 2.

Leg 2 was riskier. Yesterday, Coloprobe was at 48, and for Leg 2 of the Trifecta, his ultimate game, it had to reach 50. He decided to prime the pump. He had until 11 o'clock New York time, which was when Coloprobe would announce, sadly, that they were abandoning trials on their device to detect colon disease. After 11 the stock would nosedive and be worthless, another testament to high hopes blindsiding reality.

But what if they announced it five minutes early? Well, that was what they called Risk.

Harry logged onto his account and bought five thousand shares of Coloprobe. He waited for a few minutes and saw the stock edge up as others piled on. Good, good, good. Harry readied his sell order for his two hundred thousand-plus shares. At 7:50 the stock was at 49; at 7:55 it was at 50. He should sell. But he held. 51, 51½, 52.

Squeeze it Harry! Squeeze it!

Harry's thick forefinger trembled over the Enter key. His body strained. He was bursting, his face in the laptop screen tumescent.

Hold it! Hold it!

Harry glanced at the clock. 7:59.

53!

Harry jabbed his finger on the Enter button.

He panted. Sweat poured off his body. He frowned at the spot on his trousers. He got up, his body shaking. He went to the bathroom and cleaned up.

Coloprobe. He'd bought at 5 and sold at 53. Do the math, assholes. It's ten o'clock, and he'd just made ten million dollars for himself and twenty for his clients. That fifteen grand he spent for the tip from the Coloprobe researcher was well spent. Coloprobe: he'd never liked the name, no nuance there. Except others had gotten cornholed, not Harry Mach.

He'd renovated the Victorian when he bought it, opened up the spaces, removed walls, added windows. And when he made more loot, he added something else, something expensive like original Monets, Bose sound systems, or expensive Persian rugs. Not that he needed any of those things. But what else was money for?

Harry shakily made a pot of coffee in his kitchen. His hands never shook, but they did that morning. Ants ran up and down his spine. He steadied his hand to pour into a mug embossed in gold with "Mach Investments."

He held the mug in both hands as he walked carefully back to the dining room. He set up at the table and glanced at the pulsing window of stock quotes, which even then flickered Coloprobe's demise. 2½, 2, 1½. Soon to be grazing in the pennies.

Karl had been a sublime risk-taker. Stratospheric IQ, math whiz, his one fault gambling, in Las Vegas or anywhere on anything. He could count cards in his sleep but knew how to disguise it. After ten years of huge wins at the card tables and bigger losses at the track, he had come up with his Trifecta. It was going to be his crowning glory.

The first leg was easy, the second harder, the third leg riskiest. It was in the storied high-roller Sands poker game. It didn't take the fates passing their eye to know what had to happen. All of that life, all of the bets, all of the adrenalin came down to one hand, where Karl bet it all on aces full, and lost to four deuces. Karl walked solemnly back to his room, wrote a short note to his wife and seven-year old Harry, climbed up on the ledge on the 35th floor, and jumped.

The note mentioned the failed trifecta. Harry only understood what it meant much later.

Harry was born to take risks. Until recently, his risks were calculated and used information, lots of it. At the age of 41 Harry had houses at the Russian River, real estate in Phoenix, millions in U.S. banks, and more stashed in Switzerland. He had a life most people only dream about. He'd failed a few times, the most dramatic when he'd risked condomless sex with his ex-wife and she had produced Jeffrey—his son, a life-time irritation—and trapped him into an annoying marriage which lasted barely four years.

The risk, the game. It wasn't just a metaphor, Harry realized; it was more about life, chance, the one-eyed god cackling at the center of the universe and flipping soiled dice. At one time, he even saw it as the key to evolution, random selection, and adaptation. He didn't muse about it much, because, after all, he was in it. You can't be meta all the time.

Harry mused about his Trifecta, a smile pulling up and releasing his nascent jowls. He was waiting for it; the ground had been tilled. The details didn't come together as a result of collusion or cosmic coin toss. Last month, he saw three projects were going to mature at about the same time. Buzzword, Leg 1, was something he'd thought about for some time. Fifteen thousand bucks to the Coloprobe researcher cemented the exact date of the Coloprobe debacle; more research revealed the hour of the announcement. Leg 3, Wiley Brooks? Wiley was just lucky. He'd thought about another stock for Leg 3, but Wiley had appeared at about the right time with a different game and a different risk and, after worrying about it for days, Harry grabbed it.

When the lucre spills into your account, when the piles of dough reach to the sky, when you perform elegantly in the game, you have to spend it, and you have to tell people about it. Otherwise, what's the point? He called Shelly, his mistress, or, rather, his ex-mistress. She was frosty, but she could be bought, as she was that night for dinner at One Market.

Harry spent the rest of that lucrative morning calling his investors and relaying the good news. By afternoon, he was ready for Trifecta, Leg 3.

Leg 3 was the least lucrative of his Trifecta, but the riskiest, the equivalent of Karl's game at the Sands. Harry knew one thing: he wasn't jumping out any windows.

He punched out the number for a cab on the Elite telephone at the end of the dining room table. No way was he taking the Jag. Harry rose abruptly from his seat. He'd dressed down in slacks, windbreaker, Giants baseball cap, and Bausch and Lomb wrap-arounds. Harry walked slowly down the hallway towards the stained-glass window, which cast its mid-afternoon multicolored glow over the burgundy carpet.

Door, lock, key, straight square steps and street sloping steep into the Haight. Enveloped in his morning triumphs, he'd absently noted the day changing from side and front windows. But now he was out in the day. It was always a shock, the real world. The pesky summer fog had burned off, and it was September hot. Harry liked Parnassus Heights. He liked his big Victorian, the views of Mt. Sutro from the dining room and from the front room of Golden Gate Park shrouded in the distance. He liked the animation. But he was a single, divorced anomaly. Lots of families, lots of kids, schools, and predatory Volvos. He imagined clothes being folded, gardens being dug, sweat, lemonade, and occasional and desultory fence talk of school boards, local politics, Haight Street robberies, a murder.

Harry pulled the cap down over his face.

A few minutes later, his cab skidded to a stop.

The inside of the cab was dark and musty. Harry said, "Oak and Stanyan."

"No problem, Buddy."

Harry glimpsed the baseball cap in the cab's mirror. The hooded gray eyes under his dark glasses flicked right and left. He steadied his eyes and smiled warmly. The driver was a bland sort, forgettable. But was he, Harry, as forgettable? He looked like everyone else, but still. There would be a record. He had a lot to learn about being anonymous, about precautions.

The cab sped down the hill. The driver turned left on Haight, just missing a tattooed raven-haired red-lipped girl in the crosswalk, then shot through the early afternoon Disneyland of Haight Street with its logjams of Greek, African, and Mexican eateries, its crêperies, Ben and Jerrys, second-hand clothing stores, its clumps of pasty-legged tourists, scruffy homeless, pink- and green-haired punks, and scattering of angry winos. It was the usual disconnect in The City. Expensive, staid Parnassus dovetails into the motley Haight, tony Pacific Heights into the crime-ridden Western Addition, world-class-shopping Union Square into the wreck of the Tenderloin; rich and poor shoulder to shoulder marching through the fog towards...Harry lost his thought.

Harry leaned forward and said, "Drop me on Oak."

Harry watched the yellow cab merge with cars barreling downtown before he turned and walked back along Stanyan. Sun flashed through the waving eucalyptus in the park, tantalizing the eye and softening unrelenting traffic. People bunched at the stoplight on Haight and Stanyan and, on green, streamed into the park from Haight Street.

He found Wiley's buzzer and pressed it.

Harry fingered his keys nervously. Whenever he went to Wiley's, part of him felt like turning around and bolting. He'd egged himself on about those deals in the first place, and every time he felt the same. But no risk, no reward. His misgiving right then was whether he should have made his underground dealings with Wiley part of the Trifecta.

He saw a slender space between the door and frame. He frowned and pushed the door open with a thick forefinger. Nothing moved. Harry walked inside and closed the door carefully behind him. No one lived downstairs, according to Wiley. He took in a long breath, regarded the stairs, held the banister, and started up.

Wiley's door was open. Harry frowned. He listened for a moment and then pushed it open. He forced himself to walk into the front room. The blazing light from the front windows blinded Harry.

"Wiley!"

Wiley's flat was always without a redeemable grace note. Dark musty rooms, dark musty hallway, walls adorned in hideous masks, and obscene clown prints done in too-white whites and bright reds, clowns in polka dots, evil-eyed, smirking and winking.

That day, the flat looked trashed. Harry threaded his way through the dark furniture, the black sofas and tables, and rooms littered with overturned ashtrays, bottles, and books, his shadow shortening as he approached the kitchen.

"Wiley!"

In the dark kitchen, he stopped in front of the square yellow table where Wiley usually dished out the dough. Wiley's dark eyes, beneath his fierce widow's peak of snarled red hair, always looked slightly sinister. He had a habit of stroking the ragged attaché case with his long fingers before opening it and taking out the money and pushing it across the table. The last time, after Wiley delivered his share, they'd toasted each other with glasses of Chardonnay.

Harry stopped in the small bedroom. The closet door was open, and clothes and papers were scattered on the bed. It looked like Wiley had packed up and left. What did it mean for his Trifecta? It didn't look good: doors open, flat littered, clothes scatted on a bed. Wiley MIA.

Harry sat in a chair next to the bed and took out his Blackberry. He dialed Wiley's cell.

"¿Por favor?"

"Wiley Brooks?"

"¿Qué?"

Harry clicked off. Wiley had closed his cell account.

Harry wiped his face with a monogrammed handkerchief. He expected something odd from Wiley, but not this. What to do? Was Leg 3 kaput?

"Damn!"

A shadow darted from behind him, caught on the bed covers, tugged on them, and finally lunged to the floor. The black cat turned, hissed, then scrambled into the hallway.

"Shit," said Harry, holding his hand over his chest. His heart thudded. He breathed in and out, steadying himself.

Red fluttered in his peripheral vision. A well-thumbed red book stuck out of the covers.

Harry picked it up, flipped open the cover, and read: Property of Wiley Brooks. Had Wiley in his haste forgotten his address book?

Harry fanned a few pages, frowning. He was squinting at the numbers in the Qs, when the phone at his elbow rang.

Harry snatched it up.

"Hello." Silence. "Wiley?" Harry heard a metallic click as the caller hung up.

A distant siren cycled closer.

"Shit!"

Harry heaved up and hurried down the dark hallway.

3

Judy Ferris had a fantastic morning, the best morning in a year of scattered projects and sparse paychecks. The new owners of the defunct travel magazine Vietnam Today had offered her the managing editor position.

"Slant it," said Peter Gross, the one she knew best, a small fat man in a huge yellow power tie who bore an uncanny resemblance to the Frog in Zippy the Pinhead. Peter was at the end of the table in a boxy room of cinnamon pile carpet and puce walls decorated with posters of vanilla beaches, turquoise ocean, and bronzed, athletic couples. Behind him she could see the reversed lettering of the Asian Travel Association in the door's frosted glass. "Hit the market opening up. Call your writer friends, get them interested—it's Vietnam, after all. I see industrious peasants happy their country is going to market." Peter's eyes narrowed as if he had just seen and dismissed a happy peasant.

"Halong Bay is a magnet," said the small thin one at Peter's elbow, glancing at Peter. The small one—what was his name?—Morris. Morris Blank.

"There's a fortune here," said George, a dapper man in bright red suspenders on Peter's right. George screwed a large ring deep onto a manicured slug finger.

Peter frowned. "We cut the Vietnamese middleman and give them cut-rate packages. Make it peasant quaint and luxury Riv rolled into one."

She'd heard it before. The great American male entrepreneurs laying waste to the fields no matter what or who got in their way. You reached a point where you had to go along. A few years ago, she would have blown them off. Her eyes would have turned flinty; the words would have been harder. She would have lectured them on colonialism, the French, the stupid, interminable American action or war, or whatever it was finally called, the wasted lives on both sides. But she'd given into the inevitable. They wanted her; she needed them.

The money was good, fifty grand a year, travel expenses, work at home. She had reservations, of course, and it wasn't just about politics. The socialist Vietnamese government had arcane rules about foreign business, which meant corruption and black markets. Peter was dreaming about cutting out the Vietnamese middleman.

She'd get rid of her agèd Miata, get that Toyota Corolla, and be a solid citizen.

As she drove back to Corbett, she planned the rest of her day: long workout at Club One, a great meal, a revival at the Castro Theatre—The Usual Suspects, a favorite—and a relaxing nightcap or two at Harvey's. That's why, when she sauntered into the small boxy house high on Corbett she called home, she was surprised to see her answering machine flashing like a Christmas tree. The flashes turned out to be: an article on Cambodia for Travel and Leisure, a press release for a company that wanted to build a disk-manufacturing plant in India, and a few chapters for a Fodor guide to Costa Rica.

Judy sighed. The workout was still on, but she'd have to put the dinner and movie on hold. Lately, the gigs had evaporated, and she needed the money. She shrugged, alternately miffed and surprised, rolled up her sleeves, and went to work.

At three, she realized she'd missed lunch. She didn't want to stop, so she nuked a Lean Cuisine and spooned it into a bowl with a Quetzal motif, shook ten drops of Religious Experience hot sauce into the middle, and stabbed at it while she worked on the Fodor chapters. The Fodor chapters would take the longest, and she wanted to get them done. She had plenty of time to revise and polish.

She was spinning out details of the eco-tour when the phone rang.

It was Khris from the rental they shared in Napa.

"I'm thinking of coming up this weekend," Judy said, cradling the phone between her ear and shoulder and typing in the next subheading. "I'm celebrating." She advanced to the next page and typed: "The Gulf Coast, Birdwatchers Paradise."

Khris said, "I have a little problem."

Judy saved what she'd written. She propped her elbow on the desk. "What?"

There was a pause, then Khris whispered, "You know. Wiley, the money."

Judy backed up and swiveled her chair towards the open kitchen door.

It was bright on the tile floor, subdued outside in the afternoon light. Beyond the rim of grass and the lone pine, a light smog covered the East Bay. Judy sighed, then sifted through what she knew of Khris' idiotic liaison with Wiley Brooks and her more lamebrain "deal." Khris had made at least two lousy choices in the last month. "What about it?"

"I was supposed to call to meet him. Somebody else answered his cell, and when I called his land line, same thing. That time I think it was the police."

"Fuck me." Judy tapped an unpolished nail on the tabletop. She pushed her chair back, got up, and strode into the living room.

The living room: white sofa, white rug, glass table, artfully strewn Condé Nast. Her winged, fanged Garuda, lion's paw raised to strike, wings flared, stared at her from an end table. Above the Garuda, a trio of pointy shadow puppets pretended to clamber up the far wall. Elephant palms, rubbings from Angkor Wat. The room was a perfect counterpoint of action and contemplation. She used to like the room; lately, it seemed too polished, false.

She plopped down on the white sofa. Judy pictured Wiley at a party in his farmhouse across from the one she and Bob and Khris rented. Wiley was smirking. He always smirked. He must practice it. "What can I do?"

"I hate not knowing. Could you call some of your friends or look him up? You're so good at finding things out."

"You know what I think of him. And I don't know who to call."

"I don't know what I'm going to do," said Khris softly.

"Was it a lot of money?"

There was a long pause. It was longer than it should have been. "Enough."

"Jesus Christ."

"I feel hollow, fucking miserable. Everything's coming down on my head right now. Wait...thought I heard Bob. Fuck, what—"

Judy said, "Calm down. What's his address?" Khris gave her Wiley's address and the names of the bars he mentioned in the Haight. Bars? That was it?

After she hung up, Judy threw the phone on the sofa. She stared into the blue/white sky. She'd met Wiley a handful of times and had grown to hate him. She didn't use the word lightly. Wiley seduced Khris and almost willfully destroyed whatever Khris and Bob had. Then Wiley pressured Khris into dope deals. This was the second. It was too dumb for words. Of course Judy Ferris had made her own serious mistakes with men.

Judy walked to the picture window. She felt a funk growing. With a single phone call, she'd slipped from the giddy heights of morning and non-stop industry to a black hole afternoon. Earlier she'd felt alive. She'd laid out ideas and linked them to other ideas. Intro, body, recap. Tagline, image, cutout. It was all so simple and neat.

Judy stared at her PC, then forced herself to sit down and sketch the rest of the Fodor chapter. She kept at it, but after two hours her brain shut down. She sighed, saved what she'd done, turned the PC off, and walked into her bedroom. The bedroom was a tableau of hardwood floors, unmade bed, white wicker ensembles, faux-Tiffany lamps, and—stacked on the white chest—photos of her mother, Stella, sister Jane and kids, and a score of Judy in different Asian locales. A print of Wyeth's "Christina's World" hung over the bed, a symbol of loneliness and hope. It was the innocent Americana wing she told friends, a room where she'd buried the mines so deep, she didn't know when they went off.

A light breeze twirled her curtains above the window succulents. She slid open her wardrobe doors. White feather boas, fantasy spike heels, which she'd never worn, snug-fitting Gap jeans, Rockport hiking boots, pin-striped suits, a leather jacket. What theme could possibly fit her mission? Finally, after rejecting jeans and a white frilly blouse, she decided she felt most comfortable in impish Irish green: green Capri pants, white blouse, jade necklace, and open-toed shimmery green sandals. While she dressed, Judy rehashed her own problems with men who were magicians and opaque power fantasists. She recognized it, she talked about it, but then, almost on cue, she found another one, just like the other one.

Judy walked past her kitchen, flopped down on her white sofa under the shadow puppets, and lit a forbidden cigarette. Leg up, long ankle looking especially well turned, smoke eddying like cosmic dust in the afternoon light slanting in through the door windows.

Rare nexus. The problem was...there was no problem. Fuck Wiley. Judy Ferris was on a roll...and it was about time.

Judy drove down the Twin Peaks hill, up the hill towards Buena Vista, and down to Haight Street. She turned left on Haight, then drove through the Haight–Ashbury Disneyland to the park. She drove past the bars Khris mentioned, the Golden Paradise and Tully's. She found a parking place across from Tully's next to the Wasteland, a second-hand clothing store into black clunky shoes, Goth costumes, and feathery Halloween masks. The street was a ragged collection of homeless, winos, and clusters of punks in green, pink, and red hair teased into Mohawks, tire treads, and spikes. Two blocks away, the street refuse had snuck into the park and were spread out on the grass that sloped down towards the tunnel under Kezar Drive and the eastern entrance to Golden Gate Park. She hadn't been to that end of Haight Street for months. It was a little too dirty and ragged and violent.

She slung her bag over her shoulder, gritted her teeth, and walked through the Cala Grocery parking lot. She read the numbers on the first apartment building and saw that Wiley's apartment was in the next block. She crossed the street and stopped in front of a two-story apartment building. Wiley had a flat on the second floor, but she didn't ring the bell. Bumblebee tape draped across the entrance like bunting on a maypole.

Judy stared at the door, stunned. Something bad. Wiley in jail, Khris an accomplice. She turned on her heel and walked back towards Haight Street, its rainbow glow spread out to her left. Looking east in the late afternoon light, she could see that Haight Street was shifting gears. It was starting to preen and gussy up for the night, the dusk pastels routed by harlot neon, the bars fuller, the punks and bikers louder.

Tully's neon blinked off and on, as if it were trying to seduce her. Bars. You could find out a lot in bars. Rumors. Men. Action. She didn't want to go into that one.

She waited for an old Toyota with hundreds of tiny pink triangular-eyed space aliens glued to the roof to pass, then walked across the street. Tully's white-on-black lightning-bolt décor hemmed in bikers playing pool, punks beating on the pinball, and a scattering of people at the bar, anchored by a latter-day hippie with a gray ponytail near the street window. The hippie's nose was bandaged, and his head was draped in surgical gauze. He hunched grimly over a drink.

Everyone cast a ritual glance at her, but Judy ignored them. She was there on a doomed mission. She perched on an empty stool near the wounded hippie and ordered a Bloody Mary. The bartender was short and round, his eyes big and friendly. There was a ridge on his bald head, as if an axe had dented his skull.

A few minutes later, he placed the drink in front of her. "That'll be four bucks."

Judy dug in her green bag for her light green purse, flipped it open, and found a five. "Thanks," she said, pushing the money across the bar. She closed her purse, but kept her bag on the bar. "You know Wiley Brooks? He's big and rangy with a widow's peak of curly red hair."

The hippie turned towards her. His blue eyes were hard and flinty and punched into the middle of two black circles turning a sickening yellow. He turned back to watch the street.

The bartender's round face fell, enlarging the bags under his soft, brown hangdog eyes. "He jumped off the bridge yesterday."

She glanced quickly at the bartender. He wasn't kidding. Her hand shook while she took a sip of her drink. "I didn't know."

"Was he a good friend?" said the bartender, shaking his head slowly.

"I was looking him up for a friend."

"Ain't that too weird," said the bartender. He hitched his elbows on the bar top, and she saw puzzlement in his face. "The cops said he left his car on a shoulder off the Sausalito exit with a note. Note said he'd had 'business reversals' and was so depressed he couldn't go on."

She sipped her drink and sifted what the bartender said. "Why did they come here?"

"Matches on the front seat. Can you imagine jumping? Holding onto a piling, a football field above the water, cars behind you, people yelling, gulls flying past, the wind flapping your shirt? I get woozy thinking about it."

"I'd do pills."

A big guy two stools down turned towards her. He had black butch hair and beard, a wash of tiny pockmarks, and quick, questioning brown eyes. He was dressed in black sweatpants and a sweaty Columbia University T-shirt. A pair of wrinkled, sweaty handball gloves lay next to a half-full pint.

"You asked about Wiley," the bartender said to the big guy.

The big guy turned to face them both. He scrutinized her and leaned on the bar top. He was faintly predatory. "Hard to believe what he did."

Judy had problems curbing her attraction to big, tough-looking guys. She'd talked about it with Nora Fromm. They decided she was, as were most people about something important, thoroughly ambivalent. She hated macho men, but some tough men, not all, made her feel loosey-goosey. She'd given up rationalizing it.

"Was he a friend?" said Judy. She crossed her legs casually, then grabbed her drink and took a quick sip. She carefully put the drink back on the coaster.

He watched her for a second, as if he were thinking about her very simple question. "Mike Larew," he said, standing and extending his hand. Mike's forearms were muscular, his handshake strong and a second too long.

"Judy Ferris."

"Just met him Saturday, here. What about you?" Mike said, watching her carefully.

On her left, three bikers puzzled over a pool shot. A lightning bolt on the wall in back of the bar pointed at two tall men, who slipped furtively into the alley. She knew bars like Tully's, places where you could slip into the alley, do a line of coke or smoke a joint. You came back with a frisson of pride that you'd done something secret and illegal.

She came back to Mike. "Looking him up for a friend. What about you?"

Mike picked up his beer and flipped his handball gloves a few feet from her. He moved with an athlete's grace and economy. Locker room sweat came with him. Judy took a longer sip of her drink, then turned to him expectantly. Mike rubbed his butch briefly, as if he had to do that in order to get started. He hiked his elbows on the bar. "Chaos makes me feel alive," he said. "Drugs, bikers, punks, street people, winos, and Wiley. He didn't seem like the type."

"America is a big happy family," she said, too sarcastically. "How was he acting?"

Mike shot a glance at her. "You ask a lot of questions." Mike straightened up. He'd been crouching before. Now she saw he was inches over six feet. She felt him pressing down on her.

Judy said, "Just curious. The more I can tell my friend, the better she's going to feel."

"Humph," said Mike, eyeing her narrowly. "As I said, I just met the guy, but he didn't seem like the type to dive off the bridge."

"You got to know him fast."

Mike shrugged away a thought. "Let's just say I'm a people watcher; you are too."

Judy took a sip of her Bloody Mary. "What do you do besides play handball?"

Mike watched her carefully. "That one's easy. Been on the road for a year. You know, my world tour. My Wanderjahre. Saturday, I fly to New York for law school."

She detected a slight accent. "You didn't succumb to the charms of Haight Street."

Mike laughed. It was a shielded laugh. "Not this time. And you?"

"Writer. Mostly travel."

"Any languages?"

"French, Spanish, a little Italian. I used to travel in Central America. Now, it's mostly Asia. No, I don't know Khmi."

"Tu es très accompli."

"Pas du tout. Et c'est pas 'tu,' mais 'vous.' We've just met, Mr. Larew."

"Touché."

"Excuse me."

Judy slid off her stool and walked to the phone at the end of the bar. She was too conscious that people were watching her, even more conscious that Mike Larew had turned and was watching her too. She had to think. Acrid tendrils of dope wafted by her from the alley.

Judy dialed her number and talked into her answering machine, but her thoughts were on Wiley. She didn't like anything she'd seen or heard in the last hour.

After she hung up, Judy regarded the bar. Inside it was heating up: bikers swarmed around the pool table, punks took over a table in back, empty glasses stacked up like miniature forests. Outside, through the front door, the early evening crowds dialed up the noise. Punks slouched past the door. She felt the smallness and oppressiveness of that bar world, of a bandaged hippie sitting like a stone monument at the bar.

She walked past Mike Larew to her stool. She had an inch of Bloody Mary left. She lifted the glass and took a final sip. She shouldered her bag. She looked at Mike. "Nice meeting you."

"We could talk about Wiley some more," Mike said, raising an eyebrow of invitation.

That would be one too many balls in the air. "I have things to do."

"Seems a shame. Maybe I'll see you around."

"I doubt it."

She gave him a quick smile and left. She felt her walk was exaggerated. Invitation, rejection. Were we all side-stepping reality? Why didn't we acknowledge we were ready to lie down and fuck anyone who appealed to us? Would the world be better or worse off? She knew: too many babies, too much emotional strife, too much everything.

She stepped around drunks slouched on the sidewalk. The street traffic scratched at her consciousness. To her left, the park, with its scattering of runaways, bikers, dopers; a motley crew no matter how you cut it. To her right, the shifting tacky mirage of Haight Street.

She popped open the Miata's cranky door. She knew one thing from that night's outing: Wiley Brooks did not jump off the bridge.

4

Harry Mach walked briskly along Haight Street towards the Golden Paradise. The Paradise was the only bar he frequented in the Haight. Years ago when they still met, he took his increasingly snide ex-wife Milly there. She took one look, wrinkled her nose, and said he was slumming. He thought she was thinking of Haight Street itself, which was a post-hippie slum. And maybe he was slumming. He explained it once to curvaceous accommodating Shelly, his ex-girlfriend—sex was good, but afterwards agonizingly dull—that everything was the case. You had to know as much as you could about everything in order to act.

And Leg 3 of his Trifecta?

Harry speculated on that as he threaded through the ragtag crowds.

Inside the Golden Paradise, he shook his head no to the bartender about a drink. Jeff, the day bartender, knew Wiley but hadn't seen him. Harry didn't see any regulars. He felt pissed he couldn't talk to anyone. Jeff told him to check Tully's.

Tully's was six long blocks away, near the park.

Instead, Harry caught a cab back to his flat.

His answering machine flickered at him from the hallway.

He quickly cycled through the messages: two investors congratulating him on Coloprobe; Mark, a glad-handing broker; and an acquaintance, restaurateur Sal Ziti. Sal said it was important. Nothing from Wiley about a hiccup in the plan, nothing about getting together.

He punched out Sal's number.

Sal said, "I'd like to talk to you, Harry."

"Of course. Perhaps at Capriccio's. I love your eggplant. Right now—"

"No, no. It's not a social call or an investment. It's about Wiley Brooks."

Harry blinked. "What? What about him?"

"It's hard to talk about it over the phone."

Harry hesitated, then said, "Do you know where he is?"

"That's the problem."

Harry considered what to do. "I'll call you back in a few minutes."

"I'm on my cell. It's 415-736-8799."

That was curious, too curious. But first things first.

Harry poured two inches of Glenfarclas in a crystal glass, brought out the Sony, sat at his desk, straightened his Elite phone and burgundy organizer. He checked Tully's number online and tapped it out.

When he mentioned Wiley to Tully's bartender, the line went silent.

"Hello?"

"Yeah, I'm here," the bartender said gruffly.

Harry heard shouts in the background, a jukebox, the click of pool balls. "About Wiley?"

"I know he ain't here."

Harry frowned. He knew he wasn't there. Did that mean he did know where he was, or was this just a jocular way of talking? Harry hunched over the phone, his eyes on the laptop with Tully's location, phone number, and quotes from inebriated customers.

"Where then?"

"Cops was here an hour ago. Wiley left his car on a road off the bridge with a note about 'business reversals.' That he couldn't get out of the hole. Said he was going to jump. You know, off the bridge. The Golden Gate. That's number 871."

Wiley a jumper? Not on a bet.

Harry had to know more, and he had to think. He absent-mindedly picked up Wiley's red address book. He paged through it. He didn't see anything right away. Odd scribbles on the blank pages in back: chemical formulas, the word "Algeria," on one page a "K" with an arrow pointing to an "M," on another page three names—Potato, Sugar, and Scab—with red lines through them. The numbers in the Qs looked suspiciously like bank account numbers.

And, of course, his own name with an asterisk next to it. He rifled the address book and saw a handful of asterisks. A fraternity of the ripped-off. On a hunch, Harry looked in the Zs. There it was: Sal Ziti with an asterisk penned next to his name.

Jesus Christ.

He called Sal and told him to come over.

At six o'clock Sal sat on his right, grim and agitated.

Sal was short with a blunt face, big brown eyes, an incipient beard shadow, and a hook-nose. He was likable, excitable, and ran Capriccio's, a solid Italian restaurant in North Beach. He had framed photos of himself with City dignitaries and a handful of B-list actors. They had been friends for years, partly because Harry liked him, and also because they shared the curse of ex-wives. Sal had hinted that he had other darker connections.

The table was empty save for Sal's glass of Pinot and Harry's Glenfarclas. He'd stored everything else in the office with the Bloomberg terminal. The morning's victories cycled back unbidden every few minutes.

Harry said, "About Wiley Brooks?"

Sal ran his sausage-like fingers through his thick black hair. "Well, Harry, I'm fucked. Where's my fifty grand?"

Harry cocked his head towards Sal. "You had a deal with Wiley?"

"You joked that Wiley might be a drug dealer. As a curiosity, I found him, talked to him. I did a few small deals, then—"

"How did you know about me?"

"Wiley said this deal was a big one and you were one of the backers."

"Jesus Christ."

When Harry met Wiley and realized who he was, he was tempted. Drug money, a quick hit. He did his due diligence, if you could call it that. Studs told him Wiley was a former CIA interrogator, that he was dangerous and cutthroat, and was probably doing drug sales on the side.

The next time he saw Wiley, and Wiley mentioned his little deals, Harry went ahead. And it worked! It gave Risk a whole new meaning. Stock market risk was one thing, drug risk another. Each time it gave him a thrill he couldn't describe.

He'd been scrupulous in protecting himself. But there was Harry Mach's name with an asterisk next to it, and Sal Ziti sitting at his table. Harry ran through the possibilities of being found out. So far, only Sal knew of his connection to Wiley.

Harry leaned forward. "For the sake of argument, let's assume I had dealings with Wiley too. Why would you go in on a dope deal? You have plenty of money, a restaurant, a reputation."

"Why did you?" Sal said, shaking his head. "It seemed like easy money. In a sense, it was to pay off Virginia. You know, the alimony. Somehow it didn't seem too bad, if it didn't come out of my pocketbook."

Harry leaned back. He sipped his whisky. "You asked why I did. I'm not sure; it was because I could, I suppose. It was a different risk. Okay, we're both dupes, so let's sort out how duped we are. When was your project—let's call it a 'project' for now—going to happen?"

Sal shook his head back and forth. "Today. I was supposed to meet him in our usual place. He didn't show. I called his cell and it had been disconnected. Some Hispanic voice."

Harry said, "It's obvious in retrospect, the plot of a million movies. We only have one question to answer: What to do now."

"Right, right. But what can we do? The deal's dead."

"According to Tully's bartender, so is Wiley," said Harry. "They found his car and a note. He jumped off the bridge this morning."

Sal buried his head in his hands. "Jesus. Fuck me. Well that's it."

Harry stared down the length of the polished cherry wood table. Out the window the evening fog encircled Mt. Sutro. Sal would come to the same conclusion, if slower; he wasn't an idiot. "A big deal, our money, and I assume others' in Wiley's hand, and he disappears. Suicide? Not Wiley, and not on a bet. He could be in Cabo by now." Harry paused and looked at the Monet on the wall. Its pastels, its softness always calmed him, made him back up and sort his choices. "Or not. Chance has given me his address book. Curious, isn't it, how everything seems to go smoothly...what's the cliché, like clockwork, except it never goes like that. More like a broken cuckoo clock obeying a whacko algorithm. Back to Wiley. There's an outside chance he needs his address book."

Sal's eyes got wider as Harry talked, then he frowned as if he were working out what Harry had said. "Do you think he'd come here?"

Harry inclined his head towards Sal and shook his head. "About the address book? Our exchange was at his flat. But he's not going to think of me, at least first. Too many assumptions."

"I suppose not."

Sal looked worried. Harry said, "You're puzzled, and it's not because of Wiley."

Sal grimaced. "The tail's missing."

Harry frowned. "Tail? What tail?"

Sal looked at his stubby fingers, then at Harry, as if he had a revelation, which he did. "It wasn't all my money."

Harry frowned. "What?"

"Half of the money was from Vito Mongreve. I owed him and mentioned this deal. He put up half my part, twenty-five grand. But he insisted on insurance and had Wiley followed."

"How?"

"Wiley told me where he lived. I told Vito what he looked like, his red hair. He wasn't difficult to find."

"Which could have spooked Wiley." Harry thought about that for a few seconds, then said, "Probably not. This was well planned. What happened to the tail?"

"He was supposed to report and rotate this morning. But no guy. Vito is pissed."

Harry shook his head. "Could this get fucking worse?" Sal, Vito, the tail missing. Fuck. "Do you think—"

"You don't double-cross Vito."

Harry mused aloud, "Wiley and the tail, both."

Sal put his hand on Harry's arm and said, "Thanks for talking to me, Harry. It makes me feel better that I'm not alone. You're smart; you'll figure out something."

"It looks grim right now," said Harry. "But before I throw up my hands in surrender, I need more information, and I have to think."

"I'll talk to Vito," Sal said finally. "He'll have an idea; it might not be one that we like."

"If Vito has a problem, let me talk to him."

Sal got up. "Maybe. Vito isn't the easiest guy to deal with. Well, Harry, it looked worse when I came in, but now we have options, especially with that address book."

"Let's not get giddy. It might be something he needs, and it gives us something, however small. But right now we're out of the game." He should bail. He hadn't expected Sal and Vito...or the tail. The last thing he needed was to get tangled in some neo-noir thriller.

If nothing else, it looked like Leg 3, the Trifecta linchpin, was fading with the fog.

5

Marant Olivier switched off the oxyacetylene torch. He popped back the heavy hood. He took off the hood and snagged it on the hook near his solid steel workbench. His neck was in a vise. He twisted his head and neck to the right. He felt pain, which gradually subsided. He held the position for thirty seconds, then he twisted to the left and did the same. At the middle point, he dropped his head onto his chest, held it for a few seconds, then arched his head towards the ceiling of the garage.

He massaged his neck with both hands. His hands were long, almost feminine, but exceptionally strong. His looks—tall and lean with long black hair, black eyes, and aquiline nose—belied a physique as tempered as the steel he worked with. Years ago, he was at the top of his class in the Commando Hubert trials. Commando Hubert, the French equivalent of the American Navy Seals and the British SBS, was the most physically demanding of the French commando units. He still kept in shape by swimming two miles every day, working out, and of course, fashioning his sculpture.

While he rubbed his neck, Marant assessed the piece. Two ragged figures on a two-foot-square piece of steel. The figures were thin, jerky, spidery, linear. Giacometti resonated in his spirit, accenting a dour vein of existentialism. When he thought deeply about why, it went back to his parents who were tortured and killed by the Nazis. He thought, in those rare times, that any chance to be romantic died when they died. But like most people, the opposite attracted. He loved, or desired, curves, lushness, the cliché "biomorphic." The Le Monde critic, Berseau, loved his work, but called it retro. The French had become a nation of analysts, critics, and consumers. But curves. Curves were romantic, lush, full of life. Curves were feminine, women he loved, or caressed. His body, his soma, loved curves, and his spirit loved curves, or wanted to, and his hands made spidery straight lines on empty planes.

Marant walked into his yellow-walled Monet-inspired kitchen massaging his neck.

He stopped when he saw his black answering machine. The blinking light signaled a message. He walked over and looked at the read-out. One message. He felt a twinge. He hesitated answering it. He sat at the wooden kitchen table. Out the window to the north a quarter mile away was the small town of Fort Mahon. To the west was the flat Normandy beach with its treacherous tides, shifting dunes, and pervasive sand. He'd walked on that beach with his parents fifty-plus years ago, hand in hand, thinking of some happy future time, or not thinking at all. He could stay in Paris and rent a studio or live anywhere else, but his spirit was in Fort Mahon.

On the beach, a rivulet snaked around two tourists basking in the sun. In fifteen minutes, they would be surrounded by water. Five tourists had been lost last year from drowning in irregular patches of quicksand. Somewhat like life, Marant thought. Erratic. The rivulet was twenty feet wide and widening.

Marant walked through the house and out the front door.

His tread was even, even though his feet sunk in the sand giving him the rocking motion of beach walkers. It felt good getting out. He'd been working for over two hours without stopping. He'd always been like that: once started, he had to finish.

He realized, and not for the first time, that living on the beach encouraged the starkness of his sculpture. It was not lush. It was a flat horizon, a horizon of memories. A few gulls swooped beyond the breakers; sun and clouds made shifting shadows on the slate-gray ocean.

He yelled to the vacationers, "Messieurs, faites attention!"

One raised up and turned on an elbow, saw the water, and soon both were splashing waist-deep through a rivulet growing into a small river.

Marant walked slowly back to his house. He knew he shouldn't go near the answering machine. He could put it off, pretend he'd started his vacation in England.

He stared at the blinking light for a split second before tapping the play button.

"112.13.4335."

Ah, yes, a second message from Christian. He hadn't heard from him in over a year. Then inside a week, two messages. The first was in clear text, the subtext ominous. The second a coded number, the subtext opaque. A subtext, opacity, and riddles. Odd how innocuous things such as numbers had such import. Life and death. Elected or not. They were representations of course, emanations from our spirits. Nothing in themselves. But one had to deal with significance, implications.

A distant part of his psyche scratched at his consciousness. Rationally, he hoped he'd never hear from Christian again. But there was the irrational. Opposites attracting. Curves and straight spidery lines. At Paris salons, galleries, openings, when he should have thought only of his art, of a growing recognition, Christian and RM haunted him.

He added the first three digits, subtracted them from the last number, divided the result by five, and added that to the middle number. He brought out his Paris par arrondissement.

Tuesday. Invalides.

Marant went to the refrigerator. He poured himself a glass of Fumé Blanc, but paused at his reflection in the window over the sink. The welding hood had swirled his slick, black hair, but his appearance was much the same. His eyes betrayed him, as eyes always do. What RM gave him, however ambiguous, was purpose. Art was never enough.

The next day, despite doubts, regrets, and a postponed trip to England to admire Henry Moore's sculptures at Perry Green, Marant drove to Paris. His ambivalent mood hadn't improved on the drive, but that night he felt calmer when he slept in his apartment on the Rue de la Convention. The next day he ate at his favorite restaurant—Les Oiseaux—and, later, watched the inevitable jeu de boules in the exquisitely manicured Le Jardin de la Convention.

He took a long late afternoon nap.

His naps were usually filled with images of spidery sculpture, of vanishing curves, or his spare garden, or the most innocuous overflow of the day's meals, radio listened to, or book read. It was easy, sometimes too easy. Too insignificant.

That night his dreams were full of the past, the deep past. The first time he'd worked for RM years ago, of hot poverty-ridden South American lands and hot tribal deserts, and others, of Afghanistan, and of North Africa and the Atlas Mountains. A handful of times and a handful of dispersed places he'd used his peculiar skills. When he awoke, he wondered, as he'd wondered more since his retirement, whether any of it did any good. Or whether he was just part, a necessary part, of a process, of opposition necessary to any conflict.

At six, Marant walked through the Fifteenth Arrondissment, then down the Boulevard des Invalides. He went to the Orchestre de Paris at Salle Pleyel. That evening they featured works by, as usual, French composers: Rameau, Saint Saëns, Debussy. The music was otherworldly, mystical, and made him think of Fort Mahon and a life that was easy, almost idyllic, but ultimately barren, an almost-empty plane inhabited by a few spidery figures.

He ate dinner at a restaurant in Les Halles, then walked back in a balmy Paris night towards Rue de la Convention. He met Christian in La Soirée on the Boulevard des Invalides. The smoke from Christian's smoldering Gauloise angled towards the dull yellow canopy and past the red street sign. The street was almost deserted. A scattering of couples held onto the night. Marant ordered a Ricard and waited for the waiter to leave his drink.

Christian was a large man with a beet-red face, strong hands, graying silver hair, and a penetrating intelligence which showed itself in eyes that moved constantly. It wasn't his intelligence which made him a leader; Christian had a personality that engulfed people. He'd known Christian for thirty years. Christian was the former head of l'Action directe, the French revolutionary movement, before he started RM.

Christian looked at him and shook his head. "The Muslims," Christian said, frowning.

It was all Christian had to say. Christian was the scion, then inheritor, of great wealth from his grandfather, then father. Christian, educated in les grandes écoles, was radicalized in the 60s and became that rarity: someone who moved easily in French society, but who was a radical and romantic at heart. Twenty-five years ago, Christian brought many of the revolutionary groups in Europe, the Middle East, and South America together in a collective where they could trade information and tools.

Marant was astounded it lasted. The groups he brought in had different, in some cases opposed, goals. What did the IRA, Red Brigade, ETA, l'Action directe, and Baader-Meinhof have in common? Christian insisted they shared a key ingredient: opposition to a well-armed, entrenched, mostly capitalist, status quo.

At times, Christian was acutely aware of the contradiction of a capitalist trying to destroy a capitalist status quo. He explained it as the ease with which the human animal shuffles ideas and actions into thick-walled compartments.

A handful of years ago, against many objections, Christian brought in the Muslims.

Marant mixed water with the Ricard and it became milky, a fitting counterpoint to the point he was going to make. "I told you to be careful of GIA, the Egyptian IG, or the Islamic League, the PLO split-offs, Hamas, al Qaeda. They are crazy, fanatical, goons, or all three. Religious fanaticism scrambles the brain."

"I was considered a fanatic once," said Christian, a smile of resignation on his face. "Or, rather, I considered myself one."

"You were—are—principled, or at least I understand your principles. I wouldn't have worked for you otherwise. Sometimes that doesn't matter. Remember, you urged me to retire?"

"You were ready. You'd become too jaded."

It was true. The impossibility of their struggles, of doing anything

34

that had a hint of truth or nobility overwhelmed him. He saw now that it had started years ago when he'd assassinated a Russian general in Afghanistan. He helped save the country from the Russians for the Taliban!

Marant shrugged. "Now that we've exhumed my old spirit, what's the problem?"

"The details overwhelm the big picture. An American chemist contacted an RM operative in Algeria. The note was about a process for making a new explosive similar to RDX that combined properly would make a more powerful Semtex."

Marant frowned. Bombs. He tried to concentrate. He disliked bombs. He had an image of arms and legs, detached, waiting for someone to assemble them into a living, breathing entity. They'd started using women, girls, the ignorant. The smart ones never died, only the deluded and the innocent. "He wants to sell it to RM?"

"Who knows what his motives are? Perhaps he is a disgruntled scientist. Perhaps a corporation stole his patent. The last is the story I was given." Christian paused. There were volumes written in that pause, and Marant couldn't read everything. "Merde! Putain de merde! I don't know," Christian said, wagging his head from side to side as if it hurt. "This process is the key to something. It's obvious it's not what they say it is."

"The Muslims." Marant let that hang in the air.

Christian lit another Gauloise and regarded its smoke, which formed, briefly, a shifting barrier between them. "Perhaps. Probably. I don't know what to tell you. I asked you to come because you are my friend and confident. I wanted to talk to someone I trust."

"What about Mirabeau, your second in command?"

"Disappeared. He was last in Toulon."

Marant's eyes narrowed. Worry etched a thin line in the middle of his forehead. He didn't know Mirabeau well, but he was Christian's confident. "I don't like that. What of your contacts with the IRA, or ETA, or the new head of l'Action directe?"

"My old guard. You know l'Action directe is a shade of its former self. They sit around and talk anarchist theory. I have calls into Brody and Stavros. No one has called back. What are the Muslims doing? I feel—feel, mind you—that this business of a new explosive is a charade. I don't understand why. You're helping me figure it out by just being here."

He had worked for Christian and RM for decades, sometimes as Christian's confident and lieutenant, often alone, as an assassin for hire. Once he'd stopped a coup and saved Christian's life. Their official relationship had changed over the years, but he would always be Christian's friend. Christian was his one failing: after a certain level of cynicism or consciousness of reality, especially of what you do, you don't trust anyone. He trusted Christian.

Marant regarded Christian. They were on another level, the level of hunches, of sorting loyalties, of matching everything against a shifting sense of values and priorities. Marant hated it. He loved it at the same time. He started feeling a little of what he felt years ago when Christian sent him on his first project. At one time facing death, he thought he'd done it all because of his parents. How brave they were! Surrounded by implacable enemies who will torture and kill, one makes the sacrifice. It was about nobility. It was about standing up.

Marant said, "Why do you think it's a ruse? And why do you still want to go along?"

"A feeling."

"They want your supply lines, your information, your bank account."

"I've thought of that, of course. The problem is that I think I can hold on."

"I'm surprised it lasted this long. Of course you knew that. Tell me about this explosive."

"It's complicated, too complicated. The Muslims sent one of their own from Algeria—Kafi Bella, GIA—to look into this explosive. He reported it was as described, but I didn't think that was enough. I talked to ETA, and they sent one of their own, a woman, Teresa Ahuestia, to look into it from, one could hope, an objective perspective."

"Objective in that they both could use a better explosive."

Christian waved his hand. "Once you buy into the idea, the rest is details. Speaking of details, it now gets cloudy."

"I didn't expect anything else."

"The Algerian thought the best way to prove this explosive was as advertised was to blow something up. I suppose he had to prove it to us. So they found a remote part of the city—"

"City?"

36

"San Francisco."

Marant laughed. "Remote part? Nothing's remote there."

"Near the ocean, the fog, early one morning." Christian shrugged. "It was Bella's call. He obviously called badly. In any event, they had their test, and then complications ensued."

Marant frowned. Why was he getting all this background? "Police? FBI? CIA?"

"I think the authorities are treating it as a prank."

"It makes a good story."

"Indeed."

Christian reached in his pocket and threw a handful of papers and clippings on the table.

Marant picked them up and read them. The papers were reports in a trade journal of a new formula for a powerful explosive, which had been developed by the Mirador Corporation. The caption of a clipping read, "Windmill Damaged by Mysterious Explosion."

Marant read the articles quickly. He looked at the clipping of the windmill again. He threw the papers and clippings on the table. He took a long sip of his Ricard and placed his glass on the table. "One. You know I think explosives are stupid. You have to convince people not blow them up. Two. I find it hard to believe this Mirador corporation sent out a press release of a new explosive. Three. The chemist. It's not easy to sell industrial secrets, especially in Europe, and even more especially through North Africa. How did he know who to contact?"

"I agree with your points. Still."

"I'm glad to help you think this out. Is that all you want from me?"

"No. After I agreed to buy the formula, there was a complication. I don't know the details. The chemist refuses to hand over the formula until the complication is dealt with."

"And the complication?"

"I'm not sure. I was going to send Rafael to buy the formula, but Oman and Osama suggested you were needed for this complication. You can find out what the complication is and deal with it without attracting attention."

"Everyone is so trusting. Yet you feel it's not about a formula."

"Back to intangibles. Before Mirabeau disappeared, I heard things, felt things. The purpose of RM is slipping away. It was difficult enough to keep it together for twenty-five years. Perhaps I am holding on to something which should die a quick death."

"And you want me to..."

"Find out what is going on. Verify as much as possible that this formula is real. And if necessary, dispose of the complication. Give Kafi, or the Basque, the Swiss account number. Let them do what they want with it. Leave. You will get your usual compensation."

"Even when I helped with your internal political problems, I had specific targets, a goal."

"I would never risk anyone's life needlessly, especially yours, old friend."

As soon as it appeared as if he were going to take the assignment, Marant realized his doubts. The same doubts assailed him two years ago. "The compensation has always been a sore point for me. One wants to appear noble, righteous. But that's a problem you can't solve. I have another problem."

"Your growing cynicism? That sense of hopelessness?"

"It was why you urged me to quit. And I still feel it. But there's more. It's that I'm older, and changed. I've grown into a life of making sculpture, a modicum of fame, sipping white wine at openings. My life is settled, easy; I don't feel fast or intrepid."

Christian frowned. "Your last assignment went well."

"With the usual ambiguity. A dictator dies, the reprisals are bloodier. Che thought that was the way revolutions start. Instigating the bloodiest reprisals makes the revolution inevitable. You know what I think of that."

Christian looked troubled and shook a Gauloise out of the crumpled blue pack. "I hadn't realized. I've been training someone else, but I don't think he's ready. And I don't know a French commando with your sympathies." Christian laid his hand on Marant's sleeve. "The more I think, the more I hesitate."

"He who hesitates is lost. I'm bored. When you can't solve your own riddles, you take on someone else's." Marant got up. Christian stood. They embraced. Looking deep into Christian's eyes, he knew he'd decided to go ahead. He knew equally it was futile, possibly his last assignment. "Perhaps I'll discover the secret of the curve."

6

Monday, after making ten million dollars on two impeccably executed Legs of his personal Trifecta, had come Leg 3. Harry Mach had done his research. He knew who he was dealing with. He'd dipped his toe in illegal waters before—and twice with the flare-haired Wiley Brooks. He'd agreed to medium-sized dope deals, fronted the money, waiting breathlessly, and finally picked up the reward, the prize, in Wiley's clown-themed, dingy Haight flat. And it was exciting, a rush...more rush than shaving points or shorting stocks. It had an edge and biting, heart-stopping risk.

When Harry Mach thought about it, about why he did things, which, latterly, had been more frequent, he thought of his father. So much of what we do, he mused, is either following or reacting to one parent or another. When Karl bested two pair with trip deuces and won the biggest pot of the night, it wasn't enough. There was always a bigger thrill, or pot, or risk around the corner. Was that what made him, Harry, tick? Possibly. Many businessmen worked hard at their little service or company. He was successful because he saw every venture as a game. It gave him the proper distance; it allowed him to manipulate, to maneuver, to place the elements exactly in place.

Harry was in the game from the first day he stepped into the playground at St. Boniface to the pinnacle of Mach Investments. He owed his success to greed, motivation, and game-playing brains. Hard-core criminals had greed and motive but lacked any brains beyond a street-level sneakiness.

Tuesday morning he woke up with a hangover, completely self-induced. The mirror confirmed everything. He was Jackie Gleason mimicking Fred Basset, minus fur.

Staring at his visage in the mirror, he felt hesitant. Or, rather, it was an unaccustomed feeling of incompleteness and dread that ebbed and flowed around Monday. Everything should have been fantastic. Trifecta Legs 1 and 2 were impeccable; he was rich, or richer, and yesterday should be enshrined in the Dealmakers' Museum.

Leg 3? He knew deep in his consciousness where he tweaked risks, legal and illegal, that he should hand in his tokens. But there were complications. Sal, Vito, and the missing tail, for example. They were just the kind of complications he avoided, or should avoid. And, after reflection, he should call Leg 3 a lost cause.

But Difecta? It sounded like a Coloprobe dump.

Harry, his spirit in unusual abeyance, walked into the dining room/office. He regarded the end of the table and the early morning fog swirling in the window, before sitting and cranking up the Harry Mach circus: WSJ, Times, Chronicle, laptop, phone.

Harry opened his spreadsheets and lost himself in the columns and rows, the displayed numbers, and calculations. He transferred money from his accounts into his clients' and emailed more good news. He called the few big ones left. A hundred thousand here, a million there. Everybody was happy; everybody loved Harry Mach, Master Investment Consultant.

In late afternoon as the glory of Monday's triumph ebbed, Leg 3 yo-yoed back. Wiley had fleeced him and a handful of others. But Wiley was onto something else, something, the more he thought about it, more insidious. An hour after he met Wiley, after tapping Greg, a lieutenant on the SF Police force, and Studs Markus, a retired CIA officer, he knew a lot more about the mysterious Wiley Brooks than Wiley thought he knew. He'd smiled inwardly when he picked up his cash on the drug deals, sharing a drink with Wiley over his kitchen table, as Wiley smirked and puffed his chest about his deals. Harry tried to see who the real Wiley was behind the masks. And Wiley did like masks—clown masks and clown prints in apple reds and glaring whites. Harry felt Wiley was playing with everyone, and liked playing with everyone.

Yes he knew a lot about Wiley, his time in South America, Wiley the interrogator, Wiley the drug dealer. But as for the contours of what Wiley was doing in the last few days, besides the dope deal, he had nothing.

He was doodling about that in his planner when the phone rang.

Sal said, "Harry, let's meet. I've talked to Vito. He made some calls."

Harry frowned. "Of course, come over; we can flagellate each other."

Harry blinked at the light in the window, his dried floral display on the small table, his soft Monet print. Harry walked meditatively to his built-in liquor cabinet. His soft fingertips touched his amber single malts, a rare tequila, a scattering of dusky bourbons.

He poured two inches of Woodford in a clean tumbler and drank half of it. It was hard going down, then hot.

Even though he expected Sal, the door buzzer startled him.

Harry walked slowly down the Persian rug, past his dark, framed prints. He pressed the buzzer, letting Sal in. He walked quickly to the top of the stairs.

Sal walked slowly up the stairs as if he were Sisyphus shouldering his boulder. He looked at Harry, smiled grimly, and patted Harry on the shoulder. Sal looked behind him at the man climbing the stairs and said, "Burt, Harry."

His "friend" was shorter than Harry and had a square neat face, watery blue eyes, a fading tan, and a blond ratty ponytail. He had on a patchy black windbreaker, work shirt, faded black jeans, and black scuffed shoes.

"Harry Mach," Harry said, proffering his hand.

Burt looked him up and down, then said, "Hey man." His grip was wet and limp.

Harry wiped his hand on his pants as the three of them trooped into the dining room. Burt slouched ahead of him, cocking his head briefly at his dreamy Watteau on the wall and glancing down the hallway to the kitchen. Sal walked around the dining room table and sat. Burt circled the table, pulled out one of the chairs, turned it around, and sat with his arms crossed on the top of the chair at the foot of the table, fifteen feet away.

Harry said, "Gentlemen. Drink? Scotch? Bourbon? Beer? Coffee?"

Sal waved his hand. "Nothing for me."

"Maybe later," said Burt.

Harry sat. Burt brought himself to attention and hunched over the end of the table. "Harry, I'm what they call a fixer. Vito wants me to sort this out. Get it?"

Harry didn't like the way he said "get it." "Okay."

How long would this take? Leg 3 was moribund, and the post-mortem was showing him how moribund. He was curious about Sal, and Vito, and now a soi-disant "fixer." Harry turned to Sal. "What about the tail?

Is he back? Did he report anything?"

Burt frowned, cocked his head to one side and said, "You know about the tail?"

Harry lifted his shoulders and pointed to Sal.

"Yeah, right," said Burt.

Sal shook his head sadly. "I told him yesterday. I said he was missing."

"Okay, okay." Burt looked meditatively at the Monet. He turned back and spoke to Harry. "Lemme field this one, Sally. A hiker, I think Vito said a hiker, saw this guy, the tail, spread over the rocks near the Cliff House. Of course they didn't know it was the tail at the time. Just a guy on a rock. Took a while to get him outta there. You know the surf, rocks, fog. The guy got it good. Everything broken, and get this, his eyes were eaten out by gulls."

"Dead?" said Harry, staring. "How did Vito find out?"

Burt smoothed his blond hair back with his hand. "Not that it should matter to you, but the guy had Vito's card in his coat. The cops tried to give Vito a rough time, thought he might have done it, because, well, Vito has a rep. Vito thinks he got too close to this Wiley, and Wiley killed him. That's why Vito hired me. I find Wiley, give him to Vito, then..." Burt drew his forefinger across his throat dramatically.

"Christ," said Harry. Wiley was capable of that. He'd seen it in his eyes, in the coarse way he handled people, and in the Stud's report. "Of course. But the tail dead and Wiley a possible suicide. What's the point?"

"Nobody thinks Wiley's dead," said Burt. "You don't."

"So what?" said Harry, shifting uneasily in his chair. "He could be in Honk Kong, or Helsinki...he could be anywhere."

"Kinda leaves us looking for a phantom, or a vampire, for sure," said Burt, nodding.

Vampire?

"Listen, Harry," said Sal, "Vito hired Burt to help. What have we got to lose? He helps us for a few days and see what happens."

"I'll think about it," said Harry. Kiss Leg 3 goodbye. Of course, he had Wiley's address book, but so what? He could give it to Burt and let him try to figure out the formula, the mysterious Ks and Ms, the names with thick red lines through them.

Burt turned to Sal. "Doesn't Harry have Wiley's address book and knew Wiley longest?"

"Harry mentioned Wiley a month ago," said Sal.

"I don't remember," said Harry. "Perhaps."

"I'd like to talk to Harry for a few minutes...alone."

Sal looked at Burt, then Harry. "You okay with that, Harry?"

Harry shrugged. "I don't see what's left to do, but I'll help any way I can."

"What a fucking mess," said Sal. He got up, gave Harry's shoulder a quick squeeze, angled around the table, then walked slump-shouldered down the carpet. His wavy black hair descended the stairs slowly then disappeared.

Harry turned back to Burt, just as Burt took a silver handgun out of his faded black windbreaker. He put the gun on the table and twirled it. It spun in an irregular orbit, flashing in the fading light.

Burt looked at him and said, "Why did you do it, asshole?"

Harry's heart pounded; sweat formed on his head and trickled down his neck.

He felt hot and cold at the same time. Time stopped. There was an infinity in that short time where, were he interested in anything but that gun, he could have taken trips, read a novel, or just mused about life. His Trifecta seemed silly, sillier than ever. If he was going to die, why should he care about a hash mark on a scorecard?

The gun spun slowly, its black muzzle drilling him, then whipping away. "What?"

"You and Wiley. Vito and Sal's money, you fuck."

The silver gun rotated slowly. Harry flinched.

"No, no...I'm an investment consultant. I have clients, stocks; I read business reports..."

"And you needed money. We all need more. Isn't that right, fuckwad?"

Harry gripped the table. Everything wrong, wrong. His voice boomed from a forgotten survival space. "I don't need any fucking money. I did it for pocket change and...and the thrill."

"You know what kind of a hole my friend here makes," Burt said, nodding at the flashing gun. "Tears you to pieces. There's pain, lots of it, then the blood kinda drips out, and you fade away. Now give, where's Wiley?"

His body was dissolving. He felt insane. He shrieked, "How the fuck would I know? He just stole a fucking hundred thousand dollars from me. I lost more than Vito and Sal together."

Burt examined him, as if he were looking into his soul. The gun spun slowly then stopped, its barrel pointing directly at him. "I didn't think you did anyway. And you don't have to swear, Harry. I knew right away you were too soft to double-cross anybody."

Soft ?

Burt picked up the gun, pointed it at Harry, and said, "Bang."

Burt's body shook with laughter. "What a scene, man...ha, ha, ha... didn't think I could pull it off...ha, ha...you know it takes a sense of theatre; it takes balls...ha...look, genius, it isn't loaded. Got it from a friend." Burt stuffed it in his windbreaker, where it made a small hump. "You know, I just wanted to show you. You think you're a tough jungle type with your fucking papers and laptops. But I guess we saw who you really are. Say, got a beer?"

Harry wiped off the sweat from his neck. "What?" He couldn't believe everything was all right, that Burt had played him. "Of course." Harry started to get up.

"Stay; Wiley's for sure gonna be hard, but I can find the kitchen."

Burt came back with two Eel Pale Ales, which he lined up on his end of the table.

"Saves getting up."

Burt put the top of the first bottle between his teeth, ripped off the cap, and the cap rattled to rest on the table. Then Burt took out a joint, licked the end of it, and lighted it. Harry watched the smoke rise past the window. Outside it was darker; faint shadows covered Mt. Sutro.

"Want some?" Burt said, holding out the joint to him.

First an enemy, now buds. "No, no."

Harry was tense, his back stiff, his face cool where he'd wiped off the sweat.

Harry was good at identifying people, who they were, what they wanted, whether they could stomach risk. Burt seemed tough, violent, but had quickly become a question mark. What about the casual attitude, the joint, the beer?

"Nice place you got here, Harry."

Harry breathed slowly, calming himself. "I get by."

"You own it?"

"With a mortgage," Harry lied.

"Well I don't own anything. And you know what, never wanted to. I don't worry about it. Right now, it's me, myself, and I. Mr. Free Bird, just like the song. That's the way I like it."

Harry didn't know what to do with the stoned weak-eyed ponytail bolting down his ales and babbling fifteen feet away at the bottom of his table. But it looked like they were going to be there for awhile. Harry got up and poured himself two inches of Woodford.

After he sat and took an extra belt of bourbon, he got these nuggets from Burt:

"Cool shit, man. I hate the fucking room, but soon..."

"Fucking girlfriend...you know, wanted it all, the ring, the noose..."

"Ya know, families are shit...never knew what happened to mine... one day..."

"Hey, man, you gotta come to Donnelly's; it's my new watering hole..."

"The last gig was a bust, but this next one is the last; it's a big payout..."

The rest of that hour should have been the worst in his life, but it was painful in its monotony. Halfway through Burt's barely coherent monologue, Harry found that Burt's parents had divorced when he was ten, his father died of a heart attack at 50, and his mother was an alcoholic in Stockton. Beyond the clichéd familial dysfunction, Burt had his own fragmented history: a college dropout, a succession of low-paying jobs, and a recent spat with a girlfriend led to a single room in a North Beach SRO. And Burt, obviously, didn't know much about "fixing" anything. The only bright spot, if it could be called that, was being the former boyfriend of Vito Mongreve's granddaughter.

Harry had been sitting near the edge of his big chair. His body strained. He'd listened to Burt, and listened. Burt, casual and stoned, had caused this tension, this rigidity. He was simple and possibly loutish—at least that was his first impression—with a dash of pretend violence.

45

Harry's thoughts were a mish-mash: the "tail" spread-eagled over a rock, the gulls dining on his eyes, Burt's silver gun rotating, rotating, its black hole aiming at his stomach. The blood, the slow death. Burt's stoned babbling.

Harry realized, finally, he was mad. Mad that the idiot at the end of the table smoking a joint and twirling a brown Eel Pale Ale bottle made him sit on the edge of his chair, made him mute, made him a captive in his own home, his oasis, his palace.

He was Harry Mach. No one played him.

Harry examined that moment in the next few days, occasionally admiring what he did with a macho pride, then wondering whether that was the moment he'd trapped himself and made the rest of that ill-fated week inevitable.

"I'll be right back." Harry got up and walked slowly into his kitchen. He stood, the news draining over him from the built-in TV, the glow making a faint shadow on the island behind him, his hands clenching and unclenching. Finally, he walked to the cupboard, reached behind a raft of plates, and pulled out the machine pistol. He'd bought it on a lark—he had the top-of-the-line Brink's Home Security system—and on a lark he'd practiced at a range in Daly City. There was something complete about finding the target, the zen dictum about being one with the bullet, with knowing in some spiritual sense the center of the target. His holes were crisp, clean, unlike the messiness of life. And he was good, better than good...and steady.

He took two deep breaths and walked back to his office. He kept the gun by his leg.

Burt rotated a bottle in his hand, pleased with himself, pleased with the night, pleased with what he had pulled off over Vito, and over Harry Mach.

Harry sat, pumped, but unsure. His heart raced. He took two long breaths.

Burt sensed something had changed in the room, a slight shift, but didn't know quite what that something was. He looked meditatively at the bottle in his hand.

Harry pulled the gun up to the table top, rested his hand on the table, and pointed the gun at Burt's stomach.

Burt looked up, saw the gun, and laughed. "You're too much. What the fuck are you going to do with that?" Ha, ha, ha.

"Mine's loaded."

Burt, stoned, puzzled, pushed back in his chair, his eyelids popping up and down over his blue eyes, his even mouth working. Finally, he stuttered, "What...what are you doing?"

Harry clicked off the safety.

Harry waited a beat then said, "Soft, Burt? Hey look, my gun is aimed at your stomach now. Know what kind of a hole real bullets make?"

"Jesus. Listen—"

Harry felt his control growing. He could kill Burt. "You listen—"

"Please. I didn't mean anything. My gun—"

"Shut up," said Harry.

Burt circled his arms around his body and moaned. "Christ, I pissed my pants."

"What?"

"Pissed my pants....fuck, and my shirt."

Harry clicked the safety on. He said, "Well, Christ, get off my chair. That chair's worth more than you are."

Burt stood up. Harry could see the stain in the front of his pants. Burt's shoulders slumped. He looked beaten and forlorn, as if his spirit and body had failed him, as if he'd failed once again. Was that dejection one of Burt's defining features, that he would try, and fail? That he brayed about projects that never materialized, that he was in bald terms, a loser?

Harry knew at that precise moment that he'd inherited Burt, that Burt was his. He had a huge psychological edge over him. Why? Because Burt sensed Harry had it.

Harry got up and said, "Let's go...upstairs...don't drop piss on the rug."

Burt stumbled in front of him, rocking from side to side, slump-shouldered, his ponytail bouncing right and left. Harry wrinkled his nose at the odor of urine.

Harry directed him to the spare bedroom. "Take your pants and shirt off in that bathroom, and clean up; I'll find you some clothes."

Harry watched Burt disappear into the bathroom and close the door, then he flipped open the folding closet doors. He grabbed a blue Oxford shirt and an old pair of designer jeans.

47

He opened the bathroom door and flipped the clothes in. "Leave the ones you soiled; I'll have the maid throw them away. Come downstairs when you're done."

"What?"

"Are you deaf? Do what I say."

Ten minutes later, Burt stood at the entrance to the dining room. He looked better than when Sal brought him upstairs. He looked vaguely like a rumpled, slightly used, Harry Mach.

Harry waved to a seat a couple places to his right. "Sit."

As Burt sat, he said, "Where's the gun?"

"In my pocket; I won't have to use it. Now, why did Vito Mongreve hire you?"

Burt cocked his head, surprised. "What does that mean?"

"You're living in a room in North Beach, and you've never 'fixed' anything. The only connection I can see is that you dated his grand-daughter. Why do you think he hired you?"

Burt scratched his head. "Actually, I'm not sure..."

"That will remain a mystery for now," said Harry, "but one I'll come back to. Now, what am I going to do with a small-time loudmouth living in a room in North Beach?"

Burt frowned, "I've had a few setbacks. Even you've had setbacks."

"When I was twelve," said Harry.

Burt squinted and closed one eye, as if it helped him think. "Don't be nasty."

"If I called Vito and told him what you told me, what do you think he'd do?"

A crafty smile replaced Burt's puzzlement. "But you're not going to do that. Number one, if you think Vito doesn't care about finding Wiley, he won't care. Number two, you won't do it because you have a proposal."

He wasn't that stoned. "So I do."

Burt adjusted Harry's shirt, bunched under his chin, and said, "So, what is it?"

"How much is Vito paying you?"

Puzzled, Burt said, "You're a piece of work, Harry Mach."

"How much?"

Burt shrugged. "Five hundred bucks for now; if I find Wiley, more."

"You're going to work for me. You'll make a lot more than Vito's paying you."

Burt put his elbows on the table and looked directly into Harry's eyes, as if he could discern what was going on behind them and what he really meant. "Say that again."

"Take it or I call Vito." Harry pulled out his Blackberry.

Burt watched him warily, as if he knew Harry wouldn't call, but was curious about his actions. "I won't kill anyone...I don't think I could."

"That will hardly be necessary."

7

How does one figure everything out? Judy Ferris worried about that problem and sometimes she thought she had the answer; other times, no. Part of the problem was a question of history, her history, her decades of spiritual and emotional sediment. Conservative editor of the student newspaper at Ohio State, muckraker and serious journalist in El Salvador in the late 80s, spiritual dark ages in New York—didn't everyone have some?—and San Francisco, where the dark ages became gray and she surfaced as a free lance journalist and travel writer. Her solution to that problem, or, more accurately, her current self-image, was that of a juggler, and the balls in the air were old or newer versions of herself, which sometimes she juggled adroitly and other times she just watched fall.

Late Monday, she congratulated herself on juggling the balls adroitly. She was going to be managing editor of Vietnam Today.

And nothing was going to change that, especially Wiley Brooks.

She was going to cinch up that dark alley and get on with this new Judy Ferris. Last night, home from the odious bar Tully's and faced with the cheerless task of telling Khris about Wiley, Judy Ferris verified everything. She checked the Chronicle online and found an article about Wiley, the bridge, and the suicide note. She called Leona Wicker, a friend on the SFPD. No body, nothing on Wiley Brooks. Judy had zero proof

Wiley planned his disappearance. But she knew he did. Wiley was the spiritual brother of Miles Slimeball, the Ponzi scam artist from Pacifica, who left his creditors blown dry high, his car at the bottom of Devil's Slide, and who died ten years later choking on a steak in Bermuda.

Late Monday, she called Khris. She told her what she'd found. Judy had no idea what was going through Khris' head. Khris' clandestine fling of a few weeks was, supposedly, dead, and she was out x-number of dollars for a dope scheme Khris knew was idiotic. If she were in Khris' shoes, she'd hide in a cave for a month.

Khris asked her to come up.

Judy was dubious; she'd done her bit. She sighed then said she'd try.

Tuesday morning and early afternoon, Judy worked her projects. She finished a rewrite of the press release and emailed the finished version to her client. She found more notes of her trip to Costa Rica and poured more details into the Fodor project. Finally, she sketched out her presentation to Peter Gross and the ATA.

Around three, she gave up. She poured the rest of a bottle of Calistoga water into a blue Mexican art glass full of melting ice, strolled through her kitchen, and sat at the white deck table in her postage-stamp back yard. She took a long drink, felt the cold swat the back of her mouth and chill her throat, and placed the glass carefully on a coaster depicting a bird of paradise flaring its iridescent green feathers. Often the back yard took her away from obsessive thoughts or the letdowns inevitable in freelancing. Often the limitless view or the more confined one of Mt. Diablo, barely visible through the gray-yellow smog, absorbed negativity. It was the oceanic feeling with not quite an ocean.

That day the immensity was a dark, sullen screen. What bothered her? A thin motif of unfulfilled promise from the past, a knife-twist from the deeper past of Mom, Dad, and betrayal? No, she was dwelling on—obsessing about, she would say after reflection—Wiley Brooks. She had seen Wiley a handful of times. But those encounters made her feel sour, as if she were agreeing to something she didn't feel or believe. Some people had that power. The events she uncovered yesterday were like someone banging on a garbage can in a symphony. She felt herself going back, reaching deep through the sediment into what she sometimes called her irrelevant history. Back to South America, back to El Salvador.

She walked inside and stared at her PC. The screensaver was on, pipes growing one out of the other, dipping down, then jerking off to start another series, as if a programmer with an Escher sensibility had gone mad.

Judy mesmerized herself with her long fingers, her fingernails tap, tap, tapping on the table. Tap, tap, tap. Tap, tap, tap. Judy wandered into her bedroom. She regarded the clothes in her closet for a few minutes, lost in thought. Then she picked out jeans, a forest green sweatshirt, and light hiking boots. After she'd dressed, she grabbed her dark green backpack and threw in her purse, a water bottle, and an apple. She turned on her answering machine and grabbed her black windbreaker in the hall closet, but her momentum stopped at the door.

Judy Ferris was a balance-beam specialist, a juggler of styles and memories, an artful arranger, but never quite the Judy Ferris she admired years ago.

The word was "pretense."

Finally, she shrugged and said to her long-fanged Garuda, "Have I become an expert in self-deception?"

Fifteen minutes later, the Miata primed with regular, she navigated the hills on Franklin Street, then the dense traffic on Lombard. She stopped when she saw a liquor store. A few minutes later, she was winding through one of the double-lane on-ramps, which bound the Presidio like the Lilliputians had bound Gulliver. The soft fogless light made the bridge bacon-red and the parched hills gold. The bridge was the usual immensity, but the bridge powers were playing with the lanes, which meant it was choked with cars.

The bridge made her think of Wiley and his suicide note. She glanced at the railing and thought of what Tully's bartender said about bridge suicides. A gull flying by, cars and people passing, that moment of suspension, then a choking feeling as you released.

Wiley did not feel that, any of it.

First, the car was found on the way to Sausalito. He wouldn't jump from the bay side, if he did jump. He'd have to hike around to the ocean side, the popular side, which would have been a seriously long hike.

Someone likely picked him up. If he didn't want that, limiting the number of people who would know he's alive, there was Sausalito. He could park his SUV off-street there or in one of the long-term parking lots. She visualized him parking, checking the road, then slipping a note on the windshield and hiking into Sausalito.

The traffic eased after the bridge, and she zoned out for over an hour, letting the whistling wind and the flashing brown hills glue her to the road. Finally, she turned down a twisting asphalt road and arrived at two white frame houses. She turned into the gravel drive of the house on the north and parked in back of Bob's Bronco. She saw Bob's lanky form and Khris' petite one in the porch shadows. She waved, walked over, climbed the stairs, and pulled up a chair.

"Some mess," Judy said.

"You know about Wiley's house?" said Bob, frowning, then glancing at Khris. He saved the program he was working on, switched off his laptop, then looked at her. Bob Bower was tall and skinny with a towhead of blond hair. His hands were outsized, his arms thin but muscular, his nose too large for his angular face, his eyes gray and small. Bob was a programmer for Automate, Inc., and was the one person at the farm who never quite got away.

"Wiley's house?" said Judy, puzzled.

"Last night, I heard something. This morning, I looked in a window. Someone was looking for something. They didn't clean up."

"As if things aren't weird enough. By 'mess' I meant Wiley jumping off the bridge."

"Screw his death," said Bob sharply, his Adam's apple bobbing erratically. "If he did it, really did it, it's a boon to mankind. His friends and the police bother me."

"Right," Judy said. Khris looked detached, almost subdued. "How are you?"

"Great." Khris Kyber was five-two, with blond hair in bangs and robin-egg-blue eyes. She wore cut-offs with raggedy white edges, which dribbled over her muscular tanned legs. Her sarcasm trailed off, and she dropped her defenses. "I'm glad you're here."

Bob glanced at Khris suspiciously. It was going to be a tough night, Judy thought. She couldn't help staring at Wiley's house, the twin to their house, a two-story white frame house with a front porch, fireplace, and screened-in back porch. Memories of what happened there flickered, then slipped away. Parties, drugs, Wiley's devilish charm.

"We should call the cops," said Bob, glancing at Judy with his light brown eyes. He closed the lid of his laptop, reached over and placed it carefully on the floor, as if he'd decided it was time to pay attention.

"I thought we decided to wait," said Khris, twisting her hair with her finger.

Bob stretched his long legs, then crossed them, then frowned as if he were thinking of something else. "Now or later. We have to do it."

Khris shook her head. "We're supposed to be getting away, not throwing ourselves in the middle of some weirdness. Of course, you never get away."

Bob scowled and looked at the sky, dismissing Khris.

Judy gave Khris a quick smile of support. "It looks like the weirdness came to us." Judy stared at the sky and for a moment felt the peace, which the farm was supposed to be about. Six months ago, she looked forward to driving up. After Wiley arrived, it was noise, dope, and wild nights, most of which she heard about secondhand. Too much noise, too much hype, too many people on the make, everybody stressed and worried. Of course, it was too easy to blame it on Wiley. She supposed the seeds of the end were laid when they started. That thought made her wonder how cynical she'd become.

"What do you think?" said Khris, looking at her edgily.

"I don't know."

"I suppose it was about a drug deal," said Bob. "He bragged about them. There was something evil about him."

"No one is all conniving and bad," said Khris. "We all have mothers, brothers, sisters, parents, friends."

"You always defend the people you fuck," Bob said, stonily.

Khris folded her arms tightly across her ample breasts. "I'll never defend you."

"Truce," said Judy. "Kill each other when I leave."

Khris grimaced. "It was nice, wasn't it?"

Judy supposed she was thinking of the walks through the parched valleys, the talks where they strung out their lives and wondered how it was all connected. On Wiley's side, squirrels chased each other up and down the live oak in the front yard. Beyond, in the white sky, turkey vultures prowled the air corridors looking for carrion.

"Go to Oakland for a few weeks."

"We both thought that," said Khris.

Judy got up. "Let's celebrate that. I have reinforcements."

The mood brightened when they moved inside. Khris made fettuccine Alfredo and Bob got shit-faced on vodka tonics. They even let him bore them with a rambling description of his latest Java program. Judy's favorite spot at the oak table gave her a view of slightly warped linoleum, slightly warped screen door, and rolling brown hills dotted with clusters of dark green live oaks. It was a kitchen she should have had years ago, a place of friendliness, calm, and the easy life like the one she'd had growing up in Westfall, Ohio. Judy's sister, Jane, after ten years as a graphic designer in Chicago, ended up, surprisingly, back on a Westfall farm, married with kids and happy with sixteen-hour days shoveling shit and weaning squealing pigs.

She and Khris took a hand-in-hand walk. The sun had set, and bluish light cast soft shadows off the live oaks. They didn't talk much, but eventually they talked about Wiley.

"I don't know why we do these things," Khris said. "I knew deep in my bones."

"Some people can charm you into anything. Look at Manson or Reverend Jones." Judy released Khris' hand and sat on a rock surrounded by parched thistle. She tore off a dead thistle branch and dragged it through the dirt.

Khris walked a few feet more, stopped at the trunk of a live oak, and turned. "Bob thinks he faked it."

"You know he did."

"Just for the money?"

"I'd guess. And because he could."

"Right. Which means I'm a grade-A dupe. Fucked and fucked over. That's probably a song." She leaned against the oak. Above her head was a row of small holes punched out by a sapsucker. "I know those few days with Wiley weren't worth it, but I felt alive. I wasn't plodding down a long trail with Bob, or making nice sounds, or doing the right humdrum thing. It was a 'lonely impulse of delight.' I suppose getting fucked over is part of the territory."

"It's men."

"You and your 'opaque power fantasists.' I'll never know what that means."

Judy ignored Khris' demur. She broke the thistle in two. "How much?"

Khris glanced at her, then glanced up at the sky in supplication. "Five thousand."

"Was it a lot of money?" Judy looked at the lines she'd drawn in the dirt. She could inhabit those lines, find a smaller universe, walk up one ridge, down another. Separate universes; why did another one always seem so interesting?

"From our joint account—a baby step towards marriage."

"Shit."

"That part's okay, at least for now. The only thing right about Bob is that he doesn't care about money, even his own account. He's a nerd with bohemian fantasies."

"Were you the only one?"

"I think I was low on the totem pole. He told me the name of the dealer, Roger Nesbitt, and exactly how he'd do it. He talked a lot when he was drunk. He bragged about his other backers. A woman in real estate, a guy who owned a shop, and someone named Harry Mach. He put up over a hundred thousand. Wiley talked about stashing loot in Barbados. It sounded real. But now it looks like he was taunting me, telling me exactly how he was going to rip me off, then doing it. I'm not sure now why I slept with him; maybe to find out if he was real. You can't lie about everything, especially when you're naked, or making love."

"Seems to me that Wiley liked to fuck, not make love."

"I don't even know if he liked to fuck."

She'd seen that too. His need to manipulate, his need to hurt. She tried to calm Khris down. "It seems unreal, then it doesn't. Don't worry about Bob. He's come around before."

"If I want that."

From her room on the second floor, Judy heard Bob and Khris arguing, or maybe they were making love. Sometimes she couldn't tell the difference. Finally, the dissonant sounds died away. She stared out the window and felt at peace with the quiet and the valley oaks.

After a while, Judy started thinking about Wiley, about the few times she'd seen him, about Khris, then about what Bob said. She stared at Wiley's house. She stared at it long enough that she knew she had to do something. She dressed, slipped on flats, then the vest she kept in the country. She pulled her flashlight out of the dresser.

The moon made Wiley's gravel driveway glow against the background of quiet hills and a strangely quiet house. Judy walked across the asphalt road, then down the gravel. The crunch of her shoes on gravel reassured her in the face of the sinister quietness of Wiley's house. She peered in the small window in the garage door and saw a cluster of shadows. An oil slick gleamed in the moonlight. Racks of tools and a bench lined the wall. Wiley's? She couldn't imagine Wiley doing anything common or ordinary.

Judy snapped off her examination, then walked up the concrete sidewalk to the back porch the last owner had added to the house. The screen door was cracked. Judy listened for a beat, then slipped inside. She tried the back door, and it was—surprisingly—unlocked, as if Wiley didn't care if anyone came in, as if the house were no longer of any use. She pushed the door open.

She listened, then switched the flashlight on.

She couldn't help comparing their house across the road with Wiley's. Their house was cozy, an oasis, at least in the first year. Wiley's was almost the opposite. When she walked in for a neighborly get-together, she felt its coldness. It wasn't that it was spartan, but it was more the spirit. Scary clown prints on walls, no plants, heavy dark furniture, the only books about wingnut conspiracies, the only magazines about guns and hunting.

Those books and magazines were still there, except they were on the floor, scattered, as if someone in a rage had torn through the house.

She wondered if that someone was Wiley or one of his so-called backers. She picked her way through the front room. She stooped to examine a few of the books, the papers. They didn't tell her anything.

Their farmhouse, framed in the window, and the posts of Wiley's front porch, shimmered in moonglow. It was a spectral other world, static and calm. The front door was locked. Judy walked towards the stairs but froze at the figure staring at her. It was anxious, furtive. She shined the flashlight on her face, and the mirror made a Halloween mask. She looked intent, eyes deep and black, eyebrows antennae.

She grinned at her foolishness and turned towards the stairs.

Upstairs, she walked slowly down the carpeted hallway. It was like their house. Closets on her right, guest room on her left, window at the end, master bedroom to her left. It looked like the bedroom doubled as an office. There were piles of papers thrown on the bed. She shined the flashlight on the papers and saw a final cell phone bill—the number had been canceled—a TV warranty, a few letters, several from Arlington, Virginia. She read half of one and glanced at another. Was Wiley in the service, The Company? If so, why would he stay here? Why the drug game?

Again, the common things made Wiley more common than she wanted. The big question was why wade through months-old PG&E bills? Judy had an odd feeling about those papers. Wiley supposedly jumped late Sunday. Bob said someone was there Monday night. If Wiley faked the jump, it could have been him.

She followed the flashlight into a bathroom connecting the master bedroom to the guest bedroom. That room had clothes and books strewn on the floor. She was puzzling the wreckage when she heard a low grinding noise, like beans in a coffee grinder. She frowned, clicked off the flashlight, then walked around the bed. She picked up the side of the curtain and peeked through the narrow slit. After she focused on the moon-drenched landscape, she saw a car threading its way down the curvy road, lights out.

Stunned, she saw the car turn, then scratch its way up Wiley's gravel driveway. The car door opened carefully. When Judy saw the flip of a ponytail in the moonlight, she dropped the edge of the curtain. She heard steps on the gravel.

She heard the creak of steps underneath her. He was on the front porch. She heard the faint squeak of a door handle, then "Shit."

She heard him walk down the steps of the front porch.

She expected the car to start, but instead, she heard the back door open and close. She walked quickly to the connecting bathroom, unsure which way to go.

One minute, two, three...the stairs creaked.

Judy held herself, the back of her hand to her mouth almost as if that would disguise her breath. The steps stopped outside the guest bedroom.

57

Judy edged towards the master bedroom. The steps continued down the hall. Judy slipped back into the guest bedroom. She shut the door to the bathroom, leaving it open an inch. She saw a closet packed with clothes. Too small. She walked quickly to the door. She turned the doorknob. A light blazed in the bathroom. A hand grasped the side of the bathroom door. Judy turned the door handle.

A cell phone snapped open. The voice faded into the master bedroom.

"Yeah, it's fucking Burt. Of course, I'm here...Wiley's not; I coulda told you that much. It was a long shot. The place looked torn apart, and I came in...the back door was open. Whoever it was went through his papers. What now?"

Judy eased her grip on the knob and twisted it until the door cracked open. She carefully opened it wider, then slipped outside. She closed the door as much as she could. She waited at the top of the stairs, torn between getting away and the garbled phrases punctuating the silence.

"...C'mon Harry, I'm fuckin' tired...course, I'm not a moron...I'll check."

She walked down the first two steps.

Judy froze on the stairs. When she didn't hear anything, she walked quickly down the stairs to the landing. A light flicked off. He was in the guest room. Judy stepped over a pile of books and into the kitchen.

"Fuck, I need a beer." His laugh boomed through the empty house.

Judy slipped through the kitchen and out the back door. She jumped three steps, then after glancing at the gravel, slipped her flats off. The gravel bit into the soft pads of her feet. She grimaced but didn't make noise. When she was abreast of the car, she glanced back at the house. A light beam shot out the kitchen window. She bent over and read the license plate. Then she walked painfully around the garage.

She picked through her vest pockets and found the notebook with a pencil crammed in the coils. She wrote down the license number, the make of the car, then the fragments of conversation. Steps on the gravel. She didn't hear anything for a few seconds, as if the man were pondering what to do. Then she saw a bottle flip through the cold night air and land on the grass.

She heard the car door open and close, the engine start.

Judy edged towards the back of the garage. She heard the car back up, then turn, then just before it came into view, she slipped around and flattened herself against the back of the garage. A few seconds later, the car bent around the first curve and snapped its lights on.

Judy sat, brushed the dirt off her feet, put her flats on, then walked unsteadily back towards their house hugged by a shadow cast by the moon.

Inside their house, she walked upstairs. She closed her door and breathed a ragged sigh.

A luminous hand grasped her shoulder.

8

Marant didn't know how long he'd be gone, and he spent several days taking care of appearances, opera tickets which wouldn't be used, dinners, a date for a new show at Quai d'Orsay, and his Paris apartment. He closed the Fort Mahon house and gave the keys to his former housekeeper, the diminutive and fussy Geneviève Fourmis, so she could drive to Fort Mahon once a week to water his plants and sweep the sand out of the doorway. He'd cinched up his life many times on projects for Christian, but that time felt like déjà vu, though very different at the same time.

He spent an hour staring at his sculptures, both finished and not. His Manichean split, long-time pondered and expanded on, into linear and not, between straight-edge and biomorphic, was simplistic. But there are times when simplistic leads to more. He couldn't help feeling that time, however, that he'd reached the end, that the conflict, the spidery figures on immense plains, was more about a spiritual split which would never be bridged. It corrupted the romanticism that was the core of his nature.

Christian's extensive contacts in the Foreign Service produced papers as a cultural representative with his chosen name, Albert Rieux, a bow to one of his favorite authors, Albert Camus, his novel The Plague, and that novel's protagonist, Dr. Rieux. His few close friends, including Christian, still called him Marant but, working for RM, he changed it quickly for his adopted name. Christian told him that many in RM who didn't know him and had never met him, still called him Marant. Albert Rieux was, in theory, in America as part of that vague potlatch of white-washed ideas and antiseptic customs called a "cultural exchange."

The rambling eighteen-room neo-Spanish Biondi Villa, in Sea Cliff, San Francisco, was his base for the next few days. His two rooms were spacious, clumped up with ponderous neo-Mission couches, chairs, and dark brown tables partially covered in too-white filigreed doilies. Neither curve nor line, more a simple heaviness. More like the defiance of gravity.

The reception was typical, white wine on the terrace, amiable talk of cultural differences, and he managed to bore a few Spanish representatives with talk of sculpture, the elusive curve, the too easily rendered line, and upcoming visits to the Legion of Honor, the home of many of Rodin's sculptures, including his favorite, The Shades, of three hunched figures half in life, half not, in spiritual limbo.

Marant retrieved his purchases from the large oak armoire and dressed—in gray slacks, Ecco walking shoes, a robin's-egg blue shirt with open collars, and a stiff red-and-gold San Francisco 49ers windbreaker.

He strolled down Sea Cliff's winding streets to Clement Street. Ten minutes later, he drove west in his rented car, a forgettable Ford Escort, until the Cliff House loomed out of the fog. That early, and despite the tourists already queuing up at the door to the restaurant, the fog made it a lonely place. It was the furthest point west in the city, a hundred feet above the ocean, the end of the earth.

Marant parked and walked to the telephone near a souvenir store, which was open. He picked up the phone, dropped in two quarters, and dialed the Institute. When someone picked up, Marant hung up. He took out a small black notebook and noted the location and phone number.

As he was to leave, he glanced at the viewing deck with its telescopes. The deck, where you could watch gulls swing out towards Seal Rock—seals angling for space like living sausages of boudin blanc, and dusky cormorants spreading their wings to dry—was empty. The store, however, was full. He watched people queuing up at the register with ashtrays, I Love San Francisco T-shirts, and postcards. San Francisco was the most European of any American city. Still, even in San Francisco, there was the typical American spirit. Americans were backward, knew nothing and sold everything, especially themselves. They would conquer the world, Marant thought ruefully, despite the movements and revolutions. Americans were dietitians of the spirit, missioned to distill life into hype, sex, and food.

He snapped off his gaze, turned, and got back to the Escort. He watched the traffic wind down the hill towards Ocean Beach. When there was an opening, he made a U-turn.

It took him most of the morning to work his way east into the city. Sometimes he stopped and checked pay phones. If they worked, he noted their locations and phone numbers. He also drove by the addresses of Kafi Bella and Teresa Aluestia. Kafi was in the Hotel Rutledge in the Tenderloin, one of the worst areas in the city, full of crime, prostitution, and, not surprisingly, a grab bag of immigrants including ones from the Middle East. Teresa was in the Capri Motel on Lombard Street, the northern artery, which became an on-ramp to the Golden Gate Bridge and connected the city to Marin County and points north.

In early afternoon, Marant stopped at a phone next to a new fishing pier on the Embarcadero. Old piers marched away from that spot towards the north; towards the south, there were more piers and construction on what looked like a streetcar extension. In front of him, fishermen baited hooks, threw out crab pots, and gutted fish.

Marant took out his notebook and dialed the number for Kafi Bella. Kafi had a gruff, suspicious voice. As he talked, Marant started shaking his head. The complication became clear. Three homeless people—drunks—witnessed the test of the explosive and had to be eliminated.

While Kafi droned on in his harsh Berber accent, Marant looked at the soaring span of the Bay Bridge, the tinker-toy boats. A speck flew towards him, did a loop in the air, climbed several hundred feet, and shot over him towards a clutch of downtown high-rises. It acted like a falcon, likely a Peregrine. It knew where to go, thought Marant: downtown San Francisco with its thousands of pigeons was a raptor smorgasbord.

He interrupted Kafi. "You know how to find these people?"

"Yes, I have photos."

"How did you get photos?"

"We have our means."

Marant shook his head. He couldn't reject the contract out of hand, but it was idiotic. The revolutionary movements of the world needed fewer explosions and more passive resistance, more organizing, more talking with their enemies. It was ironic, after all, that after twenty years spent blowing the brains out of generals, chiefs-of-police, and prominent politicians, he didn't believe it worked. He couldn't get Afghanistan out of his mind. He killed a general, the Taliban took over. It made a Pyrrhic victory seem like a real one.

"All right, I'll look at what you have. Put your photos and proof in a brown paper bag. Roll the top of the bag over several times and mark it with an 'X'. Go to the corner of Church and Market. There is a phone on the corner, next to the Armadillo bookstore. I will call you there at three o'clock."

"No. You must do—"

"Three o'clock, the phone outside the bookstore."

He wasn't going to sacrifice his safety on a whim, especially not the whim of an Algerian Muslim. Marant hung up. He walked to where he'd parked, then drove down Market. At that time of day, the fog had burned off and the air was clean, the city bathed in brilliant sunlight. Market Street was animated, full of cars, rumbling streetcars, tourists, worker bees, and, of course, the ragtag homeless he'd seen all day.

He turned off Market on Church Street and parked on a side street. He walked back to Church and stopped at the Best Beans Café. The café gave him a view of the phone on the corner. He had an espresso and waited. The café was full of youthful writers who observed each other, then typed furiously on black laptops.

At three, a thickset man with very dark brown hair—and chest hair which poked out of a white shirt —walked to the phone on the corner. He walked with a limp like a crab. He carried a brown paper bag in his hand. Marant got out of his chair and went to the phone next to the café. He dialed the number of the phone outside the Armadillo. The ringing seemed to shock Kafi Bella. He looked around quickly, then picked up the phone.

"There is a garbage can near the entrance to Muni Metro across the street," said Marant. "Put your evidence inside, then go back to your hotel. I will call you in half an hour."

"But—"

"No buts. Do it now."

Kafi hung up. He looked around as if he were trying to see Marant. Marant didn't like that, but he saw it as a natural reaction. Few people in RM had seen Marant Olivier. Most knew about him, and he was sure, wondered about him. Kafi crossed the street. He put the brown bag in the garbage can and walked down the stairs into the Muni Metro.

Marant walked back towards his car but stopped at a man he'd watched earlier. The man had been grubbing in garbage cans looking for bottles. The man looked up at him, his face a mixture of impudence and caution. He had dirty hands, a face the color of mud, and bright red lips. Marant held out a five-dollar bill.

"There is a brown paper bag with an 'X' on it in that garbage can. Bring it over there."

The homeless man blinked at him, turned, and looked at the garbage can. Then he turned back to Marant. "You bet, boss."

Marant watched him shuffle towards the Muni entrance. Marant walked the opposite way down Church Street and turned the corner. A few minutes later, the man shuffled around the corner with the package. Marant took the package and gave the man the five-dollar bill. The man put his red lips to the bill and kissed it.

Marant walked back to his car, then drove down Church Street to Dolores Park. He circumnavigated the park and stopped along the high side on Twenty-first Street. The park sloped down to a large playground, soccer field, and tennis courts. It gave him an expansive view of downtown San Francisco, of the Bay Bridge, of razor thin lines of houses in Berkeley and Oakland, of the mist-shrouded hills beyond.

Marant rested the brown bag against his stomach and the steering wheel. He had gone over his last meeting with Christian Jollet many times in the past week. He did it again. He realized he was doing it because something was off. It started with Christian's hesitation. It started with the Muslims.

Their meeting was ostensibly about a new explosive, a disgruntled American chemist, and money. But it was the skepticism that made him pause. It wasn't that he disbelieved Christian; it was that he felt deeply there was much more going on. Christian's last words were to be more detective than assassin.

The first set of photos showed him a briefcase lying against the side of a windmill. It was night, and fog encircled the windmill. The second set, taken during the day, showed the thick brush around the windmill, along with its large hole, shattered vanes, and bumblebee tape. The explosive looked powerful. The briefcase was small, the effect destructive. The last four photos were of three ragged-looking drunks. There was a photo of each one against varying backgrounds of grass and trees, and scatterings of people walking, dogs, and picknickers. A group photo showed the three drinking on a scrape of grass in front of a pond. The skinny one stuck his tongue out, the others held up bottles. He supposed all the shots were in Golden Gate Park near an entrance. It seemed the homeless and drunks had established a third world society in San Francisco.

Marant slipped the photos back into the bag. He drove towards the Cultural Exchange, stopping on Clement Street. He checked his notebook, found a pay phone, and called Kafi. "You're convinced this process is real?"

"Yes, the process is real. I used a small amount to make the device. It is malleable, like Semtex, easy to use, and, according to the chemist, easier to produce. It is exactly what we need."

"Who is this chemist? I haven't seen his name anywhere."

"He already feels compromised. He uses the code name Boris."

Boris? "Hmm. A vengeful chemist. What happened to empiricism, the pursuit of truth, the reflective life?"

Kafi said impatiently, "I don't know about that. I know our struggle; I know our people."

Marant knew their people. Many fought in Afghanistan. They tried to transplant the Taliban's success into Algeria. They killed everyone: moderates, Christians, Jews, journalists, foreigners, anyone who didn't believe in a state ruled according to Islamic law. Inviting the Muslims into RM was one thing; after Afghanistan, inviting in GIA another. But he'd heard the GIA were losing members. Radicalism consumed itself. "How did this chemist get the photos?"

"He didn't tell me. He has means; he is very clever. I assume he pointed out the bums and had an associate take their pictures. The means don't matter. These bums are easy to find; they live in the park, most of the time near the entrance on Haight Street."

The chemist did seem clever. It did seem coincidental that their chemist, a well-paid, well-respected professional would live near the park.

Of course there was the American obsession with appearing different, a character full of quirks and tics. But Kafi sounded nervous, very nervous, though Marant thought it was from being in America, surrounded by enemies. "Have you seen these drunks yourself?"

"No, but these people sleep at Haight and Stanyan near the park entrance."

"Why would anyone believe them?"

"I don't know; I know Boris wants them killed. He doesn't want loose ends."

Marant shook his head. "Why did you have a test in the park?"

"My superiors wanted a test, an urban test. I tried to talk them out of it. When they insisted, we found a spot removed from the crowds. There is dense fog in the morning."

It was idiotic. Not only did religion and fanaticism scramble the brains, it scrambled day-to-day good sense. An urban explosion! "A mysterious process, an urban test, a bloodthirsty chemist, and three winos. RM never got in this kind of mess before..." Marant was about to say, "before they let in the Muslims," but he stopped himself. "I'll contact you tomorrow."

Marant looked at the phone. It was worse than he thought. His usual targets were informants, double agents, politicians, military men, government functionaries, or brutal police. Killing American drunks—innocent onlookers of unauthorized tests of an unnecessary explosive—was not part of his repertoire. But there was more, much more. What was it?

The next day, Marant decided to find out as much as he could about the chemist, the drunks, and the formula. It meant getting ready to kill at least one of the drunks. If the information was correct and there was a formula, and Christian was willing to pay for it, he had to go ahead. He couldn't see what it meant for RM in a larger picture. If nothing else, it would quiet the firebrands, which meant, for the most part, the Muslims.

Marant dressed in typical American fashion with jeans, work shirt, baseball hat, tennis shoes, and a light tan windbreaker. His outfit looked so American he didn't recognize himself.

He took buses to Haight and Stanyan and the eastern entrance of

Golden Gate Park. It was foggy and chilly, and the drunks—didn't they used to call them "winos" before an infection of political correctness?— and homeless lay in heaps near the park entrance. He walked down Haight Street and found a restaurant. He had breakfast and looked at the photos again.

Then he went back to the entrance to the park. After walking up and down Stanyan Street for an hour, he found the men in the photos. Their clothes were ragged and dirty. They seemed to spend most of their time arguing and drinking.

He followed them through the park most of the morning and early afternoon. Mid-afternoon, they stopped, oddly, at the mill where they'd seen the chemist and possibly Kafi and Teresa. The winos stared at it, as if reassuring themselves of what they'd seen.

While they sat, drank, and argued on a hill close to the ocean, Marant walked up to the mill. A man in a hazmat costume stooped inside the plastic, which covered the hole. Marant crouched and squinted at the inside of the mill. The blast would have blown into the mill causing more damage, but the walls were thick. Still, the damage was significant.

Marant walked back to the road. The winos staggered towards the bushes that surrounded the mill and disappeared into the underbrush. Marant waited a few minutes and followed them. They drank a late lunch near a small lake. Then they made their way slowly back through the park towards Haight Street.

Late afternoon, they entered Sharon Meadow, the large open field a few blocks from the Haight Street entrance to Golden Gate Park. Sharon Meadow was rimmed with trees, set off by a vista towards the east, towards Oak Street, tennis courts on the north, large trees which barely hid lawn-bowling courts on the west, and on the south, an old stone building and a playground.

Marant Olivier sat down in front of the stone building on a bench too low for his back, or any normal back. With his peripheral vision, he watched the two winos stumble past the tennis courts and shuffle down the wavy ribbon of concrete which circled the meadow.

The big one sprawled on a hill almost directly across the field. Then he grabbed a package from the smaller one. They shoved, pushed, and fought over the package as if they were a cartoon couple haggling over the TV remote.

But then divorce. The lean, bearded one yelled into the stunned red face of his companion, thrust his finger at him, then staggered along the winding concrete path towards the park entrance and one of Dante's shabbier circles.

Marant watched the skinny one disappear.

Marant got up slowly. He felt old, vital. He supposed that meant he was in a transition, a transition like the geometric gray area between point and line, between line and circle.

His inner musings were masked for a few moments by the day, which was gorgeous, full of light, people, a slip of breeze. He walked on the concrete sidewalk, which encircled the meadow. That day, the meadow hosted a handful of soccer players in shorts and gym shoes playing between two hastily constructed goals, two young couples chasing Frisbees, and a picnic spread over the grass like a postage stamp. A scattering of homeless were tucked into the bushes surrounding the field.

Marant stumbled as he approached the wino, as if he were drunk. He stopped on the far side of baby-face and looked back, smiled an idiotic grin and sat. Baby-face had an odor of the street, of clothes slept in and soiled.

Marant lit a cigarette. The wino asked him for one. He gave him two—"One for later."

"Name's Richard, but people call me Potato," he said, "cuz of the nose. You know, German potato nose."

"Buck," said Marant.

He watched the wino light the cigarette with an elaborate gesture and exhale as if he tasted a fine Havana cigar. The wino's puffy red hand circled the brown paper sack.

"Hear that explosion the other day?" said Marant.

"Hear it!" said the wino, contemptuously. "Seen it."

"Man."

"Fuckin' Wiley Brooks did it. Made money on that redhead. Fuckin' Scab wants to keep it all now Wiley's blew."

Wiley Brooks?

Marant hadn't seen the name in Kafi's papers. Potato was likely a congenital liar, or piling on street-wise hyperbole. But why lie about a name? "Wiley blew?"

"Scab said he nose-dived off the bridge. Fuckin' nobody believes that."

"Why?"

"Ain't the type. Used to live right over there." Potato pointed to a rim of trees at the eastern end of the park. "On Stanyan. Saw him all the time. Scab said he was a dealer. Hey, what the fuck you wanta know for?"

"I'm just talkin' man," said Marant. "You told me you saw the mill blow up."

"Didn't blow up on its own. He did it." Potato held out a hand, as if to correct something. "Didn't do it on his ace; crabby guy did it, but Wiley was there."

Kafi. At least that part was true. "Why?"

"We was speculatin' about that. Some secret stuff. You know CIA, FBI, ADC."

"ADC?" said Marant, puzzled.

Potato let out a long strangled laugh. His head dove towards his chest, and he crossed his arms over his chest as if he'd explode with laughter. He tried to talk but couldn't. Finally, he gasped out. "Aid to Dependent Children." This last was followed by more strangled laughs.

"Funny," said Marant.

Potato subsided into head-wagging and chuckles. "But fuck, Buck. We got some money out of him. Now he's fuckin' gone. Fuckin' redhead. He was our ticket. Our ticket to ride."

Potato guzzled the beer. A thread of foam hung beneath Potato's broad lip. Potato wiped it away with his sleeve. Potato hitched up, shifted, and planted himself next to Marant. He encircled Marant with a large arm. Potato smelled of stale beer, dirt, and coffee grounds. Too-ripe tomato face, crab hands, nails broken and discolored, distended gut. His jeans were streaked with dirt and grass, and his shoe tongues lolled on scabbed ankles. "You're my fuckin' brother, Buck. Can tell. Ever kill a man?"

Marant shrugged Potato's arm off his shoulder. "Why?"

"Know how easy it is to kill somebody in jail? Cakewalk. Killed two. Know why?"

"No."

"Cuz you can!" shouted the big wino. He slapped his knee, then fell into another series of strangled laughs. He quit laughing. He took a

68

swallow of beer. "Know why I was in last time?"

"I don't see how."

"Dooooommmeeestic aaahhhbbbuse. Punched out the old lady's lights. Hadda keep talkin', ya know? Babble, babble, babble."

"Too bad."

"Know what?" the wino said, leering at him. "Don't give a fuck, not a fuck. Out here, in there. It's the fuckin' same. Watch the cops." Potato stuffed the brown bag under his coat.

Two policemen on horses clop, clop, clopped down the pavement. They watched Potato, then glanced suspiciously at Marant. They reined their horses. Their horses stomped and moved in erratic quarter circles, enveloping them in a sweaty, earthy odor. The policemen wore long coats, riding boots that hugged their calves, walkie-talkies, notebooks, and nine-millimeter pistols on broad leather belts cinching their coats.

"You got a bottle on you," said the biggest cop.

"Nope," said Potato. "I'm clean."

"What's your story?" said the thin one to Marant. He had a clipped moustache and questioning brown eyes. His hat was pulled down hard on his head.

"Enjoying this beautiful day, officer," said Marant pleasantly. They would check his papers. Everything should be all right. Marant judged distances and routes. He could try to take them here. Then he'd have to run. He'd run past the tennis courts, double back past the lawn-bowling courts, then the tunnel, then the Haight. Potato could identify him. The others out in the field would stop their play and watch.

"Maybe we should take a look at your IDs." The skinny one was about to dismount, when his walkie-talkie scratched to life. He grabbed it out of its holster and answered it. He listened for a few seconds. He snapped it off. "Fuck, John. Robbery at the de Young."

The big one with the heavy thighs reined his horse to the left and kicked the horse into a trot. The other took the reins in his left hand. He pointed a thick finger at Potato. "Next time we see you drinking, you're busted."

He whipped the flank of his horse. A few seconds later they cantered past the lawn-bowling courts.

Potato watched them leave, then shook his head, as if he'd been thinking about them for a long time. "I'd love to kill a cop," said Potato.

69

"You know there's no difference between a guard or a cop and a prisoner. Look at those cops in Oakland; cops killing dealers and running their own dope ring. Gotta love it. Just plain luck one is inside and the other ain't."

"Just luck."

Marant glanced at Potato. He didn't like the assignment. He also didn't like Potato. Marant shrugged inwardly. Marant slipped the fugu pill out of the key pocket of his jeans. He took a five-dollar bill out of his shirt pocket. "I want your drink."

The eyes were crazed, puzzled. "Fuck you talkin' about?"

"Five bucks for your beer. You can buy three later."

"Whole fuckin' thing?"

Marant started to fold the bill in his pocket. "Fuck, yes."

Potato was puzzled, then accepting. Finally he grabbed the bill out of Marant's hand. He thrust the bag at him.

Marant took the bag. He unscrewed the lid on the malt liquor. While he pretended to wipe off the top of the bottle, he dropped the pill into the malt liquor. It made a soft plop. Christian said it had to seem natural. The fugu pills, with their lethal dose of tetradoxin, would dissolve quickly. Marant pretended to take a sip.

"Wow," Marant said. He kept his hand on the bag.

The early morning fog had vanished long ago. It was a blue-sky afternoon. Tall trees rimmed the open field, which was filling up with soccer players. The sidewalk was empty. No policemen. Marant got up, screwed the lid on the bottle, and put it in the grass out of the reach of the wino. "Leave it, man," he said, pointing his finger at the wino. He wondered if "man" sounded too accented. "I'll be back."

"You're fuckin' queer."

Marant turned and walked slowly around the big field, past the noisy picnickers and their beer and chicken, past a young woman stretching and missing a Frisbee, past the red-faced soccer players stumbling, stopping, and racing towards the goal. Marant walked up the hill past the playground towards the hustle of cars circling the park south. At the top of the hill, he looked back. Potato had fallen back, arms spread, as if he were Christ. The sack with the top of the bottle stuck out rolled erratically down the hill and rested in the middle of the sidewalk. A couple walked down the sidewalk, saw the drunk, and shook their heads. The man kicked the bottle back on the grass.

So easy, yet discordant. He didn't, couldn't, trust Kafi. Christian hinted at doubts but held some in reserve. And Wiley Brooks and Kafi blew up a windmill. Was the chemist Wiley? And was Wiley Boris? And why a suicide?

Too many questions. And he felt old, yet invigorated. Expert, yet still a novice. He walked alongside the dense traffic to Stanyan. He watched the traffic momentarily before hailing a cab. In a few minutes, he was on his way to Clement Street. He shrugged off that feeling of unease as he neared the villa. He thought of what he would do that night. First, an excursion with the Cultural Exchange to the San Francisco Symphony. Afterwards, North Beach and jazz clubs, perhaps a late night cognac in the Starlight Room on Nob Hill.

If he had to go along with the assignment, he should make his stay worthwhile.

9

Harry Mach groped for the phone. He switched it on. "Mr. Big, how's the market?"

Harry dropped the phone. It bounced once on the gold Persian rug. He stared it at for a split second, reached over and picked it up. Harry sat on the edge of the bed, his clothes half on the rug, half spread over the polished parquet floor. His curls draped lankly over his forehead. Yesterday was a thinly veiled fog through which he saw characters walking about, towards the ocean, back, their images rising from indistinctness towards recognition, like sharks drifting up from the depths.

Then there was a rock, a man spread Christ-like over it. But then an image from his past, a god, Prometheus, descended, handing him wads of bills, embossed paper, stocks.

Harry focused. "Burt?"

Burt said, "Not too sharp, Mr. Kingpin. Remember yesterday? Remember Napa?"

"Of course," said Harry, kneading his forehead. What did he remember? Burt's silver gun slicing circles, its black hole aimed at his stomach, Burt's stoned rambling, and yes, Harry Mach's turning, his own pistol, his psychological advantage. Then his proposition. He'd "hired" Burt. Had he been alcohol-impaired?

Details from the night crowded back. He'd found Wiley's address in Napa, and after prodding Burt—he'd wanted to go to Donnelly's, get drunk, and talk with his "buds"—sent him to Napa to find Wiley. "You said Wiley wasn't there, and you didn't leave the note, and the place was torn apart. That was good. But you went in. I wouldn't have done that, but what can we do now? Did you find anything else?"

"The phone bills were interesting. I wrote down the numbers and checked them this morning. Most were in California, but there were a bunch to a D.C. exchange. I didn't find anything else, but I didn't have time for much else."

D.C. exchange. That fit with what he knew about Wiley. "Good work. I didn't expect quite so much industry. Now we know, or think we know, he needs the address book. But he has to know we have it. Anything else?"

Burt said casually, "Oh yeah, Vito called this morning. He got me out of bed."

A stone lodged in Harry's throat. Too many variables. After Burt left he'd called Studs and left messages about Vito, Sal, and Burt, then done his own research. According to numerous articles online, Vito had slipped in the criminal rankings and was recovering from a triple heart bypass in San Jose. He wondered again about Vito's sanity, or reason, in choosing Burt. "And?"

"Duh. I'm supposed to be working for him, remember?"

It was like pulling teeth. "Of course. And?"

"I told him you were soft...and had money of your own. And that you have the address book, found the place in Napa, and I checked it out. He thought I was making progress and wanted me to work with you. Nothing to hide there."

So easy, yet. "Good, good." He needed Plan B for Sal and Vito, some way to neutralize them or bring them into his game.

"Say Harry, I'm beginning to like our deal, but what are you going to get out of it? I think you want more than just your money back?"

72

Did he underestimate Burt? "We'll talk about that later."

Burt said, "Okay, kingpin. What now?"

And impudent. "Keep Vito in the loop. Go to the Haight bars. Tully's is near Stanyan. The Golden Paradise is on the corner of Ashbury. Talk to the bartenders, talk to anybody. Dig up anything you can. There may be nothing there, but we have to try. Call if you have something."

"What about that retainer?"

"This afternoon. Call first."

Harry frowned. Burt was a stoned, small-time idiot, and even though he was recruited easily, he didn't trust him. Burt could have gone along with him and told Vito, although he didn't think so. Even so, he had Burt by the balls, if Burt was smart enough to realize it.

Harry put on his bathrobe, walked into the bathroom, drew cold water, plunged his head into the bowl, and blew bubbles through the water. After toweling, he felt alive, ready. He walked briskly down two sets of stairs and retrieved the papers. A few minutes later, the laptop booted, the WSJ, Times, and Chronicle spread out in front of him. He checked Coloprobe to see how far it had fallen. Grazing in the pennies. Buzzword wasn't even listed!

Harry felt right, he felt in control, but what he'd done last night cycled back. He'd done something he'd never dreamed about. He'd been threatened, he'd reacted, and he'd recruited a stoned loser to help him. But help with what? A hunch? He was performing normal Harry Mach actions, but he felt changed. Beyond the adrenalin rush, recruiting Burt, and tweaking Vito on the nose, he felt in control. Sorry, Karl. I can win at this game, a riskier game than you every played.

Harry went back to his laptop. His inbox was full mostly of congratulations on Legs 1 and 2 of the Trifecta. Trifecta, Leg 3, the elusive Leg 3, was in the works, but remote. He'd never call it Harry's Difecta.

The key to Leg 3, the only key, was Wiley's address book.

Late last night, after he'd sent Burt to Napa, he realized its importance. He'd gone through it again and dog-eared the few pages that interested him. Harry snatched it up. It was a thick book. He flipped pages and quickly drew lines through entries that wouldn't help him.

The Qs were important. They looked like bank numbers. He called Simon Mores, a bank auditor, a client, and asked a favor. Then he recited the numbers in the Qs.

While he waited for the return call, Harry worked the address book and the phone. It didn't take long to find that people didn't like talking about Wiley. Wiley had offended, or ripped off, almost everyone. But the problem wasn't just with them. He knew how to be flexible, how to extract the points, but he was flying blind. He had cues; he had notions; he was curious. He felt—a feeling, a hunch: they were what he told his clients to avoid like the Black Death—there was more at the end of the road than a hundred grand in a dope deal. But he needed information; he had to know everything about Wiley, secondarily his "fixer," and Vito Mongreve. As for leads: at that point, he wouldn't know a decent lead if it stood up, waved its thin arms, and pointed to a sign on its chest.

But the address book was interesting in an abstract sense. He'd always thought one could extrapolate from every object around a person to the person her- or himself, to form a perfect representation. An address book was a sum of those objects, a grand sum of a person's notions for food, clothing, real estate, finances. At some point in the future, there would be a program which would take every entry, every mark, every misplaced period, every doodle and come up with an exact simulacrum of the person. In this case, a violent Machiavellian drug dealer who was likely a murderer.

John Vesco called back with the names of the banks. They were safe havens, out of the country, from Switzerland to Barbados. Wiley had planned more than a simple dope deal.

He had to get back to his clients. He put his gold pen on the open page in the address book. He sorted through his email and typed out a few short responses. He was checking a new tech stock, when he stopped short. Unraveling in Wiley's address book near the tip of his pen was an obscure chemical formula—cyclotrimethylene trinitramine.

Harry paused, hunched up his shoulders, and copied the formula into his search engine. Cyclotrimethylene trinitramine was an explosive nitroamine. Nitro.

Great. What was it doing in Wiley's address book?

Harry punched out the number of Fakir Aldruzan, chemist. Fakir was interesting, bendable, and had more than a hint of larceny in his soul. Fakir was a lamb when he'd come to him to help him with the IPO of his first company, Aldruzan Plastics. Later, after Fakir realized Harry had played fast and loose with his stock, he called him names and vowed he'd get back at him. Then, oddly, Fakir called him up and asked for his help. Fakir said that Harry had taught him something and he needed his expertise, his ruthlessness.

Harry felt complimented, and after thinking about it, realized Fakir was right. If you'd just been taken by one of the bigger sharks, who else to go to for help? Since Fakir's capitulation to the ruthlessness of American business, they'd done several under-the-table manipulations of Fakir's stock options in his last company. And he'd made them both money.

He got routed to Fakir's cell. Fakir was driving across the Bay Bridge and was going to lunch before a meeting in Palo Alto.

"Let me take you to lunch, Fakir."

"Of course. See you downstairs in fifteen minutes."

Fakir's Mercedes pulled up at one. The fog had dutifully burned off, and the streets of Upper Parnassus were open and full of light.

"Head over to the south side of the park, the Sunset. There are scores of restaurants."

"You're the captain."

While Fakir steered through the maze of Haight streets, Harry mused about Wiley and how Fakir could help him.

Finally Harry said, "I have a minor problem. It could be lucrative for both of us. Tell me about cyclotrimethylene trinitramine. I know I didn't pronounce it correctly, and I know it's a member of the nitro family."

Fakir was a small man with a neatly trimmed goatee, a large nose, and keen eyes. Fakir laughed. "Are you joking, Harry?"

"I don't think I'm joking."

Fakir turned on Judah. "Your thoughts are ever on money and business and how to make more money. It is a thing to make boom-booms."

Harry frowned. "It seemed likely. Tell me about boom-booms."

"It is the area of chemistry where we figure out how to blow things up. We—Homo sapiens—have spent much time perfecting explosives; it is a mark of civilization. Of course, the big ones are nuclear, but there have been developments in what, for lack of a better word, we call military and domestic explosions. Cyclotrimethylene trinitramine, also called RDX, is used in military explosions. It is also a prime ingredient in the explosive of choice for terrorists. I suppose you're not a terrorist?"

Hah, hah, hah. "And the explosive of choice for terrorists?" said

75

Harry dubiously, wondering how he'd strayed onto that path.

"Semtex, Czech. It is also called 'plastique.' You see it in all the movies; it looks like play dough. Very powerful, easy to use but destined to become obsolete. We are always looking for a bigger bang for our buck."

Harry mused aloud. "Semtex...plastique." An explosion in the park, a damaged windmill, a notation in an address book. "Do you make it or buy it?"

"Buy it if you have the right connections. Are you considering a second career as a terrorist?" Fakir emitted a little chuckle and stroked his goatee.

Harry chuckled with him. Terrorist was absurd. An odd modicum of regret edged his tone. "I fear it is too late. It's too late for most of us. Too late to be a free-lance bridge player, too late for a career in academia, too late to be a master gardener. Too late. Too late. Perhaps one of those paths would have proved more worthwhile, or... Excuse me for meandering. No, Fakir, someone handed me a riddle. Riddles may be intriguing, but this one is irritating, and, as I said, possibly lucrative. Of course, anything could be lucrative. There's a fortune in cow farts, if you can extract the methane economically." Harry felt Fakir's interest. Good. "Let's try this new Asian Fusion restaurant on Irving and Second."

"It could be explosive," said Fakir.

Harry laughed. "Let's hope not."

It felt liberating to leave his flat. Irving Street with its doctors and nurses and students from UCSF made him slip into another world. Everything was straightforward in that blond room with those white tables and blue and green uniforms. The talk around them was about sickness, education, cures, research, and graduating. All without irony.

The noodles were steaming, spicy, and not explosive.

At the start of the lunch, Fakir talked about why he was going to Palo Alto. He had a new venture involving a diminutive plastic wireless hub, which he would sell for a while, then sell out to Cisco. It was a long shot, risky, but hadn't he been doing risks lately? For a few minutes, Harry spun out scenarios for publicity, of building up, shorting stocks, the profit.

But it seemed Harry Mach, financial genius, brilliant market tactician, was no longer concerned about IPOs and raking in bushels of money from stock.

"Fakir, help me with this riddle?"

Fakir looked at him closely. "Would it involve anything slightly irregular?"

"Mostly not; perhaps not at all."

"What is it?"

Harry pulled his arms on the table and looked squarely at Fakir. "Fakir, in your spare time today—I know you don't have much—could you stop by the mill we mentioned earlier? Find out what you can about that explosion."

"Whether it was Semtex or not?"

"That would help; and how one might buy Semtex in this area."

Fakir watched him closely. "I'll see; after the mill we could talk a little."

Harry relaxed, smiled, "Of course."

"Uh, Harry, I'm not sure the venture capitalists will help. The VCs are wary, too many casualties lately. Every time a dot-com dies, funding dries up."

Harry knew about dot-coms dying. "I see."

Fakir looked serious, too serious. "Would you possibly help?"

Good. Leverage. But doing one on Cisco and then selling out? "I'll see."

"That's all I ask."

Harry watched an Asian waiter mince through the crowded tables. "How much?"

"At least a million."

"Of course...if it seems right. Right now, I need information about this explosion."

"I'll look at the windmill later this afternoon and call some people about the Semtex."

His meeting with Fakir helped. He'd connected the explosive in Wiley's address book with an explosion in the park. Whether it was real or not, he'd see later.

First, of course, he had to find out more. He began to feel the dope affair, his Leg 3, was a red herring, or immaterial. Was there another purse, different money? He had no idea beyond his own hunches and a few hints. It was, as they say, a long shot.

But that was how fortunes are made, or Trifectas completed.

10

Judy whirled, fist cocked.

She stopped when she saw the diminutive figure huddled before her. Khris.

She embraced her, her body shaking. She steadied her breath.

Khris' eyes brimmed with tears. "I...I couldn't sleep with Bob. Where were you?"

Judy stroked Khris's hair. "Exploring, digging around, freaking myself out."

She tried to tell her but didn't tell her everything. She couldn't tell her about her hunches or why she had hunches and what, rationally, she was doing.

Soon Khris fell asleep, but Judy had a long night. When she slept, she dreamt she'd walked into the Camino Real in El Salvador and into a maze, a cluttered maze of tunnels splitting off, growing out of one another. Down one tunnel into another. She chased a phantom, which flipped around corners like a white bird. Finally, she plopped down in the middle of the maze, rested her chin on the palm of her hand, and cried.

Khris slipped out of bed around six. At eight, Judy woke up to brilliant sunlight, the brown hills of summer, a distant speck, a bird, chattering squirrels, and scraping sounds from the kitchen. She felt the way she always felt on the farm, until she saw Wiley's house. The Toyota had slipped through the Napa countryside like a thief. She shuddered when she thought of the bathroom, the hand on the door, the loud voice. Harry? Those words filled her head with puzzles as she showered. She had some of her toiletries here, but not her deodorant. She grabbed Khris' pink Sure, thought for a second about whether that was a good idea, decided it was, and used it.

Bob concentrated on making a breakfast of eggs, bacon, and toast. It was the only thing he cooked, but he'd gotten it down to a serious art. Past his lanky form, out the open door, the morning light crawled up the side of foothills. Outside it was pleasant, easy, a slight morning mist. Inside, tension cycled back.

After a few bites of eggs, Judy looked up and said, "I went to Wiley's house last night."

Khris looked at her, then Bob. Bob's fork stopped halfway to his mouth. "Why?"

"Not sure. Anyway, someone else drove up, lights out. He went through Wiley's. He was medium height, shabby, a ponytail. I barely got out without him finding me."

"Jesus," said Bob.

"Seen him before?" said Judy.

"No," said Bob.

Khris shook her head. "Think they'll be over here next?"

"Don't think so," said Judy. "I think you should call the sheriff, then go to Oakland until this quiets down."

"Why don't you call him?" Bob said petulantly.

"You have the time. I got tons of work. In fact, I have to leave after breakfast."

The phone broke through the tension like a klaxon.

Bob put his fork down. Judy stared at the phone. Khris answered it.

"Who?" Khris listened, frowned, then said, "I can't help you." She hung up.

Khris said, "Someone named Harry. Said he's a friend of Wiley's."

Judy frowned. The Harry from last night? She wondered if that was the Harry Mach Khris mentioned. Why would he know about Khris and have her phone number? Judy decided not to say his name. It was likely Bob didn't know a thing about him. "What did he want?"

"He asked about Wiley. I told him—well, you know what I told him."

"Let's leave this morning," Bob said.

"I don't want to go back yet," said Khris. "We just got here."

Yin and Yang. For and Against. Eternal opposition. "You guys hash that out," said Judy.

While Bob and Khris argued over plans to leave for their separate apartments in Oakland, Judy walked into the living room. She sat in her favorite stuffed chair. She felt exhausted, worried, and oddly pumped from last night. She relaxed into cushions. It was odd, she thought, that her apartment was almost clinically antiseptic, but she felt most at home in old chairs, rundown farmhouses, and sitting at scratched-up kitchen tables.

Judy plucked the notebook out of her vest. She jotted down what Khris told her. She wrote down "Wiley Brooks" and "Harry Mach" and "CIA." Then she noticed Bob's four photo albums—all indexed and labeled—stacked on the side table. She picked them up, one by one, and flipped through them. Most of the photos were of the good times in the last two years, everybody smiling. But there were a few recent photos, photos where Judy Ferris was absent. One was of a party at Wiley's. There was a gang of people on Wiley's front porch. Wiley wasn't there; in fact he wasn't in any of the photos, but Wiley's SUV was.

She squinted at the number, then jotted it down next to the license number she'd jotted down last night. She pocketed the pencil and notebook, then stared at the window, which gave onto the front porch. She could see a railing, sky, the second floor of Wiley's house. The last travel article she'd written—a story on Bali for Garuda Airlines' in-flight magazine—faded into the past of another Judy Ferris. Bob and Khris were part of that past. It was a mundane past, where one acted for rational reasons: getting rest, getting away, finding a new job. Was there a coherent reason for searching Wiley's house or scribbling notes in a tattered notebook?

Judy felt antsy as she listened to Bob and Khris make plans. She went to her room and wrote a check for her share of the rent for October. Half an hour later, she looked at the farm a last time, kissed Khris, gave Bob's shoulder a squeeze, and fired up the Miata.

As soon as she got on Highway 12, the peace and silence of Napa, of the farm, of that rare blend of companionship and silence drifted away. Her head filled up with what she'd done last night, a silent car, and notebook fragments. She angled down towards Highway 37 and decided to take the long way along the coast. She found Sir Francis Drake, then picked up Highway 1. The road along the coast was as curvy as the trunks of the bay laurel and treacherous as a snake. Sometimes she felt like a real snake along these roads, moving in a slow peristalsis towards quick mouth-openings and quick views of the ocean.

One wheel off and over she'd go.

Tully's. The bartender. The bridge. Would she scream or lose her breath going over that fast? Would she be terrified on the way down or,

80

realizing the hopelessness of surviving, would she make a last existential comment on her life, on its worth or lack of it? At that moment, she didn't know what she'd think. A curvy road, a cliff, a demon imp. She'd better get off that road.

Judy got back early in the afternoon and found more messages and projects on her answering machine. The Asian group called to confirm their meeting that afternoon. There was a meeting on Friday with Fodor, two messages about press releases. She felt tired, but she had a ton of work. She shrugged off last night and recharged her day with coffee.

Fifteen minutes later, after blanking out in a misty view of the East Bay, she read the supporting documentation on two press releases, wrote them, and emailed them. She still had a semi-long article on Cambodia and the Fodor chapters. She was thinking about how to approach the Cambodia article when the phone rang.

Mike Larew.

"How did you get my phone number?" Judy said, frowning. He was big, pockmarked, sweaty, and curious about why she was curious. She tried to fashion his face, the black-butched hair, the muscular forearms, the way he looked against the backdrop of Tully's noise, beer-pissy smell, and subterra shadows.

"You're in the phone book," Mike said.

"Bullshit. The number's unlisted."

"Got me. You'd be surprised what you can find on the Internet."

She'd found people herself. "Okay. What's up?"

"I thought we might meet and talk some more about Wiley."

She listened with a growing sense of alarm. Last night was bad, a warning that things could spin out of control. Now people were calling her! Her impulse was to say no. Then she felt an unaccountable frisson. Mike Larew. Talk about Wiley. It was more interesting than making nice to the ATA. "I have a meeting late afternoon. I can see you for a few minutes after that. There's a old bar called the Palms near Fourth and Market?"

"Curious. Six-thirty?"

"I might be a little late."

Mike said that was okay, and that was that.

She forced herself to concentrate on her presentation. Which writers was she going to call? Who would do the layout and graphics? She said she'd hit the ground running—everything had to be running, leaping, charging, sprinting. It was the ongoing conquest of sports metaphors. After an hour, she got up and paced in front of her picture window. She was irritated at the ATA, and she couldn't say why. Impulsively, she snatched the phone and called a friend at the SFPD. There was no record of Wiley's SUV or Ponytail's Toyota. Wiley Brooks: nada. Roger Nesbitt? Roger had a record, and her contact thought he knew where he lived. Judy did the phones and found his number in Sonoma.

That was good, but why would she call him? Judy hung up, grim and distracted.

Khris had said Wiley bragged about "special projects" and that he'd mentioned "Barbados." Judy checked the clock. She didn't have time, but she flipped through her filing cabinet. Then when she didn't find what she wanted, she picked through the black plastic case of her old diskettes. The label on the El Salvador diskette was old, very old, the "E" obliterated. She held it in her hand for a moment, then slipped it back into the case.

Judy picked the portable phone out of its unit, grabbed her Rolodex, and walked through the kitchen to the patio. She flipped through the Rolodex and found Myra Cohen's number. Myra was a diminutive Jewish woman with twinkly brown eyes, a mop of raven hair and coaster-size earrings. Myra had worked for the New York Times in Central America, then Washington, and finally on the West Coast. Myra had connections to someone in CIA Internal Affairs—CIAIA: it always made her hum "Old MacDonald had a farm..." She'd met Myra in El Salvador before they'd arrested her, Judy, and they kept in touch, but lately, any contact was rare. The last time was a year ago when they saw a remastered copy of The Third Man at the Castro Theatre.

After a few minutes of catching up, Myra listened to what she said about Wiley Brooks. Myra said she'd call back. Ten minutes later the phone rang. Judy watched it as if it were a timer signaling a sea change in her life.

Myra made her life more difficult. Wiley—it wasn't his real name, but everyone knew or guessed that—was a former CIA officer. South America, Chile, Peru. The rumors were—everything about CIA operations officers were rumors, unless you caught them in the act—he was an interrogator working with the secret police rooting out leftist cells for Pinochet, and later Shining Path cells for the Peruvians. Two years ago he assassinated the wrong Peruvian police captain and had been hung out to dry at a desk job in San Francisco. Myra guessed he was on a project, but she didn't know what the project was or why Wiley would disappear.

"Why?" said Myra. "Every time we talk about the CIA, you go into a funk."

"This is special."

"You weren't able to do anything about it before. Why now?"

Judy shook her head morosely. "Touché."

"I didn't mean that," Myra said softly.

"Help me scratch the itch. What about Barbados?"

"Beyond it being a great place to hide money, I didn't find a connection to Wiley."

"Anything else?"

Myra whispered, "Revolution Mondiale."

"Worldwide revolution? What shit is that?"

"Somebody mentioned it, and that's it. I don't know what it has to do with Wiley or with anything. I don't even know what it means."

"Well, if you find out, and if you can tell me…"

"I'll call. You've got me interested."

Judy cradled the phone.

Worldwide revolution: only a few miserable Shining Path radicals believed it. On the other hand, the stars were lining up in long military rows and marching her towards a fate she could sense but not see. A disappearance, a dope scam, a CIA project, Revolution Mondiale. That was the wrong track. There was a connection between those events and people. But the scam and a project were separate, distinct, bound together only by Wiley Brooks, one of the boys-in-men's-bodies, a Hemingway distortion now invisible, who had just tapped into the recesses of her past. A past that scared her and made her angry at the same time.

Late afternoon, the room darkening, the light softer on the East Bay hills, she felt the slight breeze from the open kitchen door. Her favorite scrub jay peered at her from the lone Monterey pine. She went back to her PC and looked at her screen saver, the pipes growing out of each other. They were a foretaste, a foreshadowing of what would happen if she got involved. It was nothing if not a maze, a Sartrian no exit, where

83

people were destined to pick at each other in perpetuity.

Before she could stop herself, she grabbed her Napa notebook and pulled out a blank piece of paper from her printer. She copied everything she'd written, the sputters of conversation she'd overheard in Wiley's house, the license plate numbers, then everything she knew about Wiley, how long he'd been in Napa, what he'd hinted he was doing, what Khris had told her, what Myra had said. When she finished, she taped it to the wall over her PC. It was a puzzle, a special Mensa problem with a high-level trick answer.

"What am I doing?" she said to the scrub jay peering at her from the backyard table. She picked an unshelled peanut from the jar and held it in her hand. A few minutes later she felt the spindly claws on her hand and watched the quick plucking of the nut, and the escape. The single-minded bird perched on the patio table, held the nut with his claw, and hammered it with its thick bill until it cracked.

She glanced at the clock on the refrigerator and saw she was going to be late if she dawdled. She took a quick shower, then dressed for her ATA meeting in a blue pantsuit, a matching jacket, frilly white blouse, and blue short heels. She got her keys and picked up her valise, but before locking the door, she looked at her apartment again, working out the same pause as yesterday, seeing the soft distant skyline, Asian accents, elephant palm, cute glass tables, and cozy white nook as foreign. She'd counted months and trips like tokens, watched stuff accumulate from a phantom Judy who lived like a ghost at the edge of Normal, normal-this, normal-that, normal-anonymous.

It meant she was nobody, a cipher, a placeholder in her own life.

11

Kathy "Sugar" Mercedes sat alone in the arboretum in Golden Gate Park. She'd slept out near Ocean Highway last night, not far from where they'd watched the hatchback crawl through the fog.

She'd thought about that early morning every day wherever she was, out near the ocean, back in the Haight, or across from Wiley's flat. She thought of the guy crabwalking up to the mill, putting down a briefcase, snapping a photo, and crabwalking back to the car. What she remembered best was waiting in the bushes. They knew something was going to happen but not exactly what or when. Course what happened was they blew part of the mill to smithereens.

It was weird, and she had to admit she obsessed about it. And the place she most obsessed about it was right across from Wiley's flat. It wasn't just because Potato died. It went right back to waiting that night. It wasn't blowing up the windmill so much as after the dust had settled when Scab announced it was their ticket to ride. She knew at that very moment fate had started tugging them in, that something bad was going to happen to them. Scab's ticket to ride. Something bad was bound to happen. Bound to.

She didn't want to go out to the far end of the park in the first place. It was cold and foggy, and they were all hungry, at least she was. But Scab brought everyone along in his wake as usual. There was always something happening around Scab, mostly of his causing.

Ticket to ride. Hah! She didn't like Wiley, the red-headed devil. He was twisted, mean, and devious. And Scab thought he could handle him!

What a laugh: a two-strike homeless ex-con alkie was going to match wits with a guy who had a couple cars, lived in a Haight flat, and was twice as big and twice as mean as Scab.

Sugar lit a roach and lay back on the grass. Bye bye, fog. It was getting towards their special summer, and it started out as a blue-sky day and stayed that way. She saw a couple vultures lazing in the currents, and a small cloud like a lamb without a head, tail, or legs floated over the treetops, over her head, and towards downtown.

And she didn't like it when Scab went up to Wiley outside his flat and told him we'd seen him and wanted money, lots of it. And she really didn't like it when Wiley, after giving them the evil eye, gave him two hundred bucks.

She told Scab not to press his luck. We got our money, she said, a lot more than we thought we'd get. We got lucky. But Scab told Wiley he wanted more, a lot more. She didn't like the way Wiley gave them the evil eye. Later, Scab said that's what America is about, what made us great—not settling for a little when you can get a lot. We're going to squeeze that redhead, squeeze him for a long time. You don't go around blowing up windmills without paying for it.

And she told 'em both it was peculiar when that short woman in the leather jacket followed them around snapping their photos. Scab thought it was a lark, and so did Potato. She didn't like it...at all. Why them? It would have been different if she'd taken a lot of pictures, but she didn't. It looked like she was pretending to take photos of others so she could take more of them. Made her feel weird.

She tried to tell Scab something weird was happening when Potato turned up dead. She told him it wasn't a coincidence. She told him Wiley had some part in it... it was the photos. He done something with the photos. Scab said what, did he put the photos on little dolls and stick pins in 'em? Potato died cuz he was a retard and drank himself to death. He was a malt liquor fatality. It was his time to go.

Sugar scratched her hip. She reached into her pack and pulled out a day-old bagel and cream cheese. Dope made her super hungry. That two hundred bucks didn't last very long, and there wasn't too much more coming with Wiley gone. That was peculiar, probably the most peculiar thing that happened in the last week. Wiley doing a swan dive off the bridge.

You know what, she told Scab and Potato, she didn't believe it for a split second. They didn't believe it either. Wiley musta planned it a long time. They still couldn't figure why he blew up the mill.

One thing she didn't tell Scab was what she saw at that flat. She started hanging around with a couple old guys—Petey and Jon—near Stanyan, and she saw Wiley's flat most days...couldn't help looking at it after what happened. First thing was she saw this good-looking basset-faced guy go in on Monday. He looked nervous when he went in and a lot more nervous when he came out. Then the cops came and roped it off. What was even weirder was Tuesday night. That's when she saw Wiley slip into his flat. Then she knew he wasn't dead. She didn't tell Scab, cuz it wouldn't have done any good. How was he, a homeless ex-con, going to find Wiley, if Wiley didn't want to be found? She wondered why he came back, cuz as far as she and anybody else knew, he was still dead. She decided he musta forgot something.

Sugar put the joint in the front compartment of her pack. It was

86

early, but she was still hungry, and it was time to go into the Haight and start the day. Sometimes she felt like an animal. She was always looking for something to eat or drink. Not like real people who had money and fridges and knew exactly when they were going to eat, and most of the time what.

12

Marant Olivier was riven with doubts. He wanted to call Christian but, according to their agreement, couldn't until he had something concrete. He had a mystery. According to Potato, the noxious park resident who liked his cheap beer a little too much, the furtive chemist might be Wiley Brooks, a Wiley Brooks who may have committed suicide, who lived near the park. And who took the photos? If it wasn't the chemist, he must have had an accomplice. Kafi said the chemist was clever. Was he more than clever?

Yesterday, he puzzled the affair over a breakfast of scones and strawberry jam topped off with a cappuccino on the fogged-in terrace of the Cultural Institute. He spent most of the morning there reading the local papers the Institute staff left outside his door, and watching the fog swirl under the bridge and dissipate. He was circling a problem that was like the fog, hiding, then vanishing, ephemeral, then revealing the solid distant headlands.

That afternoon, he drove to the Civic Center and parked on a side street near the San Francisco Public Library. Halfway across the middle of the Civic Center complex, he ran into another homeless encampment. They were everywhere! It was easy to see why a few of them may have seen the stupid and ill-advised test. Seeing them moving their carts from place to place or drinking or fighting made him think of Potato. He hadn't wanted to kill him. Potato was the lowest pawn in a larger struggle. Pawns. You could say that of everyone until you got up to the ones actually pulling the strings.

He soon found that the new library specialized in cul-de-sacs; it was a classic triumph of form over function. La Bibliothèque Nationale, Beauborg, the chain of Sorbonne bibliothèques—all real books with tattered covers and pages. The San Francisco Library had fewer books than any he'd seen, although computers sprouted everywhere like toadstools.

Marant sat at the only free computer on the ground floor and typed Wiley Brooks' name into the Chronicle/Examiner database. He came up with an article about a Wiley Brooks who had disappeared, apparently a suicide. Why would Boris/Wiley disappear? Was he waiting until the drunks were dead? But disappearance, especially pretending to kill oneself, was a risky ploy. How would he come back?

Different country? Different identity? Had he made those plans?

The article also mentioned a bar, Tully's, where the locals had been questioned about Wiley Brooks' death.

Marant found his car. He turned off the side street onto Market and a few minutes later turned on Haight Street. He parked on Page Street and a few minutes later stopped in front of Tully's. He stepped over a pink-headed boy splayed on the sidewalk like a squashed spider and pushed open the weathered brown door.

The lightning-bolt décor and ear-splitting music reminded him of a Rhine thunderstorm. After a few minutes, he saw that the denizens were smelly, loutish, drunk, draped in leather and spangles, and excelled in boozy posturing. Odd place for a chemist.

Marant bought a glass of Chardonnay and talked to the bartender, a rotund talkative man named Charlie. With little prompting, Charlie told him about one of the bar's more notorious patrons. "He's more popular dead than alive," said Charlie. Charlie picked up a wet glass and started cleaning it with a dirty white bar rag.

"How is that?" said Marant.

"Beside the police, four or five people been looking for him."

"Hmm."

Charlie held the glass up and looked at it critically, then he bent over the bar and lowered his voice. "Know why?"

"Not a clue," said Marant, amused at Charlie's secretiveness.

"Drugs."

Charlie stood back. He swirled his bar rag in a glass wiped clean two minutes ago. "Isn't everything about drugs?" said Marant.

"This is different. He was dealing. The bartender at the Golden Paradise said the same thing. He'd set up in back and make calls. Then somebody come in, and they'd go out to the alley. But you know, he was onto something else, too. It was like selling was a kinda sideline. Of course, I heard he scammed a bunch of people."

"Did you see him selling drugs?"

"I'm not an idiot. I didn't see nothin'. You can get hurt, easy."

"Of course," said Marant. "By that other thing did you mean as a chemist?"

Charlie laughed and put the glass down. "You been talking to the wrong people, buddy."

"Likely for a long time."

"Another thing. Never liked the guy. He was mean. He got in rows with a couple guys here. They always got hurt. Most never came back. See that guy?...turn slow."

Marant turned his head slowly and glanced towards the front. He saw a hippie with a long ponytail. His nose was bandaged, and he had yellowing circles under his eyes. He came back to Charlie. "Right."

"He and Wiley had an argument right in here. Next day he was like that. Guy only came back after he found out Wiley was gone."

"What did Wiley look like?"

"Big, strong, rangy. Musta been Army or Special Forces. Somebody said he was CIA, but you can't believe everything you hear." Charlie turned, reached over a few bottles of vodka, and plucked a photo off the mirror. He slid the photo across to Marant. "That's him."

His face was in a shadow, and it was hard to pick out details. But Wiley looked almost demonic with his widow's peak of snarled red hair and smirk. Marant had seen that before.

Marant pushed the photo back at Charlie. "Wouldn't want him mad at me."

"You got that right."

"Hey Charlie," yelled two punks near the hippie.

"Customers," said Charlie.

While Charlie went to serve the punks, Marant pieced together Wiley's portrait. He found that Wiley was more violent than sincere, a manipulator, a person who probably had drug dealings, and not, given Charlie's reaction, a chemist. Could he have been a middle man for someone else, the real chemist, Boris? That was a possibility; whoever the chemist was, he was playing a dangerous game.

Marant turned his back to the banging and shouting around the pool table and the juke box, and took a sip of cheap Chardonnay. Crowds jerked by the open door.

Marant took a last look at Wiley's photo, pushed it back, and left Tully's.

Marant puzzled what he'd learned as he walked to the car. He wanted to drop the assignment, but he had to find out more. If Wiley wasn't a chemist, what was going on? Was it about Kafi, the Muslims? Marant realized that he missed his sculpture, his striving for roundness, his straight lines, the Fort Mahon beach, the treacherous tides and shifting sands, small talk in galleries, his Paris apartment.

He needed a diversion. Thinking of his own sculpture made him think it was time to visit the Legion of Honor, the Rodin collection, and The Shades. Half an hour later, after regarding The Shades for a few contemplative minutes, he paid the entrance fee and headed into the left wing of the museum's extensive Rodin collection. Rodin was more like Moore or Maillol, especially the late Rodin when his figures, like those of David, seemed to emerge from the rock, as if their forms had dwelt in the interstices for millennia waiting for the sculptor's chisel.

It was a pleasant interlude, but it reminded him too much of France, Fort Mahon, of the openings he was missing. His intuition told him that he might not get back to that life for a long time. Finally, he went to the Legion's café and ordered lunch, a toasted eggplant sandwich and a Perrier. When he finished, he tried to work out what he knew about the project. He still didn't have enough information, but he had to call Kafi. He saw a phone in the patio, walked over, and punched out Kafi's number.

"This assignment is absurd. These winos are harmless, drop-outs with pickled brains. Who's going to believe they saw a shadowy character blow up a windmill in the fog?"

Kafi sounded nervous, as usual. "This assignment has not worked the way we hoped. But we need the process. The drunks could be our security problem."

"Have you talked to Boris?" said Marant.

"He was happy one wino was eliminated. He says the others must be, too. He doesn't want loose ends. He may be overly careful, but we know about loose ends."

Marant almost mentioned Wiley Brooks' name and his presumed suicide. He held back. He wanted to piece together what was going on without being spoon-fed. "The only loose end you have is the chemist. The winos didn't see you."

"Perhaps they did," said Kafi. "I placed the explosive. I was out in the open."

Over the limitless ocean, gulls swirled and pelicans glided. Marant looked at the enormous sculpture of a spider on one side of the café. It looked like it had crawled out of some crevice in the rock face and was going to attack latte-sipping museum patrons. Kafi and GIA. Why did Christian let them in? GIA was responsible for thousands of innocent deaths.

"The Americans revel in death," said Marant. "The gore, the weapons, and not least motives. Giving them more bodies could imperil our chances of obtaining the explosive. You do want the explosive."

"It's not needless. You're the expert. You will make it an accident, as usual."

"I don't usually compound fiascoes."

"A mercenary!"

Marant imagined Kafi's nostrils were flared, the mouth—given the appropriate liquids—would have foamed. It was a conundrum, he'd told Christian, that he, the mercenary, never killed needlessly, while the righteous planted bombs in schools, destroyed villages, and cut the throats of dirt-poor farmers. He did understand Kafi's position. He wanted to look in the stern faces of his fellow Muslims in GIA or the IG, or even some of Hamas or Hezbollah old guard—the flurry of acronyms which made up Kafi's side of the loose council of RM—and report that he would soon have the perfect revolutionary tool from Boris, a voice on the telephone.

The picture was unsettling. Who was Boris—Wiley Brooks—exactly? Was the real chemist using Wiley/Boris as a front? Did anyone really have the formula? And what would happen when the last wino was dead? It exasperated Marant every time he thought of it. "I'll see," he said finally. "I'll call tomorrow."

After he hung up, Marant walked out of the museum. He was about to unlock his car when he saw the George Segal installation of a concentration camp.

Marant walked over and stared at it. It was an ironic installation, the chalky-white bodies strewn over the cement, the man with his hand draped on the barbed wire facing the ocean. Not just freedom, but ultimate freedom. The plaster figure watched distant pelicans gliding, hovering, and then dropping into the ocean, surfacing a few seconds later, their gray bills full of water and fish. The Nazis had imprisoned, tortured, and killed Marant's parents, Michel and Françoise. Sometimes when he walked the beach at Fort Mahon, he thought he could feel them walking decades earlier, arm-in-arm, their footprints drifting off with the tide, planning what they would do with their lives, hoping for, working for, in their small way, some distant peaceful time.

13

Judy drove down Market Street, the wide artery stretching across the city diagonally from northeast to southwest, from the Embarcadero to an imaginary center under Twin Peaks. The street was, as usual, full of contrasts. The UN Plaza which, remodeled and spiffed up, should have been the city showing off with its sculpture, tree-lined cut-stone walkway, and fountain, was home to fifty-plus homeless who camped out with shopping carts piled with broken TVs, boom boxes, dirty dolls, scruffy paperbacks, and worn shoes. More street people hung out on the sidewalks, some begging, others screaming at each other with thick, drugged voices.

A few blocks from UN Plaza, tourists crammed Macy's, the Gap, or other stores, garish pizza joints on Powell, or marched towards the south side of Market and the Sony Metreon with its games, stores, multiplex, and IMAX. Some checked maps and shivered in the growing chill.

As she got closer to Fourth Street, businessmen and women, programmers, financial consultants, secretaries, and temps hurried in opposing streams on the sidewalks or got into or out of cabs, SUVs, and limos. Tattooed bike messengers dipped into and out of traffic. The air was frantic, and people yelled into cell phones with worry etched on their faces.

One adjusted. One went with the flow. There was pride in fitting in, Judy thought. Or coping. Judy parked the car in a secret place near Fourth Street, grabbed her valise and handbag, and went to see the Asian Travel Association. She was halfway to their office when she realized she didn't want to see them or explain how she was going to slant Vietnam Today to build up another premier vacation spot for the rich in a struggling third-world country. She shrugged, frowned, then pushed open the glass door of the Gould Building.

Two hours later, she emerged. She talked, she walked, she juggled her balls, she hid doubts in brusque competence. She hadn't forgotten about meeting Mike Larew, but she hadn't thought about him. She glanced at her watch. The Palms was a block away. She walked slowly down Market, then turned down a winding alley. She had no idea what to expect. Who was Mike Larew? What part did he play in the Wiley mess?

Judy stopped in front of the Palms. The bar leaned into the abyss. It was an anachronism in the downtown high-rent district of fancy bars and tony restaurants. A brown sign, weathered and askew, announced the "Palms" above a door flanked by withered palms in wooden buckets. Judy took a last look at the fading cerulean sky capping the alley and pushed open the door. The Palms was a large dim room with a dark wood floor and dark tables, occasionally lit by a sputtering neon beer sign in the corner. The back bar was antediluvian, the scattered natives fossilized. A miasma of fetid air rose from the ghosts of a thousand dead smokers. Mike Larew sat near the neon sign and an ancient dartboard that had a few darts stuck in it at odd angles. He tapped a plastic dart on the table.

"Evening," she said. He was dressed in a white shirt with the sleeves rolled up to his elbows, pressed jeans, and light hiking boots. He regarded her casually, almost lazily.

"Drink?" he said, starting to get up.

"I'll get my own."

She dropped her valise in one of the empty chairs, then angled through the tables to the bar. She felt Mike watching her, and she was conscious of the way her hips swung through the tables. The back bar was an interesting maze years ago, but it had given up its interest to time. It was busy with square mirrors, Doric columns, old photos, and dusty Eisenhower-era dart trophies. She ordered a Bloody Mary from an elderly, slight bartender with a bald head and frayed baggy pants held up by a pair of old-fashioned suspenders.

She paid for her drink. When she turned, Mike was tapping the dart slowly and watching her. She angled self-consciously through the tables, moved a chair out, and sat. They stared at each other across a table of a thousand splotches, beer rings, and cigarette burns. Every few seconds the sputtering neon in the corner silvered the right side of his face.

Mike stopped tapping. He made a small, half-wave with the dart. "Cool place."

Judy glanced at the man sleeping to her right. "It was the first place I could think of. Once I imagined O'Neill used to come here to drink and record the drunks, masks, fantasies, and slurred talk. It feels like a set for Anna Christie or The Iceman Cometh. But it's not romantic anymore, just forgotten. And it's a lot closer to the abyss than I remembered. The owners have long-term cheap rent, but I can't see it lasting much longer. So what's this about?" She sipped her drink and felt the rush of warmth.

His brown eyes were bright, intelligent, his expression suddenly suspicious. His gaze shifted to the dart. "Why do you think Wiley faked his suicide?"

Mike tapped the dart, as if it were a technique for third degree. She sipped her drink. The Tabasco made her feel alert, the booze calmer. "Why do you think he did?"

"Let's not spar," Mike said, leaning forward and resting his elbows on the table. His eyes pinned hers. "Wiley faked his suicide, probably for some rip-off. That's why you were in Tully's, and that's why you're here."

The cards were on the table, but what did they mean? "All right. So what? You're passing through, on your way to law school. That's your story."

Mike's face developed a condescending smile. "Mountain-climbing. Sky-diving. Canyoning. Don't you watch SUV commercials?"

"What does that mean?" she said, truly puzzled.

"Thrills, action, a hint of chaos. It attracts some people like dead

94

meat does flies. It attracts you too. That's why you were in Tully's."

"Wrong. You think Wiley Brooks is thrilling? You met him once."

"I can see that the man leaves bodies in his wake." Mike paused, as if he were searching for a word. "But that's immaterial."

"What's thrilling now?"

"You." Mike sipped his beer. The neon flashed on the brown bottle like a silver knife.

Judy flushed, then smiled in spite of herself. She clicked open her purse and found cigarettes and lighter. She threw the pack on the table but kept the lighter. She flicked the lighter, and a flame jumped up between them. The flame hid Mike's face, then his face jumped out at her when she flicked the lighter off. She felt complimented, angry, and suspicious. "OK. I'm tall, sexy, and irresistible. What's the real reason?"

Mike's chair creaked as he shifted his weight. He seemed edgy; of course, they were talking about crime or sex. Judy thought about last night. That spur-of-the-moment midnight excursion vibrated in her psyche. Why had she done it, and why did it feel great afterwards?

Mike shook his head as if she were a child, then leaned over and picked up the dart. He felt the point with his finger. "That's the only reason. You're my type, and I don't like to beat around the bush. I want to get to know you."

"First it's all about Wiley; now it's a one-night stand. I missed the segue. Erratic doesn't equal adventurous or exciting."

Someone stirred behind her, a chair was dragged, neon flickered in Mike Larew's frown. A few days ago, she was offered a job she'd wanted for years. Now, she was sitting in a dying bar trading innuendos and talking up dope deals, disappearances, and one-night stands. A vision of El Salvador flickered in her consciousness. It was a perspective of immense poverty and fear, prisons, torture. She knew that beyond her arrest, beyond the threats in the hot, dank, piss-soaked jail, that fear fed the beast, fear kept everyone off-balance, and fear kept a straitjacket status quo. Fear and terror were part of the human condition. Would always be a part.

Mike scraped his chair forward. He seemed confident, athletic. "I don't have time for the niceties," he said. Mike watched a blind man in a large trench coat tap his way to the bar and whisper his order to the bartender. Mike placed the dart on the table, then rubbed his hair. It flipped back like a brush.

Judy snatched up the pack and jiggled out a cigarette. She lit it and blew a thin stream of smoke away from Mike. It was time for her to cast out a line. "I'm not a Pepsi-moment. Wiley fucked over a friend of mine. If I were interested in him, it would be to nail his ass to the wall, not for a thrill."

"You can do that?"

"I can try."

Mike drained the last of his beer and set it on a beaten-up coaster. "Because you're a writer?" She could feel her face tighten. She rolled the cone of her cigarette around the ashtray. "Your travel stories are indexed in a handful of search engines. Some have an edge; most don't."

Judy took a long drink and saw Mike's face distort in the side of the glass. From that perspective, he seemed almost demonic. The absurdity of what she was doing ebbed back. "I used to have an edge. As for the Web, I lose money every time someone downloads a story. Eighteen-year-olds think everything is free...until they get their own stuff ripped off."

"If they have their own stuff. So what was Wiley like? As you said, I saw him once."

She couldn't figure out what he wanted, and he knew Wiley faked a suicide. That might be interesting for cocktail party chatter. But there was something else. You didn't find out more by playing coy. "I went out with him once. He was mean and a bully. He liked playing with people. He felt he could do anything he wanted. He felt he could fake a suicide."

"I guessed it was about drugs," said Mike. "But was there anything else?"

"Like what?" said Judy, frowning.

"I'm not sure. Maybe I want to be a writer too, and need more information."

"No ulterior motives beyond curiosity?" said Judy.

"Do reporters always look for ulterior motives? It's a pessimistic world view. There are times when a suicide is just a suicide, or a fake suicide a fake suicide."

"That doesn't make sense. If it were fake, that means there was another motive."

Mike's eyes narrowed. He looked serious. "Was he doing anything else before his suicide? It could have been anything."

Mike's interest made her think about the time she was with Wiley, what Khris said about him. She had to call Khris later. "Nothing else."

"Somebody mentioned he'd seen him with some street people."

Judy frowned. "What kind of street people?"

"The kind that live in the park. Alcoholics, I'd guess."

"This is the first time anyone mentioned them. He lived near the park, and park people are always panhandling."

"It may sound like I have an ulterior motive, but the bottom line is that the mysterious Wiley Brooks is gone. Whether he gainered off the bridge or faked it, he's gone." Mike punctuated what he said by snatching up the dart, cocking his arm, and throwing the dart at the dartboard twenty feet away. He threw it harder than she expected. It stuck deep in the board.

"I see you're good at parlor games," she said, crushing her cigarette in the ashtray.

"I'm good at a lot else." Mike smiled and raised his brows slightly in invitation.

She felt flattered. She was starting to like Mike, but there was something that didn't ring true, and she went with that feeling. And there it was again. That slight accent. She couldn't quite place it. Eastern European? And wanting to know more about what else Wiley was into. Revolution Mondiale? CIA?

"I'll bet you are. But that's for another lifetime. Gotta go."

"I thought we might have dinner."

"I have a real life."

"What isn't life?" he said, laughing. Mike's laugh was more rumble than laugh. He threw his arms in the air. "I can see I've lost, and I've lost before, and I can take it. If you don't know how to lose, you're in trouble. Which bus do I take to the Haight?"

She got up, snatched up her valise, and watched him. "I'm sure you know. Want a ride?"

Mike laughed, shoved his chair back, and got up. "Finally a concession."

She was glad to get outside the Palms. Outside, the sky had faded to gray, and the streetlights made dirty cones on the buildings. The night air revived her.

Her car was half on the sidewalk, half in the alley in her special unticketable spot.

"I can see it's not safe," Mike said, looking critically at the Miata.

"It's worse the way I drive."

"Good." He opened the door and angled himself into the passenger side and moved the seat back as far as it would go, but the dash hit the top of his legs, and his head was inches higher than the windshield.

She threw her valise in the cramped space behind her seat. A few minutes later, she made a screeching turn onto Market Street. "The engine's healthy, but the body's on life support."

Mike watched the pavement zipping under his legs from the hole in the floorboard. "My life expectancy must be zero."

She liked Mike's bigness, his muscles, his smell. She even liked his bluntness and thrill-seeking, if that's what it was. It was refreshing after dealing with the likes of Peter Gross and gay huggy-feely editors. Streetlights and cars shot by. Powell Street, UN Plaza, the Civic Center, Van Ness. Mike leaned against her as she turned onto Haight Street, and she almost leaned back. She made a show of double-clutching, then revved it up the hill. Gradually those up-and-down hills opened to a perspective of Haight Street with its rainbow colors rimmed with looming blackwood acacias marching west, capped by a sedate dab of swaying eucalyptus in the park.

They hit a bump near Buena Vista Park, and the glove compartment popped open. Three DeLite condoms fell out, two balanced on Mike's lap, the third disappeared through the floor.

"They're Gay Parade leftovers. I'm not a contortionist," Judy said, laughing.

"You keep surprising me." He flipped the surviving condoms into the glove compartment and slammed it shut.

Sometimes it seemed that Haight Street never slept. Punks hunkered down in groups of threes and fours, bikers straddled their cycles, drunks passed paper sacks. She drove past the Wasteland, Tully's, the Cala parking lot. The fog was just starting to creep over the trees onto Stanyan Street.

Judy said, "Kinda an odd neighborhood for a to-be lawyer, isn't it?"

"It has action on the streets, in the bars."

"That's your mantra."

She turned on Stanyan, passed the homeless encampment near the park entrance. Mike said, "You can drop me here. The hotel's a block away." He pointed to a two-story hotel, The Park Hotel. She stopped across the street, and Mike pried himself out of the car.

"I blew tonight," said Mike, resting his hand on the window frame. His body was bent slightly towards her, relaxed. Swaying eucalyptus framed his head. She could barely make out the tiny pockmarks on his face, but in that light it made him seem softer, more vulnerable, accessible. She almost felt like parking, swapping innuendoes, seeing what might happen. He saw it too. "Next time I'll start slower, bring daffodils, truffles."

She laughed, and sighed inwardly. "I'm allergic to both, and there was a lot more to tonight than flowers and candy. And you know it."

Mike shook his head, grinned. "Maybe it was all about you."

"Likely not. Good luck lawyering."

Mike lifted his hand off the car. She checked the street, then the Stanyan/Haight intersection, then put the Miata in gear. She shot forward and made a screeching U-turn. When she turned right on Haight, she glanced at her right-side rear-view mirror and saw Mike watching her. Then he started across the street.

She accelerated through the Haight for two blocks, then turned on Cole. She wasn't sure what she wanted to do. She wasn't exactly playing it by ear, but something didn't feel right. Parking karma was good. She edged into a spot on Cole, dropped her valise into the trunk and locked it. She waited five minutes, then walked slowly up Cole two blocks, then doubled back towards the park and Mike Larew's hotel. The clerk was young with two arms full of tattoos.

"Say, I'm looking for Mike Larew. You know his room?"

"Who?"

"Larew, Mike."

"Ain't heard of him, lady."

"Big guy, beard, pockmarks, athletic."

"Nobody like that," he said. "I woulda noticed."

She didn't trust Mr. Tattoo to be that alert. He could have been stoned, or dumb. "Nobody tonight?"

"Course. Couple tourists—gals."

"Right. Thanks."

Outside, Judy stared at the park. Mike said "street people." Is that where he went? She turned and walked slowly back to the Miata. The night had turned dark on her. She watched the shadows and wondered about Mike Larew. Almost everything he'd told her was a lie or subterfuge. She wondered what he really wanted, and why.

14

Fakir dropped him at the bank. He took out a few thousand and walked the mile back to the house, past the sprawling UCSF campus and over Parnassus. Harry regarded the Victorian he called home for the last five years. It was on a cul-de-sac near Ashbury Terrace and open on every side. No dim, grim, poorly lighted Victorian for Harry Mach. He'd had a handful of houses in the city after the divorce...on Russian Hill and Pacific Heights, but he liked this one best.

He knew how the natives looked at him. He had the biggest, most luxurious house, the fanciest car, the trophy women, the limos, the animation. They had bills, babies, and long commutes. They envied him, and he knew it.

He picked out a raft of letters, the Harvard Business Review, the Economist, and Bloomberg from the mailbox.

Afternoon sun brightened the front rooms and in back sketched a refracted yellow pentahedron in his Monet print. Harry sat contentedly for a few moments thinking of lunch, of Fakir's new venture—Fakir was still a dynamo, especially considering how he'd screwed him in his first IPO; a lesser man would have folded his tent, brooded, and become a lackey for someone else. Another time, he would have researched Fakir's venture. But Fakir's venture seemed bland and boring. Not like the broken and resuscitated Trifecta, Leg 3.

We all wear different hats, Harry mused, are different things to different people, speak differently to the busboy and the client. Harry didn't know how many personas he projected. He could try to find out, canvas a score of therapists, lay his self on the couch. But that would be abstract, possibly worrisome, and wouldn't do any good. He was fantastically successful, rich, poised, a thoroughly invested member of the leisure class. But...but perhaps his new persona, a persona traipsing beyond risk, deserved a second look, or some time on the couch.

How many hats did the violent, erratic Wiley Brooks pose on his flame-haired head? Wiley, explosives, and an explosion. What was that about? Wiley liked intimating there were other bigger deals. At the time, Harry thought it was typical male strutting. He certainly understood that. Once when Wiley had too many tequila sunrises—Wiley was sitting on the sofa at the Golden Paradise, Harry on a chair; the place was full of yuppies, young people with slight portfolios slumming, posing, laughing loudly—he threw out a handful of non sequiturs about Algerian politics, the small but continuing Muslim insurgency, and a new project.

Could that be a source of loot? If he could find what Wiley was up to, then find Wiley, he could leverage money out of him. Possibly money for keeping quiet. Possibly money for giving him back those bank account numbers. The address book was a chip; it had to become a stake.

Harry squared his laptop, Elite phone, and Wiley's red address book, called numbers and made notes. As the shadows lengthened, a tumbler of Glenlivet appeared beside the laptop. He was digging out information but not answers. His base was growing, but he didn't have it yet. But it was there. His years in the business of watching people, of manipulating people, greed, and stocks had given him more than a sixth sense. He was at the top of his game. He smelled money. And when he smelled money, he didn't stop.

Harry scribbled an organizer entry. He tapped the gold monogrammed pen on the table. The Napa number. He'd tried it several times only to be cut off. Those people across the road from Wiley's knew something. He found the Napa number, listed under Khris Kyber. Khris had the dubious distinction of having an asterisk in front of her name.

He punched out the number. He was switched to a cell and connected to Bob, who he guessed was Khris' boyfriend.

Would Bob know about Khris' asterisk? It could be a wedge. And it might be too early, or late, to use it. Harry started with his pat line. "I'm a friend of Wiley Brooks and—"

"I don't know who you are, but I don't want to talk to you. No one here does."

The voice, likely Bob's, was high-pitched and whiney. Harry said quickly, "I don't care about the money."

"What money?"

Bob in the dark. Okay. "Forget the money. Did Wiley mention explosives or have foreign connections? Answer it, I won't call again."

The line went silent, then Bob coughed up a tidbit. "Explosives? I don't know about them. Wiley mentioned two visitors, a man from North Africa and a woman from Uskade."

"Did they come to Napa?"

"I don't know." Bob hung up.

North Africa? Uskade? It was an interesting fact—a connection—but connection to what? He jotted it down next to the item about Algeria, the date, and asterisked it. He searched the Web for Uskade but came up with nothing. He probably wasn't spelling it right.

Harry posed his chin on his fingers, watched the sun fracture on the window, and tried putting those items into a rational progression.

He failed.

He paged through Wiley's address book again. Something was missing, something important. The bank accounts were significant. If Wiley didn't have them noted elsewhere, he was a lot stupider than he thought.

What was it?

Harry flipped through the last pages again. He'd seen light numbers in the margin, but thought they were doodles...like the chemical notations. That time he looked at the first one, a faint "1" scribbled in the margin. Between the addresses were a series of letters and numbers, which started on the left and extended through the lines down and right. Two pages after that there was a "2" in the opposite margin and another series of letters and numbers hidden in the addresses and phone numbers. Three pages after the two, a "3" and another series of numbers.

It was a simple progression, but what did the scattered letters and numbers mean?

Harry picked up the list of banks and accounts John Vesco, the bank auditor, sent him. First number, Bank of Barbados. Harry found the website and put in the bank number. When it asked for a password, he typed in the series of letters and numbers hidden on the page with the indistinct "1" in the margin.

Harry held his breath. After a few seconds, the account value, deposits, and withdrawals spread across the screen.

Harry smiled ear to ear, then laughed. It was a long, loud laugh that echoed through the house: he had Wiley's bank account numbers and his passwords!

Harry calmed himself and regarded his faint reflection in the window.

Should he be worried about this new Harry Mach? Violence, "fixers," murder? But you know, naysayers, Harry Mach has played the riskiest games, and he can play this one and play better than anyone. Trifecta, Leg 3, just needs a little more time.

Harry smiled as he checked the other accounts. He had to know exactly what he was dealing with...how much he was dealing with.

It took him half an hour. Yes, his token had morphed into a huge stake; he had Wiley Brooks by the balls. Except there was a peculiarity about accounts "2" through "5": they were empty. The first account, the "1," had roughly three hundred grand. It was certainly the drug account.

Harry sat back and stared at his dim reflection in the window.

With the password, he could transfer all the money from the moneyed account into an account he would set up. That would mean: Leg 3, Trifecta, complete at triple what he'd paid in! Wiley wouldn't know it was Harry Mach. He'd split the proceeds with Vito and Sal. And in the unlikely case Vito or Sal found Wiley, they could keep him.

Why were the other accounts empty? He guessed it was because the money would come in later. More than anything, it made him think there was more money. He didn't know where it was coming from or how much, but it was likely a wad. A million...two?

Now that was a fitting finish for Leg 3! Karl would be proud.

Brring, brring, brring. Harry frowned and answered picked up the phone.

Burt said, "Got the retainer?"

"Come up."

Harry logged off, put the laptop away, and retrieved the envelope with Burt's money from the safe and put it on table. He got an ale from the fridge, opened it—he didn't want to endure another round of Burt biting off the top with his teeth—and set it next to the envelope.

Ten minutes later, Burt sat down next to the envelope and beer. His blond hair hung loose and touched his shoulders. It gave him a slightly feminine air.

Burt opened the envelope and rifled the bills. "Jesus, it's two thousand bucks."

"I said it would be more than Vito is paying you. You weren't sure?"

"Frankly, no."

"I always keep my word. As I said, it's a retainer, just like Sam Spade."

"Hey, thanks for the beer. I've got to admit, you've got style." Burt brought the bottle up to his lips, took a long draw, shook his mane, and smacked his lips. Then, before Harry knew what he was doing, Burt took out a joint, lit it, and inhaled deeply. He coughed up the smoke, and sat stoned and dreamy, the smoke from the joint making curlicues in the gray light.

It was darkening, shadows eroding. Harry shook his head grimly as Burt went comatose. He got up and retrieved a glass ashtray from the liquor cabinet and set it in front of Burt.

Burt took another puff of the joint and put it in the ashtray.

Burt didn't look as abashed as he did last night. His ego had reasserted itself; he was in control. If nothing else, Harry's money would neutralize Burt and keep him under his thumb. The big question: Would he get anything out of a stoned Burt? He must be down to his last functioning neuron. "Let's get started. What have you found out?"

Burt twirled strands of his hair together and appeared to concentrate. "You know, Harry, you don't take time to enjoy life. What about birds, sunsets, blue skies, air, dirt? You know how many microbes are in a handful of dirt? I know you don't. Actually, I don't either. That's okay. My point? I'm not sure."

"Try to concentrate. Remember why we're here? Remember why you have my money?"

"Serious, right. Let's be serious. Sure you don't want a hit?"

Harry sighed. "Positive. Now focus."

Burt shrugged. "You know how to bring a guy down. Okay, okay." Burt put his hands on the side of his head as if he were contacting an astral plane. "Let's see...Tully's: I see a couple of bartenders and a bouncer talking about Wiley. I see them having tequila chasers... they're getting drunk, really drunk. I used to do tequila, but you know, at a certain point...and I'm not sure where that point is, you have to start taking care of yourself."

"Please. And?"

"I'm not an automaton." Burt squinted as if that helped. He hunched, his blond hair spilling past the nearest shoulder. "Ah yes, Wiley, the caper. Jesus, you just don't stop do you?"

"And!"

"Okay, okay. The bouncer, the bartenders. They thought Wiley was acting weird lately, weirder than usual, worried. Course I'm not sure what that means."

Harry nodded. "Likely pretending so a suicide would seem more natural."

"Verrrryyyy posssssibbbbbly, Harry. Verrrryyyy posssssibbbbly. Got two for ya," said Burt, eyes wide and nodding familiarly.

"What?"

"The bums from the park."

Harry shrugged. "What about them?"

"One of the bartenders saw Wiley give a couple bums some money."

Harry frowned. The crossed-out names in the address book. "Any names?"

"Nope. They were just bums."

"And number two?"

"Girl, red hair, black leather jacket. Name of Rosie."

"And she is?"

"Wiley's girl...at least that's what this bartender said. "She's been in Tully's a couple times in the last few weeks."

"That's good. A woman, Wiley's girl. He could be staying with her. She might know where he is." Harry brought out his notebook and scribbled an entry. "Vito? Sal?"

"I called Vito. Told him I was checking the bars. I haven't talked to Sal."

"I'll deal with Sal. I want you to keep digging; I need more information."

Burt said, "I'm running out of places to go. Shit, when I started I just had you. Never thought I'd find anything else."

Burt, a fixer? Was Vito senile? There was more there. Burt had some-thing with Vito's granddaughter. Maybe Vito was trying to get Burt killed. He'd wait until he made a mistake or didn't find Wiley, which was likely, and then kill him. It was a stretch, but Burt was no fixer. His usefulness would end soon, that is, if he was useful at all.

"Go back to Tully's, hang out, talk to people, listen for tidbits, and follow them up. Find out the last name of the redhead and where she lives. Right now, she's our best lead. Find Wiley's friends and ask them about the redhead. Dig, dig, dig. And find the names of the bums."

Burt shook his head. "You're a trip, Harry. I hope you know what you're doing."

Harry wondered about that. Curiosity, hunches, and confidence only take you so far. At the end of the day, or several days, you had to see the numbers, the digital 1s and 0s, the dough, or know it will come. Right then, he didn't have the dough, the millions, or know it would come. "I do, and I don't. I work with what I have, and I don't have much. If Vito asks what you're doing, tell him you're talking to Wiley's friends and that you're running out of leads. Let Vito down slowly; we want him to chalk up the money he lost, Leonard, and your five hundred dollars to experience and go away."

Burt's left eye stared at him through the blond screen of his hair. "You know, Harry, couple days ago, I never thought I'd be working for Vito. It was lucky. And now I'm working for you. Cheri, former girlfriend, would say it's synchronicity. You know, a cosmic aligning of the stars." Burt lost the train, snapped his fingers, and came back to it. "Right, aligning. You know, Harry, I think my star is aligning, and I'm gonna ride it. You know, go with the flow, make it happen, hit the homer, make it big."

Harry frowned. One chance, one gold ring. He'd heard it before, often. The fairy dust of money and success sprinkling over the lumpen, making them buy lottery tickets, and invest in gold mines and swamp-land. "This may be your big chance; I don't know. Success isn't about hope or cosmic gulf streams. If we're going to win this game, we need more information. Write down what you learn. Tomorrow we'll com-pare notes. And Burt..."

Burt looked up, puzzled. "Yeah?"

"I like to get stoned as much as the next person, but you have to be sharp for the next few days. If you want to catch that gold ring..."

"You just said that. You don't ever get stoned. You're always on point. But I like dope. It helps me think. No, it helps me fantasize and feel good about myself." Burt smiled, his mind in the ether. "Of course I can't remember much later."

Harry sighed inwardly. "Right."

Burt set down the empty ale bottle. "What do I do with all this money?"

Harry frowned. What was he talking about? "What?"

"Is there, like, any place to put it?"

God, was he born in vacuum chamber? "Put it in the bank."

Burt said, "But I want to make money, like you."

Harry shrugged, sure Burt wouldn't remember. "Find a broker and have him buy sub-prime derivatives. He'll know what they are. They're new, but hot."

"Thanks, Harry." Burt stuffed the envelope in his coat pocket, looked at him, shrugged, saluted, and left, his long hair dark, then gold in the fading light from the front room.

Fading light made Mt. Sutro a dull yellow. The room darkened; the room, his dealmaker room, was pale and remote. The stained glass made faint rainbows in the hallway. Harry was the center of his universe, his galaxy, his constellation. The seasons continued, the outside world turned, babies were born, and people died of heart attacks and strokes. It was a time Harry liked, the contemplative time of day, a time-out, a few seconds when one looked back, or forward.

The eucalyptus on Mt. Sutro moved sluggishly to an ocean breeze. That soothing motion made him forget, briefly, he was on the hunt.

15

Marant's feelings about the project were mixed. They were mostly negative, and had been negative since seeing Christian. But it was more about a mystery, a mystery he felt a need to unravel. Perhaps it was human nature. Perhaps he felt an obligation to Christian. Perhaps he'd begun to dislike Wiley Brooks and his machinations.

In the short run, his mixed feelings meant he hadn't decided to kill Sugar or Scab.

He followed them. Occasionally, he would think he was learning more about what had happened, or what was happening with the Muslims. Was it another gigantic ruse, a plot to overthrow Christian? The actors and roles fermented as he watched Sugar sip sweet wine, and Scab yell at other equally smelly and grotesque winos. Other times that afternoon, he felt like a note-taker, a scribe, an amanuensis documenting the stories of Sugar and Scab for some distant race of readers.

He felt, after three hours, as if any thoughts of fashioning spidery Giacometti figures or running his hand over the smooth, hard-cool surface of one of Henry Moore's pieces at Perry Green, or of his apartment in Paris, or a Paris opening, were mere figments, intrusive thoughts from another world which may or may not have existed. It goes to show, finally, inexorably, how brute reality trumps memory.

They led him on a merry chase that afternoon. Earlier, blocks from the dirty white scrum of the ocean, Sugar and Scab spent most of an hour drinking and shaking their heads, he supposed, over the death of Potato. But Scab settled in the midst of six or seven fellow drinkers and Sugar got up. A large woman and an old man with a thick red nose, white hair, a long flowing beard, and twenty bracelets clanking on each arm got up too. Marant followed Sugar. He followed her and her new buddies through the park and watched from across Lincoln Way while they bought supplies at a small grocery.

Sugar was feted by her companions, possibly because of the recent loss of Potato. He followed them through the towering eucalyptus and pine from one oddly chosen spot to another, until they crossed Sharon Meadow and angled back towards Haight Street and the source of most of their panhandling money. As they walked towards Haight Street, the fog followed them. When they stopped, finally, north of the park entrance, the fog encircled them like a shroud.

The spot they chose was odd considering what he'd learned. It was an equilateral triangle with the ends Potato, spread Christ-like on the hill west, Wiley Brooks' cordoned-off flat east, and Marant Olivier south. It made him start thinking again about what Wiley Brooks had done, and how killing winos fit into some plan. We all have plans, excursions into the outside world. Most plans could be explained or made sense. The ones Wiley Brooks posed were hidden like the fog that had overtaken them.

Sugar posed like a model for her loud companions, hand on ripe hip, puffy wine-face twisted into what he could only describe as a leer. It was a common affliction of Americans that they all knew they were beautiful, sexy, and mysterious. Of course in her case, she had her props, her fortified wine, her dope. He supposed there were moments of recognition, of how far she'd fallen. There would be the intense hangover, the dull body-length pain from sleeping on the ground, the stretched-out bodies around her, the musk smell of damp, soiled clothes.

Marant tucked the bill of the 49ers cap down over his face and adjusted his leather pack so it didn't pull on his work shirt. He circled Sugar and stopped in the shadow of eucalyptus. As he watched Sugar, he wondered—again, and not for the last time—why his current highly paid job involved killing a trio of the sub-humans who spread over that end of Golden Gate Park like an urban cancer. They weren't revolutionaries except in a remote asocial sense; they didn't hold cards in the oppressed underclass. They had decided not to play in any game, and that was unforgivable in some stretched societal way.

But the winos! Sugar—she looked rather more a turnip—finished her elaborate posturing, yelling at another yahoo who, naturally, yelled back. He could see she was being made incoherent by a fortified wine supplied by one of the more revered American magnates.

Marant tracked the large sandy-haired woman as she finished the bottle, threw it dramatically on the ground, and stumbled towards the dark bushes of the interior. Marant waited, circled, and closed in on his target. He stopped when he saw her head disappear behind a bush. Sugar squatted, and he remembered reading that American snipers in World War II used to wait until the Japanese were incommode before shooting them, sometimes aiming at their swinging testicles, watching them fall in their own excrement.

Cars arced through the park. Despite the fog, they illuminated the side of his face with a faint, weak white and cut a shadow across his cheek from the 49ers cap. He wasn't sure how—or if—he was going to kill her. In his pack, he had a bottle of beer which he'd salted with tetradoxin. He also had two fugu pills in a small pillbox in his coat. Suddenly, remorse swept over him. He didn't want to kill her. She was, in the best of worlds, rooted on the bottom, a burlesque. He watched the bushes on the other side of their camp shake and her head appear. Perhaps she was beautiful before the wine puffed her face. Genet found beauty in the grotesque, the maudit.

Marant watched the bushes, but deep in the shadow of the tree, thought of a time four years ago. Machiso, Guatemalan, a high-ranking so-called general, America-trained, hand-picked by Ríos Montta. Machiso had ordered multiple massacres against the indigenous Mayan population. The opposition appealed, through the Sandinistas, to Christian. They needed a sign that they could strike, that they weren't impotent. It had to be public.

He'd watched from an empty room near Machiso's square brick residence. Downstairs was a large café with a scattering of customers—most people stayed off the streets fearing arrest or worse. It was a dull, heavy, yellow morning. Three cars full of soldiers were parked in front of Machiso's villa. Machiso strutted down the walk, glancing to his right, then left as if he were an emperor. Marant shot the general in the head, and pink mist sprayed out like a halo. Machiso flopped back like a fish. He'd fired a string of shots to keep the guards pinned down. He left the rifle and a note that the dissidents had assassinated Machiso. Then as shots dug into the walls behind him, he'd taken the back stairs, which gave out on a series of alleys, and...

...and the result was more killing of Mayans, more brutality, more rapes, more dead children. Marant shivered.

He felt a pressure on his shoulder and spun around. "Hey, slow down, Chief. What you doin' sneakin' around? Come here and have a drink."

Sugar's face was rimmed with dirty straw-colored hair. Marant glanced past her puffy face and saw a group of three men walking on the pavement, which paralleled Stanyan Street. He shrugged inwardly. Sugar led him to her group.

"First off," she said, batting her eyes at him, "you have any drugs?"

"No," said Marant.

"Nothin' in the pack?"

"No."

Opposite, the old man with the staff and the bracelets nodded, his hair hung like a dirty mop over his face. To his left, a shoeless man cradled a head stippled with gray hair in his crossed hands. Sugar squatted on his right. He sat, completing the circle. Between them were Twinkie wrappers, two wine bottles, and a scattering of cigarette butts.

"Petey and Jon can't take it," she said, nodding at her companions. "Leaves us to party."

Sugar snapped a beer out of a six-pack and handed it to him.

Marant looked at the beer, popped the lid and sipped. "Thanks."

"Ya know how tough it is out here?"

"I can imagine," said Marant. Beyond the old man, the trunks of the eucalyptus, pine, and cypress appeared through the fog like legs of giants. The glow from Haight Street was soft. Then the fog thickened, enveloping them, isolating them from Haight lights and the brooding park. He had no idea what he was going to do. He rarely met his victims. Now there was Potato, then Sugar, innocents he didn't want to kill in the first place. He wondered if he could pay her to leave, go to another city, be discreet.

"Ya get in these moods, ya know? Why am I here? What do you think?"

"About?"

"Why I'm here?"

It was either an existential question, or not. He guessed not. "Why?"

"Ran away when I was fourteen. If I tried it today, there'd be a four-state alarm. Oh fuck, probably not. You gotta have money and a big house before they look for ya. Mom kicked when I was ten, and I couldn't fuckin' stand Dad. He was always tryin' to get me in bed, feel me up. Feels dirty, doesn't it?"

"It happens a lot," said Marant. He thought of his parents. They were shadows, regal, unapproachable. They had so little time. If he knew them better, they'd be more human. Warts, egocentric, mean. We all cherish illusions. "Did you hear the explosion?"

"Fuck, I was there. Potato and Scab too. Didn't wanta be. Too fucking cold. Stupid Scab. There was Wiley, the guy that blew it up, and someone else I couldn't see sittin' in a car. Scab saw 'em though. The fuckin' blast shook the ground. Piece of wood almost creamed me."

"Why blow up a windmill?"

"Shit everybody wants to blow something up," she said. She took a swallow of wine. "Takes guts."

"And this Wiley had guts?"

"We seen him a lot. Fuck, he lives right across the street." She pointed with a half-full bottle of banana-flavored MD 20-20. Marant gazed across the street at the building that had been cordoned off with bumblebee tape. "Ya know what?"

"What?"

"We got money out of him, but I didn't like it. Shit, I didn't like being at the mill that night. I knew it was wrong. I knew something bad would happen. And I didn't like him. He was mean. I seen him beat up some hippie. I mean he didn't quit. I'm surprised that hippie is alive."

He took a sip of beer and watched Sugar. "Why didn't you like getting Wiley's money?"

"Cuz I didn't trust him. And later, a little redhead, a woman, started snapping our pictures. Seemed like a set-up. I tole Potato and Scab. They didn't give a fuck. Said nobody was going to waste their time coming after us. Poor Potato. I'd feel worse, if he wasn't such a retard."

An explosion, three winos, photos, disappearance. It was an unlikely sequence. "What happened to him?"

"Dead. Probably drank himself to death. I suppose it's not a bad way to go." Sugar moved closer to him and straightened his shirt. She stared into his eyes. Her eyes were weak gray, red-rimmed, with streaks of dirt on her cheeks. Her hair brushed his cheek. Her breath smelled of wine and Fritos. "Be right back, lover."

She left Marant with his dilemma. He watched her absently as she walked to the edge of the fog. He knew that he wasn't going to kill her. She stopped near a garbage can. Beyond her, headlights crept through the fog on Stanyan.

He wondered what she was doing, then saw her open a small container. Marant patted his pocket. His fugu pills! He watched her pick the pills out of the box.

Marant jumped up. "Don't—"

Sugar yelled at him. "You didn't want to share!"

He leapt towards her as Sugar laughed, gulped both pills, and took a quick swig of sweet wine. She smiled contentedly, as if she'd had a hit of designer drug. As he reached her, she blinked and stood up straight, pirouetted, and fell like a sack of clothes.

"Merde." Marant glanced at Sugar's companions. Both asleep. Marant knelt down and picked up his container. Sugar's face held him briefly. Sugar should be able to drink her wine, whine about her past, wallow in self-pity. A loose-limbed man stumbled towards them.

Marant rose to his feet, turned and walked quickly through the towering eucalyptus towards the intersection a block away. Through the curtain of fog, cars lumbered through the park on the boulevard and bunched up at the stop light. Cars, trucks, a U-Haul full, no doubt, of the belongings of someone in transition. He'd always been fascinated with transitions. Moving, leaving...from one apartment to the next, from one city to another, from one life to a second hidden one, from the shadowy distance of a curve to a straight line, from birth to life, and life to death. The two deaths weighed on him.

He was in a transition he didn't quite grasp.

16

Judy Ferris rarely got up before seven, but that morning at six, she'd already showered. She put on sweatpants, sweatshirt, and heavy gray socks against the morning chill. She made coffee and took it to the chair closest to the picture window. She curled up, held the coffee in her hands, and saw snatches of the East Bay through the fog, which swirled like phantoms around the solitary Monterey pine.

It could be that the last few days were just an emanation from the fog, fog-created, evanescent, drifting away with the sun. A mirage.

She had to figure it out. She was at a cusp. She'd had her fill that week, but they got worse. Wiley Brooks had invaded her life. She tried to remember the first time she realized she hated him. It was a party at his house in Napa. Wiley was stoned and drunk and seemed to attract people as if he were a magnet. She wasn't a prude. She'd done her share of dope, drugs in the eighties, booze. But Wiley wasn't experimenting or having Dionysian fun.

He brought people in, used them, set them off against each other, or tricked them in some vicious mind game. That was his real fun. Wiley's smirk. Wiley's fun. It was the smirk and fun of a criminal, or twisted cop who has carte blanche to do what he wants. Wiley's personality was evident in what he'd done to Khris. He'd even tried it with her, once. Out of curiosity, she'd met him in café, where he'd tried to inveigle her with smooth talk and insinuations about her, and ended when he proposed they go to his flat and fuck.

She told him to go back to his flat and fuck himself.

But it wasn't what he did to Khris, or his dope deal, or his crassness. There was something else there, something that reached into the recesses of Judy's past, that positioned him on a corrupted side of human nature. She'd seen that side before, up close.

Judy realized at that moment that she was setting herself up as the anti-Wiley, or as a Wiley-killer. She was beginning to understand why, too. The reason was on that El Salvador diskette; it was her personal brush with the other side.

She walked to her file cabinet. She ran her fingers over the metal, then snapped off her gaze, and turned back to her desk.

Judy fetched her planner and a pen and sat down on the sofa. She listed the projects she had to complete in the next week and how much time she had to complete them. Cambodia article: one hour. Press release for the Indian manufacturing plant: one hour. Costa Rica for Fodor with revisions, proofing: a week. Calling writers, graphic designers for the ATA?

A ray of sun splashed through the fog and lit up the top of the pine.

Judy jumped up, switched on the light, and booted her PC.

Two hours later, she had the Cambodia article and the press release done. Usually when she estimated, she was off. It always took her longer. That perfect execution made her feel good about that day. She found the email address for Bud Price, typed a short cover letter, and sent him Cambodia. Then she sent the Indian press release back to HD Enterprises for proofing.

The phone startled her.

She walked into the kitchen and pulled the portable out of its base.

"Ms. Ferris, my name is Harry. I am a friend of a friend of yours."

Ponytail had said "Harry." Khris said Wiley had mentioned Harry Mach, as a backer, and "Harry" had called when she was there. "That's obscure enough to be interesting. Let me guess. You're a good friend of Wiley Brooks, and you want any information about him."

"That's exactly right! Do you—"

Judy rolled the dice. "We'd both like to know more about Wiley Brooks."

"What?" Judy felt the tension in his voice. "I can't—"

"I see," she said frostily. "You want me to help you, but you don't want to help me."

"How can I help you?"

"You give me something, I'll give you something. Quid pro quo."

After a pause, Harry said, "Of course, Ms. Ferris. Perhaps we can help each other."

"Quid pro quo," she said finally. "Let's meet. Where do you live?"

Harry's voice, hesitant at first, was strong. "The city, Parnassus Heights."

"Let's meet halfway. You know Corona Heights?"

"Most people don't; I do."

"There's a staff parking lot behind the Randall Museum and a bench near the trail to the top. See you there in half an hour."

Judy put on running shoes and a windbreaker, stuffed her notebook and a windbreaker in the windbreaker, and went to meet Harry Mach.

Corbett was an odd street. You'd think it would be exclusive with the fantastic views, but often it wasn't. Sure there were fancy houses, Victorians, stone-worked English cottages, but most of them were built low, no more than two stories, and many were pink square motel types with thin walls and big windows. The developers scored on those. She always forgot how lucky she was to live in a small, single shack with an affordable rent. She wasn't going to count on that forever. She knew about change, but like everyone else it snuck up on her.

She walked down Corbett, thinking of Harry Mach, of who he was, what his game was. She'd done a quick search on the Net. It wasn't hard to find the website of Harry Mach of Mach Investment Strategies.

Stocks, bonds, annuities, IPOs. Excellent advice, in the business for twenty years. He had quotes from other investment gurus, a reference list of economists. One webpage had a photo of Harry with some of his clients. All beaming, all the time. Of course, you don't attract many clients with frowns and grimaces.

What was he doing with the odious and deadly Wiley Brooks?

She took one of the streets that circled Corona Heights. It was easy to end up in cul-de-sacs on that hill; she'd done it before. She turned left on Levant, right on Fairbanks. As she mounted, a different perspective opened up. The fog was burning off to the east, but it shrouded the northern part of the city, downtown, the Wharf, the Golden Gate.

She liked walking, and she liked that walk. They'd published a report a few years back about how the hills in San Francisco added years to the lives of its inhabitants. That depended, of course, on whether you walked the hills or lumbered over them perched high in your Hummer.

The Randall Museum was a kids' museum, where kids could play with rabbits and turtles and white mice, experience the wild in dioramas, and listen to wounded red-tailed hawks squawk at them from steel cages. Outside, flanking the entrance, the kids had gardens, and plants were labeled with gray tilted signs unevenly lettered in bright reds, yellows, and greens.

Judy walked through the large parking lot. On her right, running the length of the parking lot, was a stand of towering eucalyptus, which acted as a barrier that hid a hundred-foot drop to a playground and dog-run. She walked past the kids' gardens, then through the scattering of staff cars behind the museum. The trail to the top of Corona Heights was at the end of the lot. It was steep and short and led up to barren, exposed rock, which, from the right angle, looked like the polished head of a bald man. The bench at the trailhead was a couple of cinder blocks and a plank. Grass hid the legs. A hundred people had sat there last week admiring the hundred-and-eighty degree view of Oakland, Berkeley, and the city, their feet scraping half-moons in the dirt.

Harry Mach was already there. He was a middle-aged, tall, curly-headed man, whose head was canted to one side and whose right shoulder drooped slightly. From the back, he looked like the Harry she'd seen online.

"Harry Mach?"

Harry turned. He beamed, his face expansive. It was Harry's business face that ritually, or from habit, hid what he felt or thought. But we all needed some mask or other, didn't we? He got up and extended his hand. "Ms. Ferris?"

"Thanks for meeting me here. It was an easy walk, and I have a long day."

"I should have walked," said Harry. "And I should get to the gym and lose a few and eat better. I feel appropriately guilty."

"Shall we?" Judy said, gesturing to the bench.

They sat down stiffly at opposite ends of the plank, as if they were on a blind date.

"I haven't been here for ages," said Harry, breaking the starchy silence. "My flat looks west, towards Mt. Sutro, the park, and the ocean. I've forgotten this perspective. It's limitless but more overwhelming, full of freeways clogged with cars, and people clustering closer and closer together. I thrive on that hustle and bustle. I know more of those economies of goods and spirit than flat, structureless ocean."

"I've seen your website. I know what you do. I don't know everything."

Harry looked at her sharply, as if in his musing he had revealed too much. "It would be less than cautious to reveal everything. I've seen your articles. I use the Web too."

"Our public face. But secrecy and mysteries seem the order of the day." She shifted so she could talk to Harry directly. Behind his curly head, a stone wall held back the hill topped off with eucalyptus. A straggle of bushes arced down the steep barren hillside. "Wiley Brooks rented a house across the road in Napa. I didn't know much about him. I didn't like him. That's how I know him."

"You know Bob...and Khris?"

"We share. Yes."

Harry pursed his mouth. His eyes calculated what she'd said. "I see. I know where you live and who you know and that you write travel pieces about exotic mostly Asian locales. But a person is not the sum of what they show. Who are you?"

"Back up. Remember, you called me."

Harry shrugged, rubbed his finger along his nose. "You've seen the website. I'm an investment consultant with a hundred clients. Mutual funds, IPOs, real estate, the Melton high-rise..." Harry waved his hand, as if a recital would go on for hours.

What was he doing with Wiley?

Harry puzzled her. She decided she wouldn't get any more out of him without offering him more about herself. Self. Identity. Identity—that was rich. It was changing that morning...by her being here. "I'm a journalist, lately a travel writer. As you've seen, I've made it easy for rich people to find just the right tequila sunrise on the right white beach with the right five-piece combo. Wiley Brooks ripped off a friend of mine. But there is more. I'm not sure I could explain it to myself, but I want to know more about him, what he was doing, why he disappeared, and who he really is. I'm not with the police or undercover or any semi-secret agency."

It was a long speech. Her mouth was dry. She took out the water bottle, screwed off the cap, and took a swallow. She recapped it. She didn't know what Harry Mach might say.

Harry reached into his pocket and brought out a box of Altoids. "Do you want one?"

"No." She calculated: if Harry were up to something with Wiley, he could, possibly, give her more than she could give him. And she had nothing to lose. She decided to go for it. "Do we both know what happened Monday?"

Harry popped an Altoid, narrowed his eyes, and calculated his response. "Ah, yes. The reason I called. Well, Wiley Brooks was a friend of mine—"

"Who left his car on an off-ramp near Sausalito and a note that he was going to jump off the bridge. We also know he ripped off a bunch of people in a dope deal. You're one of those people; that's why you called." It was a leap of faith, but that was all she had. If she was right, she had an investment consultant on her hands and a busted dope deal. What fucking country was she living in?

Harry smiled, shook his head. "I see you pride yourself on directness. One needs nuance, subtlety in these matters."

"Let me be more direct: bullshit. What's nuanced about a so-called investment advisor getting ripped off in a dope deal?"

Harry frowned, then smiled thinly. "I suppose it is difficult to understand. Sometimes, I find it difficult to understand myself." Harry looked at her, calculating what to say. "I was in for pocket change, thrills, my personal trifecta. I suppose ultimately it's about thrills and energy. And, of course, there's the money."

She'd heard it too often. Life style. Harry was Peter Gross of the ATA. Harry was every white "entrepreneur" who had to have a little extra and was willing to risk others' money. The skin on her face tightened. "So you got taken too. If I didn't hate Wiley, I'd say good for him."

Harry shook his head and laughed. "Have I stumbled onto an undercurrent of outraged morality? The same people who, let's say, write travel articles for rich people and glamorize peasants in third-world countries are the same people who go batshit altruistic when businessmen talk about making money, or how they make it. Outrage is greatly overvalued, Ms. Ferris. It makes one feel good. It rarely has an impact on the real world."

"I'll let that sophistry pass. But why don't you quit? You've given me a laundry list of wheelin' and dealin' and, I assume, you've got a bulging bank account. It has to be more than greed. Or, it's possible your 'business' isn't doing that well, and you need the money? And we know you want to go on. You didn't bug my friends in Napa because you want to quit."

"It is hard to explain," said Harry, eyes narrowing. He looked past her, as if he were trying to explain his deal with Wiley. "Let's say I feel compelled to go on."

"If you want to find out about the dope deal, I have Roger Nesbitt, and I guess you don't."

Under the curly black hair flecked with gray and hang-dog eyes, Harry's head expanded to a well-shaven chin and a hint of jowls. He cocked his head at her. "Who would that be?"

"Wiley's dope contact in Humboldt."

Harry's eyes widened. He thought about that for a second, then said, "I'm not sure that will help me, or us. How do you know that?"

"I dragged it out of my friend. Wiley brags a lot when he's drunk."

"Your friend would be either Bob or Khris?"

"Let's just say someone I know."

"No need to be coy; I happen to know who it is. Khris' identity doesn't concern me. What else do you know of this man?"

Judy frowned. Why was Harry so sure about Khris? He knew about Napa, and he had Khris' phone number. She assumed Wiley tore apart his house looking for something. Address book? Judy shrugged inwardly, dug in her pants and pulled out a card. "Roger Nesbitt. I did some digging and found his phone number. Do with it what you want."

Harry cocked his head at her. "Why don't you use it?"

"It doesn't interest me. Frankly, I don't think that number will do much good."

Harry nodded. "I see why. Why don't you?"

"Cuz there wasn't a last deal, and your money is likely in a bank in Switzerland."

Harry said, "Or Barbados."

"Say, do you know someone named 'Burt'?" Harry was momentarily startled, then recovered into a noncommittal smile. A car sneaking along the blacktop in Napa, scratching up the gravel. "Medium build, retro blond ponytail, baggy clothes."

"I'm not sure why you—"

"Is he a colleague? A partner?"

"Please, Ms. Ferris. Let's drop Burt."

"Okay. Let's recap. Wiley scored your money and my friend's and other people's money then disappeared. Somehow you and your friend Burt ended up with a handful of phone numbers. My guess would be that you have Wiley's address book."

Harry frowned, calculated. "Possibly."

"Most people keep backups, even for old-style address books. And Wiley must know that if someone else has it, they could make a thousand copies." Judy ruminated about that, then she stared at Harry. "We're different animals, Harry. But I think we're helping each other. I'm getting more of a feel for what Wiley was doing." Judy took another sip of water. "Before we go on, let me reassure you: I don't give a rat's ass for Wiley's dope charade."

Creases appeared in Harry's forehead. He looked at her intently as if he could discern what she was thinking. She supposed he did that with his clients. "What then?"

"Wiley II."

Harry thought about that, nodded. "I know there is something else. I call it Wiley's dark side, Mr. Hyde's side. He has an elixir, and it's not tequila sunrises or fancy vodkas. When he takes it, he turns into something different, very different."

"Same ruthlessness."

"Undoubtedly," said Harry. "Let's chat about Mr. Hyde. I can't see how it can hurt."

"Good," said Judy.

Harry frowned, "Why the curiosity? Why?"

"Humor me."

Harry shrugged, was silent for a few seconds, then said, "I've unearthed pieces, fragments, names with a single letter, exchanges in Washington."

"Toss me a bone."

"I doubt I can help you, but we must churn. It's like those little birds, phalaropes, that spin in a circle and bring the fish up to them. Wiley was interested in explosives, something called RDX and C-4."

Humph. "Funny. Explosives, explosion. The windmill."

Harry said, "That came to mind. Does that connection mean anything to you?"

"No. Anything else?"

Harry seemed to hesitate. She knew he was thinking about how much to tell her. "Do you know anyone named Sugar, Scab, or Potato?"

"Those are real names? They sound like street people or the kids in the park. They give each other weird names. Of course we all have, or had, nicknames."

"As far as I know, they're real."

Mike Larew's street people? "Nope, never heard of them. Anything else?"

"I think not, Ms. Ferris. We seem to be churning in your direction."

"As you said, one churns in the hopes of dislodging something." Harry shrugged, and he started looking as if he wanted to leave. "Wait a second." Judy took out her notebook and made a few notes on what Harry said.

Harry stared at her. "You're not quoting me?"

"No way. Right now I have fragments."

"That's clever, and opaque. We both think Wiley was multitasking; the question is what he was multitasking at. Now, why are you interested in these things, Ms. Ferris?"

"Clarification."

"Clear to you, not me."

Judy looked at him curiously. She made up her mind. "I was a reporter in Central America in the eighties. I saw what fear, terror, and suffering Reagan/Bush foreign policy produced there using people like Wiley. Funny, the policy is still there. Even funnier, people like Wiley are still fucking people over using grandiose words like regional security or U.S. security. Wiley is up to something, and I feel compelled to find out what it is."

"Ah, yes. A typical straight-shooting liberal with that lethal dose of altruism. I don't care about your politics, Ms. Ferris. You're chasing a different Lazarus, and I might say, with the same likelihood of success." Harry paused, stared into smog hiding the Berkeley hills. "I used to believe one could make a difference, but isn't that a stage? We grow up, mature, become compromised. This is the key: at the end of your search for Wiley II, if you're still alive, and if you truly find Wiley or expose what he is doing, you will feel good about yourself. At the end of my search, given the same conditional expectations, I'll have dollars to rub through my fingers."

"Call it arrested development. One final question: Do you know Mike Larew?"

Harry stared at her. "No. Who is he?"

She felt her eyebrows arch, a frown crease her forehead. "I'm not sure."

Harry shrugged. "How do you know him?"

"Tully's, a bar. He was curious about Wiley, too curious."

"Possibly another victim. It could be a long list." Harry stared at her for a long second. "I feel good about our exchange. I don't know if this Nesbitt will be a lead, but I appreciate it."

"What about a look at Wiley's address book?"

Harry laughed. "We've reached the end of how we can help each other, but you never know." He pulled out a gold pen and a business card with "Harry Mach" embossed in gold in the middle and scribbled on the back of it. "'That's my private line; if you have something substantial, call me. We'll work out something. Goodbye, Ms. Ferris. "

Harry got up, turned, and trudged up the small hill towards the museum parking lot.

She put his card in her pocket. She took a sip of water, pushed the plastic bottle in her pocket, got up, and started after him.

She crossed the lot deep in thought, trying to sort everything out.

17

Harry Mach walked back slowly from his meeting with the earnest Judy Ferris, his thoughts on what he'd learned. It rounded out what he knew about Wiley's dope scam. Others were scammed; he knew that. Look at Sal and Vito. Look at the asterisks.

But Wiley II, Wiley's dark side, or in Machian terms, Leg 3, Trifecta, take 2. They both knew there was something there. He'd felt there was something there before the dope scam. He had to give it to Judy Ferris; she'd figured out a lot, and she didn't have Wiley's address book with its arcane scribbles, passwords, and asterisks. She had Khris in Napa, one of the ripped off, and she likely had friends in journalism and possibly the police force.

But realistically, Judy Ferris was out of her league or playing in a very different league. What if she did find Wiley and learn the details of Mr. Hyde's dealings? What would it get her besides a self-administered pat on the back or a bullet in the brain?

And what about that well-known, well-heeled, risk-taker Harry Mach? He was brilliant, manipulative, and he was unconsciously projecting scenarios, possible lines of attack, lining up his ducks. But shorting a stock was one thing, playing games with Burt, Wiley, Sal, and Vito Mongreve another. If he was being realistic, he was playing in a different league too. Judy's fate could be his as well.

On the other hand, he had the bank accounts and passwords. He could take Wiley's drug money, and Leg 3 would be complete. But no. Harry Mach always—always!—went for the bigger slice of pie, and he knew a pile of cash was waiting for him.

Upper Parnassus looked the same, but as he neared his flat, his eyes swiveled towards the shadows of trees, somber walkways between Victorians, slow-moving BMWs. Incipient paranoia? Just possibly. Wiley wasn't dumb; violent and edgy, not dumb. He ransacked the Napa house and had plenty of time to sneak back into his flat and check anywhere else. If he thought he'd lost the address book in his flat, he'd think about who was there Monday morning. He wanted to find Wiley and forge a deal, not be blindsided by him.

Back in his house, seated at the head of the dining room table, laptop, and notebook squared away, he scribbled notes about his meeting with Judy Ferris. They were mostly about her, what she'd told him, and what kind of a problem she could become. He checked Wiley's address book for Mike Larew. No Mike, and no asterisk. Another complication.

As for the rest, they didn't amount to much. It was interesting others were chasing Wiley. They were the x-factors. Judy didn't know about the tail, Sal, or Vito, and she didn't know what he knew about Wiley, which fit with what she told him about South America. She knew about Burt. His colleague—hah! She must have seen him in Napa, but he couldn't see how, unless she saw him get out of the car. But she'd said his name. She couldn't know that without overhearing him. She must have been in the house. That was extremely bad karma.

Harry squared his Elite phone, nudged the laptop an inch, and looked at the number Judy Ferris had written down. She'd given him that number as a token, as a chit to extract information, but what good would come of calling it? Did he really want to talk to Wiley's dope contact? Was it a real contact? The only way it could help was if Wiley was there, or if Roger Nesbitt had been ripped off too and had an idea about Wiley's whereabouts.

Harry regarded his faint reflection in the window. His image was flanked beyond by waving eucalypts on Mount Sutro, a few Victorian roofs, a branch of sunlight. He looked prosperous; of course he always did. But that day, he saw in his square shoulders and curly hair something solid, something important. He played his own games for a long time. It was time to play a different game with different stakes. He knew he could. There would be difficulties, but obstacles made one better.

Harry punched out Roger Nesbitt's number. He had become good at indirection, at probing for clues, but that conversation didn't need nuance. A raspy-voiced woman said Roger was in jail and had been for three weeks. When she asked if he was Roger's parole officer, Harry punched off the phone and dropped it in its cradle as if it were a hot skillet. Roger in jail? Roger was in jail well before Wiley's last deal, which meant no dope, and Wiley had planned to take their money all along...if Roger Nesbitt was Wiley's dealer.

Oddly, Harry felt stronger after that dead end. He combed the pages of Wiley's address book and his organizer, knitting items together. As he flipped pages, he felt its nagging schizoid quality. There was the Jekyll side with pure and articulated lines of force extending asterisks from him to Khris in Napa to Sal Ziti/Vito and possibly to Roger Nesbitt and an overseas bank, number 1. But the lines of force didn't lead anywhere; they were like connecting the dots in a child's game. Tweaking Jekyll on the nose were Mr. Hyde's pages, pages full of mystery and darkness, pages full of question marks next to chemical formulas for RDX, explosions, Algerians, and crossed-out names.

Mr. Hyde's side was less story than collage. Mr. Hyde in Algeria? And what was Algeria? He'd spent three days in Algiers on a business/vacation trip; he hadn't moved far from the Sofitel. The desk brochure had touted the exotic land butting the Mediterranean, but hadn't mentioned the waste of desert. It was a land of a dim French colonialism, burning sun, and compliant, but sometimes deadly, Berbers. He knew that romantic vision had gone by the board; was Wiley connected to the nastier present of militant Islam, Jihadists, and slaughtered peasants?

And what about the mysterious "K"—linked to the equally mysterious "M"? He'd called the number twice and left messages.

Harry rang Fakir.

Fakir answered on the second ring. "Fakir, Harry."

"I couldn't get close to it; the mill is wrapped up like a Christmas tree. It could be Semtex. No gas explosion—that was the official line. The authorities must know that too."

"I'm not sure that matters. Someone may have set it. That's helpful. Semtex suppliers?"

"I had to be discreet, but the upshot is the military or some other government agency. Be careful, Harry. I wouldn't want anything to happen to you."

Harry smiled, "Looking out for your funding."

"And yourself, of course."

Beyond the concern, Harry detected the wheedling in his voice. That was good. Fakir was an entrepreneur, a good one, but didn't have the necessary ruthlessness or knack for scheming that made one rich. "Don't worry. Right now I need more information. Don't call this number; I'll call your business phone and leave a message. Understand?"

"Of course. I'll need the loan soon."

"This will happen soon."

Harry flipped through his email, rummaged through his snail mail. Finally, irritated that he hadn't found anything, grabbed Bloomberg, the Journal, and the Chronicle and strode through his spacious front room, his spirit troubled, his mind a blank. He sat in his favorite stuffed chair near the window, the light over his shoulder. He ignored the faint blue sky, the serried roofs of upper Parnassus, the view of the Haight, the distant park. He flipped through the papers, crumbling the ones he'd scanned and throwing them on the floor.

He stopped when he saw an article in the Chronicle's Bay Area section. A second homeless person had died; her name was Kathy Mercedes, aka Sugar. The first was Richard Spudino, aka Potato. Harry scanned the article fast.

"Jesus!"

Harry hurried into the dining room. Three names crossed out. One left. Explosion in the park, winos in the park. He had to know more about the park.

He dialed Burt's cell. "I want to brainstorm."

"I'm shopping."

"No you're not. Remember the gold ring? Pick me up. Ten minutes."

Harry dressed down with a brown Tesi downturn hat, old Armani slacks, and an old pair of designer Tom Ford sunglasses. He was about to leave, when he stopped. He called Studs and got his answering machine. "Shit." He left a message about Rosie.

Downstairs, he found Burt hunched behind the wheel of an old gray Corolla. That day, Burt wore a blue work shirt with the sleeves rolled up, revealing a few tattoos. Burt's ponytail was tightly snubbed, and his milky blue eyes looked serious. Despite the tattoos, Burt looked different from the first time he saw him. He was cleaned up. He began to look more like a typical sun-loving, slightly weathered, 90210 L.A. denizen instead of a stoned gofer.

Harry wondered about his gofer. Was Burt actually trying to catch the gold ring? Of course there was still his situation, which was that Burt, zoned on dope, dreamt big and didn't have any money...except Harry's.

Harry flicked a Penthouse onto the floor and angled himself into the passenger seat.

Haight Street unfurled block by block on the window of the Corolla. For the first time since he'd seen Burt's raggedy body a few days ago, Burt wasn't stoned.

Harry went along with that. "What's new?"

Burt turned, eyebrows up, eyes narrowed. "I know you think I'm an idiot, but I'm not. I've had a few setbacks; everyone does."

"You're not an idiot. But you have to be sharp for the next few days, not drifting through the Haight in a dope fog."

Burt looked miffed. "I'm not stoned all the time. I got the D.C. phone exchanges, didn't I? I took notes this time, not that I learned much."

It was time to be cautious with Burt. He knew Burt wouldn't lie down and roll over. Back in his room, he would be plotting, trying to see how he could win, how he could best Harry Mach. Burt may have been dumb, stoned, and perhaps reckless, but he was a child of his time... always on the make. "And what little did you learn this time?"

"I talked to guys in Tully's again. They didn't have much, except they didn't like Wiley. Shit, we knew that."

"The Golden Paradise?"

"They didn't talk. Arrogant fuckers. It's not a real bar, not like Donnelly's."

"Hmm. I wonder how many Golden Paradise patrons got taken by our Lazarus."

Burt snorted. "I could go in with a sign-up sheet."

Harry laughed. "What about the winos?"

Burt stared at the window and cocked his head as if he were sifting ideas. "Carl, Tully's bouncer, saw Wiley give 'em money. They've been hanging out for years on the street and in the park. I asked a couple winos, but they didn't know them."

"Good, good. I may know why you couldn't find them," said Harry, smiling.

Harry settled into the seat and watched the Haight Street carny. Bikers and homeless paraded by as if they didn't have a care in the world.

It was the usual observation, especially in America. The poor and rich were the carefree ones. The middle class striving, always striving. Where would he be without the middle class trying to get more? Even Burt, who was not quite middle class, was touched by the bug, the gold ring, the Hollywood fantasy.

They drove by Tully's. There was a body curled on the sidewalk and winos hanging out in front. He'd been there; he didn't like the riff-raff, the watered drinks. He could see why Wiley did. Wiley was mean and violent; you don't trot out your macho or deal dope at the Top of the Mark. It made him wonder, again, about Wiley II. Why would the CIA give the erratic, violent, flame-haired Wiley a project, especially one which might be worth a lot of money?

Harry pointed to the sprawl of homeless, punks, and winos at the park entrance, and a few seconds later, Wiley's apartment. The juxtaposition of winos and Wiley's flat was important. The winos would have seen Wiley come and go. Was Wiley killing them?

"Turn on JFK Drive, next left."

They drove towards the innards of the park.

"Stop," said Harry.

Burt slowed towards the side of JFK Drive and stopped opposite the park's Moorish-Gothic McLaren Lodge.

Harry looked back towards the end of Haight Street and drew imaginary lines according to what he remembered. "That's about where the woman, the wino Sugar, dropped dead."

"So she was one of them. Scratch her. What's with the winos?" said Burt, leaning towards Harry and narrowing his eyes.

Harry scanned Sharon Meadow, the thin lines of concrete circling it like a hug, a few spare slim green benches, a ragged soccer game with backpacks for goalposts, four or five Rastafarians beating on drums on a bench near the tennis courts. "Another wino died near that bench. The paper said Mr. Potato died from an overdose. But isn't that too convenient?" It was more than a geographic connection. What part did the winos play in Mr. Hyde's world?

"Let's go," said Harry. "Left, off JFK."

Burt eased into traffic. "Come on, Harry, what are we chasing?"

He had to let his "fixer" in on some of it. Context could be helpful. "Later. Drive to the beach. I want to see the windmill."

"The windmill?" Burt frowned. "I read it was a leak."

"Hmm," said Harry.

The sharp afternoon sun, shaggy outlines of eucalyptus, and furious surge of cars distracted him. If the fog concealed, the bright sunlight didn't reveal. Everything ordinary and harmless, despite the dark overtones.

The light flickered rhomboids on Harry's designer sunglasses as they drove through the eucalypts, pines, and cypress. They drove by weedy ponds loud with migrating shovelers, scaup, and the always-present mallards.

Burt, a smile cracking his fading tan, his hands twitching as if he were already shuffling through a wad of cash, drove up to the Queen Wilhelmina Tulip Garden. He pulled up a score of yards from the cyclone fence with a "No Entry" sign. Inside the fence was a fragile twist of bumblebee tape.

The mill leaned on an invisible crutch. There was a broken window, a sheared-off vane, a ragged hole. A sheet of plastic covered the hole and barely disguised the damaged infrastructure, a hanging wheel, a splintered beam.

Harry said, "A formidable opponent for mad knights, not modern explosives."

Burt said, "We know it wasn't Quixote."

Harry sorted what he knew, how much to say. "This is the origin, the seminal event. It was early in the morning, thick fog. I'd guess the winos were in those bushes, secreted, unseen. There are a couple right now."

The bushes moved, and a woman appeared briefly, then disappeared in the foliage.

Burt shook his head, smiled. "You sound like you were here."

"Imaginative re-creation. Then somebody, possibly someone from Spain or Algeria or even Wiley himself, put an explosive next to the mill and minutes later blew it up. The winos saw everything, of course. They tried to blackmail Wiley, and he is killing them or having them killed. Why? He disappeared; how could they hurt him? There's one left: Scab."

Burt smiled appreciatively. "That's a lot of supposing."

Harry shrugged. "Imagination only takes one so far. What we lack is motive."

"Isn't that more?" said Burt.

Harry smiled involuntarily. "The eternal motive. But there are different, sometimes circuitous, routes to more. Everything that happened this week was done for a reason. They might be stupid reasons, or addled reasons, or reckless reasons, but reasons nonetheless. We know the middle part; we don't have the ends, the why, and where, how the "more" comes in...or how much more there is."

"Blowing the mill, killing a trio of winos. You think that will lead to Wiley and a purse," Burt said, dismissively. "You're smart, Harry, but you have to know that's a stretch."

Harry decided to go ahead. He doubted Burt would remember what they talked about after his next joint. But Burt was changing, or had changed. Of course, one can think they've changed and even act it for a few days. But after fifteen or sixteen, one's character is fixed. Burt could act different for a few hours or days, possibly a week. The odds were he'd revert to type.

"Why blow up the mill? It's innocuous but far from prying eyes... most prying eyes. It was a test, possibly of an explosive, the cyclotrimethylene trinitramine in Wiley's address book. Why? We have connected actions with efficient motives but not ultimate ones." Harry glanced at his watch. "Let's eat a late lunch. Turn right up here; we'll go to the Cliff House."

Burt turned right on the Great Highway, and Harry saw the Cliff House perched on its promontory, headed bravely out towards the ocean. But even as he watched that landmark rise in his view, he made mental notes of the short journey and tried to see the whole. But when he tried to shoehorn in the windmill blast, cyclotrimethylene trinitramine, Algeria, and winos into a larger context, he failed. It was a clubfoot in a wingtip.

It was crowded at the Cliff House, and they were lucky to find a seat out of the sun on the north. Out the window, beyond their reflections, cormorants and pelicans swarmed over craggy Seal Rock, and a score of seals lolled on the slim stretch of sand like detached thumbs. Towards the north, over the mouth of San Francisco Bay, the Marin Headlands stuck out into the Pacific like a crooked brown finger.

Burt ordered a steak sandwich and fries. Thinking of his weight, Harry ordered a chef's salad. When it came, he ate contentedly for a few minutes, then put down his fork.

"What do you think of what we've seen? The blast and winos—it sounds like a chic clothing store on Union Square—is intriguing, but the immediate motive opaque. Opacity; why is everything so cloudy?"

Burt took a bite of his steak sandwich and chewed deliberately for a few moments. "I should have told you earlier, but I forgot."

Harry frowned. "What?"

"When I was chatting up Tully's bartender, he said Wiley bragged about being CIA. I thought it was just bragging, but with the explosion and the winos, it seems more interesting."

It seemed odd Wiley was so free with his real identity, or old identity. Now that old identity cycled back and fit like a linchpin with the mill, explosion, and winos. "Really?"

"Everybody lies about stuff they've done. I know I do...did. But the mill doesn't fit with the drug deal."

Burt was catching on fast, possibly too fast. "It doesn't. The real question is why they bombed the mill."

Burt wedged three Texas-cut fries into his mouth. A cormorant landed on the roof. Burt watched the cormorant angle his beak towards the sun and spread his wings to dry. Seconds later, Burt looked at Harry, as if the bird had helped him organize his thoughts.

"Say Harry, honestly, what's in this for me? Look, I'm not stoned, I'm not drunk. I took a big risk taking your money. If this doesn't work, I could be in big trouble."

Harry was surprised at Burt's seriousness. He certainly wasn't the drunk, stoned dolt who twirled his gun and threatened him days ago. "Never say 'honestly' to anybody."

Burt frowned, his mouth grim. "Don't play me, Harry."

Harry regarded Burt. What was he? The casual gunslinger, the stoned barfly, the hired hand? Was Burt playing Caliban to his Prosperous? He was more than he seemed, but on the other hand, he did buy him, and, if necessary, he'd buy him again.

Harry shoved his salad towards the middle of the table and folded his arms over his stomach, as if he were ready for a real talk. "I don't know, Burt. Right now, you have two grand in your pocket, and Vito's five hundred. If we find more, which is pure spec, you'll get more."

Burt smiled wryly, then went ahead as if he'd rehearsed what he was saying. "Listen Harry, I'm in this for good. I can make money with you, and I want in. I don't give a shit about Vito. I never thought I'd find anything anyway, and I'm not sure he did."

Burt had intimated that before. "Why did he hire you?"

"I told you, I'm not sure."

"I think you have to be very careful of Vito. Vito hired you, who are obviously not a fixer, for a reason. What is it? It could be to appease others, to show perhaps that he cared about the tail, Leonard. If that is right, Vito is less of a problem."

"That's just more spec."

Harry waved his hand. "I'm not done. Did Vito encourage dating his granddaughter?"

Burt frowned. "Not exactly."

"That could be another problem...for you. Vito could have hired you knowing you'd fail. Then he could have you disposed of. I know it's spec, but it's a possibility."

Burt, worried, smoothed back his blond hair. "I hadn't thought of that."

"Again, pure spec. What we have to concentrate on now is Wiley. I need more information. Did you tell me everything?"

Burt relaxed, then took out a notebook with a few scribbles on it. He looked it over for a few seconds, then shook his head. "That's it. You got the juicy pieces."

"I'll be back," said Harry. He went outside and called Studs. He left a message about Wiley and a new CIA project, the explosion, and the winos.

Harry walked slowly back into the restaurant.

After he sat, Burt said, "Who'd you call?"

"Someone who might help," said Harry. "Believe me, you don't want to know."

Burt said admiringly, "You've got connections."

"Some. Back to the CIA. If Wiley is part of a CIA project, why jeopardize it with a dope deal? It seems counter-intuitive. And why would anyone trust Wiley with a CIA project?"

"As for the dope, it's an easy way to make money; you never have enough."

It was the cardinal law. Still. "Even easier when you rip off your backers."

Burt nodded, pointed a fry dripping with ketchup at him, and winked. "Right." Burt chewed the fry slowly, swallowed, pushed his plate next to Harry's in the middle of the table, planted his elbow on the table and propped his head on his hand, as if he were ready for a real conversation. "So tell me, Harry, how are we going to make money on this? So what if we find Wiley is on some weird-ass CIA project. Where's the money?"

Burt was starting to annoy him, but he had a point. "We have numbers, bank account numbers. Wiley's address book. I'm sure that's why he went to Napa. We have, in other words, a big chip. But there's much more. It's not evident yet, but it will be."

Burt leaned forward. "You didn't tell me about the accounts."

"I didn't know what they were until today," Harry lied.

"From what I see, percentage on the CIA thing is low."

Harry decided to give Burt another tidbit. It might help; if not, it didn't mean anything. "I had someone check one of the accounts. It was empty."

Burt shrugged. "So?"

"If other accounts are empty, that means the money's coming in... and it could be a lot. But you can see it's spec, totally spec. Right now, I'm chasing a mirage, but I have a hunch."

Burt nodded. "It makes more sense, now. We want Wiley cuz we can deal the numbers, and there might be something else. Interesting. I like that. Say Harry, I got an idea."

"What?"

"Do you think Wiley knows about Vito?"

"He knew about Sal, of course. Vito was a silent partner."

"If somebody was following me, I'd want to know why, wouldn't you?"

"The tail. Your point?"

"If this Wiley thinks Vito is after him, wouldn't he try to get rid of him?"

"Interesting point. And, of course, we are after him. Would Wiley come out of hiding to remove Vito or Sal? I don't know. If I'm right about the winos, someone else is killing them. Why would Wiley have someone kill them and kill Vito himself? It would depend whether he thought he was a threat. It would complicate our project."

"Maybe Wiley will get rid of Vito for us."

"We can't count on it. And we can't count on why Vito hired you."

Burt smiled devilishly. "And the bank account money would be all ours."

"Not without the passwords."

Burt frowned. "Right." The sly look Harry saw earlier spread over Burt's face, broadening it. "Even if Wiley doesn't get them, Vito and Sal don't count. We'll cut it up."

Burt wanted to cut it up. What was that about? "They have means. Vito—"

Burt set his jaw. "The more I think about it, I think you're right. Vito never expected me to find Wiley. He sure isn't paying much. You think he might want to get rid of me?"

"It's a possibility, but right now we have no way of knowing."

Burt laughed. "We're both speculating."

"You have to be careful. Right now, keep Vito in the loop."

"I know what to do."

Was Burt playing him? He'd gone this far. Maybe he'd gone too far. He leaned his curly head on his hand. Burt's uneaten fries stared at him. Dead, cold.

"Let's see if there's a there there. We have to find Wiley. I'll go over the phone numbers again. I know one of those numbers will lead us to the redhead." Harry caught himself. He was about to say "...or lead into the project...how North Africa fits in, what Wiley's project is, why blowing a windmill is important..." but he didn't. "We have to find the little redhead. The wino might help us. Try to find this last wino and bring him to me. Tell him I have money for information."

Seals basked in the sun. Gulls, pelicans, and cormorants arrived and departed from Seal Rock. Tourists trailed past their table to the Cliff House toilet.

Harry felt as if he'd reached another level in l'affair Wiley. He had to be very careful. He had to be especially careful with his fixer, his lackey, his Caliban.

Burt popped in a cold fry and chewed for a few seconds, then said, "Been out of it for a long time; maybe I've never been in it. But now I'm part of it, and I'm staying part of it."

18

Marant dressed slowly. His apartment in the Cultural Institute with its clunky neo-Mission furniture was a big room made into two by an equally heavy screen. The sitting room gave him a view of the ocean and of the patio below, which in its turn was part of the restaurant. He'd eaten early inside the restaurant—not the patio with its thick fog—then returned to his room. He read in bed—Hesse's Steppenwolf, for the third time. He'd always thought of himself a Harry Haller, a wolf from the steppes, someone unfit for normal society.

And he did have malarial attacks of everyday, conventional morality. He opened the French windows of his small balcony and through the fog caught glimpses of a gray ocean, flashes of gulls, the distant lighthouse, and finally the patio below, which, despite the fog, had attracted late morning coffee sippers and scone eaters.

He felt unsettled, alternately angry at what he'd done and had to do and puzzled by it. But there was more, a more he couldn't quite place. He'd called several of RM's old guard. Most of them were missing, gone. It disturbed him. The one he did contact, Olivier Paragon, didn't know anything and didn't want to know. He'd retired from the wars, from being in eternal opposition. He wanted to live out his life in peace. Marant understood that.

Late morning, Marant dressed in a casual outfit—dark slacks, dark shoes, a white tennis sweater with thin burgundy trim—and took a long walk, which ended when he stumbled on Mountain Lake on the southern border of the Presidio. In a small park near the lake, chess players raised their voices in a three-sided shelter with built-in chessboards. He welcomed the diversion. They were older, most of eastern European extraction, and devoted to chess and their own idiosyncrasies. He stopped and chatted with them in German. The open side was an ever-changing picture of colorful spandexed men and women jogging, well-wrapped babies in strollers, gossiping mothers, and a vagrant mascot swan.

He played Sergei, a friendly, snow-haired white Russian descendant with a blunt nose. He could have won his match easily, but he prolonged it, because he liked watching, and, despite a desire to pull out his game at the last minute, let Sergei win. That was as it should be.

That afternoon, unsettled and nagged by an image of Sugar swallowing the fugu pills, he went back to the Cultural Institute. He changed and drove to Davies Symphony Hall for a subscription concert at the symphony. There he met Dr. Bob Newsome and his wife, Jana, several of San Francisco's more serious culturati, and had a pleasant conversation about the Puccini festival at the opera, especially La Bohème and its relevance to modern-day America. Could artists really starve in America? Could they develop intractable, romantic, mortal diseases? Bob thought not. But wasn't that a good thing?

Later Marant had a double espresso in a café in Opera Plaza on busy Van Ness Avenue. The Opera Plaza nook was a place of refinement and culture, with a fine book store, but still marred by a view which took in street refuse, the homeless, and a few panhandlers who always said "God Bless" when people ignored them and their illegible signs.

He appeared calm on the surface, but Marant couldn't escape the feeling which followed him everywhere that the contract was a ruse, a giant cloud—didn't the Americans say smoke screen?—not unlike the morning fogs which every morning had covered his view of the ocean.

Marant got up and walked to the pay phone on the corner. He dialed Kafi's number. Before he could say anything, Kafi surprised him by saying he felt he was being followed and was a security risk. It was time, Kafi said, to bring in the Basque.

"Who is following you?" said Marant, incredulous.

"I may be overcautious, but we must be careful."

"It's a trouble, as an Australian mercenary once told me, one I couldn't have invented," said Marant, incensed. Everything went wrong. But when everything went wrong, that meant it was supposed to go wrong.

There was a pause. "The woman can't finish the assignment alone."

"Why not?" said Marant, frowning.

"She is a woman, weak, troubled, emotional. She shouldn't be here at all. If we wait, it may slip through our fingers. Help her. Guide her through the final meeting."

A typical Muslim attitude towards women. That didn't bother him. Everything was working out too conveniently. "What does Teresa look like?"

Kafi seemed surprised by the question. "Short, round, curly brown hair, big eyes."

"Fine," said Marant. "We'll see about your explosive."

"Don't you want to know where she is?"

"I know already."

Marant hung up the phone, tapped his finger on it for a few seconds, then walked through the Civic Center complex. He walked past the library, then turned north. A few minutes later, he was deep in the Tenderloin. He approached the Rutledge Hotel carefully, then saw a Vietnamese café half a block away on the basement level. He walked down into the café, ordered a coffee from a surprised diminutive Vietnamese woman, and took it to the window, where he edged into a corner away from the four Vietnamese men who drank coffee at the other end, dragged deeply on cigarettes, and blew smoke over the sidewalk. He watched the Rutledge through the shoes and feet of the whores, pimps, drug dealers and Asian, Palestinian, and Third World children who walked the sidewalks of that notorious triangular district of the city.

Half an hour later, Kafi left the building. Marant left his second coffee and followed him. Kafi walked towards downtown with his odd, crab-like walk. It was easy to stay back several blocks. When Kafi reached Union Square, San Francisco's commercial hub, he sat down on a bench in the middle of the square. Macy's, Nieman Marcus, Levis, Borders, the Disney Store rimmed the square, which that day was crowded with tourists and shoppers. A Latin band at one end attracted a small group of dancers who bounced and swayed to the music.

He expected Kafi would meet Teresa, but a few minutes later, a tall man with a long jean jacket and a beret sat down. The beret couldn't cover the red hair that dribbled down the back of his neck. One mystery had been solved: The whereabouts of the chemist/Boris/Wiley Brooks. So many names; how many identities?

Marant watched their animated conversation for a few minutes, then walked back a few blocks so he wouldn't be seen, then onto Market Street. He took a bus to the Civic Center, where he picked up his car. He drove back to the Cultural Exchange.

He stopped on Clement Street and called Christian from a pay phone.

He called Christian at his usual number, then the Neuilly number.

Christian didn't answer. He had several other numbers—revolutionaries had to be quick or dead—and an emergency number. He tried the number in Nice, and that time Christian answered.

"Why are you running all over France?" said Marant, truly puzzled.

"What has happened?" said Christian, ignoring his question.

Marant told him about Kafi, the elimination of the first two winos, and his reluctance to kill the last one, that Kafi thought he was being followed, and that Kafi met someone who could have been Boris, the chemist, one Wiley Brooks, who was also a drug dealer, and that all his personas may have faked a suicide.

Marant said, "This Wiley could be an intermediary. But there is something wrong here, something we're not seeing. Everything seems too purposeful."

"Yes, it seems obvious. But the Basques, some of the Muslims, and others think the new explosive is la pièce de résistance of revolutionary movements. Politically, I can't give it up until we know it's a fraud. And there's still the possibility, more and more remote, that it isn't."

"You're more worried than when we met. Why?"

"Being followed, being assassinated, RM being split or taken over. I've strung out all these scenarios, and all are possible. We both know something is wrong, but we must know the exact shape of what is wrong."

"I couldn't locate Peron and Lové. Paragon has retired and wants nothing more to do with RM. I should come back."

"Stay. The existence of RM is at stake. Get close to the Basque. Find out if there is anything else. Find out what she knows."

After they hung up, Marant watched the crowds—mostly Chinese—on Clement Street and thought of RM, how long it had survived. It was a law of nature that everything changed. People got older, turned from being hotheads to stay-at-homes toasting their feet near the fire. Businesses, companies, local politics, governments...there were always struggles, competitions for the top spot, for resources. In Christian's case, the opposition was the Muslims. Christian was trying to gauge the depth of the opposition. As for RM, maybe it was time for it to go.

Marant parked close to the Cultural Exchange. A few minutes later, he changed his clothes and looked out the window towards the Golden Gate Bridge. The fog had lifted, and the view was a mix of sky white and ocean gray. He normally felt drawn into the view, but he felt irritable, edgy, and unsatisfied. He hated the assignment, and it seemed to get worse. Kafi announces he is being followed and immediately leaves and meets Boris/Wiley Brooks in Union Square. It was odd, but not that odd. Wiley was odd. A chemist/drug dealer? He acted more like a drug dealer than a chemist.

He didn't think a new liaison would answer his questions, but he had to find out more about the project, about whether it was ruse or real.

It was time to talk to the Basque.

The next morning, Marant drove to Lombard Street and waited for Teresa Aluestia. A woman who looked like Kafi's description came out around eight o'clock, he supposed, to go to breakfast. She wasn't fat, but more a round woman, a Maillol. He watched her as she entered a diner. An hour later she came out.

He followed her in his car, then stopped a few yards in front of her. He rolled down the window. "Teresa?"

"Yes," she said, surprised.

"Get in. I want to talk to you."

"Who are you?"

"I normally don't give out my name. I'm here to help."

"Are you Marant?"

Marant sighed. He'd kept his identity secret for years. Many didn't know he existed. Many thought he was a phantom. "Yes."

Teresa hesitated, then looked ahead, as if she had forgotten something, then she opened the door and got in. "Where are we going?"

"Someplace where we can talk."

"I want to know where." Teresa was holding a small, silver gun. It looked like the lance of a deadly insect. He could have taken it away from her, but he wasn't sure what would happen to the car, the disturbance afterwards.

"A French restaurant in Ghirardelli Square. I like to talk in public."

"I know where Ghirardelli is. If we don't go there—"

"I'm driving there now," he said.

Teresa put the gun away, but kept it where she could get at it. She seemed sullen and uncooperative. If she were on the other side, she could kill him. But her tension seemed genuine, and it didn't appear to be about him. He drove in silence, and Teresa watched him closely. After making sure he wasn't followed, he parked on Polk Street. As they walked the few blocks to Ghirardelli Square, he could tell she seemed calmer. He walked through an interior mall to an open French café he'd noted in his earlier tour of the city.

He rarely dealt with women. There were none in the Muslim countries, of course, but in Europe they were very effective. Teresa was from ETA, the active wing of the Basque nationalist movement, a specialist in the spring assault on the Spanish railroad. At least she had a goal he understood: the elusive Basque homeland, Euskadi.

After they ordered, Teresa broke the silence, "You look very different." The remark surprised him. Teresa was small with dark brown eyes and a broad forehead. Her angry exterior was quickly replaced with a quick smile and the curiosity of a squirrel.

"And what did you imagine?" said Marant, amused in spite of himself.

"I've heard of you for years, but few people have seen you. I'm not sure. I supposed that you were big, muscular, and frightening."

"Instead of thin, weak, and simple," said Marant, feeling drawn in.

He hadn't met many of RM's operatives in the field. When he worked, he worked with Christian and a telephone.

Teresa looked aghast, then she laughed with her whole face. "Just different. You're more cultured, slightly more handsome, older."

"Older, certainly. Let's talk about the project," Marant said, embarrassed.

Teresa drank a Coke in a tall crystal glass. The restaurant was elegant and empty at that hour. They sat in a small café annexed to the restaurant with white marble tables and a scattering of Persian rugs thrown casually over the polished floor. Past Teresa's curly head was a small terrace and balustrade, a whitish sky, a thin gray slash of San Francisco Bay. He liked the view. He could see the abbreviated hill of Angel Island, a slip of Alcatraz. A section of the Golden Gate Bridge filled the window to the left of the terrace. Marant calculated: two miles to the bridge, another mile to the institute. The Cultural Institute was almost three miles due west. They formed an isosceles triangle with a military emplacement on the Marin side.

"Kafi doesn't like you," she said, Basque accent ascendant. "But I don't like Kafi."

"I don't care what Kafi thinks," said Marant. "Why don't you like Kafi?"

"He thinks I should be draped in a black bag from head to foot. When I say anything, he butts in. He thinks I should keep quiet."

"I can tell that you don't."

"Don't what?" she said, brow bunched in tight waves.

"Keep quiet," said Marant. He sipped his espresso and watched her. He didn't have to pretend with her. Sometimes he thought he was living ten lives at once. Cultural representative, sculptor, pianist, and different personas for his work. Would the real Marant Olivier stand up and say what he was doing in America? Thinking of multiple personas made him think of Boris/Wiley, chemist and drug dealer. They were mixing and matching like a Morpheus jigsaw.

Teresa let out a laugh he could only describe as loud and slightly too long. "I have three cells under me in Bilbao, and my superior is a woman."

Marant knew he had to be careful. He took a sip of espresso. "ETA—your political arm—has always supported RM. Isn't it odd how you have stayed in it so long?"

Teresa watched him carefully, then seemed puzzled. "I don't know what happens at RM. That is for the politicians. But you're right; I find it strange it's lasted this long."

Marant had seen that before. If it was a question of RM surviving or ETA, Teresa would, of course, choose ETA. Only Christian could keep such disorganized, fractured, virtually autonomous movements together. The question which lay unanswered between him and Christian was whether it should continue.

"What do you think of the chemist?" said Marant. He wondered if he should ask Teresa what Boris looked like but decided it would sound suspicious. He sipped espresso and watched her over the rim of the small cup. "Do you believe him?"

Teresa looked at him quickly, then grasped the long blue straw with her lips and took a sip. The straw caught on her lip, and she flicked it off with her tongue. "I only met him twice. He was as angry as his red hair. He seemed angry at what his company had done to him, angry the courts were on their side. I had no reason to doubt he was who he said he was."

"And the formula," said Marant, getting to the heart of the issue. He was being blunt, but he wanted answers. Trust was always conditional, but he would trust Teresa, not Kafi.

"I'm not an expert in chemistry," said Teresa, frowning. She seemed to think of her answer, which made him think she had doubts, too. "But I know how to use plastique. I saw Kafi put a small amount of this new explosive into a valise, and I saw him place it on the side of the mill. I saw him detonate it remotely, and I saw the results. It was impressive. Yes, I believe there is a formula. Yes ETA needs it."

Teresa seemed less fanatical than Kafi, but she had her passions. She was likely a saint, a good Catholic, part of the semi-autonomous cells of work-a-day terrorist-on-call which kept the counter-revolutionary squads pulling their hair. "Did you see the homeless people I'm killing?"

Teresa looked uncomfortable, then said, "Boris said he saw them, and so did Kafi. I didn't. I don't doubt they are real. Do you?"

Marant shrugged. "It seems stupid to kill them. No one would believe them." Marant was thinking of Sugar, of his hesitation. He didn't want to kill her or Potato. They weren't generals, police captains, or counter-revolutionary assassins.

"I agree," said Teresa. "But those are his conditions. We go along, or we go back to Europe our hands empty, our tails between our legs."

Marant shrugged. "Tell the chemist the last wino will be dead today. Tell him it is time. Arrange a meeting, so you can get the process and leave."

"Are you running this project now?" Teresa said angrily.

Marant was surprised at her intensity. She was still angry from working with Kafi. "Don't you want to get the formula and go home?"

"It has taken so long," she said, shaking her head. Sorrow drew lines around her mouth. She was almost downcast, disconsolate. It was the last thing he expected from the woman who had trained her gun on him a short time ago. Kafi may have been right that she was troubled. "I go to a diner in the morning, another diner at lunch, a café or bar in the evening," she said suddenly. "It is not like our cafés where people talk about life, about problems. Here they are all laughing, drinking, and posing.

I sit like a post wondering what I'm doing here."

Teresa threw her straw down. She noticed the view for the first time and got up and walked from their table towards the small balustrade, as if to compose herself. Earlier, he thought she looked hard and sturdy; now she looked small and vulnerable, oddly round, certainly not a terrorist. He heard yells through the open window and imagined the chaos of bandy-legged, camera-toting tourists, mall stores, street artists drawing caricatures, queues for cable cars, and the broad gray bay below.

He wasn't sure why he got up and walked up to her. He stood next to her, then looked down. He felt how isolated they were from their perch. They schemed; they watched the human carnival. "Don't mistake my hesitation. I will help. If the process is there, we'll get it."

"I feel better talking to you," she said, turning and searching his eyes. "Would you go to the meeting with me?" she said suddenly.

"That isn't part of my assignment. Why?"

"Nothing, nothing. It is my project." It was obvious she wasn't weak. However, he could see why she might want his help. She was alone in a strange country on a dangerous mission. It was a logical development, one that might help him answer some of Christian's questions.

"I'll see," said Marant.

She looked at him, her brown eyes wide and inquisitive. "Can I ask you a question?"

"We're not in school. Of course," said Marant.

"How did you become what you are?"

Marant regarded the scene below, a family of three, two parents trying to shepherd a boy through the carnival. He thought of his own parents, the distant Fort Mahon beach. He had, at one point, thought he was justifying his parents' existence, their noble struggle. "I was trained in the French special forces," Marant replied, off-handedly, thinking of something else.

"Why did you quit?"

"You are inquisitive." Marant hadn't thought of that for years. Commando Hubert, the orders to blow up the Greenpeace ship, his refusal, the year in prison, the dishonorable discharge. "I can't say, but after I quit, someone from RM asked me to work for them and I said yes. I lean towards the left and the underdog. I'm not sure that's an answer."

"We heard you assassinated Castello."

Marant thought again of security, whether it would make any difference if she knew. The papers had already reported that he had assassinated Castello. It would also form a bond between them that might be useful. "The chief-of-police. Yes."

"The torturer. Many of my friends went into his station and never came out. We were all grateful. You perform incredible acts but get no recognition."

"If I did, I wouldn't be alive. Remember that I get paid for what I do. Castello was one man. There is always someone to take their place."

The silence was thick. Teresa gave him a queer smile, then turned to watch the bay, and so did he. They watched the imperceptible movement of the bay, a matchstick lighthouse on the distant shore, a rim of faint light. It was immense, a brute reality, impenetrable. "An Ecclesiastics perspective. We are all atoms scurrying, trying, failing," he said, suddenly depressed.

She turned towards him. "We don't have time for doubts."

"Of course we don't. I'll call you when I'm done. Make the arrangements."

"I will, Marant."

They were silent in the car, but Marant felt as if Teresa had opened something he thought closed years ago. After he dropped her off, he returned to the Cultural Exchange. He paused in the lobby, and saw himself in the heavily decorated neo-Spanish mirror. He was smiling. He was thinking of Teresa, her naïveté, her seriousness, and her questions. But, he thought as he ascended the stairs, where would they be without the passion of the young? Dragging one's feet through a dusty square worrying about old age?

It was a trouble.

19

Fog held onto small areas in the Marina and near the bridge, as if the fog had reached a point of uncertainty as to whether it should spread, or wait until people had relaxed their vigilance and donned light summery clothes.

When Judy Ferris landed in San Francisco, she thought people who lived there were schizophrenic. Living on a fault zone? Chilling fogs, flesh-burning sunlight? But she got used to it; maybe it was her own need for living on the edge.

Harry Mach. Smart little boy, adult body. The little boy part was spinning out of control; he had found an unlikely game and liked it. She'd seen that before. Drug deals? Burt? If nothing else, he handed her violence and mysteries. Explosives—the explosion in the park? And who lived in the park? Street people. Possibly street people named Sugar, Scab, and Potato.

She draped her windbreaker over her blue ergonomically correct computer chair. She bought the chair in a fit of cleaning, and cleaning up. But she'd never liked it. It was an antiseptic intrusion in the space she made home.

She made a new pot of coffee. She liked to make it slow, pouring in the hot water herself, watching it bubble up, the steam rise, the water drain. The warm smell made her think of good things, normal things. A warm bed, coffee, watching the sun rise or set, the scrum of the ocean.

She poured the coffee into a bird-of-paradise mug.

Outside was her white table, her crooked pine with its soft, puffy needles, the bay, the fabulous view. Inside was cloistered space, a square tube, antiseptic chair, left-brain constriction...and mystery. She told herself she wasn't going to continue, that it was crazy. But then she found herself calling Myra, taking down license numbers, spinning out theories, meeting Mike Larew and then Harry Mach.

She sighed, looked longingly at the sharp light in the kitchen, felt the soft breeze, and gave up the healthy carrot outside for ashes and mystery. She sat in front of her PC. She booted up and went straight to her browser. She plugged in "Barbados." Several of the Barbados sites, besides extolling tourist pleasures, talked about drug dealers and Barbados banks. Wiley mentioned Barbados to Khris, and Myra said drugs. Wiley, drug deals, and Barbados rounded out Wiley, Caper 1. Harry didn't think much of getting his money back and neither did she.

Next she went to the San Francisco Chronicle website. She typed in "Wiley Brooks" and re-read the report of his faux leap off the bridge. She was about to close it, when she saw a note about a body on Point Lobos. Leonard Marsh was found on a rock a few feet away from the surf. The body was mangled. The authorities were calling the death "accidental," although there were suspicious circumstances. Coincidence? She thought of Wiley's smirk, his coldness, the way he manipulated people. She felt there was a connection, but she didn't quite see it. Perhaps Leonard was part of the drug deal, and Wiley killed him. She shook her head, as if to rid herself of the image of Leonard on a rock, the waves lapping at his legs.

Mr. Hyde. She checked her notes, then tried Myra's info first. She didn't think it would do any good, but she typed in "Revolution Mondiale." The screen lit up with websites and chat rooms. Half the sites knew it existed, and half knew it didn't. When she tracked down the positive ones, she found confusing and conflicting takes on what it did, where it was based, but the wobbly consensus was that it was an umbrella terrorist organization that shared information, weapons, and explosives with older radical organizations, lately, perhaps, with Muslim terrorists. They also mentioned an assassin, a Carlos-type who had never been caught.

It was a slim lead. She punched out Bob's cell.

"Did that guy Harry call back?"

"Why do you want to know?" said Bob, irritated.

She understood Bob. Nice guy, one-dimensional. Didn't want his manicured and buffed digital world messed up. "Humor me. What did he want?"

Bob sighed. "To know if Wiley had contacts in Europe. I told him he mentioned someone from Algeria, and from Askadi. I pronounce it differently every time."

"Thanks. You guys going to stay in Oakland?"

"Not sure; actually, I'm not sure about anything. She's at her place."

"Right. I'll call her later. Thanks."

Bob and Khris were always yo-yoing. It would be worse because of Wiley. As she was hanging up, she was typing "Yuskate" into her browser. Nada. Then she tried "Uskade" and got nothing. Finally she typed in "Uskadi," and her browser asked her if she meant "Euskadi." She said she did, and when she clicked on that link, the browser displayed a page full of websites. Soon she found that Euskadi was the not-yet-existent Basque homeland.

Khris had slept with Wiley and probably knew more about his slips than anyone. She should have called her in the first place. She punched out Khris' number.

Khris didn't help. She said they'd talked to the sheriff, and Wiley's house was roped off as a potential crime scene. But they didn't question Wiley's suicide; they thought it was a drug bust-up, and it might have caused Wiley to jump. Khris didn't know why Wiley was interested in explosives or any more than Bob did about Wiley's foreign contacts.

She punched out Myra Cohen's number and told her what she'd found on the Web and what Harry said. Myra was intrigued but had to do her own research. She said she'd call back.

Lots of details, mostly obscure. What was Wiley doing? Then she thought of Mike Larew. What was he doing? Who was he? Why did he ask her about winos? It was an incredible long shot; there must be a million Mike Larews. She found a people search site, narrowed the search to Manhattan, and plugged in his name. Too many hits; she dug down on a few likely ones, but they piddled out.

Judy filled a glass full of water, sat on her sofa, and stared at her picture window.

She felt itchy, restless. She wanted to know more. She wanted to find out about Wiley Brooks. She didn't want to play travel writer, or pretend with the ATA. Finally with a sigh, which turned into pursed-mouth resolve, she plucked the phone up and punched out the number of the Fodor editor. After twenty minutes, she'd convinced the editor, Connie Fang, that Merri Lawson could replace her.

Then, after a final frisson of misgiving, she tapped out the number of the ATA. She had a less-than-warm talk with Peter Gross. She said that something had come up, and she couldn't start for at least a week. Peter said they'd lose money if she did. "That's absurd, Peter. The magazine has been defunct for six months. A week won't make a difference."

"To you, maybe," said Peter. "But you don't have all the facts."

She'd been down that road. The big, bad white men dole out crumbs to the masses and keep the pies and cakes for themselves. She thought of Wiley, Peter Gross, and Harry Mach. It made her too pissed off to think. "Take it or leave it."

"Sometimes I think I'm in a Puccini opera," said Merri Lawson. "Or want to be." Merri was staring at a poster of Miu Miu, the tragic heroine of Madame Butterfly, one of twenty-odd Puccini opera posters that camouflaged the yellow walls of the Café Puccini.

Judy smiled ruefully and took a bite of her eggplant Parmesan sandwich. The Café Puccini was two blocks from Washington Square and a block from Ferlinghetti's City Lights and the faded center of the Beat movement. She wondered how many people had made the trek to the café since La Bohème played at the San Francisco Opera. Merri was an eager, friendly, hardworking petite woman with short blond hair held back by two fake tortoise-shell barrettes, and had a quick, self-deprecating smile that tugged on the left side of her face. Merri reminded Judy of Khris. Judy had known a few big women who had smaller friends. She wondered if there was some unconscious reason that she might choose smaller women, a macho reason like being taller or more superior. Possibly; there were some things she'd never know about herself.

On the other side of the huge plate-glass windows, tourists hurried towards the wharf or tried to figure out whether to eat Italian or try to pick a Chinese restaurant out of the hundreds in Chinatown, a few blocks away.

"It's such a romantic way to think about life," said Judy. "But Puccini's heroines die in the end. It's a fat price for a few delirious moments of pining or weeping."

Merri smiled her off-balance smile, wrapped her nail-bitten fingers around her fork, and picked at her salad. "Why can't we go through their trials, hopes, and fears and be alive, ready to enjoy life?"

Judy watched a batch of tourists, a family, look at the menu in the window and then look inside the café. They must have decided that the opera posters, the old juke belting out arias, the scattering of writers, and sockless poet in the corner were too much local color. They slipped back into the crowds. Merri was young and, if not naïve, less cynical. "That's a very romantic, or very American, way of looking at life. We want to experience everything, skydiving, rock climbing, becoming a yogi, being vegetarian, driving a truck, and being a movie star in Beverly Hills. It's as if we haven't lived if we haven't sampled everything. Life as smorgasbord. Dying is too final, but our medical system is trying hard to make death an option."

Merri laughed at that and picked at her salad. Merri was, like most American women, on a diet, in fact, had been on a diet since Judy first met her. Judy knew she was lucky to be lean. "You have a way of looking at things. What are you really looking for?"

It was the cycle of whence/whither questions. "Something I lost."

"What is that?" said Merri, frowning. Merri speared a garbanzo bean, popped it into her mouth, and chewed thoughtfully.

"An idea, a stance, a real person. Revolutionaries—I don't know why I've been thinking about them so much—want to change things, maybe to make them better. It's a noble effort, but then you can't have real change without taking risks, without hurting someone. I don't like that part, but then we're right back to wanting it all but not wanting to pay for it."

"Is that why you gave me the Fodor contract?" Merri said dubiously.

"My time to take a risk," Judy said.

Merri laughed and her left cheek stayed bunched up longer than usual, then relaxed when she said, "It must be something important..."

Merri was digging, trying to pinpoint her obsession. Judy didn't mind. "It depends what you mean by important. It has to do with little boys."

"Isn't it always about little boys?"

"It's more than that. Right now, most of the time, I think most men are insolent, stupid, and so self-involved that they don't see or care about their obvious contradictions. They let testosterone overwhelm them. Anyway, someone I know—and don't like particularly—tapped into something that happened to me long ago. Now it's colored the time between then and now. I think it's added a continuity I've been missing."

"What's it about?"

Judy saw her reflection in the window. Long, elegant face, curled lip, green V-necked sweater and whiter skin. She'd felt an inner turmoil for days, but she looked relaxed, more animated than she felt. "The CIA, assassinations, Latin America, something that happened to me, something I wrote."

Merri put her fork down. "I don't believe in any of that, although I

149

do when something happens. You read about Iran-Contra or Ellsworth Ames and tut-tut about how incompetent the CIA is. When I think of them as sinister, I feel helpless."

"That's one of their games, making people feel impotent."

"I'm not sure 'impotent' is the right word." Merri pushed her plate to the middle of the table, then the lines in her forehead bunched in a frown. "Could we talk about Fodor?"

"You bet." Judy didn't care about boring or convincing everyone she met. Neutrality had its good qualities. They talked about the Fodor project, but Judy felt her attention drifting. Finally, she gave Merri the files on a CD and told her to call if she needed help.

Judy hailed a cab. The ride to Market Street was uneventful, but as she rode towards the Castro, she wondered if she really wanted to spend the rest of the day inside wound up with her thoughts and the events of the last few days. Despite the beautiful sunny day and people walking with smiles on their faces, she felt a funk growing.

In her apartment, she felt drawn to her filing cabinet. She looked at the black plastic case. She should leave it alone. Finally she gave in and took it out. She found the diskette. A few minutes later she slipped it into the floppy disk drive. She'd gone through two PCs since she wrote it. She was sure the file format had disappeared. She found the directory in her "A" drive, then tried to open it in her word processor. The word processor stopped, as if that diskette had caused a crash, then it converted. In less than a minute, the words "CIA Orders Assassination in El Salvador" in twelve-point Courier flashed on the screen.

Her meticulously documented exposé summed up a chapter in her life and a chapter in Central America geopolitics with footnotes on The School of the Americas, the Altcatal Battalion, the war on drugs, El Salvador's Contras, Guatemala's civil war, Haiti, Panama, Peru's Shining Path, Chile's Pinochet, and ad infinitum, ad nauseum. It was about murder and assassination for national security and spurious regional balance, dead peasants, sugar, copper, and insulated elites.

Those crisp words hid her own terror when she was arrested and jailed. The fear tunneled deep into her psyche, and she knew she was going to die. When they released her and threw her out of the country, she felt reborn. Then she felt anger, then hatred. And it brought back her doomed struggle to get her exposé published with the Washington Post higher-ups. Later in New York and San Francisco, she realized her project was about more than one incident, the assassination of Dr. Ignacio Ellacuria, or hundreds of similar incidents. It was about terror and fear, certainly, but it was also about the smirking disdain of Americans for people who were different. In larger terms, it was about women and men, toleration versus testosterone.

Don't look at the notes.

She went to the "Notes" directory, almost as if an invisible presence were making her fingers type on the keys. She opened it up. The file was near the bottom. It looked so innocuous on the screen. Just another file with a path. Just more text. Just another atrocity.

Judy left the diskette in the drive. She went to the kitchen and took down the bottle of vodka. She poured less than half an inch in one of her blue Mexican glasses. She picked it up and drank it. It burned. It fogged her brain. She couldn't keep doing that.

She felt listless. She'd exhumed most of her past except for those notes. She knew she wasn't going to make it any worse.

She picked up the paper from the kitchen counter and walked into the living room. She flopped down on the couch next to the wide-eyed Garuda. Judy Ferris was ready for a local redemption, for dueling, once again, the powers-that-be, for cauterizing an old wound, or maybe opening it up.

But she didn't know what to do next. The top of her glass table was full of drifting reflections of clouds and a pissy smog, which had settled over the East Bay. She looked at the paper, then threw the classifieds, the business, and the sports sections on the table.

She rifled through the paper, hoping to find something, anything. She stopped when she saw the article about the accidental death of a second homeless person in Golden Gate Park. Kathy Mercedes, known as "Sugar" to her friends, was found near Stanyan. The cause of death was unknown but was likely a drug overdose. It was the second homeless death in a few days. The other homeless person was Richard "Potato" Spudino.

Her chest felt tight. Harry Mach's street people. Two dead. That left one: Scab.

She had something to do.

20

Marty "Scab" Slovak spent most of the morning stealing from SUVs, vans, and cars around Golden Gate Park. He cleaned himself up, so he wouldn't look suspicious as he walked slowly around them. He did his best, but the car windows still showed his face drawn and dirty, tears in his smudged plaid shirt, and faded Bic tattoos on his ropey arms. Fuck 'em, he thought. Nobody said a word, except the cops, and he didn't see a badge all morning.

He looked for cars or SUVs whose drivers didn't lock up. Idiots.

He netted fifty dollars, potato chips and Twinkies, a radio, and a six-pack of Miller Lite. Not a bad morning's work.

Right after he'd sold the radio, eaten most of the Twinkies and chips, and settled into the first Miller Lite, his mood, always volatile, turned dark. In fact, he was pissed. The two people he hung out with most of last year were dead, tote, on slabs in the morgue.

Potato. That could have been cuz it was Potato's time. Shit, they all lived short timelines, even though day to day, they thought they'd live forever.

Sugar. Fuck. Sugar said there was something going on and it was Wiley who was doing it. It might not have been Wiley, but somebody Wiley told to do it. He remembered that little redhead runnin' around snappin' their photos. On the surface they both died of too much drink, too much dope, too much of everything bad for you.

The coincidence gnawed at him and made him extra-special careful. There were new people in the park, especially one guy, tall, didn't quite look American, who had been hanging around. He asked a lot of questions. A kid said they saw him with Potato out where he died.

Not that he gave a shit about Potato, or Sugar. Everybody goes sometime. His big worry was about Marty Slovak.

He met up with another ex-con that afternoon, Johnny, and they shared the Miller and a few hits of crack.

Scab pointed his can at Johnny. "What pisses me off was Wiley taking that swan dive. The fuck. There was a lot more money there, Johnny."

"We know one thing; he planned it."

Scab scowled. "Suppose so. I saw him blow up that mill; that was my ticket, my ticket to ride. But you know, I don't know why he did it."

"Sure wasn't a terrorist. Terrorists have to say something, and they sure have to blow up something more than a fuckin' old windmill."

"Red-haired fucker was up to something. More I think about it, more I think it's a good thing he took a powder. People got hurt around him, not that he scared me."

Johnny nodded. "You squeezed him for some bucks; that was good."

"Sure wasn't enough. I started thinkin' where else I could get money for what I saw, and I came up with zip. Police don't want to pay nothing, or reporters. They just call it a story."

"It's hard to get them to believe you when you're on the street."

"Fuck yes. Tell you, Johnny, Potato and Sugar dying so close together made me careful, real careful. Fact, I gotta plan."

Johnny killed his Miller, crushed the can, and threw it on the grass. "Yeah?"

Scab leaned in. "First, I got my protection."

Johnny whispered, "Gun?"

Scab shook his head. "Not saying; better that way. I got more than that."

Johnny said, "The cops find it on you..."

"Don't worry about them; I don't."

Johnny shrugged. "Just saying."

"Nobody gonna take Marty without a fucking fight. He'll be dead before I am."

Johnny laughed. "If it is a he."

"You're a riot, Alice."

"So, what's this plan?"

"You could be part of it. Fuck I hate these fuckin' lite beers. Jesus Christ, they made everybody a fuckin' wimp and made 'em like it. Well, hand me another and I'll tell ya."

21

Burt was a common sort of loser, no money, doper, corralling a few bucks here and there, wasting it with "buds" in run-down bars. Stoned he added 2 and 2, got 5, and thought 5 curiously more interesting than 4. But a person is always more than the caricature we make of them. Not that it made much difference in the big things, and Harry knew about the big things. The real question with Burt was about the switch. Had one been thrown? Harry had a switch thrown (or had thrown a switch—wasn't that the pesky problem of fate?) that led him to pluck out his pistol and play tough guy. Had a switch been thrown with Burt...one that amplified his ambition, his desire to succeed, and his handmaiden greed? Did Burt really think, considering his lack of skills and experience, he could snag the elusive gold ring?

Speaking of which, Harry Mach, how far would you go for completing Leg 3 and changing the Di- into the Tri-, as in Trifecta?

But, backing up, he had to figure out what was in play. He'd placed pieces on the board and the jigsaw was becoming a picture. But it was a picture of Wiley's other persona, Mr. Hyde. Explosions, dead winos, upper case letters K and M, and empty bank accounts. He saw opportunities, resemblances, shadows. He saw proximate causes and effects, but not the whole, the motives, the endgames. But the obvious plot and the shadow were mixed, bound in one man, and they, the outsiders, Harry Mach, Vito, and Burt, and even Judy Ferris, saw different men.

Sal and Vito were chasing dope-dealing Dr. Jekyll. At least he thought so. Sal certainly, but Vito? Was Vito playing at finding Wiley? Harry Mach and Judy Ferris were intrigued—obsessed?—with the mysterious Mr. Hyde. What was in play in Wiley II?

Harry walked slowly up the hill towards his house. Something caught his eye, a shadow. He turned. He'd had the feeling, unconscious until that moment, that someone was following him. He was desperately trying to find Wiley, but was Wiley trying to find him?

Harry's mood, mixed and protracted by his excursion and tête-à-tête with Burt, stayed with him as he stopped in front of his Upper Parnassus

Victorian. The house was a polished oasis where he was a king, an arbiter of deals, a doling out of laws and riches to clients and the Harry Mach carny.

He didn't expect that to change.

As he walked up the stairs, he felt a subtle change. Small things askew. The second floor was messy, but it had gotten messier as he'd stumbled through Wiley's dark side. He saw a clump in the doorway to the living room. Clump? His heart hammered his chest. The clump was a pyramid of books. Other pyramids had risen like mushrooms through the flat.

Harry stopped.

Tick, tick, tick.

He held his breath. Harry inched forward.

"Wiley!"

Harry was still. "Wiley!"

Tick, tick, tick.

Harry breathed raggedly.

He stopped at the edge of the dining room.

The dining room had documents spread over the floor. His file room was open. He expected more damage. What he didn't expect was his razor-sharp Wusthof butcher knife pinned to the center of the dining room table like a slender erect penis.

Harry's heart dropped to his knees. He stood motionless, welded to the spot.

The room swirled. The table lurched up.

The dust, the strewn papers, the floor.

Where was he? Harry rolled over and looked at the ceiling. Why was he on the floor?

He rolled over onto his elbows. The butcher knife stood proudly erect in the middle of his table, his table of Grand Deals. Harry gulped. His whole body shivered.

He came up to his knees. Holding onto the side of the hallway, he made it to his feet. Using the wall as a support, he stumbled into the front room and fell into a chair near the doorway.

He edged the handkerchief out of his pocket and mopped his face. The handkerchief felt good, as his face cooled. He kept it in his hand as he vacantly regarded the living room. Some books were open, their white pages exposed, or face down, their spines ragged and punched in.

The afternoon sun spread over the front of the room. He was a part of the detritus, a furnishing, an accessory, which had been rejected and left with the other lumps.

No, he thought, finally forcing his mind to grasp what had happened. His game, his amusing game, had become too dangerous.

Wiley must have guessed Harry Mach had the address book, the bank numbers, and the passwords.

And he'd be back. That's what it meant. And it meant that Harry Mach was a walking target, a dead man. His head dropped to his chest.

No game was worth it. It was time to get out, and get out fast.

22

The Haight Street end of Golden Gate Park was settling down after a long day and night. The usual inhabitants, the winos and runaways and homeless, had done their eating and drinking and drugs finding surcease, banishing the glimmer of recognition that their lives could in some small way be different. They lay in humps on the patchy green grass, like buffalo felled by long rifles. Arc lamps from Stanyan and Haight streets shone through a rare fogless night and made short shadows on the far side of their sleeping bags and brushed the eucalyprus and the surrounding darkness a chalky prison white.

Marant Olivier thought the luminosity sinister. He knew it had everything to do with his assignment. He was tangled in a mess that got worse when he tried to understand it.

RM. Kafi and Teresa. Boris/Wiley. Three winos, two dead. Phantoms.

He tried to call two old friends in RM, but both numbers had been disconnected. He tried to call Christian again, but Christian was at none of the numbers in Paris, Neuilly, or Nice. Emergency number?

No. He called Teresa and told her the project was off.

"Why come this far and leave empty-handed?" Teresa implored.

"What makes you think Boris has the formula? He could have lined the valise with C-4 or planted explosives inside the mill."

"I hadn't thought of that. Kafi made and planted it. Why go to that trouble?"

Teresa's urgency made him hesitate. And it was possible Kafi met Boris/Wiley to reassure him that they were serious. Except...except. There were other problems, serious problems. If Kafi was concerned about being followed, why did he see Wiley half-an-hour later? More importantly, was Wiley Brooks a drug dealer, a chemist, both or neither, or was he fronting for the real chemist?

It defied comprehension. On the other hand, there were the articles about a new explosive, the blowing up of the mill, RM's desire for the explosive. Marant shook his head and grimaced. He hesitated telling Teresa about Wiley and the drugs. If she was on the other side, they might take that as meaning he knew it was a farce. And, of course, he wasn't sure. Americans wanted to be all things. What was wrong with being a chemist, a drug dealer, or a front for a rogue chemist? "All right. One more wino, one more day. Then we'll meet and I'll hand you the key." After he eliminated Scab, he would give either Kafi or Teresa the account in Zurich. They could get the process themselves.

"Hey man, let's go," said Scab. "If you got the scotch, I got the will!"

They lurched through the light towards the underpass. Marant was dressed in the American costume of jeans, work shirt, a torn leather jacket, an old pack, and walking stick. His outfit reminded him of a latter-day Johnny Appleseed.

Scab was, he supposed, wearing the same clothes he must have worn at the Queen Wilhelmina Tulip Garden on that day when, according to Kafi, the three winos had seen him blow up the mill. Scab's plaid shirt was torn and dirty, his black jeans torn, his tennis shoes new, too-white, and probably stolen. Earlier, despite reservations, he'd followed the continuously inebriated Scab through the park. Marant made sure neither of them were followed and set up in Scab's path with a bottle and pack of cigarettes. Scab quickly adopted him in the same way Potato had. They sat on a hill overlooking a dell with a pond, sidewalk, patch of grass, and a grove of tree ferns. It was an empty, false Eden.

The more Scab talked—like Potato about killing people in prison, how he had fucked up so-and-so, beaten someone to death with a baseball bat—the more Marant didn't care about killing him. This one lives, that one dies. It was odd to think that he was making judgments about life and death. Of course he'd made those judgments before, but then he had the distance of a concrete cause; without a cause, life-or-death calls made him feel old, as if he were edging through a dim, moral land.

Scab also talked about the explosion, how he would fuck up Wiley when he found him. Marant tried to find out more about who Wiley was, but it was obvious Scab didn't know.

Marant had taken out the fugu pill, when a camera-toting batch of tourists shuffled down the path, camped on the patch of grass, and took out cellophane-wrapped sandwiches.

Scab lurched to his feet and insisted on finding friends. Later, near the spot where the greedy Potato had downed the fugu-laced malt liquor, they shared their bottle with a ragtag group of four or five. They all commiserated with Scab when he talked of the boozy adventures of the erstwhile Potato and the sorrowful Sugar. Scab watched the paths that led around their hill, as if Potato and Sugar would soon show up to fight over the bottle.

"Man you are something else! I don't know where you got all that money. But I don't mind. It's nice not having to worry about it for one day. I seem to spend most of my time doing that, but it's nice having a buddy again. Say, how much money do you have? Can't be too careful with these creeps." Scab's wave took in the bushes and heavy shadows within shadows of kids, winos, and dogs strewn over the hill like battlefield dead.

"A few hundred," said Marant, uncaring. He was finally going to get Scab alone. Marant tapped out a Jacques Brel ballad from Le Crime de Monsieur Lange, making echoes in the stalactite-toothed tunnel.

Scab was following him, a sycophant, drunk, bold. "Good thing you're with me," Scab said, shaking his head. "Can't be too careful, Mortie, my man. Can't be too careful."

"You can never be too careful," Marant replied.

"You're gonna like this spot," said Scab. "It's my favorite. Got that bottle?"

He handed Scab the bottle. Scab took a drink and thrust the bottle at Marant. Marant, stifling his objections to Scab's odor, took a sip. He'd substituted a good scotch for Scab's malt liquor and fortified wine. The scotch warmed him, but he began to feel drunk himself.

They staggered down the sidewalk as it curved gracefully past the bushes and cypress around Sharon Meadow. Stadium light from Kezar Stadium on the far southeastern corner of the park rimmed the flat cypress and dangling eucalyptus swords and offered a theatrical backdrop for a playground where plastic dragons, turtles, and geese were thuggish monsters of the night. They passed the playground and the heavy building with stained glass hanging in the windows. Then they were in a narrow wooded area. It was dappled with shadows, and the moon tried to break through low-level cirrus disguised as fog.

Marant stopped and Scab ran into him.

"What the fuck!" Scab barked.

Moonlight touched the wrought iron fence, an old bench, a winding road. The shadows encroached on the flat surface of the grass lawn-bowling courts. The courts, the soft shrub line, and the single, looming flat-topped cypress, were uncommonly serene, a bonsai of the giants.

"Just looking," replied Marant.

"That's where we're goin'. Hey, give me that bottle!"

He gave Scab the bottle, and they walked across the curving street.

Scab opened the gate to the lawn-bowling court and walked on the grass carpet towards the shadows thrown by the cypress and gnarly bushes.

Marant followed him and walked into one of the shadows. It was an interesting space, one of immense peace. It was as if he'd been transported to a Japanese scroll painting with its ritual enveloping mountain, distant rivulet, and dwarfed figures. It was soft, not point, line, or curve. He realized in that moment that the world view he always came back to was a simple Manichean one. Curve or line. There was so much in between.

But his purpose flowed into that rare moment of recognition. Peace, yes; softness. It would also be a good place to kill Scab. It was far from the entrance. He was reaching for the fugu pill when Scab said, "Drop the stick and hand it over."

"What?"

159

"Don't play dumb, Mortie," Scab growled. "I've got a gun aimed right at your head. Drop the stick and hand over that pack."

Marant turned. Scab had put the bottle down and had a gun in his right hand. He was close enough to get off a good shot. Marant dropped the stick. It became a white snake on the grass carpet. "Don't use the gun."

"Put the sack down and turn around," said Scab.

Marant felt adrenaline pouring into his body. Scab's show had been real and ruse. Marant unfastened and threw his pack on the ground and turned slowly. Out of the corner of his eye, he saw the contents scattered, the wallet pulled out. Scab grunted as he pulled out the money.

Scab's smell preceded him. The gun teased the bristles on Marant's neck.

"You're queer, Mortie, but you messed with the wrong honcho."

"Tell me more about Wiley," Marant said, trying to gain time.

"Why the fuck do you care, shithead?"

"It's important."

"I know what you're doing," Scab said. Scab's voice dropped as if he were trying to figure out what Marant was doing. When he found the words, they came out low and menacing. "You killed Potato and Sugar, didn't you? Just the same way you're going to kill me. You're from that fuck Wiley. Guess what, asshole, I knew that. Hey guys!"

The shadows moved, and three shabby men emerged from his left and one from his right. They were carrying two-by-fours.

Scab's gun jammed into Marant's neck.

Beyond the tangle of plants was the trunk of the cypress. It was huge, solid, thin-ridged. Would he walk into the darkness beaten, shot, with that ridged bark seared into his brain?

Scab said, "Guys it's time for some fun. Fuck him up."

The three advanced warily. They were a body's distance from him when Marant flattened his hand, ducked right, and jabbed his rigid fingers up into Scab's throat. He heard a clap, and felt a bee sting his arm. Scab gagged and staggered back. Another shot slapped the cypress trunk. Marant whipped around Scab, caught him, grabbed his head, and snapped his neck. Marant snatched the gun out of Scab's hand as he fell.

Scab's three accomplices halted and stared at him.

He pointed the gun at the one in the middle. "Gentlemen, go back

160

where you came from."

"You're gonna pay for that, asshole," said the bearded one on the right.

"Now!"

The three turned, shuffled into the shadows.

Scab lay on the ground, his body softening into a contour.

Marant knelt warily, like an animal over his prey. Nothing moved. Distant voices, cars honking, Haight Street. Marant peered into the shadows around the lawn-bowling court, then the road and the luminosity hovering over the trees nearer the city. That's when he saw the spreading patch of blood on his arm. He felt the pain. He'd deal with it later. He picked up the gnarled stick, his pack, and his money. He looked at the pistol, picked it up, then looked for the spent shells and found them. He stuffed the scotch in his pack. He didn't have time to hide the body. He walked towards the road, but paused at the wrought iron fence.

He regarded the sweep of the court, and a moon-dappled slug halted in its nocturnal crawling. Marant admired the contour for a moment, the soft lines, the object which was a sculpture, but not full of Henry Moore's life. Years ago, he took pains. He always thought, but maybe that was just his own vulgar bragging, that his plans were perfect, that point A and point B were attached in an elegantly logical way. That the bullet path was straight from rifle to victim. On that project everything went wrong. Worse than wrong. The subjects were wrong. The execution was wrong. He was wrong.

Marant felt old. He thought for a few moments of the finality of that night's adventure, then the thought was gone like a rustle of leaves.

Marant retrieved a spare shirt from his pack, took off his shirt, and tore it into strips. He bound his wound—it hurt, but it missed the muscle—and put on the other shirt. He walked towards the faint light of the inner road. In the distance, a police car stopped, then accelerated. Clouds passed. An argument erupted from the shadows. Was it another Scab and Marant playing out some skit, a one-act play that would end in death?

Marant hurried towards the light.

23

Judy drove over Buena Vista and down into the Haight. The street hadn't changed since she'd dropped off Mike Larew. Homeless, winos, punks, and bikers. Hair in pinks and greens. A scattering of tourists mixed with the local fauna. She turned left on Stanyan and glanced at Mike Larew's hotel. Why had he lied about where he was staying?

She turned right on Page Street and soon negotiated the difficult turn onto Kezar Drive. Kezar Drive turned into Lincoln Way, and soon she was headed towards the ocean three miles away, the park on her right, the Sunset on her left.

A block from the ocean, she made a sharp turn on Inner Drive, which pointed her back towards the city. Two blocks later, she parked across the street from the Queen Wilhelmina Tulip Garden. Cyclone fence, a warning. Bumblebee tape wrapped around the mill with a sign labeled "Danger." There was a huge hole in the near side of the mill and, through a plastic sheet covering the hole, she saw splintered remnants of the innards. Surrounding the mill were cypress and pine whose tops were swept towards the city by ocean breezes. The underbrush was dense with bushes and thick gnarled leptospermum. Two homeless people emerged from the undergrowth on the far side of mill. They looked at the mill then slipped back into the brush.

Judy took bills out of her purse and a couple of business cards. She slipped the purse into the glove compartment and locked it. She vaulted out of the Miata, skipped across the street, and ran towards the bushes. She dove into the same opening as the homeless people and found herself hemmed in by thick ropes of leptospermum and smaller branches sprouting small oval acacia-like leaves. She crawled over the first trunk, then crouched under another. Finally, she emerged at the intersection of two narrow trails, one edging back towards the ocean, the other into yet another mass of undergrowth.

Judy frowned, looked up and down the trails, and when she didn't see anyone, pushed through the underbrush at the other side of the trail. She stopped a foot from angry red eyes in a streaked grimy face.

Judy's heart raced. They stared at each other.

"What the fuck you want?" the face sneered.

"A few answers."

"What?"

"Did you know Sugar Mercedes or Potato?"

The dirty face coalesced into a man in Army fatigues. He was thin, hunched over, and had a too-large nose anchored by those washed-out red eyes, which now dinged back and forth in deep eye sockets. "Sugar was okay, a little screwy." He made a slow, tight circle around his ear. "I also know both of 'em are dead as doornails."

"Scab?"

"You find him, tell him he's an asshole."

"Name's Judy. I'll give you five bucks for information."

His eyes softened, and he seemed to talk to himself. "John. Vet. Been living here two years. Kids rip us off, punks beat us up, set us on fire. In election years the cops throw us out. I try to cook, have a lean-to."

Judy felt a pang of sympathy. John was at a dead end. "What about this Scab?"

"Scab and Sugar and this other guy, this Potato, lived closer to the edge than me. They were gonna die sooner than later. I guess two of 'em did."

"What about the mill, the explosion?"

"I wasn't here, but I heard it. Sugar said she saw it. Said this guy blew it up on purpose. She said Scab was going to get money from him. I thought it was a crock."

"Maybe that's why they died."

He looked at her, puzzled, then shrugged. "That's a stretch, lady."

"Has Scab been here today?"

"Nope."

"What does he look like?"

John put his hand to his jaw, as an aid in thinking. "About fifty. Average height, skinny, long stringy hair, mean lookin'."

"Where does he hang out?"

"He sleeps out here sometimes, but they hang near the fountain, or at least used to."

Judy said, "End of Haight?"

"You can't panhandle here."

"That's close to where Wiley lives," Judy said, more to herself.

"Who?"

"Doesn't matter." Judy dug in her jeans, pulled out a five and a business card. "Thanks, John. Could you call me if you see him?"

"Sure, but I ain't got no change."

Judy dug quarters out of her back pocket. "There's more."

"One thing," John said, stuffing the quarters in his pocket. "Scab is not the nicest person. He's ripped people off and he's mean, especially drunk."

"Thanks, I'll remember."

Judy slipped underneath the branches. She took the trail for about hundred yards back towards the city. She saw four or five lean-tos, but no people. Everyone had their schedule. Finally she turned and headed back to her car. She walked by the mill and across the street. Judy stared at the steering wheel, trying to absorb what John told her.

She started the car, then popped the Miata into gear. She drove slowly through the park, stopping every now and then when she saw a homeless encampment. When she arrived in the city years ago, she lived in the Sunset and took long walks every Sunday. That end of the park was wilder, full of homeless, and gay pickups staked out near trees or in half-hidden glades.

She drove slowly past artificial lakes filling up with migrating ducks. She turned on JFK Drive and a few minutes later made a right turn on Stanyan. She parked on Stanyan. That area reminded her of Mike Larew and the Palms. Bits and pieces of that night filtered back. There was the musty dead bar, the neon flickering in the corner, the living relics, their give-and-take, the drive into the Haight, three De-Lite condoms.

She turned towards the street people spread over the hill sloping down towards the tunnel under Kezar Drive. She used to jog through that tunnel years ago and always thought the false stalactites—papier-mâché and wire that hung down like icicles—were funny, not a ridiculous attempt to make the park exotic.

The ragged batch spread out in front of her were not funny. She wasn't sure exactly what to make of them. She'd given her share of quarters and dollars to the homeless she saw every day, and certainly the younger ones had good chances to get off the street, find jobs, get in programs, go to school. But the majority seemed, as the article in the paper said, intractable. The Sugars and Scabs didn't want to change. There was nothing she could do about that.

Judy squatted down next to two spread out on a dirty blanket. They were young with pink and green hair and soiled hands. A half bagel with a few bites out of it lay between them.

Zeke had green hair, washed-out brown eyes, soiled hands, and wore jeans and a dirty "Daffy Duck" T-shirt. They were stoned, but intelligible.

Zeke knew Sugar. "She was kinda plump, you know, and always gettin' in trouble, like she had a screw loose. But you know she was okay. Kinda fun, too. I miss seein' her around."

Janey had pink hair, a round, dumpling face, rings on each finger, and wore patched jeans and a dirty "Jerry Garcia is God" T-shirt. She piped in, "When she got too high, she was weird. And the big guy was a drunk, a real alkie."

"Did they hang out with a skinny, older guy?"

"They was always fightin'," said Zeke. "Scab's an ex-con, at least he said he was, kinda ornery, always in-your-face. Said he carried a gun."

Janey peered up at her. "Why are you asking, lady?"

"A lot of people ask me that. I'd just like to talk to Scab. Know where he is?" They looked at each other, gauging, Judy guessed, whether she was a cop or a social worker. "Believe me, this isn't anything official."

"Sometimes, he sleeps near the ocean," said Zeke. "People don't bother you there."

Janey looked at Zeke, then blurted, "He was here earlier with some guy. This guy had slicked black hair, a walking stick, money. We seen him in the last few days. He was always watchin'. He ain't one of us."

Ice snaked up Judy's spine. "How long?"

"A couple hours," said Janey.

"Any idea where they went?"

"Nope," said Zeke. "It's a big park, biggest in the country."

Judy got up. Couples walked slowly under the stalactites, babies were pushed, runners emerged. It would take her weeks to find Scab.

"Could you spare a couple bucks?" said Janey, looking up at her dolefully.

Judy looked down at them and dug in her jean pocket. She gave them a twenty. "You know about the Haight Street Youth Center, or the one on Larkin?"

"We're gonna go next week."

Gonna go. Next week.

She hoped they would. "Okay. Thanks, guys."

Judy turned and walked swiftly towards the tunnel. She felt pumped, animated, but also knew her mission was hopeless. When she emerged from the tunnel, she checked the small baseball field near the children's playground, then the picnic area near the stone lodge, which at that time of year was busy with people cutting glass and making stained-glass birds and butterflies. She walked quickly past the lawn-bowling courts with their clusters of players decked in white, and took the sloping drive to the big baseball field. At the baseball field, she scanned the stands. A few winos watched little league games, but they were too young to be Scab.

For the next two hours, she walked through the Botanical Gardens sculpted acres, the music concourse, the deteriorating Rhododendron Dell, around a pond with a small waterfall, the tennis courts, and through the trees rimming Sharon Meadow. She emerged despondent and tired across from McClaren Lodge at the park's Oak Street entrance.

She turned right on Stanyan and walked back towards the park entrance. Zeke and Janey were gone. Mike Larew stared at her car. He looked up and stared at her, then he snapped off his stare and walked briskly towards her.

"You look like you've seen the ghost of Judy Ferris."

Mike looked at her quizzically. "Not quite a ghost. What are you doing here?"

"Being crazy, following a will-o'-the-wisp. You know those street people you mentioned? I know their names, and two have died in the last few days. I'm looking for the last one."

Mike looked concerned, then puzzled. He rubbed his head, and the black bristles flattened, then snapped back. "I didn't mean anything by the street people. You shouldn't be parading through the park on some will-o'-the-wisp."

She felt his concern was a front, but why? "I haven't been rational for days."

The traffic was heavy at the intersection. Their images flicked past in car windows. They were both tall, but the faces were hazy, the features a smear, the attitude of the bodies faintly depressed. Suddenly she felt lonely, as if she'd been juggling her balls so long that they were starting to mesmerize her.

"What are you doing now?" Mike said.

An in-line skater shot down the path and into the tunnel. A woman pushed twins in a carriage out and stared at the homeless. Judy felt like a fool. She'd let herself get crazy. She wouldn't find Scab in a year. Even if she found him, what would she do with him? "I think I'll go home and mope."

Mike shook his head, then smiled devilishly. "No fun. C'mon, I'll buy dinner. I promise not to bite or make an obvious pass."

Judy looked at him for a long second, and he looked back. She wanted to trust him but didn't. She liked him and feared him. On the other hand, he could help her find out more about Wiley. Lots of reasons. "If I choose the restaurant."

"Done," he said, sweeping his hand towards her car.

Market Street and Castro was crowded with Jaguars, BMWs, and SUVs, one of which was double-parked and loading up with supplies from the Great Grains health-food store. Thirty years ago the Castro was a dying Irish/German neighborhood where you could buy a Victorian for $25,000. Now it was gay, million-dollar condos, chic shops, fancy SUVs, and, of course, a scattering of homeless.

The Thai Village was somber with walls of dark wood hung with photos of Thailand and an old photo of the current king and queen. High on the side of the balcony was a shrine with a statue of Buddha, three oranges, and a glass of water. The photo on the wall over their table was of a ruin of the ribbed pointed towers, a Khmer intrusion at an unidentified place in Thailand.

Judy was nervous. She was in control, but not exactly. She felt loose goosey, but knew she shouldn't be. It added up to a burst of babbling... about photos of ruins, Asian trips, the nagging guilt of writing about fancy hotels perched on the edge of relentless poverty.

Mike was attentive, then amused. After the food arrived, they ate silently for a few minutes. Finally Mike said, "You're less uptight than last night."

"Unfocused, you mean. I'm on an emotional sine wave; that's not something most men worry about." She speared a piece of tofu in coconut milk and green curry, then ate it. "I farmed out most of my projects, so I can find Wiley and maybe write a story about him."

She shot a quick glance at Mike, tried to interpret his frown and couldn't. "What kind of a story? Wiley is gone, vamoosed, history."

"It will come together. I'm having second thoughts, but the punch line is that I've been impersonating myself. I need something to shake my life up. I suppose you never feel like that."

Mike watched her as if it were a trick question. "You mean 'Who am I?'-type questions? Stuff like that happens when you're not looking. You find that you believe in this or that."

"Typical male response. You're all stoics, unflappable, whatever happens happens." She was secretly pleased that Mike's special with very spicy sauce made droplets pop out on his brow. He wiped them off with his napkin.

Mike said, "And one day you'll impersonate an impersonation. Which one is real?"

Judy took a long drink of rosé. It heated her throat then her face. She warmed to Mike's physical presence. "Who is that elusive Judy Ferris? Was there a time when I was just me with no add-ons? My therapist thought the defining moment was when Dad split. Mom never recovered and is still mordant and pessimistic—that's where I get my own less-than-rosy disposition. Or was it after college, when I parlayed fluent Spanish into working for the Washington Post Central American bureau? Or is the real Judy Ferris the touchy one about what the U.S. does in the world, the one who hates little boys in men's bodies, the CIA, and black-and-white militaristic ideologies? Or is she just a curmudgeon?"

"Talking about oneself in the third person is the first sign of insanity. Besides, curmudgeons aren't good-looking."

Judy laughed, then felt silly she'd laughed. "You'd see if you were around me more."

"Shit happens. My father doesn't even live on this continent. There should be a statute of limitation on who-did-what-to-whom twenty years ago."

"I don't disagree."

Mike looked at her over his glass. "Ultimately, your story isn't about Wiley, a mysterious bad man, a boy-in-man's-body, a chameleon; it's

168

about you. You know that."

"A priori, it has to be about me. That doesn't invalidate the story."

"What has Wiley done besides scam a bunch of people?"

Judy frowned, "What about the winos?"

"What about them?

Judy said, "Two of them are dead. That's not just curiosity or a theory."

"They could have had natural deaths. You want to fit them into a theory."

She doubted if she should tell him but decided to. If she didn't tell anyone, it was like that plane going down in the desert. And whether he admitted it or not, Mike was part of the story. "Wiley, explosives, CIA shenanigans, and dead winos. It's one story among many."

Mike's shoulders raised perceptibly. "You have to believe it, and you have to write it."

"For dissent and redemption. Two things I can tell you don't think about."

"How do you know what I think?" Mike said. His rugged face was an odd mixture of opposites, of frowns and smiles, clear, big brown eyes, and pockmarks, which didn't make him less appealing. And the more he talked, the less she knew about him. Mike shrugged. "Okay, write your story. It will be just another plaintive cry against the powers-that-are."

"You can't be more pessimistic than I am. What do you think of Harry Mach?"

Mike stopped eating. He gave her a suspicious, almost angry look. "Who is that?"

"He called me. I saw him. I think he has Wiley's address book."

Mike put his fork down. "Really."

"Why are you interested in Wiley and pretend you're not?"

Mike took a sip of rosé and placed his glass on the table. He shrugged. "Isn't everyone curious to a certain degree? Drug deal, murders. It's human nature."

"Let's see, world tour and a serious interest in Wiley. You are not too believable. You must know that."

Mike picked up his fork and looked at the end of it, not her. She wondered if he was going to tell her the truth, and decided he wouldn't. "I bounced between divorced parents for a while, then I discovered the

169

edge in martial arts, climbing mountains, skydiving, and banging into handball-court walls. And of course there are wild parties, an experiment or two with drugs, and I drink too much. As for law school, it may be too tame. That's why I'm curious about things like dope, murder, and renegades like Wiley. I'm human, not a monster."

She gave him a lop-sided grin. "I'll reserve my opinion on that one. What would you do if not law school, if that is a real option?"

"You don't believe much of what I say, do you?"

"Enough to form an opinion. Isn't that what we do? Form opinions on the scantiest of information? Mostly, it reinforces what we want to believe in the first place."

She'd had too much rosé. She lifted her glass and finished what was left. She was trying to figure out where the night was going, when the brown-skinned waiter with the soft almond eyes came with the bill. They both grabbed for it, but Mike was faster. "You're embarking on a long, possibly foolish, and likely unpaid journey. I'm flush, at least for now."

"Mr. Larew, you are a gentleman after all. You want another ride home?"

"One last risk for the night."

They walked to her car. She felt loose walking next to him. It was as if their bodies were sending signals neither of them could articulate. "Is there someplace we could go for a nightcap?"

She looked at him curiously and rolled the dice. "I live up the hill."

"I'm game."

Soon they angled up the winding streets of Corbett Avenue. Luckily she found a place near her apartment. A few minutes later, they were inside. She told him to look around while she went to the bathroom.

When she came back, she found him staring at the paper taped over her PC.

"Wiley, CIA, explosives, Algeria, Euskadi, Revolution Mondiale, dead winos, and, not least, Mike Larew. I wonder how many people have my name taped to their wall."

"Mine is a puzzle, not a target. Go out on the patio while I get nightcaps. Yours?"

Mike seemed to reluctant to leave the paper, almost as if he were entranced by it. He turned, smiled, and said, "A beer, if you have one."

"Okey dokey."

Mike walked through the kitchen, opened the door, and walked to the edge of the yard. The yard dropped off steeply to a retaining wall. The other houses and apartment houses on that block were cantilevered into the hillside. It was a view framed with dark East Bay hills, washes of twinkly diamonds, and boats that were fireflies crawling over the dark glass of the bay.

Judy brought out the drinks—a Bloody Mary for her and a designer beer for him—then they pushed the glasses around the table. She felt the usual peace in the bay view, the dark haze, and the awesome space.

"Fantastic view," he said finally. "If I ever live here, I'd want a view like this."

Judy looked at him over her drink. "It's never just a background."

Mike looked at her uneasily, then rubbed his head, and seemed to make up his mind.

He turned to her, and Judy watched him back. If she'd been bright, she would have cut off that sexual undertow. But sex wasn't about intelligence. "I'm a pragmatist, and you're an obsessed idealist. I told you I want to get beyond the surface with you. I don't know how you feel. We make these snap decisions and later realize it was because someone wears the same deodorant or has a hooked nose which reminds them of their mother."

"Another two-night stand," she said, oddly pleased.

He got up and crouched down next to her and looked at her. She felt his magnetism up close. It was the animal grace, the muscular build, the way he moved, his heavy hands. He put her drink down and turned her chair around. He leaned over and kissed her once, long.

Judy said, "That was fun. Want some more?"

She could see that the night had several cusps—a little like other cusps she hadn't expected in the last few days. He fingered a curl near her ear. "Sure."

"Bad boy. You just love 'em and leave 'em."

"Guilty and out of lines."

"Guilt—what would we do without it? You wonder whether this is all on a card stashed up there." She pointed to the clouds. "Wait a minute."

A few minutes later, she slipped back in a robe and marched up to him. She played with his largest pockmark, something she'd wanted to do. He stroked her breast. She slipped onto his lap. "You don't mind making out alfresco, do you?"

"Out here?"

"You're such a baby."

"I didn't say I didn't want to, Judy."

"I like it when I hear my name like that."

She hadn't realized she was horny. It was oh so exciting. She unzipped his jeans and got him hot and bothered. Her sex was itching. She coaxed him to the ground, then perched on him like a sphinx. He was hairy and big and smelled of salt, musk, and sap.

She had a strange control of herself, and when he was inside, she guided him to a secret clit-purchase. Then she grabbed his head, closed her eyes, and relaxed. He ground away. She just let it happen. No doubts. No second thoughts. It was the way life should be. Then she popped her eyes open, and he was staring at her, as if he were feeding on her soul. Beyond his dark head were the bay and the lights. After a while it seemed as if she were flickering with those lights from flashy reds to cobalt cold blues. It was an ultimate mix of here and there, distance and intimacy.

He looked poleaxed, then straining, then a dribble of pleasure escaped from his lips.

As for the rest of that night, after that perfect moment outside, sometimes it felt as if they were sparring, trying to unlock secrets. When they got into softer games, it was easier, except when Mike stared at that yellow sheet. She supposed she'd do the same thing if a lover had her name scribbled into a spider's web of murderous events.

He turned slowly towards her. Lights flickered through the curling drapes. "You're not just an obsessive writer," he said.

"You're not just an oversexed, arrogant thrill-seeker. On the other hand, maybe we just wanted to have some fun. Life can seem so dreary and evil."

Judy took his hand and kept it in hers, as if he were going to fly away. A few minutes later she heard his soft snoring.

Her summer was not trailing off the way she thought it would. She bunched the orange pillow so it supported her neck and let her mind drift. What was next? She wasn't sure she told off the ATA from a sense of justice or to cauterize a wound that had never healed. It may have been momentum, or curiosity about that dim, underground river in American life, or even, as Mike said, a thrill she felt about the chase itself.

24

Harry Mach got the message. The black-handled Wusthof butcher knife pinioned deep in the flawless, waxed Table of Big Deals thrust into the heart of his spirit, gutted it, and left it to twist slowly in the wind.

Harry roused himself and stumbled through piles of books, suits spread over floor, pillow cases ripped open. Wiley couldn't have done that much damage on his own. Maybe he had help from his supposed girlfriend, Rosie.

Harry felt wraith-like, expendable, an exposed underbelly.

Why the Trifecta? The avatar of his father? Karl had wanted risk, more risk, the ultimate risk. Harry wanted...what exactly did he want? He wanted vitality, he wanted to feel alive, he wanted an engine pumping adrenalin through his body and spirit.

But he'd hit the wall. The Wusthof knife was a Damocles Sword swinging over his spirit suspended on a frayed thread.

He called his maid, Dolores. While he waited, he yanked the knife out of the table, then stored the sensitive stuff in the office, which was also in tatters. When Dolores came, he explained he'd been robbed. After she shook her head sorrowfully, he told her to start in the kitchen. Harry rolled up his sleeves and started in the living room.

His books were in the saddest state. Economics, investment strategies, capitalist theory, his dabbling in pragmatism, bridge books—his premier collection of the Aces—and from his wall of short stories and novels, his hardboiled collection: Dashiell Hammet, Chandler, Jim Thompson, James M. Cain. Had noir fantasizing egged him into the middle of a modern noir saga? Was he, say, a henchman to some slick Peter Lorre, beguiling Mary Astor, a foil for the unstoppable and incessant explainer, Bogart?

On his table, the Table of Grand Deals, a thin layer of dust surrounded the knife cut, and where Sal and Burt had rested drinks, were faint swirls and ridges. They looked like the tracks of tiny ATVs spinning in circles.

He cleaned the table himself.

It took the rest of the day. When Dolores drove off in her rat-trap Honda at nine that night, she had an extra three hundred dollars in her pocket and a warning not to say anything about the robbery.

Harry—troubled, his mood mixed—shuffled upstairs. He locked the bedroom door and crawled into bed with his clothes on. He tucked his head deep in the down pillow, drew the covers over him, and closed his eyes.

Friday morning.

Harry Mach was quitting. Yesterday was one of the worst in his life, perhaps the worst. He took a long shower. When he got out, he wiped a small space in the fogged-over mirror and regarded his faint jowls.

Harry frowned.

He turned towards the bathroom door and threw his robe on the floor. Harry wiped a small space in the fogged-over full-length mirror, which revealed his cock.

It had always been big, and long. His flaccid seven inches aroused was close to ten. It was why he always chose big women. Harry the cock...it was why he was so confident; it was why he could play his games; it was why he was rich, and it was why he could play in any game.

Harry flipped his cock and watched it swing from side to side like a metronome. He was quitting, wasn't he?

Quitting. The word grated on his spirit. But there are times when reason trumps expertise, knowledge, and risk. He'd told his clients that for years; it was tough taking his own advice. Yesterday was his wake-up call, a calling card stuck deep in his spirit.

Harry donned his robe and walked slowly downstairs.

As he walked towards the dining room, the phone rang. Harry hurried and picked up. Just as he said hello to John Barnes, a client, a second line lit up. Harry frowned, put John on hold, and found line two was Sal Ziti. He was thinking of how to approach Sal, when line three lit up.

Burt.

Harry stared at his telephone as if it were in a state of electrical revolt.

He told John he'd call back.

Line Two: Sal Ziti.

Before he could say anything, Sal said, "What's Burt doing?"

"About?"

"You know. Is he trying to cut me or Vito out? Does he have other plans?"

Harry concentrated. "Not that he's revealed to me. He's difficult, not too bright, but resourceful. I'd rather not work with him—you know that. But I went along with you, and him."

"He hasn't come up with the smallest lead. So what if someone wrecked Wiley's Napa house. What does that tell us? I'm in the fucking middle on this one, Harry. I would pack my bags and call it a loss, if Vito wasn't involved."

"I'm already packing my bags."

"But what about Vito, Harry? You got to help me with this. He is involved, whether we like it or not. But I don't think he cares that much about the money...in fact, I'm not sure he cared about Leonard. It may be pride and family. Thing is, Harry, Vito picked Burt, and I don't think Vito liked him, and I don't fucking like him. I know one thing; he's not a fucking fixer—what the hell is that anyway?"

Harry went ahead, gingerly. "You're not sure Vito wants to find Wiley?"

"That's going too far, I think."

"Possibly. But you had all the reasons. What is a 'fixer'? It seems to me that if Vito really wanted to find Wiley, he would have hired someone he knew better...at least more competent."

"Right. But Vito did have Wiley followed, didn't he?"

Harry said, "True, but we reach a point where going on is problematic."

"Regardless, tell me if Burt steps out of line. I'll talk with Vito."

Harry frowned. Burt versus Sal and Vito. And Harry Mach held the middle. At that moment, Harry realized how hard it would be to get out if he wanted to. He ran through quitting scenarios: he could pay everyone off; he'd be out a hundred thousand, maybe a little more. But he'd have his sanity, his millions, his good, rich life. He could, he supposed, grab the money in Wiley's drug account, the three hundred grand. But with Wiley so close, that was problematic.

Wiley was the big problem. He could pay everyone off but Wiley. Wiley's address book was gold mine and albatross. Vito wanted Wiley, and Wiley wanted the address book. Where did that leave him? "Of course."

Sal said, "Do you have anything new, any tidbit for Vito?"

Easy, Harry. "I've told Burt all I know, Wiley's bars, his place in Napa, and I've dug through Wiley's address book. I haven't found anything else, although I've wracked my brain."

"I didn't expect you to do much. Call me if you find anything."

If he didn't expect Harry Mach to do much, he didn't know him at all.

Line Three. Burt, his soi-disant lackey, qua Caliban, had morphed into a secret.

"Anything new?" Burt said coldly.

Harry stared out the window. Tell Burt about the break-in? No. Should he continue? He knew that answer before he asked the question. "Nothing new. But we have to act quickly."

"And you don't know why, or if there's any money."

"There will be. Forget the wino, keep trying to find who the redhead is and where she lives. She has to be the key." He wasn't going to forget the wino, but Mr. Hyde's side was murky. As for the drug money, that might take care of itself. He had big tokens with the bank accounts and passwords. It was a question of when and how to play them.

Harry Mach was back in the game.

25

Gulls swirled like vigilantes around the garbage cans, yawked at tourists from the pollarded, stunted sycamores, and contested the top of the refuse food chain with a scattering of blackbirds, pigeons and the maligned, but fecund, European starling. There were heavy crowds in the Golden Gate Park music concourse and in the museums flanking the concourse. Most visitors to the Academy of Science were pointing at the dinosaur dioramas, videos, and installations inspired by the success of the movie Jurassic Park. Across the concourse, crowds of tourists streamed through the de Young entrance attracted to the Asian Art Museum and crowds oohing and aahhing at the sand mandala and its seven hundred-plus deities being knocked out grain by grain by curry-robed Tibetan monks.

Marant Olivier was disguised in tourist attire himself that day—Hawaiian print shirt, which barely covered his wound, tan slacks, and Minolta. But his role and character were disjointed. The clothes felt draped, not worn. He surveyed the crowds at the entrance and queuing up in the gift store and was convinced he wasn't being monitored. He used the Shades International Dialing Card to call the RM emergency cell.

Christian was at their emergency number, and to make things worse, asked him how "Loki" was after they'd finished their salutations. The Scandinavian trickster was their signal that all was not right, including that phone call. Christian gave him two encoded cell numbers. He translated them and waited ten minutes. The wait seemed interminable.

Finally, he dialed the first number. It was busy. Christian picked up at the second.

"I had a slight accident," said Marant. Marant felt hollow as he told Christian what had happened since their last talk, of being cornered by drunks, of killing Scab.

"The police," said Christian, with a slight accent of worry.

"I doubt they'll care. He lived in the park, a wino. And the others wouldn't talk; if they did, no one would believe them."

His arm throbbed. He perspired. His shirt clung to him. He had been watching shadows all day. He'd been injured before, but that time it was more a marker, a sign he'd made a mistake taking the assignment. A sign, in other words, he was too old. He needed his lines and the ever-receding curve; he needed talk in Paris galleries; he needed quiet time; he needed music.

"A GIA operative contacted a young member from the Red Brigades, Gino, about joining a new group, a Muslim-controlled RM," Christian said. "Gino told me this week."

Marant touched his arm and winced at the pain. "A purge."

"I haven't gone that far yet," said Christian softly.

"Yes you have."

There was silence on the other end. "There are two problems," said Christian finally. "Some of RM's members—not Muslims—are yelling for this process. Two. If there is a purge, they will see you as on my side."

Marant shifted the phone to his left hand. "Do they know who I am?"

"They know you're there; I don't know if they know who you are."

Marant thought of Teresa. She guessed who he was, and Kafi knew a voice on the phone. He hadn't seen Kafi, but he could have been watching the Capri Motel when he picked up Teresa. That was another mistake. He shook his head. All wrong.

Christian said, "It's hard for anyone to remain completely anonymous. I'm sorry for that. It worked well for so many years."

Marant felt cold, much colder since their conversation started. What to do, where to go? Did they know about Fort Mahon or his flat on Rue de la Convention? Did they know Albert Rieux equaled Marant Olivier?

"I was lulled into thinking life could be normal and peaceful." Marant thought about what he'd have to do, how long it would take. If the explosive was a ruse, he would be dead or taken. If it wasn't and there was a purge, they would look for him. Not good options. A tourist watched him, impatiently moving from one foot to the other, wanting to use the phone. Marant smiled thinly. "A moment." To Christian: "Let's play this out and see how far they are willing to go."

"It's about more than an explosive."

"I'll contact you at two o'clock tomorrow."

"Call this number," said Christian, who gave him a new cell.

Marant looked at the phone for a few moments, replaced it on its hook. He felt hollow and walked aimlessly through the first gallery. He stopped at a sign indicating the museum would close for a major renovation. It made him think of the ending of an era, the start of something new. Christian's RM was an anomaly when it started. And now? And Marant? They were the old; what, or who, would be the new?

His mind was blank, oppressed by what he'd learned. Fort Mahon, his sculpture, his limitless vistas, his doomed attempts to fuse line and curve. All gone.

As he reorganized what Christian said, he began to realize that outcome was there from the beginning. Both had reservations. Both distrusted the Muslims. And both went ahead. He'd said that one who hesitates is lost. He was complicit. He had agreed to everything knowing this could be the result.

They had to play it out. If there was a scheme, they had to know the full extent of it. Christian was right that it wasn't just about Christian and RM; it was about Marant Olivier. They would see him as a deadly member of the old guard. He would work on a sculpture, a car would cruise Fort Mahon's sandy streets, men would slip into the shadows. Plop, plop, plop. The void.

Marant roamed through distant galleries far from the crowds. He felt wooden, his frame lanky and disjointed, his arm ached. He absently remarked on the poor quality of the American paintings. From limitless landscapes to portraits, they all seemed too burnished, the vistas too congratulatory, the towns a mawkish stylized naïveté, the portraits too self-involved.

He stopped at a painting of a Puritan minister draped in black. He had a tiny, hard mouth, banked cheekbones, gray marble eyes, a square white forehead. The man exuded rectitude and self-righteousness. Their iron-bound religion burned witches, spoke of the avenging glory of their god, and grim hells populated with sinners. Why not call it what it was?—fanaticism. The newer members of RM didn't have a corner on that market.

Marant walked out of the de Young Museum, hailed a cab, and returned to the Cultural Exchange. There he shed his tourist costume and changed his dressing. The wound hurt, but it was clean and looked like it was healing. He donned slacks, a dark turtleneck, and deck shoes. He watched the ocean from his window. Forces swirled around him like a North Atlantic storm. It was the old hubris. One watched from a mountaintop, played like a god, drank the ambrosia, until one day you woke up Laocoon, snakes like cords binding your arms and legs, and pulled through scenes and plays like a marionette.

The phone shocked him. He was even more shocked when he found it was Teresa. She was in the lobby of the Cultural Exchange.

"How did you find me?" said Marant testily.

"I followed you the other day," said Teresa. "I told the Institute's reception I'd met you at a party but couldn't remember your name. We are not all incompetent."

"Apparently not."

"Is your real name 'Albert'?"

He laughed. "No. I'll meet you downstairs in five minutes."

Marant scanned the hallway, then walked slowly to the staircase. He paused then walked down the sweeping staircase. He scanned the lobby and then the area behind the staircase. There were no cold-eyed lurkers with their hands inside their coat pockets. Teresa was sitting sedately in a chair opposite the staircase. She had changed her dull, casual clothes for a brighter skirt and white blouse, higher heels, makeup, and a hint of jewelry. It gave her a gypsy-like air. Her deep brown eyes were more alive than he remembered, but flecked with worry.

"Woman transformed," he said, slightly mocking, walking up to her.

She laughed, less loudly than yesterday. "I don't always wear sack-cloth and ashes."

"In that case, you deserve a drink on the Institute's patio."

He led her through the Exchange lobby to a table on the patio, near the balustrade. They were in the sun. Right was the Golden Gate Bridge; opposite, the brown hills of Marin; in front, the sluggish ocean bordered in thick white mist.

They ordered coffee, and while the waiter was getting it, he surveyed the other tables. He felt silly for being cautious there, but last night showed him something. At first he thought it was the project, the stupid killing of three winos. But it was more than Potato and Sugar. Scab and his friends showed him he was not the same Marant as five year ago.

The coffee service was set in front of them. They regarded each other over the white tablecloth. "People normally don't follow me," he said. He poured her coffee, then his own. "My anonymity protects me, or did. I should have stayed retired."

"I'm sorry if I disturbed you," Teresa said seriously. "Your anonymity is safe with me."

Marant sighed. "It's enough you know I'm Marant. Why follow me at all?"

"I need to talk to you."

"The project?"

"Partly," she said. Her worry descended into a kind of harried misery.

She seemed more vulnerable, curiously attractive. "We always wondered about you, why you didn't belong to RM but worked for us. You were for us, but not of us."

Marant wondered whether she was grilling him about his sympathies, although he doubted it. It was a strange conversation, but he felt comfortable with it. He was the aging assassin, she the novice asking advice or wondering about a different life. "I told you I favored the left and I favored the underdog. Isn't that enough? It's what RM is about."

"You didn't join a movement," she said, her eyes troubled.

"I could never spout the party line. I don't like taking orders."

"I probably shouldn't talk to you like this, but I must." She seemed agitated, frowning, vulnerable, then her words rushed out. "I was arrested once and tortured."

Torture. It never produced reliable information, only terror and fear. "I suppose it is necessary for both sides. But I never condoned it or thought it useful. I'm sorry."

"It was the usual. Beating, rape threat. They put a bucket over my head and hit it with a hammer. I felt like an animal—worse. I didn't think I would ever be human again."

"I'm sorry," said Marant, troubled. He'd seen the results first hand. The torn skin, the amputated limbs, the gouged eyes, the bodies. They jolted him when he saw them; then, as a reflex, he saw them as just bodies.

"A week later, after I left the hospital, I helped blow up the railroad south of Bilbao. My parents, my cousins, my comrades called me brave. I suppose that if I hadn't done anything, they would have called me a coward."

"They see no middle ground. Either A or B, but not A-plus or D."

"There has to be more, doesn't there?" said Teresa, looking at him blankly. "I was brave and scores of people were hurt. I didn't want to know if anyone died."

"You worry about continuing," said Marant.

"It's not thinking I might die, but the unbearable tension. It's being an animal again. It's many things. Is it right to kill innocents? Will I be effective if I worry? Do we need more explosives? You have solved those problems."

Marant barked out a laugh. He found the conversation apropos but unsettling. He sympathized, but worried. "No I haven't."

"Then we must forge ahead and worry about the innocents later?"

Marant was thinking of the Greenpeace action, the one he refused. His parents acted knowing they might be tortured and die. He'd thought it was noble. He'd modeled himself after them. If they hadn't acted, he would have his parents, marriage, a different life. "Everyone reaches a point where they have a choice of playing safe or doing what they think is right."

"Then I think it is right that we need this new explosive," she said determinedly.

"All right," Marant said. "You must know I think it's silly."

"I know, but we're so close. Boris is ready to exchange the process for the money."

"And," said Marant.

She looked at him nervously, then stared past him. "Help me."

She asked him before, then stubbornly decided to do it herself. Was her change of mind too pat? Christian wanted him to help, but when he was about to offer his services, Teresa asked him again.

"Why?"

"I usually work with someone else; we support each other."

He understood that. He wasn't sure he wanted to help; it would entangle him. "You seemed more sure a few days ago."

She looked at him with a smile of regret, then shook her head. "I hate appearing weak. I thought the project would take a few days, and it has dragged on for over a week. I hate the motel. I don't like this country. I feel as if I'm being manipulated." It was a long speech, and he could see she meant it. "Boris wants to meet at Point Reyes, a wildlife area, far from the city."

Marant frowned. "If I help you, it must be in the city, in a crowded area. We have gone along with his silly demands so far. It is time for you—us—to worry about security."

Teresa tilted her head to the noise from Baker Beach. "Where?"

"I'll find a place. If he doesn't like it, tell him we have enough plastique to blow up half of America. You must be firm."

"All right. I didn't want to bother you, but there were other calls."

"Other calls?"

"From someone named Harry. He left this number."

Marant glanced at the number, frowned. "I thought only Boris, Kafi, and your friends in Spain had your number?"

"I mentioned it because of that."

Marant dismissed her concern with a wave of his hand. "Possibly a wrong number."

Puffy cartoon clouds, rare for that season, poked over the Golden Gate, and a large hawk flapped twice and landed in a scrawny pine on the hillside near the villa.

Marant got up and walked over to the balustrade. He rested his hand on the white marble and regarded the hawk as its fanned red tail closed slowly. It had strong talons, a streaked back, a large chest necklace. Its outsized eyes bored into his. It was the perfect predator. There were no random attacks of second-guessing, morbidity, or lassitude.

Teresa was behind him.

He looked down at her, small against the massed white cubes and tall windows of the Institute. She had a disturbed, abandoned air.

"I will help." He wondered why he'd said it; there were so many reasons not to.

"Thank you," she said warmly. She slipped her hand into his.

He shook his head, smiled a crooked smile. "Anything else is not necessary."

26

The Pacific High was south and the coastal current warmer, which meant the fog-producing machine off the coast of San Francisco had bedded down for another season, and the day broke clear, clean, and sunny.

Judy Ferris sat up in bed and watched her filmy white drapes tease the sides of her windows and fall back and caress her succulents. She was hypnotized by their undulations and the quick flashes of light and tiny sails in the bay vastness. It was like a magician whipping his cape back to let his audience peek into the hat.

Mike Larew, magician, had slipped out of bed and left. She puzzled that for a few minutes. She was chasing a phantom. And as a last flip of her nose at that floating-along, boring Judy Ferris, she'd bedded a gruff mystery, whose pockmarked visage and animal grace had just vanished into the background. She remembered waking up once, no twice, to Mike's shadow in the hallway. She knew he was staring at her notorious and cryptic sheet taped over her PC.

She got up and threw open the curtains. She shut her eyes against the blinding morning sun. The sun warmed her body to an otherworldly sensuousness. Breast, sex, belly, face. She basked in the glow, the heat. Finally, she opened her eyes and let herself into the day. The lone pine shimmered in the searing sun. Beyond, dimly, a boat cut a line across the gray/blue bay from the south towards the Oakland docks. Mt. Diablo, fog-obscured in the last week, rose in a luminous triangle towards the sun.

Judy, body warmed and softened, turned and plucked her robe off the cane chair. She walked deliberately down the hallway, glancing at her feet, the blue veins, the arch. Is that what he saw?

The light in the kitchen was crisp and highlighted dirty glasses and the colorful bowls painted with Quetzals, the Mexican firebird, in which they'd eaten Ben and Jerry's Funky Monkey ice cream at midnight. She walked into the living room and held her hand against the intense light which streamed through the picture window. She lowered her gaze to the strip of concrete and the grassy yard. A half-full glass of Bloody Mary, a half-empty beer bottle glowed on the patio table. She remembered the tugging and pulling, two bodies pressing through the other, the wavering line of sexual conflict, the transcendent space of the bay, the after-sex glow.

Judy piled dishes into the sink and brewed up her special low-acid coffee. While the water was dripping, she donned her sunglasses and went to the back yard. She removed the evidence of last night's mutual seduction. Finally, she poured a mug of coffee, plucked her portable phone out of its charging unit, and set up outside. She sipped coffee in a spiritual space washed clean by the blazing sun. Then, holding the mug in her left hand, she punched out information for Mike Larew's boutique hotel, hoping the night desk clerk had been wrong about him staying there. Sorry, no Mike Larew was staying there, or had stayed there.

Judy let the phone rest against her leg and stared into space.

Judy shook her head, sighed, then dialed Myra Cohen. Myra answered, paused, laughed.

Judy frowned. "I'm not that funny."

"If I thought it was true, I wouldn't laugh either."

"C'mon," said Judy, irritated.

"I checked and re-checked Revolution Mondiale and Wiley."

"And?"

"My source in the CIAIA told me he heard from a friend that Wiley was on a project to catch a mythical assassin, Marant Olivier, for the mythical Revolution Mondiale."

Judy frowned. "What is this 'friend of friend' and 'myth'? I guess you, or your source, don't think either the assassin or Revolution Mondiale is real."

Myra was obsessive/compulsive. Touching this, arranging that, diving like a loon into her huge bag. Judy could see her meticulously arranging number-two pencils, a yellow pad, squaring her legal-sized pads, and absently touching every fifth key on her keyboard. "If Marant Olivier existed, he's dead. Secondly, Revolution Mondiale doesn't exist. Third, no one, not even the CIA, would give Wiley that kind of power."

Myra was eager before. Judy wondered if she'd been told to quit asking questions. As for giving Wiley that kind of power, the CIA was capable of any idiocy. There was the Bay of Pigs, the plot to make Castro's beard fall out, poisoned cigars, Allende, assassination plots, Iran-Contra. Little boys in big bodies. "Deniability. The elite's mantra."

"The CIA has its share of fuckups, but they don't use time bombs," Myra said finally.

Bomb? How appropriate. Judy saw the mill, the fence, the bumble-bee tape, the hole. She saw Wiley as a little boy stuffing a cherry bomb into the mouth of a hapless frog. "I suppose not," Judy lied. She knew about American whackos in South America, cigar-smoking, gun-toting alkies. Me Manly Man; you Little Guy.

"I've just been adding it all up. Blowing up buildings in an urban area, taking photos of winos, having them killed by an assassin. Believe me, it's a fantasy. What I do know is that Wiley knew enough about the drug trade to tap into it. It's not a new trend. And he may be alive; but you don't want to find him for that."

"Drugs, the universal solvent and explanation. What would we do

185

without them?"

"It's far-fetched, Judy; you know it."

"And what they've done before is unbelievable; you know that." She didn't want to freak Myra. "Oh, I suppose you're right."

"You don't believe me. And you—"

"I know you can only do so much. If you hear more and it doesn't compromise you, call me. You will always be an anonymous source. Anyway, let's do something to forget about this. The Golem is part of a German film festival in two weeks at the Castro."

"If only we could turn Jewish men off and on like a Golem," said Myra. "Pencil me in."

Judy grimaced into the phone after Myra hung up. Myra had reached her level of usefulness. If nothing else, Myra had given her Marant, RM. It could be a fantasy, but it was enough to keep her going. Judy tapped her long fingers on the table. Who to call next? What information did she need to start writing?

When the phone rang in her hand, she almost dropped it.

It was Mike.

"Manly Man, my Hemingway hero. You just love 'em and leave 'em," she said. She turned to her left, so that the sun wasn't directly in her eyes. When she blinked, a squat, grim-faced woman came into focus. She was bent over, holding a watering can in the nearest hillside garden. Judy smiled, the woman frowned. Judy held her robe and turned one-hundred and eighty degrees. Hunter's Point, South San Francisco, not her favorite perspective. She wondered how many neighbors had witnessed and disapproved of last night's romp alfresco.

"I've broken hearts on three continents," Mike said sardonically. "I'm leaving. I have to pack, call landlords."

"Piffle. At least you don't have to worry about checking out of the Park Hotel."

There was a long pause. "What do you mean?"

"You're not staying there."

Mike said, "The hotel was a precaution."

"Whatever that means. We'll pass on that one. Why call?"

"To check on your obsession. How's it going?"

Judy grimaced, remembered Mike staring at the Wiley sheet. "Why?"

"A platonic interest. It makes a good story."

"And the more you deny it, the more I know it's true," she said grimly.

"Dead people who aren't dead, fantasy revolutionary groups. Are you on something?"

"A truth drug," she said, thinking she should have said "serum." "I haven't started writing yet, but I'm close. And I don't really care where you stay, or who you are. Come back, I'll take a day off, then you can fly away, and I can get back to my obsession."

"That sheet looks like a treasure map."

"You were nicer last night."

"I have things to do," he said, more softly.

"I know, you're chasing Wiley. You don't, or won't admit it." It slipped out; she did and didn't want to know. Tully's, the Palms, staring at her sheet. Ambivalence shaded her character like the shadow that reached to the patio door. Janus her protector, Janus her enemy.

The pause was long and slightly menacing. "You don't believe me?"

"I didn't expect to." Judy clicked off and threw the phone on the table.

She got in the best line, but she had ashes in her mouth.

But no time to brood. She called her SFPD source. They hadn't found Wiley's body, but sometimes it takes weeks for bodies to wash in. They had found another homeless man.

"What?"

"John Dubrik. It was a murder; broken neck."

"Did he have a nickname?"

She heard papers rustled, then, "Scab, ex-con. He had a reputation inside and could have had a lot of enemies. There was blood at the scene. It wasn't Dubrik's."

"Any leads?"

"Are you kidding?"

"I suppose I am."

Christ. One, two, none. "Great, just great. Thanks."

Judy stared at the table. In the last few days, it had gotten dirty. Drinks had made rings, a bird had left an unwelcome grayish smear on the front edge. She cinched her robe and followed her shadow to the kitchen, wetted an old sponge, came back and sponged off the table.

If she'd persevered. If she'd told the police. If, if, if. Poor Scab: she wouldn't have liked him, but he didn't deserve to be a pawn. She stared at the sheet taped over her PC. She ran over the scrawled items. The fragments pointed to her own trajectory, placed her not in the boring comfort of a boxy room on Market Street, but in her home, wedged into a series of unlikely and murderous events, searching for the real Judy Ferris.

Didn't she go through this years ago?

She ripped down the Wiley sheet and etched—she couldn't shake Mike's description out of her head—Scab next to Sugar and Potato, and Marant Olivier next to "Revolution Mondiale." It was either a treasure map, or a semantic diagram in a meth-scrambled brain.

Judy taped the sheet back above the PC and stared at it for a few seconds. She was still wearing her robe. She decided not to change, pulled up her chair, and fired up her PC.

Non-system disk or disk error. Replace and strike any key when ready.

The El Salvador disk. Notes.

Judy popped out the disk and hit the enter key. When her system was ready, her hand trembling, she shoved the disk back in. She opened her word processor and navigated to the "Notes" file of the disk. She clicked on it. The word processor started converting the file.

A few seconds later, the first page of twenty pages of Salvador notes flashed on the screen. Dates, murders, tortures, disappeared, the women who paged through loose-leaf binders of missing relatives.

The one she didn't want to look at was on page 10.

It was a standard report of the massacre of villagers, peasants, dismembered limbs, decapitated heads on poles. In one household, they decapitated the entire family, including a baby. Then they'd set the bodies at the dinner tables with their heads on the plates in front of them, and their hands on their heads, as if they were stroking them. What kind of people did that? What part of human nature? It frightened her to the depths of her soul.

And that was the point.

She closed the "Notes" file.

She was held for a scary moment by the screen with its imitation blank page, then her fingers started picking out keys. It was odd, but she didn't think much about what she was writing. The story was writing itself. It was an old story, the oldest. Greed, disappearance, duplicity, murder, outrageous "actions," macabre jokes. Every nation had done it, but people in every nation had stood up. She felt aligned with them, those others, mostly dead, ghosts who had their own crise de conscience.

Her story started with El Salvador because she knew that story of assassination, of fear, terror, of the horrible tenseness of living in a country at perpetual war with its own citizens. San Salvador, the American embassy's "grimgram" body counts, decapitation, dismemberment, mutilation, terror. Duarte, Melino, D'Aubuisson. The entire daily horror story of Central and South America from the disappeared in Argentina to Shining Path Peru, from Pinochet's Chile to Columbian drug lords. It was also about her own arrest and imprisonment.

She decided, after her story was rejected by the Post and the Times, that it wasn't just that the story was buried and would stay buried. It was also about her arrest and fear. Rejecting the story canceled her own experience, made it a waste, made it as if it never happened.

It made her livid, again, and her fingers flew across the keys. She realized after a time that she'd repressed everything she'd seen and heard, or, more soberly, rationalized that one couldn't be a professional pessimist or cynic.

Tap, tap, tap.

Her fingers slowed when she got to the present. She was typing not a narrative of surreal violence and fear—where, despite the subject, sentences and paragraphs made continuous sense—but local fragments. Wiley, one of those boys-in-man, killed Leonard Marsh in a dope scam, then three winos in a plot to capture a phantom assassin. It was insane, as insane as thinking we could manipulate an entire continent with fear and terror.

She stopped typing.

It was total conjecture, vaporous as the lifting of a weak fog. Meetings with terrorists, blowing up a mill, photographing winos, a shadow assassin. It wouldn't hold up in a legal court or the court of public opinion. Fuck Myra. Fuck Mike.

She ate lunch, sat on the sofa, and brooded. She ran over the events in her head again. From hearing about Wiley's disappearance to Mike, to Harry Mach. Algeria, Basques, explosives. How, or why, were they related to Wiley's capturing, or killing the phantom assassin Marant

Olivier? The only thing she could think of tying those disparate items together was "Revolution Mondiale." Mike knew about it; Myra scoffed at it but knew about it.

Judy stewed for a few minutes, alternately grimacing and shaking her head. Then she snatched up the phone and called Khris. Bob was staying with her. The yo-yo was in full swing.

"No, I don't remember anything else about Wiley, Algeria, or that other place. Can't you forget about him?"

She'd be working for Vietnam Today, if Khris hadn't called. Odd. A simple call had pushed her off the tracks. That happens. Something clicks. Something rolls over. "Soon, soon. Humor me. Did he mention anyone else he was seeing? Anywhere else he might stay?"

Judy could see Khris' frown of distaste. All Khris wanted was balance. Judy understood that; one day she'd have it too. But not then. "He mentioned someone who was helping him. She had a place on Russian Hill. I think her name was Rosie. Now can I go?"

"Of course. Thanks."

Rosie? That could be a lead. But no last name. She wondered whether Harry had her name in Wiley's address book.

Harry Mach had given her the most information, but she didn't expect much more from him. She found Harry's card and the phone and set up on the sofa.

She punched out his number.

"Harry, this is Judy Ferris."

"Ms. Ferris. How can I help you?"

"Did Roger Nesbitt help you?" Judy said.

"Not exactly. He is out of the picture, believe me."

"That's tough. You don't know a Rosie, do you?"

The silence on the line told her he did. She was in the book.

Harry said, "Possibly. Do you know where she lives?"

"Not a clue. Whoops, there's my other line."

He'd given her enough. She called information and got the number of the Golden Paradise and Tully's. The Golden Paradise was a wash. But Charlie, Tully's rotund bartender, told her that Wiley and Cueball used to get loaded together, and Cueball was there.

She held her breath. Cueball came to the phone. "What?"

"Hi! You don't know me, but I'd like to ask you something."

"Hey it's my turn."

"This won't take long. I met Wiley's girlfriend at a party and ended up with her pipe, you know the ivory-encrusted one."

Cueball said, exasperated, "How should I know about her fuckin' pipe?"

"Well, I want to give it back. But I don't know her last name or where she lives."

"What the fuck am I, the phone company?"

"All I need is her name," said Judy.

"Rosie McCoy. Wiley said she lived on Russian Hill." The phone went dead.

That was almost too easy. She dialed information. Disconnected. She called her contact at the Chronicle, June Williams, who had a contact with the phone company. She waited five, ten minutes. June called back. Rosie McCoy lived at 1213 Vallejo, right off Polk Street. Judy would have yelled "Eureka!" if Leonard March and three homeless people were still alive. Polk Street seemed her last best hope. She was halfway to the bedroom when the phone rang.

She hurried into the living room and snatched up the portable. It was Mike.

"The last wino was murdered last night," she said, wondering what he would say.

"Park people have short life spans," he said cynically.

She wondered if he was really that cynical or whether it was an act. If it was act, what was he hiding? She should have been more careful, more discreet. But she'd gone beyond controlling everything she said. "You keep playing games. You know that's not it."

"I'm not playing games. I don't believe in far-fetched CIA plots."

"Whatever." A lump bobbed up into her throat. She thought of last night, the restaurant, his cock inside her, ice cream at midnight. Cock and ice cream. It could be a way to go. "I didn't expect I'd have a good time last night, but I did. Have a good life."

"Don't hang up," Mike said. Softer, "What are you doing now?"

She hesitated telling him. "I know where Wiley's girlfriend lives. I'm going over there. You know, a real stakeout, just like the movies."

There was a long pause. "I'm not doing anything. I'd like to see you again."

Judy felt her heart skip a beat. It wasn't much of an invitation, but she did want to see him again. She didn't want him to leave that morning. "It's not a great invitation, but I'll be a sucker one last time. It's at Vallejo and Polk. I think there are cafés on the west side of Polk and an old bar called Dino's. I'll buy you one for the road."

"You know the old ones. See you in an hour."

27

The paper said Marty "Scab" Slovak had been found murdered in Golden Gate Park in the middle of a lawn-bowling court. Harry shook his head and let the paper fall to floor. Since he'd decided to play out the game, he had to find Wiley. Soon.

Scab could have helped him with Wiley II, Mr. Hyde. Could have were the key words. Three winos down. He would scramble his brain trying to find out why they were killed. The explosion, yes. The winos saw it, yes. But Wiley had evaporated; why risk having them killed?

He called Studs Markus.

Harry said, "Have you found the redhead, the girlfriend?"

"Have you got a deal, Harry?"

"Is there a prize?"

"There is," said Studs.

Harry's voice rose; the hand holding the receiver trembled. "A few hours ago, a prize didn't matter. Wiley came after me. I was ready to quit."

"Shit, that was close. But you'll play, and it'll be soon."

Harry strummed an erratic beat on the table. "I know about timing. Why the suspense?"

"Because nobody plays you, Harry. This is my one chance."

A smile creased Harry's jowly face. "I'll take that as a compliment."

Studs said, "Number 1: Wiley and a CIA project. He's not well-liked. But they thought he would be perfect for this project."

"Project? Blowing up windmills? Killing winos? Are they insane?"

Studs said, "Buying a phantom assassin from a phantom revolutionary group, Revolution Mondiale. They want to sell him; we want to buy him."

Harry frowned. The winos? The explosive? He needed a keystone. "Why would our erratic and violent Wiley be perfect for this project?"

"Deniability. And he's already screwed up. The project should have been over weeks ago; they're letting him go, because even now if it works, it's a feather in everyone's cap. No one really knows if Revolution Mondiale even exists. They get this guy, it's proof."

Harry ran his hand through his hair; the curls settled gradually, an errant black one edged towards the middle of his forehead. "The pot?"

Studs said, "Money for the exchange. Right now, I don't know how much, but it's substantial. They wanted ten mill; we bargained down. Not sure of the final figure."

"That he'll pay these Revolution Mondiale people for this guy?"

Studs said, "Exactly."

"How would we grab some of that loot?"

"From what I know of Wiley, he's going to keep most of it."

"Isn't he monitored? Why would they give him that power?"

"What I said before, deniability. And, of course, they don't want to spook the spook. Too many people, and he'd disappear. And you know, I don't think they care if he keeps it or not. I get the feeling it's more of an exercise, proof that they're still viable."

"Craftily insane then." The empty bank accounts. How much should he tell Studs? Eventually, he'd have to tell him everything. If he didn't, Studs would find out. "That's the Wiley I know. Any idea how blowing up a windmill and killing a bunch of drunks fits in?"

"I said he's already screwed up. No one knows exactly what happened," Studs said.

"Now all we have to do is find Wiley. You wouldn't happen to know where he is?"

"That's my second piece of good news. Rosie, her last name's McCoy, lives on Vallejo on the Russian Hill side of Polk. I didn't get the exact address, but it's 12-something."

"Fantastic." Harry considered, then decided. "I'll find her. Even if Wiley isn't there, she's the connection. Find out about the money, find out about the exchange."

"That's a tall order, but I'll do my best."

"You always do."

"You're the chief."

From the abyss to the game. And in the game, everything was coming together. A to B, C to D. But the next steps were chancy, especially with his erstwhile partners, Burt, Vito, Sal...and Wiley. What was he going to do when he found Wiley? He would snatch the money for the address book, divide it, and snatch part of the CIA loot. What then? Would Burt hand Wiley over to Vito? Or would Burt flip out and try eliminating Vito? Could they track it back to him? Via Burt, possibly. But then, he was Harry Mach, a respected investment consultant. Burt scratched fleas in a room in a North Beach flophouse.

Harry mused about the affair as he watched a few wisps of fog mix in the eucalyptus on Mt. Sutro. The money from Wiley II would surface. He was going to make it, and he felt exhilarated. Really?! Or was it a malarial visitation of the broker's creed—that the market is headed undeniably, and always, up? His moods had been mixed lately. He was down when Leg 3 tanked, but up when it hadn't, down after Wiley left his butcher knife embedded in his table, and now up even further. Had he lost a connection to reality?

Viewed from any rational angle, he was already in a fantasy land. Except, except, he knew he could do it. And their best bet was Rosie McCoy.

He called Burt's cell and gave him the address. "I want you there on Polk Street."

"Cool, a stakeout. The people in Tully's are starting to think I'm a cop."

Harry said, "Then get out of there. We don't want to attract attention. Rosie lives on Vallejo off Polk Street, going up the hill. It's 12-something. Be discrete and find her name on a mail box. There are several cafés on Polk. Meet me in the one closest to Vallejo. An hour. If you find Wiley, you know what to say. If you see the woman leave, follow her and call me."

"I'll say that you want to talk to him, and have his address book and a proposition."

"You're getting good at this, Burt."

"I've got a great teacher."

Harry smiled. It was the Fakir syndrome. Show them how to make money, and you become a wizard. But he felt Burt, besides being iffy with his dope, buds, and connection to Vito, was starting to admire him, Harry, enough to become an acolyte.

Odd, Harry thought, he felt responsible for Burt's transformation. Maybe Burt would have been better off stoned, fantasizing, and playing tricks with empty guns.

Harry's cab pulled up at the Great Beans Café.

He'd lived on Russian Hill and knew that perspective of Polk Street dropping off into blue-and-white sky. If you walked a few blocks past Vallejo towards the north, you would see Polk Street unwinding downhill towards the wharf, the top of the all-white Art Deco Marine Museum in Aquatic Park, the flagpole with the flag of California curling in the ocean breezes. That day, the sun was shining, the traffic brisk on Polk Street, the shops open and bustling.

Burt had a table in the middle of the café.

Harry angled past tables crammed together on the sides, walked to the counter, and waited in line. Then he ordered a biscotti and latte from a bored bald young woman with a dragon tattoo crawling up her right arm, nose plug and twenty earrings tacked to her right ear.

Burt's table was angled to watch the comings and goings on Vallejo and Polk streets. Burt moved his legs, and Harry pulled up a heavy chair with a ratty-looking white cushion perched on it like frosting on a cupcake. Burt was wearing a new dark windbreaker which accented his fading tan, a white shirt, and pressed jeans. He looked cool, composed.

Burt hunched over the table and said, "I checked the mailboxes. Rosie McCoy is at 1213. I've been watching for half an hour. So far, nothing. But the big question, Harry, is what do you do when we find Wiley, and he says okay Harry, what's up?"

Harry frowned, took a bite of his biscotti. "If nothing else, we trade money for his address book and bank numbers."

"Right, I knew that. But why should he go along with that?"

He couldn't tell Burt about Wiley wrecking his house. "I'm planning so he will. I can't stay here long; I have other things to plan. If and

195

when you find Wiley, don't go batshit on him. Tell him it is important. Tell him my proposition will help him."

Burt said skeptically, "And he should believe that?"

"He will because he knows about me. Of course, he ripped me off, but he knows that I have connections and money."

"Sounds like you really know him...just like you know me."

Harry reassessed Burt. Not stoned, he seemed almost too competent, as if the money, his money, had notched another gear, had made him smarter, or foxier. It was an interesting transformation similar, he realized again, to Fakir crawling back to him, tail between his legs.

"What do we know of anyone else? We know surfaces, we know what people want us to know, not what they really are, if that exists. We always have the surface."

Burt smiled thinly. "You think you know everything about me, don't you?"

"How can I say yes?"

Burt laughed. "I feel different around you...and I guess you know that."

Harry said, guardedly, "Possibly, possibly not. We all conceal something. It might be a shameful thing, or things, or it might be a barely discernable core. But down to cases. When I leave, stay at least another hour. There are a couple bars on this side of the street; you can have a beer and watch." What he didn't tell Burt was that he wanted to keep him busy. Finding Wiley on Polk Street was at best a long shot. Studs would know more soon.

"Okay," said Burt, then, slyly, "How about another retainer?"

Harry smiled crookedly. "And what have you done to deserve another retainer? Not much. But it shows you're ambitious. No, we have to come up with something first. If we find Wiley now or in the next few days, your retainer will go up. As you said, a lot of what we're doing is spec. But spec has paid off handsomely in the past, and it will pay off this time."

Burt picked raisins out of a carrot muffin, leaving crumbs scattered on the glossy table top. He turned and watched the street, his neatly bunted blond ponytail a contrast to the dark walls. Burt turned towards him and said, "I've thought of scenes like this, stoned. Somehow I can't believe I'm really here. And now that I'm here, I can see it's easy, and getting easier."

Harry waved his hand. "It seems easy when you're finally in it, but mostly, it's getting there that's hard. But don't think it's that easy."

"Sure seems easy now."

Harry stared at the painting of an angelic creature on the wall to his right. It was one of ten similar paintings on the walls of the café. It was a local artist, thought Harry, one who couldn't quite shake an obsession with divine intervention or woman-as-angel.

Harry waved at the paintings. "What do you think, Burt?" Burt's jaw was set, his blue eyes filmy, his hands neat and recently manicured. "Are women Mary Magdalene or Mary, Mother of God, whore or saint?"

"Makes it easy, too easy." Burt stared at the angels, then the crowd, which spilled from the café into the street. "Thing about women, Harry, is they feel a need to be used. It's the only way they can indulge their emotions. It gives them something to talk about, something to complain about to their friends."

Harry laughed. "You'll be a sex therapist in your next life."

Burt laughed. "I have to get through this one first. Know what I like, Harry: one-night stands. There's the hunt, the capture, the fun... no messy aftermath. It's always fresh."

Burt sounded different, as if he'd been pretending all along. Was that part of the change? "If you can get one-night stands."

"It was a problem with that fucking room, not with the apartment."

"You didn't put the money in the bank?"

Burt shook his head no. "I'll work this out first. I'll have more for sub-primes later."

"Possibly. Is this your rebirth?"

"Or birth. When I think about what happened Tuesday, I'm still surprised. When I saw you, I thought you were rich, easy, pampered. Then when you pulled the gun..."

Burt gazed at the street as if he were turning a thought over in his head.

Harry remembered the silver gun twirling on the table. It was a melo-dramatic turn on Burt's part, but effective at the time. Then Burt gave himself away when he chattered about his "deals" and his North Beach flophouse. Odd how that seminal event led to Harry Mach sitting here with Burt, waiting for Wiley to pop out of his cave.

Harry said, "People have different thresholds of risk. Risk is about controlling adrenalin. There's adrenalin in a good trade, and adrenalin in life or death, fighting or fleeing."

Burt held up his hand. Harry stared outside. Red hair, a jogging outfit, fancy blue tennis shoes. Harry shook his head no.

Burt turned back to him. "Let's talk about this other deal...the dead winos, the mill."

Harry watched Burt closely. "Really? What do you think?"

"I think Wiley had the winos killed because, as you said, they saw it. But not exactly because they saw it; who is going to believe a bunch of winos? And the redhead running around taking their pictures. You were right; he did that so someone could get rid of them."

Harry shrugged. "You are putting it together. Good. Everybody wants to know more. I told you at the Cliff House Wiley was multitasking. We may be right in every conjecture, but we still don't know if there's a prize. It might be lucrative, possibly not. But right now, we don't know what it is, and more importantly, we don't know how much."

"You think it's a lot more?"

Harry calculated how much to tell Burt. Too much information was bad, but the more you say the more you can find out. "I do. The CIA, someone from Europe, three dead winos. I don't know if there's money, but there is an empty bank account. The details are vague, naturally, and there are untold machinations."

"But you have hunches."

Harry smiled. "I do. Plots within plots, mysteries within mysteries. It's attractive, but whether it will lead to anything is questionable. What you should concentrate on is that you have a retainer for going along with something which might be fairy dust. And if we don't find anything, you still have the money from Vito. That's called win-win."

"I guess it is," said Burt, nodding and smiling with an inner Burt. Burt kept his eyes on the street but lowered his voice. "But I need a lot more than chump change. I'm going to retire on this, Harry. You know there's money in it, if not how much. I have to be in."

"Why should you be in?" said Harry, frowning.

"Because I know a lot. I know Vito, and I could tell Vito about our arrangement."

Harry smiled, thought, then said, "We seem to have each other, don't we? If, and it is a big 'if,' there is something there, you'll get a part of it. Right now, we don't know what it is, or how much, or if we can tap it at all. As I've said, it's pure spec."

Burt nodded and seemed to talk to the wall. "I'm too close to give it away. Sometimes you have one chance, and you can't blow it. Say, how are you going to find out?"

Irritated, Harry said, "I told you, you don't want to know."

"Well, I see it's more than spec."

Harry grimaced. "Explosions, plots, murdered winos...nothing has gone according to plan. That's the question mark. Wiley's screwed up, and he's screwed up more than once. You want your enemies to act in a certain way and not screw up. Screwing up renders the odds questionable. You may think you know me and know I know something's there, but if it doesn't happen soon, it will disappear like the morning fog. And your golden ring becomes brass."

"It won't."

Harry regarded Burt. Burt's blue eyes had developed a hardness. He could feel it in the way Burt held himself. The playfulness was gone, the dope an afterthought. "Certainly we have knowledge and curiosity...and hope. But you can't bank hope."

"Everyone needs hope, Harry. But you need the gold ring, the money, the good life. I can see it stretching before me. A lot of people have it; a lot more don't. I'm going to have it."

28

Marant sat in his room with the French doors open, his long legs crossed and almost touching the wrought iron of his tiny balcony. The ocean seemed to sway that morning as if it were a sluggish giant awaking from a long, drugged sleep. Gulls, wings canted into a soft Bauhaus "W" drifted in circles on imaginary slipstreams.

Marant scanned the patio below with its scattering of tables. He saw a simulacrum of Teresa and Marant. Teresa probed; he felt light-headed. Her fingers toyed with a spoon, her eyes searched his, then she moved her chair a fraction and looked past him, as if she were exploring her own space or trying to see where their table, their one-on-one, fit in some larger inner discourse. Was she truly concerned about larger questions or simply maneuvering with smaller, strategic ones? She had held his hand. She had pressed her body to his. She was a triumph of the curve. He was the archangel of distance.

The assignment? It was absurd from the beginning, but its absurdity had increased tenfold. A mill, an explosion, murderous chemists, the political quicksand at RM. Christian holding on to an old idea, the Muslims trying to destroy him. He felt like a hapless tourist on the beach at Fort Mahon, eyes shut, the sun baking his skin, the off-shore breeze ruffling his hair, while the remorseless tide snaked through low points in the sand.

Marant uncoiled his legs. He took a last look at the ocean, retrieved a black windbreaker from the closet—if there was residual bleeding from his wound, it wouldn't show. He had a big morning ahead of him.

First things first. He couldn't use fugu pills in close, risky encounters.

He walked down from the Institute to Clement Street and his car. Twenty minutes later, he opened RM's long-time storage locker at Gate Storage. They'd kept that storage location for fifteen years while he worked in Central America. He hadn't been there in years. He was certain no one else had used it. The packages, the guns encased in plastic, the high-powered rifles. He didn't like weapons; he used them well, but they were a too-simple way to manage problems. He retrieved the Walther PK, disassembled it, and put it in his backpack.

Then he went to scout locations for the meeting between Boris/Wiley Brooks, Kafi, Teresa and, he thought ruefully, Marant Olivier.

He drove down California Street to Market and found parking on a side street. He bought a raft of papers and scanned them in the Boulanger Café, which jutted into the sidewalk. Infrequently, his eyes drifted from the page towards the purposeful, rushing crowds, the eclectic hovering high-rises, the blue-white sky, and he'd think of how he could be crafting a sculpture on his solitary Norman beach, making small talk in L'Exhibition, driving through the English countryside, or running his fingers over Moore's curves at Bowling Green.

For the meeting, he needed a public place with crowds and escape routes. He checked the local newspapers first, then the Bay Guardian, a schizoid local paper part hedonistic entertainment guide, part muckraking screed.

He drove down Mission to the South of Market area around Ninth Street.

He'd driven through the area before but thought it a poor location for anything, including nightlife. The area was a wasteland of closed-up factories, rag-tag homeless, and garbage strewn carelessly over the streets by some urban Pollock. But at night—most likely because of a hint of the outré, and danger—the deserted factories became huge discothèques which, apparently, attracted thousands of people, mostly young, some not so young.

He drove around the five-block radius for half an hour. He stopped at the entrance to a disco called the Hive. It was closed to the public at that hour, but open for cleaning. He asked the manager, Greg—thin, goateed, ponytailed—if he could check it for a large party. Greg, ever the engaging capitalist, obliged.

Marant walked into the cavernous space. Guggenheim-like balconies painted gold and black rimmed a huge, slick dance floor. There were multiple stages on every floor, banks of mirrors, strobes, and lasers. Open exits showed fire escapes dovetailing to a welter of alleys on the east and north. The third floor had a small stage and dance area and a club called the Labyrinth, which encircled the top floor. Inside the Labyrinth there was an explosion of blacks and reds, hideously painted faces, roaring twenties disco globes, a large open room, and smaller rooms spinning off with names which continued the labyrinth theme such as "Theseus" and "Minotaur," and a long corridor full of small private rooms and cul-de-sacs. It was, he concluded, a safer representation of the desolate area outside where, for the right money, one could have one's thrills, walk on the wild side, and still be in one piece at two in the morning.

Greg informed him the Labyrinth was open Sunday night, cost fifty dollars, and was the rage among the new bar-hopping, hopped-up with-it set. When Greg excused himself to talk into his cell, Marant checked the smaller rooms.

He decided it would be a good spot for the exchange, not that he was without his doubts. While Greg chatted on the phone, Marant walked down the narrow corridor to the end and two small rooms. He noted their names: Hercules and Jason. He slipped into the Jason and checked it. It was barren except for two speakers bolted to the wall. He unpacked and reassembled the Walther PK and silencer and secreted it high up on the back of a speaker.

He checked his cell phone. He called his flat in Paris and was relieved to find his answering machine pick up.

The fire escape door was open, and he checked outside. The fire escape on the east didn't extend to the ground and led to a closed-in, gated back yard full of refuse, discarded cars, and a hug bin of broken glass. The sun made the razor-sharp glass appear as a thousand crystal knives. Why the glass? Recycling? A lunar event with hoods, secret handshakes, and chanting?

Marant found another fire escape on the second floor. Through its open door, he saw a confusing tumble of intersecting and closed-off alleys, and the distant Bay Bridge.

Marant thanked Greg and explored the alleys. They could be excellent escape routes, if an escape route were necessary. One alley led to an all-night taxi stand five blocks from the Hive.

Marant called Teresa from a pay phone and told her they had to complete the exchange in the Hive's Labyrinth after midnight Sunday. He would give her the exact location Sunday night. She told him to call back in an hour and he hung up and drove to the Embarcadero. He walked the Embarcadero for an hour and watched Chinese fishermen on a pier. One reeled in a fish, and he watched it flop from side to side on the pier. The fisherman came over with a thick stick and hit the fish two, three blows. The fish's tail quivered and its mouth gasped slowly and lay still. Marant shook off an ominous feeling.

He called Teresa from the same phone he used to call Kafi a week ago. In that week, he'd killed Potato, Sugar, Scab. The plot had thickened. Instead of handing over a key to Teresa or Kafi and flying to Paris, he was part of the exchange. Was it destined to happen that way? At least it would conclude with a bit of symmetry like a piece of music ending on the tonic. Teresa said Boris agreed to the place; it would be in the Labyrinth at twelve-thirty Sunday night. Marant was to bring the number of an account in Switzerland with passwords, and Boris would bring a technical document on how to produce the new explosive.

"Fine," said Marant.

"Could we meet again?" said Teresa.

He should have said no. But no one had followed him—could he be sure?—and he could take precautions. It was obvious Teresa was out of her element. Besides he might be able to learn something about RM. Then he realized he wanted to see her. He was fascinated with Teresa, with her youth, with the strange attraction she seemed to have for him, with her command of the curve. They seemed such polar opposites. He supposed that meant they had to attract.

He told her he'd call her at five o'clock at the motel. He returned to his room at the Cultural Exchange. The Cultural Exchange had offered him some solace during his short time in the city. The next few days, there would be no place, no real security. He packed, had final words with a German representative and the concierge, then locked his suitcases in the car.

He drove to Clement Street, parked, then called the airline to change his ticket. His new route involved a flight to Toronto, a five-hour delay, then a flight to Berlin. Once in Europe, he would make his own plans to get to Paris. His flight left San Francisco at five Sunday morning; that would give them time to make the exchange. If their security had been compromised, he would rent another car and drive either to Los Angeles or Portland and fly out of there.

He hesitated, then spent another ten minutes booking a ticket for Teresa.

At five o'clock, Marant called Teresa and told her to go to Mission and Sixteenth, one of the shabbier and busier intersections in the city, wait until six o'clock, then walk west on Sixteenth Street. Marant waited at Seventeenth Street in a small café, and watched the intersection. Teresa came at ten minutes to six and was alone. The intersection was an outdoor drug exchange where dealers, buyers, and cops played their games. Teresa looked out-of-place with her determination and tight-mouthed seriousness.

At six she started walking west on Sixteenth Street. Marant watched carefully, then got up and walked to his car. He followed her slowly up Sixteenth and watched her walk up one, then two blocks. He caught up with her on Dolores Street and motioned for her to get in the car. "I apologize for the precautions," said Marant.

"I know what security is about," she said, slipping into the car. "Sometimes it feels like a game, but it is a deadly one. They are constantly trying to infiltrate ETA, and we are constantly trying to find sympathizers in the police."

"What do you wish to do?" said Marant, glancing at her.

Teresa seemed reassured in the car. "I don't want to go back to my motel. It is so dreary and impersonal; there are so many cars. Would it be a breach of security if I stayed with you?" She looked at him quickly, then turned away, embarrassed.

"The Mata Hari approach," said Marant. He grinned at her, but felt strangely flattered. "I suppose I'm enough of a fool to let it happen. But I understand. I've been in many cities like this one, not often in America. America is worse. If you don't have money, you're relegated to anonymous tracts of tacky motels run by the immigrants du jour."

"Thank you."

"I haven't said I would. Let's start with a place to eat."

He drove to North Beach. A doctor he'd met at the opera had mentioned the Trattoria off upper Grant. It was close to the jazz clubs he'd visited a few days ago, and that's where they went. The restaurant was small, possibly too intimate, but he liked the animation and the big window where you could watch the street. He ordered a bottle of Chianti, and after they tasted it, Teresa put down her glass, stared past him for a second, then looked directly at him with her dime-size brown eyes. "I'm asking too many questions, but so far you don't mind."

Marant shrugged. "I enjoy conversation more than I thought."

She sat back in her chair and smiled. "Do you have second thoughts?"

The unspoken but always-present subject was what they did, what he did. "Of course," he said, trying to plumb the look in her eyes. "We ask ourselves the same questions and get the same ambiguous answers. I'm not an automaton. I play a game of cards with someone named Jacques, and a few moments later I kill another someone named Jacques. Was the first Jacques better, the second worse? They both had families, mothers, people who hated and respected them. It is subjective and situational. It is the same riddle with terrorists. Look at the Israelis versus the British, the Vietnamese versus the French, then the Americans, the Palestinians, the IRA. All branded with the terrorist brush once—some still are, of course—but most are now greeted at the bargaining table, or are stable respectable countries."

"That is what our fight is about—respectability, to sit down at a table."

He thought of the insurgency at RM. If GIA approached Gino, they could have approached Teresa. No one could sit on the sidelines. On the other hand, if they fractured into three or four groups, that would be the end of RM. They quit talking when the waitress, a woman with a pasty face, a tumble of curls, black eyes, and wide hips came to take their orders.

When the waitress left, Teresa said, "We ask the same questions now that we did centuries ago. That is what I worry about. There are larger questions. Will planting bombs do any good? Or, why do I have to plant bombs? I know I can; why should I?"

"Why should you?"

"The Popular Party will never allow a Basque homeland. Until a few years ago, the Basque language was outlawed. My relatives have been hunted, killed, tortured. The police deny everything; it is the same everywhere, even in America. Sometimes I think the same type of groups are everywhere: the police, the insurrection, the murders, the denials. Everyone has a part to play, and sometimes, rarely, they switch parts."

"That's very cynical."

"I don't think it all the time; I believe in our struggle. I believe in my family, my compatriots, the Basque homeland."

"What do you think of the three people who died to get your explosive?"

"What do you mean what do I think?"

Marant shrugged, then said, "Bombing a train may kill people, but it makes a point. What point is made by killing three people to get a questionable process, which you will use to make a better bomb to blow up more people?"

"Means to an end," she said hesitantly.

"And that means they're not human," said Marant.

"I didn't say that," said Teresa. She frowned and took a quick sip of wine.

"Their names were Potato, Sugar, and Scab. They were not the best human beings. They may have killed others, they didn't contribute much of anything; they were more likely a nuisance, but they were still human beings."

"I didn't know their names," she said sullenly.

"I'm not trying to make you feel bad," said Marant. "But we all unconsciously try to create a range of evil, a moral calculus, points on a line. But it's thoroughly subjective." He was amused at her strength, but he was serious himself. "That is why I want to make sculpture, to try to capture the ineffable, the curve. But I am as bad as everyone else. I make straight lines. It is because I know them."

"Sometimes I think we don't have a chance, that we'll never have Euskadi. That we're destined to always be opposed, to always play our roles."

Marant sifted his ideas. "Or that you'll never know when you've lost. Culture wins wars, not explosives or high-tech weapons. And America will win. They have found the lowest common denominators: food, sex, cars, entertainment. It is the most recent triumph of bread and circuses. Soon culture—all cultures—no matter how esoteric or ethereal, will be stitched seamlessly into the American Frankenstein."

"You're more depressing than I imagined," Teresa said, frowning.

"It boils down to body versus spirit. No one can agree about objective rules of the spirit; rules destroy spirit. It is a conundrum. So the Muslims, for example, have their spiritual laws forged in steel. The Catholics have their spiritual laws encoded and proclaimed. They will fight to the death over their rules. Then the Americans—despite their churches and antique morality—say spirit is body, material things, things we can all touch, listen to, drive. All of a sudden, people fight to get the latest Madonna CD instead of fighting each other."

"That's horrible."

"But true. The Americans will win by accretion; but even the Americans with their Reeboks, CDs, and Gap jeans, their soap operas and their silly Hollywood movies, their science and their bloated armies can't hold back the flood."

"The flood?"

"Of bodies. The American economy—I sound doctrinaire, but I will shut up soon. The American economy, the world economy, is fueled by a tiny secret."

"And?"

"That their spirit—the spirit of capitalism and materialism—needs more bodies to survive. More people, more food. More people, more houses. More people, more cars. More people, more Madonna CDs. The world of the body is fueled by bodies and is already full."

"Marant is an environmentalist," said Teresa, laughing.

"Possibly, more a pragmatist. And I won't be around when it gets bad; neither will you. The bodies are already changing the earth, and they will keep changing the earth until it is unlivable. And, as far as I can see, it is inevitable. But for now, we have this moment, a moment I didn't expect. Ah, the food."

They ate silently. The Trattoria grew darker, the candles threw more light, and the light from the kitchen at the end of the dark room glowed intensely. Every few minutes someone would pass under the red-lettered sign of the Trattoria but quickly disappear behind the blue drapes, which cut sharp triangles in the sides of the window.

"About tonight," said Marant, after finishing most of his ravioli, a house specialty.

"I was foolish to ask," said Teresa. "I think I just wanted to be a human being, a woman for a few hours, and not a stump sitting in a dingy motel room waiting for phone calls."

Marant regarded her. What she suggested appealed to him. He had urges, although he couldn't quite believe that she, a thirty-something terrorist from Bilbao would want to spend the night with a retired assassin who played the piano, went to the opera, made linear sculptures, and small talk in Paris galleries. Of course he was simplifying.

The real problem was security. Teresa had followed him, but he was sure no one else had. He hadn't seen Teresa use the phone, and she seemed artless. Still, he wasn't sure which side she was on. He tried to envision what they would do later, the uneasiness, the tentative groping, the animal act, the post-coital smoke. It made him feel how old he'd become. "I know a place we can stay," said Marant. "If you want to."

"Not the Cultural Exchange?" Teresa said, seemingly innocently.

"I've checked out," said Marant. "Security."

"Of course."

Marant had to be careful. "What if some of our associates wanted a new RM?"

"We always want to be more self-sufficient. RM has helped when they could."

It wasn't actually an answer, but he couldn't ask more. The Trattoria was filling up. They ate slowly and watched other people, listened to them order from wine-splotched menus, watched heads appear and disappear in the front window.

After they finished dinner, Marant drove to Church and Market. He'd seen a sign for the Church Street Bed and Breakfast. He parked, and the gay proprietors did have a room on the top floor. After they checked in and while Teresa used the bathroom, Marant spent a few minutes on the rooftop patio checking the fire escape. The small back yard fronted on another yard, which had a slim opening that led, he supposed, to the next street. He realized he had never taken so few precautions. Was someone matching him perception for perception, move for move?

He extracted the bottle of Calvados, his favorite liqueur, which he'd packed carefully in Fort Mahon, and poured a healthy amount of the beige liquor in one of the provided glasses, while Teresa was in the bathroom. He set up on a little patio and followed cubist lines of the backyard rooftops. It reminded him of one of his favorite paintings, a Juan Gris nature morte at the Museum of Modern Art. The skewed lines created a pleasant tension around an apple, an orange. It was Cubist, one of the most linear of artistic fashions, still a triumph of the curve.

A few minutes later, she joined him. They shared his glass and watched the sky, which, in that part of the city, glowed from edge to edge. They chatted amiably, as if they were old-time lovers, he about Normandy, although he was careful not to name the town, she about Bilbao, her friends, her Alsatian Carlos.

Strange, warm, embarrassing. He wasn't sure he wanted to make love—or could. But then, in bed, the lights out, the glow from beyond the rooftops creeping into the room and over the large antique four-posted bed, she found him. It was, as she'd said earlier, that she wanted to connect with someone she understood.

Their lovemaking wasn't what he'd envisioned. It was less tense, easier. His mind drew lines, made difficulties, but his body had an innate affection for the curve. And her body was full of curves. She closed her eyes; a smile caressed her face.

He watched her for minutes after she'd fallen asleep. He watched her breathing and thought of dinner, the Trattoria, of what they'd said, of the larger themes that touched all their lives. He felt a pang of guilt that he had to be venal. He dressed and slipped out the door. He walked down Church Street to the pay phone where he'd called Kafi days ago. He called Christian collect.

He didn't expect the news from Christian would be good, and it wasn't. The Muslims had recruited others and had a strong position within RM.

"And this stage play?" said Marant.

"We can't alert them to what we know. Besides, others are clamoring for the process, and we have to show it is either real, or not. Have you found a secure place for the exchange?"

"'Secure' is a question of degree," said Marant.

"Do you want to come back now?" said Christian.

"No. For all the reasons we mentioned. We don't have to go over them again."

"Call me when it's over. Goodbye my old friend and good luck."

Marant walked slowly back along Church Street, still animated at that time in the evening. He felt an after-sex glow. It reminded him how constrained and narrow his universe had become. He resolved that he had to change. He would bring more people into his life. Perhaps he could get Teresa to model for him.

Teresa was in the same recumbent position, but she could have contacted someone on the outside, someone like Kafi. He checked the rooftop patio, then listened for stray noises, footsteps, the creaking of boards. It was quiet, except for the city hum, which seemed part of the city glow. He fell asleep with that same glow resting like an extra blanket over the bed.

29

The cab driver was a nut-colored, happy-faced Indian named Jamu. Judy Ferris told Jamu to drive through the Presidio. Jamu was a talker and for a while, that helped her not think about what she was doing or going to do. He told her where he lived in India, what he liked about the U.S. He was studying programming, but worried there were too many programmers. She spun out Jamu scenarios. Jamu would become a programmer. He would marry Ravi in India. Bring her back. They would have nut-colored babies, buy Explorers, back the Forty-Niners. Gain an edgy acceptance with neighbors.

She wanted people like Jamu to make it, but making it in America meant the wealth dream, greed, more, the juggernaut. He would become compromised, if he wasn't already.

Jamu's monologue lapsed, and she sat back and let the San Francisco street scene pebble the surface of her mind. Soon they were deep in the eucalyptus, pine, and cypress of the Presidio, gaps in the trees revealing postcard views of the bay.

She was in a strange mood, had been in a strange mood since Khris called her on Monday. Everything she'd planned—or hoped for—had fallen away. Khris had inadvertently hooked her to Wiley Brooks, an erratic, violent ex-CIA officer. Their lives and destinies had become linked. She couldn't sort it out or rationalize it. She was climbing away from the present towards a past in the future. She was a few handholds from the top of a sheer rock face. At the last moment, Wiley would look over that edge, smirk, kick her hands off the edge, and watch her, arms flailing, disappear into the void.

She let her mind go blank in the soothing rhythm of the ride, the flashes of trees, hidden barracks, and darkening bay.

As they emerged into Crissey Field, she told him to take her to Aquatic Park. Jamu turned east towards the Marina Green and Fort Mason. West, in the distance, tourists aimed their camcorders at the tide swirling around the huge bridge pilings and jumbled rocks and spume of Fort Point. A freighter edged massively under the Golden Gate Bridge. Jamu drove by the flat expanse of the Marina Green, anchored on the bay side by the Yacht Club, with its joggers, late-afternoon kite fliers, and intent obstacle-course runners. Jamu angled right around the Marina Green, then past Fort Mason, a jumble of old piers and white barracks converted into galleries, theaters, and exhibition halls.

Van Ness, Aquatic Park. She gave Jamu a healthy tip and told him to keep studying.

A few short days ago, she'd driven to Aquatic Park after the ATA offered her a job she thought she wanted. She was happy, secure, infolded in ordinary scenes of fishing poles, crabs, and kids hunting treasures in the rocks that drew gray parentheses around Aquatic Park's lagoon. Now, she was deep in a murderous sequence of events that she couldn't somehow escape. She let those mundane scenes wash over her for a few seconds, then she turned and walked up the steep part of Polk Street.

Fifteen minutes later, she was at Union Street, high up on Russian Hill. Past the Marina, gulls swarmed like insects near the bridge. Closer, lights popped on like a relay down Union Street, and domestic scenes welled and subsided in the hushed cobalt of TV sets. A couple read the paper over dinner and glanced up to watch the news on television. The man poked his finger at the tube. That huge distance and those tiny scenes made her feel the hopelessness of her quest. What difference did Scab or Wiley or the assassin or our strategic maneuverings make to that man or woman watching television, or Jamu poring over Java code?

She walked up Polk towards Vallejo Street. At Vallejo, she saw Rosie McCoy's white three-story apartment building was on the north side of the street. She gulped her last breath of fresh air and went through Dino's swinging doors. Dino's was an anomaly in that gentrified section of Polk. It was old and crusty—not as abandoned as the Palms—with a long wall across from the bar hung with twenty-year-old pictures of the owner shaking hands with Tony Bennett, former mayor Art Agnos, and, oddly, Quentin Quisp, the performance "Queen" of England.

The curve of the bar gave her a view of Vallejo. She ordered a Bloody Mary.

It was late for the after-work crowd, but Dino's was full and smoky. The overworked bartender tugged on his suspenders, scratched his salt-and-pepper hair, kept a running chatter going with regulars, and busily filled drinks. Scenarios formed and evaporated, leaving gaps punctuated with the clicking of pool balls. A TV sportscaster tried to make a pennant game interesting. A baseball game. Home run statistics, ERAs. Mortality figures. Births, deaths. The world outside continued with its own landmarks, which didn't correspond to hers.

The mirror surprised her with a moody reflection. The eyebrows were at half-mast, the long nose looked fragile in that light, the green eyes puzzled, her mouth unusually rippled. Where was she on the arc?

From pigtails to pixies, from fantasy pink toenails to work-a-day clear polish, from idealism to en passant cynicism to confusion. The puzzle of mirrors. She supposed she could dissect the image staring at her, if she tried, but she felt herself edging towards blind acceptance. She'd have to get used to this new, or at least resuscitated, Judy Ferris.

She saw a ponytail flip around the window. She pushed her stool back and was halfway to the door, when Mike's husky profile appeared between the swinging doors.

"A last goose chase, before you hit the road," she said, too loudly.

"You could say that, lady."

She angled back to her stool, and Mike took the next one.

She said, "You skipped out fast this morning." She watched him order a beer, then gulp half of it. It reminded her of another bar, the first time they met. Tully's, his handball gloves, his bantering, the undercurrent about Wiley. He had the same sureness about his actions, which she liked but was leery of. She remembered how he'd stared at the sheet over her PC.

"I had things to do."

"We all have projects. I almost had a good one. Sometimes I feel like the Mazda," she said, thinking of her mirror image. "Tattered body, but the inside is okay, or seems okay. Other times, I feel like it looks."

Mike shook his head. "That car is too risky."

"Too risky for I-like-to-take-risks, I-bang-off-handball-walls?"

"Is that what you think of me?" he said, grinning.

"Your PR."

"Win or lose, black and white."

"And it's not close to real life. And you don't believe it, either."

"You're going to be tough to forget," Mike said. He rubbed his head and scanned the bar, almost as if he were looking for something.

Two in the morning, a shadow in the hallway. Tully's, his questions about Wiley, staring at the Wiley sheet above her PC. She'd never know exactly who he was. But isn't that like most people? What do we know of what's inside the show, the grinning visage? Were we all like Harry Mach, fast with a smiling face, an agreeable front, the soothing words?

She didn't want to spoil the illusion. She liked Mike's smile, his bigness, his sureness. She would have said the same thing: you're going to be tough to forget. But she knew somewhere deep in her psyche, it would only make it worse.

Mike said, "Anything new on the sheet?"

She turned and watched him. He wasn't just being nice, coddling her obsession. He had scrutinized the sheet. It was time to do her own churning. "Two new names."

He seemed surprised, as if he didn't expect an answer. "Oh."

Judy smiled a knowing smile. "Too casual; you're interested."

"To pass the time, while we wait for Wiley to buy us a drink."

She watched him for his reaction. "Scab the wino, recently murdered."

"I admit there might be something there. The other name?"

She paused for effect. "Marant Olivier."

She wasn't sure she expected a reaction. For a second Mike was stunned, then he disguised his lack of composure in a smile and brief head rub. "Who's that?"

"As if you don't know. The reason. The man driving Wiley's scheme. An assassin for Revolution Mondiale, RM. I know, you don't know RM either."

"This Marant; how did you find out about him?"

"I'd guess Wiley or the CIA has a scheme to catch him. That's what one of my sources thought. But the same source thought it was a fantasy. If I wanted to guess, in my fantasy, this Marant was tasked with killing winos. I don't know why. But since they're dead, if anything else is going to happen, it's going to happen soon."

"How did you find that out?"

"A friend at the CIA."

"They think Wiley is trying to catch this guy?"

"My source heads a long queue of doubters. You're not far from the front."

Mike turned away and watched the street, almost as if he were composing himself. She could tell the name meant something to him. She didn't see why. She was equally sure Mike wasn't going to tell her.

The bar was crowded when she walked in, but the after-work crowd was thinning. A few people played pool; a few others played with half-full drinks at the bar.

"What if I said that I know something, but I can't tell you?" said Mike finally.

"Then I'd feel I was on the right track, and I'd be even more curious."

"What if I was on the wrong side?" said Mike.

She hadn't thought of that. "Why not visit the Ferris museum tonight?" she said, not looking at him. "We'll forget about it for a night."

She felt Mike turn towards her. "Would more games alfresco change who we are?"

"Or help us figure that out. Nothing's going to happen here. This is my last best hope, and it's another shot in the—"

She caught a movement on Vallejo Street. A door closed, a gate clanged. Two people emerged from the shadow of Rosie's building. The short one was wearing a spangled motorcycle jacket. The tall one had one a green Army jacket, a floppy hat, and dark glasses. It was hard to see faces in the growing darkness, but she was sure she saw Wiley's rangy, muscled form, rippled red hair, long face and smirk. Her skin crawled.

Wiley was play-acting with Rosie, gesticulating, leaning over towards her snarl of red hair, laughing, as if they were just another couple ready for Friday night on the town. When they passed the light of a store on the corner, she saw Wiley's hunched back, his wavy red hair.

She grabbed Mike's arm. "Wiley!"

Mike turned and watched. Then he got a queer look she couldn't decipher. He glanced towards the back of the bar, as if he wanted to leave. "Call the police."

"The one time I need my cell. No time."

The window frame clipped off Wiley and Rosie's images. Judy held herself for one, two, three beats, then bolted for the door. She felt Mike's arm on hers. "Don't."

"What are you doing?"

Heads turned. The bartender stopped wiping glasses and frowned. "It won't help."

"I can do what the fuck I want," she said, wrenching her arm away.

She slipped through the door in time to see Rosie and Wiley stop on the corner of Broadway and Polk. She felt Mike behind her. "Don't fuck this up. If you're not going to help, stay the fuck here."

"This won't help," he said, anger cutting his words off like a knife.

"It's the only thing that will help."

Polk Street was graying, the darkening shadows occasionally lit up by cars and by the stream of cars on Broadway. Judy hurried down the west side of Polk Street, slipping between shadows. Wiley and Rosie seemed to disagree on what they were going to do, but finally they turned towards the Broadway tunnel.

"Wait until they're halfway to the tunnel, then cross," she whispered.

"This is ridiculous," Mike said. "Call the cops. They'll be waiting when he comes back."

"If the cops do anything, if Wiley comes back. I'm not letting him waltz away."

Mike shook his head, but a few seconds later, on Broadway, she felt Mike beside her. She hugged the darker shadows along the buildings. She and Mike followed Wiley and Rosie in tandem until they stopped. Rosie looked back and they traded stares. Wiley turned, slightly, then turned quickly back to Rosie.

"They're going to take off," Judy said. "I'm after Wiley."

The traffic on Broadway was relentless. The lights of Chinatown and North Beach glowed over the top of Russian Hill. Rosie and Wiley dashed towards the gash of the Broadway tunnel. At the steps, which split and went over Russian Hill, Rosie broke left and took the steps two at a time. If she'd wanted to catch Rosie, she could have. Rosie was not a runner. Wiley—the corded muscles of his neck popping out with effort— streaked towards the pedestrian walk through the Broadway tunnel.

Mike surged past her.

She watched stunned. Then she pursed her mouth and ran after them into the tunnel. Soon, they were far ahead of her. Wiley and Mike appeared in the headlights of oncoming cars, then disappeared in the cavernous shadows of the tunnel. Pedestrian traffic backed against the wall. Mike gained on Wiley. She ran faster. Her breath came in gasps. Her neck was wet.

Wiley grabbed an Asian man on a bicycle and threw him against the side of the tunnel. Wiley got on the bike, wobbled for a few feet, then peddled furiously towards the Chinatown entrance a hundred feet away. Mike jumped over the old man and picked up speed. Judy was in shape, but she slowed down and gulped air. She was halfway down the tunnel, when Wiley then Mike vanished from the semi-circular tunnel opening.

At the end of the tunnel, the bright lights of North Beach blinded her. She blinked and saw Mike duck onto Stockton, going south. She had a gut-wrenching feeling about letting Mike get close to Wiley. She ran down Broadway, but as she started across the street, she had a funny feeling. She glanced north, focused, and saw Wiley walking north towards Columbus.

If Wiley made it to Columbus, he could go in five directions. She ran after him. It was tough angling through the Chinese markets. Chinese moved slowly carrying pink bags of groceries tied in neat bows. She rushed through more markets. She saw a black jacket flash in the shadows of an alley. She peered into the recesses and made out a figure in a ponytail. She rushed in. He turned around. It was a young Chinese man.

She ran back to the opening of the alley and up to the intersection. Columbus, Green, and Grant sprayed off in every direction.

She scanned every direction. No Rosie. No Wiley.

30

The ocean breeze slipped through the eucalypts and caressed Harry Mach's smooth face. There was a summery bounce in the step of the people who walked dogs, biked, and strolled the streets of Upper Parnassus. Harry Mach watched them curiously. He was an intrusion in that neighborhood. But he liked that. He enjoyed the contrast; it set him apart like an emigrant in a foreign country. Their world was work, babies, mortgages, Volvos, worry about crime and roof rot. He played that game pre-divorce. Everything fought over, everything with a nuance of opposition. For the last five or so years of Harry Mach Investments, his world was the Russian River getaway, first-class flights to Thailand, Tokyo, and Berlin, starched white tablecloths, cornucopia displays of Eggs Benedict, soufflés, all-butter croissants, heavy cream, and endless champagne at sumptuous brunches, comradely musical matinées, dinner in the finest restaurants, soft nights spent sampling his squadron of unblended scotches, the random girlfriend, usually Shelley, the odd bitter word with his ex.

Yes he felt good about his life, where he lived, his wealth.

Perhaps it was middle-age spiritual agitation. He built up to his personal Trifecta over a year. He wanted the first legs to be lucrative but tame. He needed real risk for the last leg. It had worked out that way. Legs 1 and 2 were tame; big money-making and clever certainly, and not without risk. But Leg 3. He'd jazzed himself with his illegal flings. Partly, it was being bored. He also explained it, rationally, objectively, as a natural progression of the business world. It was about money, about having more. Why let a few manufactured laws get in the way?

There were legal complications, of course. But if one succeeded. What was that saying? "All great fortunes are based on a crime." Look at slavery and those fortunes. Taking Indian lands and shuffling Indians off to reservations. Land grabs, robber barons, Kennedy loot! And now look at the Russian billionaires and their gangster tactics, theft, assassination, intimidation, illegal stock manipulation. The progress in illegal moneymaking was endemic in every culture.

Especially in America. So many gold rings, so many ways to snatch them.

That day, a short time after he decided to give up Leg 3, he saw the endgame. Legs 1 and 2, the money, the ten million secure in the bank were forgotten. He was closing on Leg 3. All he could think of was the demonic Wiley Brooks and what looked like a far-fetched CIA plot. He'd put himself here, finally, because he had brains and drive. He was controlling it, but he was also enmeshed. When he worked on investments, he was inside pulling strings. Pulling strings outside, or trying to, was different.

He was playing on another level, the only caution personal safety. If one could kill with impunity and reap the rewards, who would not do it?! Religion intruded into his thoughts. He'd never thought much about it, whether there was a higher being and each action necessary in some abstract philosophical sense, but that morning he felt his steps, a combination of rational projection and impetuosity, were significant and preordained.

Fakir gave him the C4, and he stitched the explosion at the mill to the elimination of the winos. Burt had given him details from slumming on Haight Street and checking Wiley's Napa hideaway. And Studs gave him Wiley the CIA agent, the project, and in the last few minutes the location of the exchange.

He had to talk to Wiley of course, and before the exchange. But that would come to him too, likely from his slacker lackey, Burt, who was rapidly morphing into an acolyte.

Sunny and full of life outside, brimming with adrenalin within.

Harry walked up the steps with his paper but hesitated, briefly, at the door. The last time he opened that door, his sanctuary was trashed. He turned the key, opened the door, and listened…no, no.

He trudged up the steps, walked into the dining room, and dropped the paper on the dining room table. He walked through the rooms of his house, pumped like a prize fighter.

Details nagged at him. If the prize was Wiley's money, from whatever source, when would it come to him? Would there really be an exchange? Who had the money, where and when? But he had chips to play; he had bank account numbers and passwords. So mundane, so necessary for the mundane.

Harry was hosting himself to a glass of Glenlivet when his doorbell buzzed. Burt.

Burt quickly appeared at the top of the stairs. So much had happened from that first night that Sal and Burt had trundled up those stairs. And later when Burt had threatened him with the silver gun which spun around and around ever so slowly.

Burt smiled as if he were a Siamese who had swallowed ten canaries. "I got it, Harry."

Harry frowned. What exactly did he have? Burt was more than just a slacker. That had become evident. But greed can make anyone appear smart and foxy.

"And?"

"Got a beer?"

Harry shrugged. "You know where they are."

Burt soon joined him with an ale clutched in his hand. He reached into his coat with his other hand and pulled out a photo. He flipped it so it spun around in front of Harry. Burt walked to the far end of the table, his ponytail flipping on the back of his jacket, sat, propped his legs on a chair, and perched his head on his hand.

Harry glanced at the photo. The photo showed him a small woman, who he supposed was Rosie McCoy, and a man with red hair in a green Army jacket, a floppy hat, and dark glasses. He had Wiley's build and hair, but the face was obscured. Odd that Burt had the wherewithal to have a camera, but there it was.

But where was Wiley? "First things first," Harry said. "How did you find him?"

"About an hour after you left, I saw him come out and followed him...and her."

Harry slipped his fingers through his hair. His curls, released, draped lankly over his forehead. He smiled. "We have our Lazarus," said Harry. "We know he is a walking, talking, sentient, and murderous being. Now where is he?"

"I talked to him," said Burt.

"Excellent. But where is he?"

Harry tasted the unblended scotch, noted the smoky hints, let the warm glow spread down his throat and up through his face, then placed his glass next to his organizer. Something was wrong. Wiley should be sitting at his table, not Burt.

Burt watched him and made little hash marks on the top of the table with his hand. He'd underestimated Burt. But Burt was still the hired hand.

Burt smoothed the top of his blond hair back. He said, "Someone else followed them."

Harry sat up. "What?"

"Big guy and a woman."

Harry frowned and shook his head. "Was she tall, lanky, good-looking, long face?"

"That's her. We lost the guy, but she almost nailed us."

We? "Please tell me what happened."

Burt smirked. "I followed all four of them, then Wiley recognized one of them, and he and Rosie took off. Wiley ran into the Broadway tunnel with this woman and the guy after him."

"And you ran after them."

Burt smiled, laughed. "Nope. I had a hunch. I've had a lot of hunches lately. I took the girl. She ran over the hill. Know what, that's some hill, and she was faster than she looked."

"And? Cut to the chase."

"The woman lost Wiley and Rosie on Columbus, and I found 'em."

Poor Ms. Ferris. "I see." Harry shook his head. Harry grimaced. "All right, we know what happened, that you nabbed Wiley and Rosie. Now, where's Wiley?"

Burt looked sly, as assured as when he first sat down with Sal. "I told Wiley who we were and that we wanted in; a chunk for us for his address book, or just the bank numbers, and we keep quiet about the other thing, you know the CIA stuff. That okay?"

Us? Harry sighed, "No, that's not okay. You don't know my proposition."

Burt frowned. "It's about the address book or blackmailing him with the CIA gig. C'mon Harry, I'm right here. I know what's going on."

"Part of it, but not the part about the winos and the explosion. This has to be done right; that's how you extract the money. What did he say exactly?"

Burt said casually, "He said to give me the address book, he'll give me the money after the exchange, and I'll meet you here and split it...and if you say anything about the CIA thing, you're toast. I told Wiley about Vito. You know what he said? He said not to worry about Vito."

What did that mean? Harry shook his head and laughed bitterly. "Come on, Burt. You have no idea who you're playing with. Wiley is dangerous. He's already killed one person, and certainly set up three others. And you and he are going to cut it up. Wiley and I are playing on another level. We have stakes, information, and protection. You don't."

Burt frowned grimly. He squinted at Harry and said, "Don't play with me, Harry."

Harry frowned, sighed. "I'm not playing with you. My proposition is for both of you."

Burt lifted his feet off the table and leaned over it. "What?"

"I know about Sunday night, the exchange. And if anybody starts getting cute, I have a high-ranked CIA agent and several other people on my side. They have documents outlining the scheme and can get to the right people, if anything goes wrong. That is, if anything happens to me. And they know about you."

Burt looked miffed. "What do you know about Sunday night?"

"The location, why the exchange is taking place, and how much."

Burt's eyes lit up. "How much?"

"I won't say. I will say that I have a very nice proposition for Wiley... and you. You'll have enough money to stay in that new apartment, and take a long vacation. No more North Beach flophouses."

Burt was anxious. "So where is the meeting?"

"Don't play games. It's at the Hive, a disco in SoMa, in the Labyrinth, a club."

Burt grimaced, shook his head so his ponytail whipped slowly. "Fuck, I thought it would be over. It sounded too good."

"When and where?"

"One of the private rooms in the Labyrinth. I don't remember which one."

"Interesting place for an exchange; it's like a bad Greek tragedy."

Burt regarded the bottle in his hand and said, "I know it's a cliché, but I feel alive...ever since I got your money. I haven't been to Donnelly's once...those other guys are losers, and I was a loser. But ever since that night, it's all coming together...I'm this close," Burt held up two fingers with little space between them, "to that gold ring. It makes you alive, but it almost makes you kinda dull, as if you've traded everything else in for that one shot."

Harry frowned and hunched over the table towards Burt. Normally, he wouldn't give a rat's ass, but for some reason, at that exact moment, he felt sorry for Burt.

"Burt, there are lots of different games. There are some games you might be good at and suited for and others not. You fell into this game whether through dating Vito's granddaughter, pissing him off, or the tail dying. There were many people in this game before you, and they are all watching their stake, not just me, especially Wiley. Don't be reckless. You've cleaned up your act, as they say, and you're bright, ambitious, and young. If you stay away from the dope and your buds, you could have a successful career."

Burt smiled thinly. "More advice from the master."

Sometimes he was craven, sometimes not. "Simple advice."

"Wiley wanted him and me to wear clown masks."

Harry laughed. "To hide his identity. He always pretended to assume a trickster persona."

Burt shrugged. "I suppose so."

One more try. "Don't forget he is a trickster. He's taken off with other people's money, pretended suicide, killed, and is masterminding a CIA project. You have to be careful, very careful. Once he finds out I didn't go along with his proposition, you might be disposable. Tell him I want you there."

"I see," said Burt, frowning. "I'll be careful."

Burt rose out of his chair, looked around the room, shook his head. "Amazing. I was here less than a week ago with five hundred bucks in my pocket, and now I've got your two grand and will have more. It's luck, or twists of fate. I don't know exactly, but I have to go with it. I don't think I can stop." Burt strutted over and stuck out his hand. Harry took it. Burt's hand was moist and limp when he first shook it; that time it was moist and strong. "See you Sunday, Harry. Don't forget the address book and those propositions." Burt turned and jogged down the hallway.

Burt's ponytail bounced once then disappeared down the stairs. The light was blazing in the front windows; it highlighted streams of dust, the furniture and his rows of books.

Harry worried about Burt's words. He told Burt he had already fixed it with Studs and Fakir, but he hadn't. He'd hesitated doing so, because too many people would know.

He set up the laptop. First he surfed the Web looking for information on The Hive. He found it easily. Chic, with it, happening, sweet. The Labyrinth was on top and the "in" place to be on the weekend. Harry scanned a few of the photos, then noted the address.

Harry called Judy Ferris.

He got her answering machine. He told her to call him. He needed to know how much she knew. If he was going to The Hive, he didn't need wild cards. Wild cards? That was good. Who was Wiley but the wildest of cards?

After he hung up, Harry cobbled together some dinner. Then he wrote out a short explanation of what had happened, leaving off his involvement, and detailing where Wiley and Burt could be found, when and who the documents should be delivered to, popped them into large envelopes, and mailed them to Studs and Fakir.

It was late when he collapsed on his bed. He let the TV drone over his body, as if it were a mummer or medicine man casting his spirit into another world.

31

Marant spent Saturday taking care of details. He drove to the Hive and watched it for more than an hour. No Kafi, no CIA and FBI, no Boris/Wiley. Of course, they could make arrangements quickly. To be effective, he had to suspend his disbelief about the reality of Boris's process. Unaccountable things had happened starting with Boris/Wiley's disappearance, but paranoia does things to people.

He called Teresa, and she asked, again, if she could see him. Marant looked at the phone, the blue patch of sky, the rush of cars on Market Street. He'd stayed alive for over twenty years because of secrecy and anonymity. He blinked. Wasn't that what the Americans said? He said he'd pick her up a block from the Capri Motel in an hour.

He drove through the Presidio to Lombard Street. Could he trust Teresa's artlessness, which vanquished the worry that marked her young, round face? That day, again, her brown eyes were bright, her face animated. He didn't know her, except they connected on a level he couldn't describe. If she were on the other side, she was an accomplished terrorist and a clever actress.

The day was easy and made him homesick for Normandy. He realized, again, that he'd led a distant life, had few women friends, and spent his leisure time—when he wasn't working at his sculpture—at equally solitary pursuits. The last woman he'd known was Brigitte, and their characters matched so well that he felt he was staring at the simulacrum of Marant Olivier. He could sense Brigitte's distance, her inevitable loneliness.

Teresa was moodier than Brigitte and more needy, but he enjoyed the surcease from their assignment. Teresa grew distant later in the afternoon when their intermezzo drew to a close as he chose the slim, hazardous cliff near Land's End for a late-afternoon drink. The slender finger of the cliff pointed towards the setting sun. The sun made their faces glow, and they watched it disappear as if for the first time.

The sun was a thin disk, already towards the south, less intense in the few days he'd been in the city. He remembered similar suns in that fabled time of his youth at Fort Mahon, the beach chalet, the sand swirling in the streets and on the sidewalks, the hourglass of beach twisting towards Le Touquet and rumors of quicksand and eddies which trapped the unwary on vanishing islands. It was a rare moment—was it two times he'd walked with his parents on that beach, three, more?—of peace before his parents had died and he was whisked off to an orphanage.

Marant savored his Calvados and watched the sunset. He had been the man who guessed edges. The one who always fell this side of death. Was he doomed to scurry around cities making arrangements, to be constantly in motion?

"You are reflective, Marant," Teresa said while watching the fading coin of the sun.

He regarded the diminutive woman with the large brown eyes and knew that she was worried about making the right choice. Teresa was curiously attractive, and he underestimated her. Her revolutionary passion made her seem naïve at first, but she was more than a wide-eyed novice. And she had a nuanced command of the curve.

"I used to be happy when an assignment was over and I was alive and I could think about more than tactics and death. But I'm becoming like you: this assignment is endless."

"But soon it will be the end of our time together," she said with a sorrowful twist of her mouth, then a biting of her upper lip with her teeth. She watched the crashing waves and the spume that billowed towards them, then collapsed in the rocks below.

She seemed more like him in her resignation. "Will you return to Bilbao?" asked Marant.

She watched a gull drifting over the crashing waves below. "Yes."

"One day you will tell stories to your children of a devil named Marant."

Teresa turned to him and laughed. "A devil, certainly."

"Bilbao is very much like the coast of Normandy," said Marant finally. "You could stay with me, model for me, help me with lines and curves."

She looked at him brightly. "I'd like that," she said.

He wondered why he felt so depressed. He walked to the point of the slim arrowhead, seeing the uneven islands of hard rock and the white spume below. The problems with the winos had made him more reflective. He was older, unsure. Had he approached that edge, finally? Was the gun in the moonlight, the wavering hand, a last joust with the other side?

Teresa was behind him, her hand on his shoulder.

Suddenly, he felt alone, as if he were immersed in a last game with himself. He was unsure of the next card—ace, deuce, queen of spades? He always played to the end. It could have been his body on the grass. There was the chance, the play. What had it been about? Had he been trapped, finally, by his own conundrums?

He regarded the rocks as one who is about to start a long journey. He felt it would be a perilous one down a narrow path with the rocks splitting and tumbling off the edges, and the edge disappearing. He felt a sense of lassitude, which Teresa had glimpsed or perhaps had inspired. The games were, sometimes, too much for the experts.

He took her hand.

32

Mike Larew, mystery, MIA. Dispiritedly, Judy Ferris hailed a cab on Columbus. Ten minutes later, she walked into her living room. Such promise early that evening. She'd spent a week trying to find Wiley, and when she did, she lost him.

"Fuck!"

She stared at her reflection in the bay window and wondered what was next. At that moment, she realized that she hadn't been ready. Confirming Wiley was alive wasn't enough. She needed a photo, she needed proof...if she found Wiley again.

She'd kept the police out so far; maybe it was time. She knew a detective, Bernie Valentine, a Vietnam vet, from her amnesty group. It was late, so she dialed his home number. Hunched over the phone, she sat on the sofa, wondering how to explain it all. She told him she was chasing a man who faked jumping off the bridge on Sunday, that she'd found him with his girlfriend, Rosie McCoy. She gave him Rosie's address. That's when Bernie asked her why she was chasing him. It was the first time she had to explain to a normal person what she was doing.

She grabbed her hair, vaulted off the sofa, and stood at her window. Her reflection showed her talking, explaining, as if she were another sepulchral person. Her story sounded ghostly too. She told Valentine that Wiley had ripped off friends without going into detail. Finally, gesturing, she sketched out the other Wiley, the CIA, the homeless deaths.

She read doubt into his silence. Finally he said, "We can check this Rosie McCoy and see if this guy is still there. If he faked his suicide, then he'll go to jail. The CIA thing sounds far-fetched. Why are you doing this again?"

"It's complicated. It has a lot to do with another Judy Ferris, one buried in old files."

"A ghost from the past, the worst kind."

"I think you're right. There's my door. I'll talk to you later."

She threw the phone on the sofa. At the door, she checked the peephole. Mike Larew.

Judy opened the door and said, "You sure are a bad finisher. How could you be so close to him and think he turned right on Stockton?"

Mike seemed sheepish. "It was crowded, and I thought I saw two of them."

Judy laughed. "Two Wileys? Jesus, let's hope not."

Mike frowned and said, "Well, you had your chance. I'm surprised you found him."

"My persistence occasionally pays off."

"And now?"

Judy stepped into the kitchen and leaned against the counter. Mike followed her. "I'm not sure. I'm pissed I missed him, and I'm not sure what's next. Maybe I'll give up."

"That doesn't sound like the Judy Ferris I know."

"So many Judy Ferrises." She had to be careful, but she couldn't ignore the reality of what Mike had done that night. He was deep in the Wiley chase, and he may be the last hope she had to find him. She had to dig, but not appear eager. Judy sighed, touched his shoulder. "You certainly tried to stop me. I guess you were protecting me in your manly man way."

Mike said grimly, "Wiley is dangerous. What were you going to do if you caught him?"

Judy frowned. "It was a little like a dog chasing a car. Is that the only reason?"

"What if there were larger issues involved?"

Judy shook her head. "Everyone says that; the CEOs say it; managers say it. We're all pawns and should stay pawns. Yep, I've heard that before. What could you possibly know that justifies what Wiley has done?"

Mike relaxed against the counter. "You want Wiley because of a personal trauma. Maybe I don't want him at all. Maybe I have to know more about him in order to stop more people from dying. Should I let you expose him, so you can cauterize your trauma?"

"Why do you want to stay with me? Just to fuck me?"

"I can like the person and hate the crusade."

Judy shook her head sadly. "I suppose it does look like a crusade. And I'm not sure you even like me. Sometimes I do, sometimes not. I know you're using me."

"You're not using me?"

Judy smiled. "Standoff. I like the bit about liking the person and not the crusade. I'm not sure it's true, but there's a lot I'm not sure of."

Mike said, "It sounds like I'm still persona grata?"

Judy paused for a second. "I'm not quite ready to give up on you. We never know what we're getting into. C'mon."

A few short minutes later, they were both naked, facing each other. Judy eased into bed. "It's always more than just sex," Judy said, tracing her finger over a scar on his chest she'd never seen. "Or we'd all have vibrators."

"You'll always be more than warm places," he said. "There's the real you."

Judy laughed. "Her! Who's the real Mike Larew again?"

He rolled into bed, grabbed her, and rolled her on top. She'd forgotten his strength. He clasped his arms around her back and spread her legs with his knees. She could feel him growing. "What would life be without secrets? You have yours."

"I'd never keep anything from you, lover," she said, spreading her legs farther.

He laughed. "Now I feel paranoid."

"I've felt paranoid for days, but it hasn't stopped me. It's either stupidity or a death wish. We can suss that later; right now, we have other business." He took one of her breasts in his mouth and ran his tongue around the nipple. "Be democratic."

She didn't remember much else that night. They were both beat. She'd forgotten how good it was, how much fun it was even tired unto death. Their bodies were separate from their minds and spirit, and they found each other, and they found new places, and new positions. She might not miss the mystery; she was sure going to miss the man.

A crimson strip of dawn edged through the drapes. The sun threw razor-like shadows from her window planter of cacti and aloes over Mike and a tangle of yellow covers. He made her feel secure, at least for that morning. She tried not to think of the rest, of larger issues, whatever they might be.

Their clothes had formed his/her clumps around the bed, a few adventurous pieces making it to her wardrobe. A couple meetings, two nights, a shared adventure, which he thought was crazy. She'd reached the next stage of closeness without wanting to. What had she done when it was over? She supposed, when the stranger had made his mark, the dialogues over, the pleasantries memories, she picked up, set her cap, and forged on. What would happen this time? The big black-haired, risk-taking man under the covers was more stranger than lover, and that was good. But the next stage was there, appearing without her volition.

The airport doors swished shut, a last wave at the blank glass, the empty stage feeling, then the loneliness demons, the faceless ones, rushing in, yelling the alarms.

As she gazed absently over the lumps on the floor, she saw Mike's wallet peeking out of his rumpled jeans. She eased out of bed.

Mike didn't move.

She walked towards the doorway, crouched, and slipped his wallet out of the worn back pocket of his jeans. She glanced at Mike's unmoving back and stepped quickly through the hallway into the bathroom.

She fingered the money and quickly went through the cards. He might have been a Mike in San Francisco, but most of the cards had Michel emblazoned on them. Michel Orjollet. That slight accent she heard, his fluent French in Tully's. There was a faded photo of an older, heavy man, and an older frowning woman.

She checked under the flaps and came up with a small address book. The International Exchange; a hotel in the Tenderloin, a motel on Lombard, a small hotel on Russian Hill. Her own number. The back page had a series of names on it. Kafi, Teresa, and MO. Marant Olivier? Under MO was a scribbled line. "The Hive, midnight, Labyrinth. Check flights."

Judy shuddered. Was that the endgame? What part did Mike play in it? On what side?

She replaced the address book and slowly opened the bathroom door. She edged down the hallway but stopped when she got to the bedroom. Mike had moved to other side of the bed. He faced her. He was still sleeping, but she guessed not for long. She kept the wallet behind her and as she walked past his jeans, crouched, and tucked the wallet deep into his jeans pocket.

She walked quickly around to the side of the bed and slipped quickly under the covers, touching his leg in the process.

Mike stirred. The bed rocked. Mike's square face and dark eyes turned and emerged from the sheets. He propped himself on a muscular arm.

She rolled over to the side. Mike came up behind her. She could feel his sex against her back. Mike put his hand on her neck and stroked. She closed her eyes and let him massage her neck for a few minutes.

Judy said, "That feels good." She turned and faced him. "Let's forget it and seize this day. Don't you leave tonight?"

Mike looked stunned. "Shit. I can't leave tonight. I have too much to do. I've got to leave right now. Can I come back here? It might be late."

"Earlier would be better. If you have to go, you have to go. And I'm going to be nice and not ask what you're going to do."

"I'm not sure I like that change."

"What would life be without mystery?"

After Mike left, she booted her PC. The Hive was a hip place in SoMa, and the Labyrinth the crown of the Hive. Would Wiley be there? Marant? Was Marant part of those larger issues? She had lots of questions, and few answers. It looked like the Hive was her next stop. She'd be ready. She'd have a camera and more ammunition than a desire to find Wiley. She didn't scribble the Hive on her sheet. She didn't want Mike to see it.

She opened her word processor and had started refining her exposé, when the phone rang. It was Merri, who asked for advice with the Fodor script. It was an intrusion from another lifetime. Maybe that was what she needed, a connection to something real.

She showered. Quick drive down to Market Street. An hour and half spent with Merri in the Front Café. They were wedged between two lesbians on their right, and two Asian men—Thai? Cambodian?—who talked into a cell phone at the same time, stopping every few minutes to peck each other on the cheek.

Back on Corbett, late afternoon. Answering machine.

Blink, blink, blink.

She flipped it on. The first message was from Valentine. Rosie wasn't at her place and neither was Wiley Brooks. He'd reported what she'd said to the Park Police, who were handling Wiley's disappearance, but they said that until they saw Wiley Brooks, he was still dead. She expected as much from the police, but it didn't make her feel better that Wiley could cruise around town, go to movies, get drunk, and kill people with impunity.

The second message was from a soft, hissing voice.

You're going to die, if you keep going.

She stared at her answering machine. Of course they knew it was her. Wiley had her phone number, her address. A board snapped. She glanced towards the back yard and saw a lanky form flip around the corner of the house.

She froze. Her answering machine spat out another message. It was Harry Mach.

The doorbell shocked her. She pressed "Erase All" on her answering machine, and turned, trembling, raced to the door, and slid home the bolt.

"You weren't that spooky when we left," Mike said through the door.

She looked through the peephole and saw Mike standing there with his backpack. She unbolted the door and let him in. "It caught up with me."

When he walked into the living room, he had that athletic stride that

230

she'd seen that first night. Mike stared out the window. She walked into the room and carefully curled up on her white sofa and rested her head on the sofa arm. She didn't want to fight. She didn't want Mike to think she was crazy. He wanted to say something, but thought better of it.

The tension was too much, considering her state. At least they should be outside, not trapped in a spiritual limbo inside. "Let's sit outside. Get a beer. I'll be right out."

She grabbed the portable phone, snagged her jacket, and walked into the bedroom. She pulled Harry Mach's card out of her jacket and dialed his number. No answer.

Puzzled, she went into the kitchen, mixed a Bloody Mary, and joined Mike. Beyond Mike, her neighbor was out watering. No one on the other side. Wiley couldn't have been there.

Minutes later, they moved drinks around the table, the way they had that first night.

A haze obscured downtown; across the bay, light smog nestled in random pockets of Berkeley and Oakland. Mike's beard was longer than when she met him and matched in texture his butch haircut. Above his shading of pockmarks, his brown eyes were worried, and his brows, normally thick and flat, were bunched in check marks, check marks which matched her own lighter ones. Their legs stretched out and almost touched to form a V.

"What do you think?" she said. "Do we need lots and lots of injustice in order to produce justice? Look at El Salvador. If we hadn't supported injustice then, perhaps it would be worse now. An accumulation of small evils makes for a secure good."

"That's your ghost," Mike said. "And you don't believe it."

"I was thinking of what I'd do if I gave up. I would have my workouts, write little stories, work with the ATA, sip lattes at the Front Café, brag about my publishing history."

"You're not going to do that," said Mike. He took a pull of his beer and put it on the table. He folded his arms and looked at her. She liked Mike, beyond the mystery, but there was something she didn't like. Maybe it was a problem with every man she'd known.

"What were you going to tell me, inside?" she said.

"You don't miss much."

"Intuition. Can't be measured and is mostly pooh-poohed by the testy folks. It works."

"I was going to try to convince you to give up your chase. But we've tilled that ground. You'll either do it or not do it, regardless of what I say."

"You don't have that kind of power. I'll do what I have to do."

"I guess you will." He touched her knee with his forefinger, then played with a small blond hair on her ankle, one she'd missed when she shaved.

Judy said, "We can stay out her all night and argue about larger issues, who we really are, and whether Wiley is worth it. But let's play it simple. We have new positions to find."

33

The next morning, after a restless night of Boschian images of crackling fires, severed limbs, anguished cries, red-headed demons, and endless, endless torments, Harry Mach woke up. It was late. A panelist on Washington Week in Review droned over his body about the great things to come in the Bush Administration, tax cuts, tough on crime—but with compassion—tough on the environment, tough on everybody, and tough, tough, tough.

The slicing sun popped and danced through a dust storm hovering over his bed.

He plunged his head into a bathroom sink of water, dried off, smiled at his swinging cock, put on his burgundy bathrobe, and walked tiredly downstairs. He retrieved the Sunday papers, threw them on the table, and repaired to the kitchen. He stared into the cavernous refrigerator until three eggs coalesced before his eyes. He flipped on his forty-two-inch built-in TV and listened to the local news as he fried the eggs. He ate toast and eggs hurriedly in the dining room as he flipped through the Chronicle. He stopped in mid-bite when he saw the article on a North Beach restaurateur—Sal Ziti, owner of Capriccio's—murdered outside his restaurant.

Everything stopped. His fork rattled on the plate. He heard the tap, tapping of a drip in the bathroom; the sun blazed in the window and was a wall of light. Had Burt gone batshit? No. Burt, despite his growing ambition, was not a killer.

The only possibility was the remote one Burt mentioned: Wiley.

Wiley found out about Vito and Sal from the tail before Wiley killed him. What did that mean about Vito? Wiley told Burt not to worry about Vito.

Harry pushed his plate out of the way. He fired up the laptop.

San Jose Mercury News.

Vito Mongreve was found dead, execution style, in a Palo Alto ditch. He'd been tortured. There was a hefty bio. Harry didn't read it.

Harry felt fragile, ghostly, his insides airy. He stumbled past his Monet print into harsh September sunlight. He shielded his eyes and squinted, looking for anything normal. Scenes unfolded in the patchwork quilt of back yards on Mt. Sutro. A woman in a halter top with white skin and soft heavy breasts, a short man in a tattered work shirt teetered on a ladder, two girls in pigtails, shorts, and loose tops played with yellow trucks on clipped grass. A couple drank coffee in a screened porch, a paper spread out in front of them.

Life without, death and emptiness within.

The torture reference lodged in his head. What for? Studs had said Wiley was an interrogator for the CIA. Wiley likely wanted to know if anyone else was following him. Of course, he knew about Harry. Wiley had already trashed his house looking for the address book, and Burt just told him he had it, and bank account numbers.

On the other hand, no one knew about his Wiley deals except Sal and Vito...and, of course, Burt. Wiley had just gotten rid of a possible complication and added a layer of protection for Harry Mach. Drug business: RIP.

What should he do? Was he next?

And what should he do about Sunday night and the chic party room, the "Labyrinth"? As if he hadn't been in one for a week. Harry knew one thing: if he was passive, he would lose...and not just his Trifecta. He had to act now. He had to dictate what would happen.

So here's how it goes. I set up bank accounts for two in Switzerland: Burt and Wiley. I go to the Hive with the deal. If Wiley takes it, I'm up x-million, and Leg 3 of the Trifecta is finished, gloriously, and I'm alive.

He had no time to lose. He had to set it up fast.

He called Studs and left a message about that night. Ditto Fakir. Then he spent hours creating bank accounts in Nassau. Then, as additional insurance, he logged on, used the password on the drug account and transferred the three hundred grand into one of the accounts he'd set up.

Finally, he dressed in slacks, boots, and a neatly pressed blue Oxford shirt. He regarded his form in the mirror. He cut a figure. Fashionably curly hair, molten gray eyes, upright figure, soft fleshy hands, huge cock, and tough.

The sunny bright day had turned into a balmy, beautiful evening, an evening spent tapping nervously on his table and staring at faint whorls of dust. When he looked at his watch, it shocked him to see it was almost ten. Harry remembered Judy Ferris.

He poured out two inches of Laphroig and punched the number.

It rang twice. Then Judy picked up.

"Ms. Ferris, Harry Mach."

"Finally," Judy said brusquely. "Is it true?"

Harry frowned. "Opaque as usual. What does 'it' mean?"

"I'm coming," she said. "Don't pretend you don't know."

"I'm not sure what I'm pretending. You must be more—"

"In two hours, the Hive. I have my means."

Harry held the phone gingerly. Best not to talk too long. How did she know? He tried to see if she would be a complication and decided he didn't know. "How do you know?"

"I have my sources, confidential sources, just like you."

How did she know? Mike Larew? He hated things he couldn't control. "Let me give you a piece of advice. Give it up! Are you stone-cold fucking crazy? Wiley's going to kill you, cut you in two, stuff you into box, and mail it to Central America."

"What about you and your little games, dimwit? You have his address book. Think he's going to thank you for keeping it for him?"

"I have a plan; you don't. What's your plan? Are you going to wag your finger at him and tell him he's a bad boy?"

"I want a copy of that address book."

"You're crazier than I thought."

"It doesn't mean anything to you now, and it does to me. You can sort through it and throw out stuff you don't want me to see. I need it for research. If you do, I won't bother you, and I'll let you do whatever you want at the Hive. If you don't, I might, totally inadvertently, mention your name in my exposé."

Harry laughed. "An exposé no one will read."

"Or I might just put it on the Web. Remember, someone had to tell me about tonight."

Point taken. And he didn't see, right off, how he could silence her without something dramatic. He'd had enough drama. He had a plan; she didn't. And he had to get out of the affair clean—that was part of the deal. He had to morph back into Harry Mach, Investment Consultant, worrying points and schmoozing clients. "I've pored over the address book; there's nothing left but taquerias and cafés."

"You're squandering your luck, Harry."

Harry clicked off. He took a quick sip of scotch. Ferris could screw up the entire plan, but he couldn't do anything about her. Maybe later.

34

Saturday night, Marant and Teresa ate in the Beach Chalet on Ocean Drive. The Chalet was a recently remodeled low-slung neo-Spanish tile-roofed building transformed into brew pub and restaurant. The entrance felt spare and touristy. He admired the blocky depression-era murals of Golden Gate Park and laughed at how they satirized his spare canvases and spindly figures. Those murals defined an era, innocent in its own way, when life was too serious for satire.

Teresa was edgy and picked at her sandwich, occasionally glancing resignedly through her reflected image at strollers on the beach. He felt her hesitancy, her feeling that they were at the end. After dinner they checked in at the Surf Motel, from where they had a distant view of the Cliff House, Seal Rock, thousands of gulls, cormorants, and pelicans, and a thin horizon line of gray ocean. The evening, the crashing surf, the few hardy surfers seemed a tame end to a project to obtain a new explosive to blow up adversaries and unlucky passersby. Marant hadn't questioned his actions for years. Teresa drew his doubts and hesitations to the surface.

Why kill? Why play chess with one Jacques, then later kill another? Did situational ethics matter, or was it a throw-away rationalization? He'd articulated the arguments, but forgotten their meaning. They had become words, placeholders in his consciousness.

Teresa fascinated him. She was weak, but strong when she came to a decision. She was courageous, but doubted her courage would lead to a worthy goal. He felt a strong desire for her, but the rational part of Marant Olivier knew she could be on the other side, or would throw him over if her own security were threatened. It gave their love-making an indescribable quality, of life in death, of throwing the gauntlet in the face of mortality.

Sunday morning, Marant dressed in jeans, a dark blue shirt, a dark blue sports coat, white socks, and a pair of tennis shoes. He looked, for all his casual American costume, with his slick-backed dark hair, nut-brown eyes, and classic, fine aquiline nose, very European. He thought of a hat, then discarded that idea, then decided on a washed-out work shirt, which made him seem rougher and not quite as polished. He would get rid of his other clothes later. To complete his costume, he put two extra vials of tetradoxin in the inner pocket of his coat.

They ate breakfast in the Cliff House restaurant. It was almost as if they were getting ready to return to Fort Mahon and Bilbao after a weeklong vacation in America. As they ate, instead of talking about this or that monument or tourist trap, about the Wharf or cable cars, they went over what they were going to do at the Hive. Finally, they talked about strategies for leaving America. He knew she had a ticket, but if something happened, she could use the one he'd reserved for her to Toronto. He explained the alternatives, the holdovers, and the possibility of renting a car and flying from other airports in L.A. or Portland. Teresa was surprised he had thought of her, and took his hand. It gave their last few minutes a bittersweet aspect.

He drove her to the Capri Motel around noon.

"I wish I were staying with you today," said Teresa. She'd said it earlier, and they had discussed the reasons she couldn't. The traffic on Lombard Street was heavy; the cars near the Palace of Fine Arts turn-off backed up. It was hard to talk, but neither of them wanted to part.

"We may have already compromised ourselves. We have to arrive at the Hive separately. For my sake, and yours. Kafi must not know, nor anyone else." Marant looked in her eyes, smiled, then said, "I wish we could have this day. We must snatch as many moments as we can."

"Perhaps later," said Teresa.

"Take what you need. You can always buy clothes."

"Of course," said Teresa.

"Oh, and take this." He handed her the small fugu pill.

"If I'm captured?"

"You don't have to use it, but it's an option. More for me, than you."

"You really think this is a sham, don't you?"

"Yes."

"Are you going through with it because of me?"

He could have said yes. "Several reasons, not you."

She frowned, brightened, then he bent over and kissed her longer than he'd intended. She glanced at him tenderly, let her fingers drift over his hand, opened the door, and left. He drove slowly down Lombard and saw Teresa walking swiftly towards the motel. When she disappeared inside, he turned off Lombard and drove up to Lake Street, then right towards Mountain Lake Park on the edge of the Presidio.

He parked and walked. The day was clean and bright, the fog vanquished, the golf course on his right an unearthly green dotted with too-white sand traps. The quiet street was accented with serious women pushing strollers who frowned at the random in-line skater or skateboarder.

He was in a strange mood, and his thoughts returned to what would happen that evening. The small park was full of strollers, volleyball games, football games, and barbecues. Signs with arrows and balloons pointed to a birthday party where gray picnic tables were draped with bright yellow paper and heavy with chicken, potato salad, sodas, and lead-colored kegs.

Marant walked to the small three-sided concrete building with the built-in concrete chessboards. He sat alone for a few minutes and watched the small playing field and the paths that wound through the park. Sergei was there and interrupted his reverie. He motioned him to join him for a game. Marant joined him and while making his opening moves watched the baby buggies, the silver-haired matrons with their feisty dogs, the swan which made Sergei point his finger and alert his friends.

That time Marant played to win. He played different gambits, was improvisational, elegant in his endgames. Marant understood that he was practicing for evening, exercising his left brain, the straight edge. He left Sergei wondering about his play, angry he had been tricked by maneuvers so simple in retrospect. The chorus of eastern European voices was muted when he said his goodbyes. If only that evening would be as simple as winning chess games.

Sunday afternoon, he went to a matinée performance of the San Francisco Symphony and heard the three Bs: Beethoven, Brahms, and Benton, and an American twelve-tone composer of note. He exchanged observations about the performance with Tom and Delia Morton, two people he'd met earlier in the week on a Cultural Exchange excursion.

Around six, he parked in the Sunset area and left his two suitcases near a homeless encampment—giving back to those he'd killed?—and took a final stroll through Golden Gate Park. He had been in the park frequently that week, but he hadn't looked at it as a tourist. The park was artificial, he found from a brochure. The trees, the flowers, the beach grass, the arboretum with its thousands of plants had been brought in and made to grow on sand dunes. It was all artificial from the ridiculous fake stalactites at the entrance to the park to the shattered windmill near the ocean. On the other hand, weren't all gardens artificial? Weren't most things man surrounded himself with merely echoes, reflections of his own concerns?

At least gardens partook more of curve than straight edge.

As he walked and observed, he tried to ignore the hard reality of what might happen that night. When he thought of that evening, he had little but apprehension. He had suspended his disbelief for days. His security had lapsed. But he didn't want to avoid the Hive. There was something important to find there, something which would have an impact on everything that RM did, something which would have an impact on his life. The die was cast, the pieces positioned. One didn't play an entire game, then decide the endgame was too chancy.

He drove downtown and dropped the car off just before the agency closed at eight o'clock—it was important to tie up loose ends—then he strolled along Market Street for several hours, drank an espresso on the Embarcadero, and finally ate dinner at the restaurant atop the Fairmont Hotel. He lingered over the view, the dots of light, which spread to the rim of the bay, the darkness of the bay itself.

At eleven-thirty, he walked out of the Fairmont and caught sight of himself in the window. Despite his too-American clothes, he looked European, the slicked back hair, the sensitive, inward-looking aspect, the lazy brown eyes. And despite his reservations, he felt steeled, ready to find out what the last week was all about.

The cab descended swiftly from Nob Hill. He had the cab driver stop several blocks from the Hive. He watched the entrance to the Hive. The occupants of the cars on the streets seemed young and were passing joints, drinking, and gesticulating. If only life were again as simple.

The Hive was, as expected, an incomprehensible mass of sound, color, and screaming children. It was a perfect public spot for a rather innocuous exchange of a key for a process. A key to the universe, a universal process. It had a scant symbolic meaning he hadn't appreciated. The lopsided universe and its very big bang echoed weakly in their little trade. The trade would mean more maneuvering, more straight lines skewing off, hemming in convenient fictions.

He waited on the ground floor and kept watch for a watcher, not a drinker. There were a few husky-looking men, who circulated and left.

Teresa walked past him. Her glance back at him was full of meaning. His, not. He thought it too controlled, and realized, again, her hold on him. She made his lines waver, unimportant. A writer once noted that the lines can't last. They are artificial, necessary, a left-brain extrusion. We trap reality in rigid straight lines and distort it.

He walked the lower floors for a few minutes, lost in his musings, bumped by revelers, by the packed-in crowds. He began to detect something important, beyond the project, beyond throwaway existential cynicism. He saw it, indistinctly; it came over him like a cloud, a mood, perhaps a fog.

He walked slowly towards the third floor. It got darker and warmer. The dance floor was littered with balloons. A crowd bunched up at the crêpe-hung Labyrinth. It reminded him of scenes in Fritz Lang's

Metropolis, with waters flooding the city and subterra workers clawing over one another to reach safety. This crowd was clawing its way to fleeting hilarity, the over-hyped, and always hyped, American pastime. Three women in tinsel costumes with black boots fought through the crowd, laughed, whispered secrets, then walked regally towards the stairs.

After the feints, shadows, and fogs of last week, it was time to find out what was real.

35

Men flitted in and out of her life, and afterwards, she thought that was a good thing. In New York, post-El Salvador, post-apocalypse, there was the occasional tremor—after a few dates, intimate nights, hand-holding at farmers' markets or sharing a movie—that she'd found the right one, that marriage, the kids, the rest would follow seamlessly. But no. Opaque power fantasists, little boys in men's bodies. Her specialty became a cheerful one-night stand, mostly with boozy editors or poets from Village bars or Chelsea clubs. With San Francisco came exotic variations. There was the black photographer in Vietnam, the irrepressible Mirachi in Sulawesi, the wavy-haired, brown-eyed stockbroker in Cabo San Lucas, whose overwhelming desire, announced post-coital, was to be a millionaire at thirty. Three nights, a few hours during the day, a handful of words. Maybe she was vulnerable, but she had gut feelings about Mike Larew partly because she didn't know who he was.

Sunday morning post-breakfast over a last drip of coffee, he disrupted her leave-taking fantasy. "I'll take the shuttle."

"That's silly. I'll give you a ride," she said casually.

"In your death trap? When you get money, get a real car."

She didn't understand why he was so gruff. He wasn't flying anywhere. "Take the shuttle. It'll save me a trip."

Mike dressed in a very dressed-down pair of jeans, a black sweatshirt, and a pair of black tennis shoes. He looked grim, as if he were going to put his dog to sleep.

He turned to her, serious lines etched on his face. "I feel like a shit for leaving, but I have to. You've got to work on something else. Tell those jerks at the ATA you had a bad day, that you made a mistake."

"Why do you care?"

Mike shrugged, as if he knew any advice would be rejected. "If you keep going and find Wiley again, which I think is doubtful, they might get rid of you...permanently."

"Admonitions from Mr. Risk," she said, shaking her head in mock scolding.

Mike sighed, as if he were remembering meeting in Tully's, their so-called dates. "Who will remember, for a while, a tall lady, a rippled mouth, odd theories about missing persons and CIA puzzles. There's been bed, you and me, your chase. It's as if I've been seeing two people."

"And we met because of Wiley. Maybe I'll thank him."

Mike harrumphed, then looked too serious. "You should drop it, but I admire that you don't. But it's over. If we see each other again—"

"Don't go there. When it's over, it's over."

"I suppose in a few days or weeks, the last few days will be just an-other incident among many," he said. There was a dart board, a neon sign sputtering and silvering the bottle, his head.

Maybe that was his way of making it easy, she thought, grouping the last few days in some category of, say, the last leg of his trip, or women he met and bedded in the last two months. It sounded too objective when she explained that to herself, but then Mike was, after all, a man and not emotionally complex.

"I'm sure you're right."

The doorbell surprised both of them. They looked at each other. She hadn't expected him to be sorrowful, regretful, but that's what she saw. She kissed him hard, until the doorbell rang again. Mike got up and they walked hand-in-hand to his bags. She watched him haul his bags to the door and open it. He took a last look around, then at her, then they kissed a last time. He loaded his pack in the shuttle, got in, waved, and a few minutes later the shuttle vanished around the first curve on Corbett.

Despite knowing he wasn't leaving, she felt empty. She wondered whether she should go to the Hive. He could turn up on the other side; what would she do with that?

241

Her apartment had become an impenetrable reality, her rooms strange and distant and empty, the result of the fussing of someone she didn't know. Her mood took her to the back yard, where she stared at two empty chairs.

She was pissed. She calmed down, then set up at her PC and worked her story. Every hour, she checked the patio, the encroaching yards. No lanky lurker. No trim ponytail, vulturish Wiley, or stubby redhead. She knew they were out there sharpening their knives, getting ready for the last chapter of what Harry called Wiley's dark side. When she'd wormed her way to that conclusion, to Potato, Sugar, and Scab, and CIA plots, she wondered again whether she was doing it from a noble sentiment or dribbling out an atavistic Ferris death wish.

As Mike said, there is a time when survival trumps risk.

It was a morose Judy who stared at her from her bathroom mirror from inside a rim of dried roses, poppies, yarrow, and round Botero ladies.

She took a last look at the sheet taped over her PC, shook her head at the name "Marant Olivier," then walked into the bedroom. She put on a pair of slacks, a shirt, boots. At the last second, she dug through her closet until she found her old leather jacket. She hadn't worn it since New York. It seemed a fitting gesture for a Judy Ferris renaissance; besides, it had deep pockets where she could store stuff. No way was she taking a purse.

She thought about what she needed. What do you need for a date with a murderous CIA agent, terrorists from Spain and Algeria, and an assassin? She was trying to be light about what she was doing, but every few minutes, she'd pause and wonder if she shouldn't give it up. Mike was right: She could die that night.

She pretended she was going anyway.

First, she needed a camera. She kept her photo equipment in the hall closet. She couldn't take the bulky stuff. She looked through the bag and finally emerged with the digital Olympus with built-in flash and zoom. She loaded in the spare battery, tested the flash, checked the photo, deleted it, and put it in one of her front pockets. She found a big pair of sunglasses: anonymity might help later.

Audio. She rummaged through her drawer of electronic throwaways

242

and grabbed the smallest tape recorder she could find. She inserted a new tape, tested it, and shoved the recorder in her jacket pocket. If she was going to get a story, she might as well have the right accessories. At the last minute, she grabbed her cell. She hated cell phones and only used hers when she was traveling. She put in the spare battery, switched it on, and called her portable. When it rang, she clicked off, then used the cell to call a cab.

She double-checked her pockets. She was missing one thing. She looked through the kitchen cabinet and finally pulled out the Mace. She tested it outside and saw it still had oomph. She clipped that inside her inside pocket.

Feeling armed and ready, Judy strode to the door. She paused at the door. Too many pauses that week, too many hesitations. She'd started something that would only finish when she exposed Wiley Brooks or published her story. She was so far from where she was a week ago, she felt like another person, not even the idealistic one she knew years ago in El Salvador.

She opened the door a crack and watched the street until the cab pulled up. Then, as if she were closing a chapter in her life, she saluted her winged Garuda and pulled the door shut. She gave the driver the address of the Hive and sat back and watched the houses clip by, the long sloping descent into the Castro, then dog-walkers, a queue in front of the Castro Theatre, gay couples holding hands. The cab ride down Market was fast, as if the driver knew she was closing on the punch line of her story.

The driver turned right on Ninth and headed for Folsom Street. He pulled up in front of the Hive. The area was remote and sinister. There was a queue, and a heavy rock beat seemed to shake the building. At the front of the queue, when the brawny crew-cut security guard waved her in, she rolled the dice.

36

A sense of fatalism stayed with her in the high-decibel, intensified space of the Hive, and in the subterranean, maudit frenzy of the first clutch of tattered punks, gruff leather-and-spangled bikers, and tattooed Rastafarians. The huge space was caressed in muted red strobes, and laser beams clashed beneath the cages of dancers. A green amoebae-like projection kissed the balconies with an enormous glistening mouth.

Judy scanned the writhing bodies on the dance floor then the shadows, hoping to pick out Wiley or Rosie or Harry and his ponytailed friend. They could have been there; she couldn't tell. If anything, they'd be in the Labyrinth later. She walked up tubular steel stairs to the second floor followed by that green mouth, which, creeping from the piazza around stairs and corners into the recesses of the floors, made the inside a gut, a place of attack and digestion.

She found herself, finally, high on the third level, where the cavernous space and huge crowds receded. The third floor had a strip of blue/green flickering light on the piazza side which cast jerky shadows over a dance floor and a rim of tables to a stage where Johnny and the Nightshades, dressed in Early Walking Dead, ground out whiney, faux-Nirvana, grunge lyrics.

The bartender said the Labyrinth was a special party area behind the stage; it was full of separate rooms, piped in heavy metal, and opened at midnight. It cost fifty bucks, was "sweet."

"Right now my sweet is a Bloody Mary," said Judy. "Extra Tabasco."

She paid for the drink, tasted it, and let the heat spread through her body. She sat down at a tall circular table near the bar. She let herself go with the moment and tried to separate out the strains which reached that third level—punk, rock, rap—and listened for a few beats to Nightshades screaming about their mother, her badness, their white-knuckle rage. The Nightshades would have to go, come the revolution.

She tuned out the Nightshades, sipped her drink, and picked out the figures hugging the edges hoping, yet afraid, that she would see Wiley...

or Mike. It was a mixed crowd, mostly young and punk. There were a few bikers, a few yuppies tasting the forbidden fruit of danger in SoMa, a few people in Phantom of the Opera masks. A woman in a butterfly costume fluttering around a table of half-full glasses, and leering blacks. It was a low-rent bal maudit. It was an odd place for Wiley's project to end, if it was about capturing Marant Olivier. If Harry was still playing because he thought he could win, he was making poor life choices.

Around eleven-thirty a curly-haired man with an appealing basset-like visage stared across the dance floor; he took in the people dancing, the people in shadows, and walked casually across the floor to the bar. Then he found a table and chair of his own. Harry Mach tasted his drink and scanned the crowd again, finally seeing her. He heaved up and walked quickly over to her. She reached inside her jacket and clicked on the tape recorder. Harry stopped at her table and made a gesture towards his ear. They waited for the last Nightshade riff of yet another song of rock star angst.

Harry shook his head, then whispered, "Turn off the recorder, Ms. Ferris."

"I used to be cleverer." Judy reached in and turned off the recorder.

Harry looked above her as if he were gathering his thoughts. "I'm surprised you're here. Death apparently isn't much of a deterrent."

"You ditto. We're in different leagues with different motives. What's your point in being here, Harry? Drug money? A weird conclusion of Mr. Hyde's side? Or, are you still unraveling that little boy's desire to prove yourself?"

"I forgot how caustic you are."

"Games and boys, boys and games. You can't help your hormones."

"You will have the fleeting comfort in thinking your story real and noble, before you die. Good for you."

"What about the address book?...I suppose you don't have it."

Harry looked around again, put his hand inside his coat pocket, and brought out a folded sheaf of papers. "Consider it protection against mentioning my name in any way. It is a copy of the most innocuous pages from Wiley's address book. There's not a lot you can use."

"I still don't see what you plan to gain in all of this. There must be a payoff in it, or you wouldn't be here. It's a stupid game for an investment consultant."

Harry smiled thinly. "And what are you going to do? Make a citizen's arrest? You've bulled your way in; now what?"

Judy stuffed the papers inside her jacket. "I'm playing it by ear."

Harry drained his drink. "Good luck, Ms. Ferris. You'll need it."

Harry walked slowly across the floor as if he were considering every step. That was another mystery: how was Harry was going to profit from Wiley's scheme?

Judy scanned the floor for Mike Larew. Would he come, or had he sent someone else?

She had to stay. She had conjecture, loose ends, stray bits of dialogue, homeless deaths. That night the theory faded away and left her with the meat-and-bones finale. She hadn't thought of her own safety up to that point, except in the abstract. It was still a mind game, puzzling a piece of paper taped to wall.

Then it wasn't.

The Trifecta started with a brilliant ten-million-dollar morning, a dealmaker's dream, and ended in an noisy dive in SoMa.

Trifecta, Leg 3, conclusion.

Harry Mach's handsome hangdog face showed confidence, as usual, but his gray eyes were inflected by doubt and hesitation. But you don't flinch in the endgame. That was how you won; you line it up and ram through the deal.

His residual doubts were about who was managing whom. Burt and Wiley: he didn't like thinking about what they could come up with, or had come up with. What did he have on his side? Money, Wiley's address book, bank numbers and passwords, the story of the caper carefully set down and given to Fakir and Studs, and his propositions. He had insurance; the big question was whether anyone would believe it, or whether it would be too late.

He fortified his spirit with a healthy shot of scotch.

Harry rested his chin on his hand and waited. There were many husky people who didn't seem interested in the rage of the Nightshades, and he wondered if they were CIA or FBI or if there was an Algerian or even an assassin in the mix! Burt, he supposed, and Wiley were already inside adjusting their clown masks. Judy Ferris couldn't find them. It was a plus for his side.

A few minutes before midnight, the Nightshades finished their last set—to storm home and beat their mothers?—and gathered their equipment. Part of the crowd drifted away. Music—horrible, weird, cacophonous—drifted over the balcony, providing a fitting accent for the chaos of lights, heat, and air of local disaster which lingered over the dance floor.

A rotund person in a tux with wide shiny lapels strolled into a spotlight, as if he were Joel Gray in Cabaret. He grabbed a microphone and looked at the assembled tables and bar. "Off to the left of the stage behind the curtains is a door." He motioned grandly and drapes parted and a spotlight bloomed on a small door festooned with crêpe paper.

"Through the door," the MC continued, "is the Hive's Labyrinth, which opens at midnight Sunday night. Pay fifty bucks, get two drinks, and party. It's awesome, the awesomest party in Babylon by the Bay."

Hidden lights swept the floor. A drum roll crescendoed. "Let the games begin!"

Some left, but most pumped their fists, shouted, and lined up at the bar. They threw down their fifty bucks, got their first drink, and, still pumping their fists in the air, strode defiantly through the chaos of lights towards the Labyrinth door. Harry, his face etched with thin green, red, and blue laser beams, went to the bar, paid his money, and ordered a double scotch.

While people disappeared in the Labyrinth, balloons floated through the strobes, bursting, hovering, and bouncing. It was their Fourth of July, the punch line, the stripper popping out of the cake.

Harry squared his shoulders and strode across the floor towards the little black door.

At midnight, a cherubic MC emerged from the curtains behind the bandstand. He smiled an ear-to-ear smile and made his pitch. Lasers, balloons, and the doorway. It was black and decorated with crêpe as if it were the entrance to a party in hell.

There was a costume ball queue at the bar and two extra bartenders taking money and giving out drinks. Judy watched the progress of a woman dressed as a ballerina in a pink tutu make her way through the line. She seemed part of a Fellini set, an amalgam of all his films where he worried about life, women and woman, and garish sexual fantasies.

She wondered where that woman went at the end of the night. Did she turn into a school teacher, drop a tab of ecstasy, or just tiredly collapse on her bed and dream about being in a queue in a pink tutu?

Judy watched her turn, wait in line at the black door, and disappear into the Labyrinth. It was Harry's turn. Harry paid his money, got another drink, then strode to the end of the line. He was either very sure of himself or making a great pretense of it.

Judy Ferris patted the pockets of her leather coat to make sure everything was in place. Recorder—she was going to have to practice turning it on and off—camera, pepper spray, the copy of Wiley's address book. Then she got up, kicked a balloon so it swooped up and fell towards the black door, and walked to the bar.

She waited for a few minutes as one of the new bartenders poured drinks for two Labyrinth-goers, then, nodding towards the Labyrinth, said, "How long has this been going on?" The crowd under the dark door made a surging, lopsided delta.

"Couple months," said the bartender. "It could be over tomorrow."

"Another sign of the decline of the West."

The bartender was a big guy, almost as big as Mike with a shaved head and dragon tattoos crawling up his forearms. The bottles stacked behind him shone red from some hidden light; it felt dark and gloomy on her side.

"Want a drink?"

"I've had my quota," Judy said. She looked at the bar top and gathered her courage. "I need whatever wits I have left."

"You sound depressed, lady. What about a water?"

"Confused possibly, not depressed. I'll take a water, thanks."

The bartender uncapped a Perrier and poured it into a large glass with ice and a plump slice of lime. Judy thanked him then picked up her glass and edged onto a barstool. She watched the Labyrinth entrance. She was at another cusp, and at that moment, it felt as if her life were a series of cusps, of halting forays into the outside world and fractured explanations, or a handful of discordant routines. And she supposed that was why she was there. It wasn't just the story, the motive gap, the missing connections; it was finding what little meaning was left.

Judy said, "Have you seen a large red-haired man?"

"Funny you should ask. He was here early. He and this other guy had masks, clown masks. I've always hated clowns. He's a popular guy. Everyone is asking for him."

"Really, who?"

"A tall guy, a curly-headed one. I think it's a surprise party."

Judy said, "But for whom?"

They were all gathering. She knew, more than ever, Wiley was inside. Judy paused, caught again by the immensity of what she planned. Was she ready to sacrifice her life to expose Wiley Brooks? Even if she found him out and wrote a new exposé, what would it accomplish?

It was a long moment. She could have gone back to Corbett Avenue, taken out her money, gone to Vietnam, talked to the ATA. She didn't want to die for a blowing-in-the-wind story. There was a basketful of reasons to leave.

After a few more minutes of wondering about that and watching gaggles of punks, transvestites in stiletto heels, and butterfly costumes stroll in and out of the Labyrinth, she leaned over to the bartender. "I'm a reporter. Mind if I go in for a few minutes?"

"We can always use press. Come over afterwards, and I'll buy you a real drink."

"Maybe," said Judy, smiling. The bartender signaled the guy at the door. Judy glanced at the dance floor, slipped off the bar stool, kicked her way through the balloons, and joined the crowd. A few seconds later, the doorman winked and let her in.

Harry Mach walked uneasily into the Labyrinth. He pretended he had control, but there is only so much you can pretend. He had his ducks in order, but how did they fit with the other ducks? The prize wasn't all about the money; it was knowing he could do it. It was playing a riskier game, the riskiest, and winning. He thought of his father. Would Karl have rolled the dice on this game with all its subterfuge, killings, and torture?

He was in a large room with other rooms spraying off like spokes on a wheel and a long corridor ahead. He was surrounded by more colorful characters in green and red hair and spangles, more nouveau riche dilettantes in joker costumes and masks. It was as if they were at a party of the damned. The music, if it could be called that, was twice as loud as the Nightshades, the lyrics indecipherable.

On his left was a large room filled with partiers. A neon sign announced the Minotaur Room. Labyrinth, Minotaur. Clever.

And on his right, dimly seen through the smoke and crowd, the Theseus Room.

And there a smaller room, the Atreus, where he saw a man in clown mask with a pony-tail sticking out the back.

Harry walked slowly over to the room and went in.

A second man in a clown's mask was standing in back of the table on the right. Red hair cascaded out the back. He had his Lazarus. But Wiley seemed different. He seemed taller, more menacing, and his hair—it was possibly the red light—seemed longer.

There was a valise on the table.

It was the finale, the climax. The movements of Burt flashed before his eyes, Burt the Flunky, the rotator of pistols, the stoned gofer, the re-born chaser of the gold ring.

"Harry," said Burt, looking at him. "I have to hand it to you. It took balls to follow this through. We need the address book, and you get your cut." Burt nodded to the valise.

"A little exchange," Wiley growled. "What could be simpler?"

Harry barely suppressed a laugh.

Burt frowned. "Your hundred grand's in the case. Give us the address book and get out."

"So now you're with Wiley," said Harry. "How you've grown. I half-expected something like that, but I didn't think you were ready."

"C'mon Harry, give us the address book," Burt said menacingly. He reached into his pocket and pulled out the silver gun.

"Déjà vu all over again," said Harry.

"Except this time it's loaded," said Burt. "Care to see?"

"I'm sure it is," said Harry. "Excuse me, Mr. Burt and Mr. Wiley Brooks. I wasn't born yesterday. You've already laid out my cut? Just take it and leave? Bullshit."

Burt hesitated but said, "I didn't use it last time; I will now."

"Certainly not here," said Harry. But at that instant, Harry wasn't sure. Everything he'd done could have been for naught. But he knew people. He knew a second later that he'd injected a sliver of doubt in both of them. "I know a lot more about you both than you think."

"What?" growled Wiley.

The hesitancy he'd felt earlier ebbed. He was on his ground. "I don't trust either one of you. And I don't trust you to the extent that I have documented everything that has happened in this past week. As for Wiley, I knew from the first time we met that you weren't just a dope dealer. I have friends in the Armed Forces, in intelligence, CIA. It's surprising who you meet in the world of moneymaking. I know all about Wiley the CIA interrogator, South America, your mistakes, and this project. As for my friend and accomplice Burt, you were a stoned slacker who bragged to boozy friends and lived in a North Beach SRO. I say "were" because you've grown up fast, perhaps too fast. You are documented as well. Am I getting through to anybody here?"

"Right," said Burt, who looked angry and uneasy at once. He turned to Wiley, and Wiley shrugged. Burt's gun wavered. "What's next?"

"I seriously underestimated you," said Wiley menacingly.

"That's an understatement, Red. You see, I knew about you hours after we met. You're violent and untrustworthy, just right for making money with drugs, and just right to hang out on a limb with this scheme to capture this mythical assassin."

"You fuck," said Wiley.

"Let me finish," said Harry. "The papers implicating you are with two of my friends. They are very good friends. One is an ex-CIA officer. If I don't call one of them in an hour, they send the papers in. They contain, by the way, résumés, photos, a description of the drug deals, and a description of blowing up the mill, and speculation about this ridiculous caper involving assassins and lots of money."

Wiley adjusted his mask and leaned back against the wall. "I sense a proposition."

Harry took a step forward. "Which will benefit you both," he said expansively. "Let's do the numbers. I understand you have between five and seven million for this trade, and I'd guess you're only giving part of it for this assassin. Let's say you take five."

Wiley said, "Your information is—"

"Impeccable," said Harry. "Forget about the four accounts you've set up. I've set up accounts for both of you using an overseas corporation,

251

a blind trust, and a holding company in Nassau. There are details, but you don't need to know them."

"This is crazy," said Burt.

"Shut up," said Wiley.

"Assuming you're going to skim five off the top, I suggest the split is two, three. Two mill for me, three for you, and you can pay off Burt out of your split. I would suggest a hundred thousand. Believe me, it's the most money he'll ever see. You work out the percentages. Tell me tomorrow after you transfer the money into the account I'm going to give you. I'll put it in the accounts I've set up and send you the account numbers and passwords in a few days."

Burt said angrily, "A hundred thousand isn't enough."

"Yes it is," said Wiley. "Too much."

Burt to Harry, "What stops you from taking it all?"

"Because you know where I live. And there's a bonus."

"Better be good," said Burt. "Give."

"I'll launder the money and structure your accounts so you'll receive about ten percent a year. On three mill, it's three hundred grand; on hundred thousand, it's ten thousand. You can both retire to the beach of your choice. As a bonus to Wiley, I'll give you the account number where I've stashed the drug loot. I assume you haven't checked recently, but it's not in the account you put it in."

"You've been busy," said Wiley.

"That's the drug loot minus my hundred grand," said Harry.

"Of course," said Wiley.

"Deal," said Harry.

"I should have talked to you earlier. I can't see how it's not a deal," said Wiley.

Burt said, "I want more than—"

"Later," said Wiley. "You helped me ditch Ferris. Help me with the assassin and your share will go up. As for Harry's deal, I like it. It's one-stop shopping and sets us up for life. And if he doesn't, we know where he lives. There's one thing, Harry."

"Yes?"

"This trade has to go through. I have to show them the assassin or his body. That's my proof; otherwise they hang me out to dry."

Harry nodded. "I know there are contingencies. If there is a problem,

252

call me by six in the morning. I'm flexible; I'm not going to do anything rash."

"I didn't think you would," said Wiley.

"One more point," said Harry, looking directly at Burt. "I didn't think you were ready for tonight, but here you are. If you go ahead, remember this is your gold ring. This is not a fantasy, or bragging in a rag-tag bar. This is your one chance to stay out of a one-room SRO."

Burt smiled, flipped his ponytail, and said, "I can feel the gold ring."

"All right," said Harry. He took out a card with two numbers on it. "Here's the account and the password—transfer the money before six, or call. We don't have to meet again. And now, I believe you have an assassin to catch."

Harry turned and walked slowly towards the door. He paused and turned, frowning. "One more thing," said Harry. "Judy Ferris is here and has a hard-on for exposing you."

"Really," said Wiley. "We'll take care of her."

"Adieu," said Harry.

Harry walked slowly to the door. He was cool outside, shaking inside. His play could have been cut short. Burt was erratic, and Wiley was dangerous. But he had aces in the hole. He had Wiley's account numbers. And he had greed on his side. It was an elegant proposition. As for Judy Ferris, all he said was that she was there. If any harm came to her, it wasn't his fault. Yes, he'd played their game, a tough violent game, the riskiest game.

Trifecta, Leg 3, was within reach.

37

Marant took a last sip of Porto and placed the glass back on the bar. He walked towards the entrance to the Labyrinth. The queue was short; most were already inside.

His stomach felt hollow. This was going to be the last night of his life, or at least one of the worst. He didn't know what to expect, but the last thing he expected was to exchange the number of an account in Switzerland for a new recipe for Semtex. There were too many variables. But it also had to do with Teresa. He'd watched her pay at the bar, shake her head no to a drink, and slip through the small door. Teresa touched something which had been dormant, something about the meaning of revolt, about the meaning of life, and the round shape of a breast. It canceled the straight lethal lines he'd drawn for RM, and for himself.

Marant walked to the small door. He waited a few minutes for the bikers in front of him, then slipped into the Labyrinth. He was in the large room studded with the doors of other rooms. A dim corridor stretched into the distance. It was full of partiers demonic in the red light. He angled his way through the crowds and checked the Theseus room first. Projected images blurred the line between real people and caricature, living body and two-dimensional image. Roaring twenties globes and lasers scattered polka dots and criss-crossed lines over punks, bikers, and a sedate older crowd who were, as one would suspect, reliving youth by proxy.

The music was deafening, the crowds loud and animated and representing all colors of the rainbow. He shouldered his way into the Minotaur room. Reds and yellows danced through the crowds and soon covered Teresa's wide face and were reflected in her dime-size eyes.

She turned, then moved close to him. She touched his hand. "Finally."

"Boris?"

Her hand tightened in his. "Boris is here, and Kafi, too."

"Why is Kafi here?"

"He decided to come at the last minute. Where are we doing the exchange?"

"The Hercules room. It's the last room down the main corridor on the right. It's far enough from the crowds that it will be empty. Kafi said he wasn't coming and came anyway. I don't like that, but there's not much we can do now. You bring Kafi and Boris."

"I never thought we'd get this far," said Teresa.

The crowds and light diffused their goal. How could they find anything real in the chaos? And how real was a non-existent formula for a non-existent explosive? How real was Teresa? The words were hollow, as

254

if spoken by someone else. "It's been a crooked path," he whispered.

She cupped her hand over his ear and said, "Let's hope it's straight now." Teresa backed up and looked at him strangely. The more he looked at her, the smaller she became. For the first time, he felt that she knew their mission was hopeless.

He waited for Teresa to angle through the crowd, then he left. He walked along the Labyrinth corridor and saw, as he'd suspected, that the crowds thinned away from the entrance. Couples occupied several of the smaller rooms, and in one room three people hunched over thin white lines. It was strange, he thought, what we do to ourselves...to forget, or to change. Our bodies sought a state of rest, and our minds were in constant agitation.

Marant slipped into the Jason room across the corridor from the Hercules room. That night a light bulb covered with a Chinese lantern allowed enough light to see but kept the room dark. The walls of the room were encased in billowy dark drapes, which may have hidden windows. Drafts occasionally disturbed the surface of the curtains and made waves that crested into nothing.

Marant retrieved the Walther PK and silencer he'd left high on the speaker. He screwed the silencer on and put the gun inside his jacket.

He flipped out his cell and called Christian.

"We intercepted one of the plotters. GIA, IG, Hezbollah, and a handful of recruits have already started a purge," Christian said. "I suspected, of course, but...but this damn explosive! They intend to find me, torture me for the accounts, and take over our supplies, contacts, routes."

"This project?" said Marant, tendrils of fear snaking around his heart. If Christian were tortured, they would know about Marant Olivier. He'd never be safe.

"Designed to neutralize you. Gino thinks Kafi is selling you to the Americans."

"The delays," Marant muttered. He shifted the phone to his other ear. Automatically, his eyes lowered in concentration. The drawn-out killing of the winos. He'd felt it that week. The arranged explosion, the winos—they must all be killed, Kafi said—Kafi and Wiley Brooks in Union Square. Everyone had played roles in a murderous drama. It made sense once you supplied the missing ingredient: timing a purge.

"I have allies, but I don't know about RM. We've talked about it being an artifact. If nothing else, this will change who we are."

"It was inevitable," said Marant.

"When you come back, you'll help me."

"If I come back," said Marant. "Whose side is Teresa on?"

"I don't know," said Christian. "Good luck, my friend. I've sent..."

"What?"

The line was dead. Marant snapped off the cell.

The room felt like a tomb. The possibilities for that night had narrowed quickly. If he was captured, he saw a life of torture, bad food, and small antiseptic cells. At that point, it looked like the fugu pills would claim another victim. He felt a moment of rage, which he quickly controlled. Rage was a useless emotion where survival was the issue. If he could get from that door past Kafi and Boris to the Labyrinth door he would have a chance. If he could get from the Labyrinth door to the second floor, he had a better chance. His odds improved as he descended, but might get worse outside.

He scanned the crowd at the other end of the corridor, then not seeing anyone, glided out of the room. He was at the edge of the Minotaur room, when Teresa and Kafi exited from the Theseus room in front of two men in clown masks. The large man must be Boris/Wiley. Teresa, worried, glanced behind her, then at Wiley Brooks.

She saw him and looked straight ahead.

At that moment, he knew she knew the plot was a ruse. And she protected him.

Marant slipped into the Minotaur Room.

38

The Labyrinth was an expressionist nightmare. Judy took off her dark glasses. Garish red light, walls covered in grinning satyrs, malevolent Cyclops, Hydras, and toothy hell birds. They were distinct, but warped, globular, bloody. It was part Hades, part Christian Hell, a hothouse fever, an acid trip in a melting, hostile world. The spiked-hair punks, spangled bikers, smirking yuppies, and show-offs of every sexual stripe—all seemed part of it, each one a kaleidoscope of melting colors, knives, and chains. And the drugs were inside, a spiritual parallel of the multicolored skin chaos. There were happy-dopey smiles, snuffling coke snorters, doomed vacant-eyed meth addicts, and smack freaks going down, down, down.

She thought she saw Wiley in the Theseus Room and anger boiled up, then subsided. Maybe it was the colors, but she began to feel that anything real, anything she thought important was being sucked into a big red happening machine. The light made a lot of people redheaded.

Judy Ferris felt antsy, light to her stomach. She was in a no man's land, part parody, part not, trying to feel her way towards something real. But underneath the leather and the dark glasses, she felt she was looking for meaning in a country with too many enemies or unknowns. And even there, deep in what she hoped would be the finale of her story, she couldn't help thinking of Mike. They were connected by invisible character threads. Had she mistaken irony for cynicism, affection for acting, energy for brutality?

Was he Hero or just another Labyrinth Monster?

Judy wandered into the Minotaur Room and elbowed her way through a dense mass of revelers, a swaying mass of skewed arms and dripping faces frozen every few seconds by a cobalt strobe. She scrutinized people when she saw them, but so far when she looked beyond the makeup, she'd only seen slack faces or happy ones.

She saw a tall man who looked different, possibly European. He was talking to a small woman, who scanned the room nervously. Judy moved into deep shadow of a hanging speaker. The small woman ducked into the crowd, emerged near the door, skirted a group of skinheads chugging longnecks, then disappeared.

The tall man followed.

Judy had a hunch and followed him. When she got to the corridor, they had disappeared. She started down the corridor. Halfway down she saw the partially open door to a smaller room. Through the cracked door, she saw two men in clown masks. Masks. She saw, or thought she saw, Wiley's red hair, and she saw the ponytail. She rolled the dice and stepped inside. They both looked up.

She couldn't detect any expression under those masks. They both stared at her, the black holes of the masks burning into her. Judy felt the culmination of the week, of her quest. She snapped the recorder on.

Burt said, "Harry was right."

Judy ignored Burt. "The elusive Wiley Brooks," Judy said. Her right hand fumbled inside her jacket, felt the Mace, then the camera.

"Wiley's dead," the big man said. "And will stay dead!"

"National Dope Deals? National Rip-offs. You faked suicide, killed Leonard Marsh, and murdered three homeless people. Fuck national security, and fuck your idiotic partner."

Burt snarled, "Let's kill the crazy bitch."

Burt reached into his pocket, but Wiley stopped him. "Not here." He strode towards her.

Judy felt her legs freeze; she was rooted to the floor, mesmerized.

Wiley was five feet away, when she woke up.

She whipped the camera out, turning it on at the same time. The lens zoomed, then retracted. She closed her eyes and pressed the button. The flash exploded in red-edged darkness and etched Wiley and Burt's shadows on the wall.

"Fuck."

Judy opened her eyes and watched as Wiley staggered towards her. Judy raced into the corridor. She clicked the camera off and tucked it back inside her jacket. She snapped the recorder off and headed back to the entrance.

She ducked into the Minotaur room.

She hugged the wall, put on her dark glasses, and hid in an alcove with a ragged group of bikers passing a joint. Smoke obscured faces distorted with strobes, globes, and masks.

Burt slipped by the entrance. Wiley stopped, scanned the room, and loped in. He seemed taller than she remembered, and his long arms ended in hands splayed like claws. She turned up the collar on her leather jacket. Then she huddled with the dope smokers. An oily hand passed her a joint. She took the joint and bent over it making a show of inhaling. Wiley's mask scanned their group, hesitated, and passed on.

She backed against the wall, flipped the recorder on, and recited what she'd seen and what was happening. Two of the bikers glanced at her, but quickly went back to their joint.

She waited a beat before starting for the door. She took a step away from the wall, when the tall man came into the room. He passed their group. Then he glided along the walls and slipped out of the room.

Deafening shots froze everyone in the room.

The bikers broke up and hustled towards the doorway.

She followed them to the door of the Minotaur room. Outside, she saw that the door to the Labyrinth was tight with people trying to get out. Beyond the heads of the people she saw the tall man dip down. She glanced down the corridor and saw four people on the ground. One was dressed in street clothes, the others in costumes. Blood spread over the floor like an oil slick.

The front of the Labyrinth was a mob scene. All those people stretched thin on dope, or coke, or smack, panicked, clawing past each other, screaming, yelling as if they were being attacked. For a brief moment, she saw that impossible scene as the end of the world.

She calmed down. Call 911. She pulled out her cell, flipped it on, and squinted at the readout. No signal.

"Shit." She closed the cell and glanced hurriedly around her. She wasn't getting out the front. She scanned the corridor for Wiley and forced her way through two bikers back into the Minotaur room. She hurried towards the other entrance. She looked out into the corridor. To her right towards the entrance, men bent over four people spread on the ground. To her left, the corridor was empty.

She started down the corridor. Strobes, lasers, and red lights flashed and glowed in empty rooms. She got past the first empty room. She had almost reached the exit, when a hand snapped out of a shadow and caught her on the side of the jaw. As she fell, she looked into a hideous warp-nosed mask and Burt's angry red eye.

Marant kept to the right of the Minotaur room. On his left, revelers danced, rock music blared, and a cobalt strobe splattered the room with steely balls of light. He reached the far entrance of the room, waited for a group of four young men in tank tops to exit.

As he exited, he glanced back down the corridor. As he guessed, they had discovered he was not in the Hercules room and were looking for him. Kafi, two masked men, Teresa, and several others marched towards him in a tight group. A masked man yelled at Kafi, and Kafi, in a sweeping gesture, grabbed Teresa from behind, pulled out a knife, and held it at her throat. Kafi whispered to her, and she stopped struggling.

Panic overwhelmed him. She would die; he would be captured. His aim, his age, the chaos of lights, meant any shot would have to be straight, the straightest of his life. A line like a laser. He would likely hit Teresa.

He hesitated for a moment longer, then pulled out the Walther and yelled Kafi's name.

Kafi squinted through the crowds, relaxing the knife on Teresa's throat. Marant aimed an inch to the right of Teresa's cheek.

He fired. The bullet found a straight path through the crowd, zipped several inches from a Rastafarian nose, and bored through Kafi's left eye. Kafi's knife trembled then dropped. Teresa jerked away as he fell. The two masks, possibly Wiley and his friend, pulled out guns and sprayed shots at him, but hit people in front of them. Two bikers, puzzled, tumbled to the ground.

Teresa disappeared. He didn't have time to find her. He hated to leave her, but his impulse was to get away. He tucked the gun away and fought his way through the entrance. People were rushing the stairs, and the bartender stared at them, uncomprehending. Marant walked to the bartender and said loudly, "Several people have been shot inside."

Two husky men in the corners flared their jackets and ran towards the entrance of the Labyrinth, but had trouble getting through the crush at the door. The bartender snatched up the phone. Marant walked quickly across the dance floor, but he turned and regarded the Labyrinth entrance. He should go back; then both would be captured.

Marant stood to the side as men rushed upstairs. He walked quickly down. On the second floor landing, Marant snapped open the cell and dialed 911. "My name is Wiley Brooks. There is a fire in the Hive disco at Eighth and Folsom. At least one person has been hurt. Hurry."

As he turned towards the second-floor fire exit, there was a scream, and the third-floor lights went out. Marant frowned, but hurried towards the open door. Two women worried, looked past him, and held their cigarettes up to let him pass. Marant walked through the gap they'd left.

Marant's footsteps made tinny sounds on the rusted rungs of the fire escape. When he reached the ground, a distant siren split the night air. Marant strode towards a distant alley.

He heard a jumble of tinny sounds.

A voice yelled, "Dead or alive. Dead is better."

Marant glanced over his shoulder and saw two men, one a hulking form in a hideous clown mask, jump off the fire escape and lope towards him.

The alley was a long block away, coned with streetlights. Marant ran a jagged pattern towards the first street light. In the cone of light, bullets slapped the pavement ahead of him.

He couldn't turn and shoot.

More shadow. It was odd, he thought, in that race, light was death, and darkness life.

The pain woke her up. She was being dragged upstairs by the collar of her jacket. Her butt and legs bounced off the steps.

Burt screamed, "My big break. No one fucks this up...no one."

Judy's head throbbed. She was going to die. It made her mad; adrenalin rushed through her body. She dug in the side of her jacket with her bruised right hand and found the Mace.

"...a busybody...never thought I'd ever kill anyone, all pretend...until tonight...first time for everything. Money, sweet money. White beach, girls, mai tais. No fantasy. It's yours, Burt."

Burt adjusted his grip.

She dug her feet into the back of the steps. Burt pulled her, but she'd stopped his forward motion. She stepped into a half-crouch. She wrenched her coat away from his hand, turned sideways, and sprayed where she thought his mask was.

She heard a scream. Some of it must have leaked past the eyeholes.

"Fuck...what the fuck...fuck."

She turned and saw Burt's frame in the red glow from the fire exit light, the mask stuck out like a grotesque hand. Burt clawed at his mask. She aimed at the mask eyeholes and squirted again. She edged past his groping hand and raced towards the exit. She grabbed the exit door handle and wrenched it open. A siren screamed through the Labyrinth.

"Bitch...I'll rip your eyes out."

She started down the fire escape but saw that it stopped fifty feet from the litter-filled ground. She had a moment of supreme panic. It was too far.

Burt lurched towards the door. Then she saw the ladder to the roof.

She jumped for the ladder. It slid past her. She scrambled up.

Burt burst onto the landing. "Where the fuck are you? Goddamn it."

Judy counted one rung, two, three. Her body was shaking. Six more. Five more.

"There you are."

Burt fumbled inside his jacket and she stopped, pointed the Mace at him again, and sprayed down continuously for three seconds. The cloud fell slowly and wrapped itself around Burt's mask.

"Ahhgg...ahhgg. Fuck."

Burt took out a silver gun and aimed it up the ladder. Judy grabbed the thin railing, twined her foot in the rungs, and swung out over the yard below. Her arm felt it was holding the world up. Three bullets dug craters in the concrete between the rungs. His next shot was wild.

"Fuck, fuck." Burt ripped the mask off and rubbed at his eyes. His ponytail jerked wildly.

Judy heaved herself back, rested a split second, then scrambled up two, three, four rungs.

She was a rung from the stop. She felt Burt was aiming at her and swung out once again to her right. Two more bullets slapped the wall.

Burt bellowed again as Mace trickled from his forehead to his eyes. She swung back, grabbed the last rung, and scrambled up and over the top. When she collapsed on the roof, she heard another shot carom off the fire escape.

She saw the curved handrails of a fire escape on the far side. Too far. There was a door in the middle of the roof, but she was sure it was locked. She looked at the rung in front of her.

She held the Mace in front of her and leaned over the edge. A hand shot out and grabbed her jacket. The Mace went caroming off into space. Burt's hand twined in her jacket.

She pulled back. Burt didn't have leverage. She wrenched her jacket away from him.

Burt screamed, "You fuck!"

Burt's anguished face appeared squarely between the curved rusty handrails. His mouth twitched into a sneer. He grasped the other rail with his other hand. In a split second he would be on the roof.

Judy watched him disinterestedly. Women gave in. Women were encompassing; they didn't fight. They nurtured. Burt was the type she'd railed about for years. Opaque power fantasists, testy testosterone, boys in men's bodies.

She stepped towards Burt. He was surprised, then he reached for her. She punched his arm aside and kicked him hard in the head and made his ponytail whip into the air. The blow stunned him, then his body came back from the hit. He grabbed at her. She waited, clinically, punched his hand away again, and kicked him hard in the face. She could see he was bleeding.

"Fuck...my money..."

He reached for the gun he'd put in his pocket, and she smashed him in his nose.

Burt gurgled, whipped his head from side to side. He swung out to his right, his left hand flailing. At the furthest extent of the swing, she jammed her boot on his fingers.

She felt the crunch, then she saw his fingers clench spasmodically, then open.

"Fuck...no...no."

She looked over the edge. He hit the railing on the landing below, then caromed off into space. He seemed suspended in the air, as if he'd performed an act of levitation. Then his hands clawed the air, and he fell into a bin where light reflected off a thousand broken bottles. An anguished shriek split the night air.

Burt, bloodied, his neck twisted, his ponytail splayed out behind him, lay Christ-like in the middle of the bin.

His body convulsed, shivered, collapsed.

Marant was at the last cone of light. He felt a bite in his leg. The pain didn't stop him. Shots ricocheted off the pavement on his left and right. Marant dashed into the alley. He was close. One more turn, a second. The taxi stand. He'd angle towards Market Street.

There was the beach at Fort Mahon, the lingering images of his parents arm-in-arm, the sand, the treacherous rivulets snaking through the sand...there was the form, the roundness; lines fell like scales from his eyes...

Teresa. They would torture her, terrorize her. They would make her an animal, again. Marant shuddered. Ahead were the straight lines of escape, this way, that way.

He turned back, exited the alley.

One of the men chasing him lay clumped up on the ground halfway to the Hive.

Boris/Wiley faced him.

Was he face to face with an assassin? CIA? Opposite sides, same work.

Wiley said, "Finally, face to face. The big bad assassin."

"It was some game," said Marant. "Overall interesting, clumsy in execution."

"You're my ticket. Dead or alive. I think it would be better dead."

Marant pivoted around Wiley's long gangling arm and gripped him by the throat.

Wiley punched him hard in his stomach.

Marant doubled over, and Wiley hit him hard in the face.

Marant went with the blow and dug his elbow into Wiley's exposed side.

Marant realized he couldn't win. He was too old, too tired, too used.

Wiley grabbed him by the back of the neck and twisted. Marant felt the pain and knew he would soon black out and die.

Suddenly Wiley released him.

Another man had grabbed Wiley. There was a struggle, an epic struggle against the encroaching chaos of that night, against the backdrop of dark alleys, cones of light, and the Hive looming in the night.

Wiley unsheathed an assassin's knife, camouflaged, serrated. The knife raised, hand grasped wrist. A bone cracked, then another. The mystery attacker held Wiley up with a muscular hand, twisted the knife, and shoved the knife up into Wiley's throat. Blood gushed out, spraying. Wiley's knees buckled; he fell back and landed hard on the street.

The man crouched over Wiley and removed the mask. He looked closer at Wiley, felt Wiley's red hair, and yanked off a wig.

The mystery attacker said. "Not Wiley. A man in a mask and a wig." He looked up at Marant. "Vite, Marant."

264

Marant, stunned, stammered, "Qui—"

"Michel. Le fils de Christian. Un peu pas tardé."

Marant glanced at the Hive. "Teresa."

"In the car," Michel said. "I grabbed her when I blew the lights. She wasn't easy to convince. I took her out the front. Vite."

Michel grabbed his arm and propped him up as they hurried towards the all-night taxi stand. A hundred feet short of the stand, Michel turned up another alley.

Michel stopped at an anonymous white car. The motor was running. Teresa was inside, her broad face tear-stained, her quarter-sized brown eyes stunned. Marant opened the door and slid onto the driver's seat. He looked at Michel, as if to ask why.

"I'm your redundancy."

"He never told me," said Marant. "Why you?"

"Besides you, I was the only one he trusted."

"Will he be all right? RM?"

"Christian needs both of us. RM won't survive as RM."

"I felt that," said Marant, sadly.

"There will be something else," said Michel. "There always is."

"Perhaps."

Marant wasn't sure what happened, but his control of risky actions in this ephemeral world had been passed to another like a baton in a race. A few minutes ago, he'd felt old, exhausted, spent, ready to die. An immense stone had been lifted from his back, as if he were Atlas, or Sisyphus, condemned to either hold up the world or roll it endlessly up a steep hill.

He took Teresa's hand.

He embraced the curve.

Judy Ferris became aware of several things at once. Sirens. Gunshots. She looked at Burt sprawled in the bin, then walked slowly towards the other fire escape. She didn't feel remorse, but something different, something she would have to spend time with. She stopped when she got to the other fire escape. There were shots, cries, and shadows moving and dodging in the streets and alleys north of the Hive.

That fire escape went down to the second-floor landing. She crawled down and stepped onto the landing. A crowd of people hung over the rail. They were pointing at a body in a cone of light down the alley. Fire and police sirens rent the air.

She climbed down the fire escape carefully. Ground. It felt as if she'd been floating for hours, or had just gotten off a boat after a nauseous trip. A fire truck careened down Folsom Street and wheeled up to the front of the Hive.

What to do? She hadn't thought of the ramifications of what she'd done, but she was in as deep as she could get. She didn't forget why she was there. She turned on her tape recorder and began recording everything she'd seen and was seeing.

She walked like a zombie towards the body. She approached it tentatively. There were more shots fired. The man looked dead; a thin trail of blood leaked out of his mouth. She waved at the first fireman who appeared at the entrance to the Hive. He hurried over to her, and she left him to work on what was probably a dead man.

It was a moonlit night, and the shadows, artificial light, and moonlight dappled a handful of alleys that spun out in front of her. She didn't know what was up ahead, but she guessed it wasn't what she expected.

She walked tentatively into the first alley. She hadn't been that foolhardy since El Salvador, but it felt right. Police sirens converged on the Hive. Soon she would have to stop, go back, figure out what she was going to tell the police. She stopped at the first alley.

It was the man in the mask, Wiley, with a knife in his throat.

But it wasn't Wiley.

The mask was off, a wig spread over the ground like a grotesque flower.

She felt numb, blasted. She turned to call the firemen when, a few blocks away, she saw a big dark-haired man watching a white car turn the corner. She hurried up, trying to hug the shadows. The man she'd seen at the bar and the smallish woman were in the car.

But her attention was riveted on the fey figure who watched them. Mike Larew.

He turned, saw her. They exchanged stunned stares, then he smiled a gruff smile.

She said, "How did you get here?"

"I was here all night."

She clicked off the tape recorder. "I killed someone."

"Good. Let's go," he said, taking her arm.

She gestured towards the dead man, stunned. "It's not Wiley."

"I know," he said, moving her along swiftly.

"But what was it about?"

"You said yourself, they'll always have an answer."

She let herself be led around the corner. A police car approached them and she almost called out to it, but she let it speed past them. Mike saw a cab going in the opposite direction. He signaled it. The cab made a U-turn and came to rest at their side.

Judy felt lost. She'd chased a chimera; there was no resolution. Except, except.

For the first time, she glanced at the night sky. The stars were stuck in heavens like diamond pins, and moon glow covered the earth. A soft wind caressed her face as if it were the hand of a night sprite.

She was alive.

"I'm not sure I care about Wiley, and don't know if I want to know more about who you are or what you've done," she said, glancing at Mike as she got in cab.

"I don't know if I can tell you."

39

Mike had the driver drop them two blocks from her house. He was different in black, an underworld creature, tense, focused. He scanned both sides of the street, then walked slowly up the west side of Corbett. She understood. There had been death that night, Burt and a Wiley Brooks stand-in, and the escape or death of an assassin. It was unreal, as if determinedly humdrum, staid, curvy Corbett Avenue with its boutique houses and vistas had become an ominous place of stealth and death.

There was less grace to Mike's movements than sureness, as if he knew this country and had lived in it for a long time.

Mike flattened himself on the ground and squinted under the Mazda, then he scrambled to the front and popped the hood. He dropped the hood back into place.

He walked towards her, concern biting lines in his pockmarked face.

"What are you doing?" she said, although she'd guessed.

"Making sure," he said. "Keys?"

She found the keys wedged under the tape recorder, drew them out, and dropped them in his cupped hand. Burt was dead, the roof, the struggle, flailing arms, a bin of jagged edges. That image would haunt her. The grasping hand, raised boot, the snarling hate would cycle back in nightmares and waking things like watering plants, sipping coffee, driving, writing a story.

Her story: it seemed further away than ever. She held Mike's arm. "The guy who worked with Harry Mach chased me, and I killed him."

"That makes you more than a reporter."

"Don't make fun of me," she said angrily.

"You did what you had to."

"What about Wiley? Where is he? Who was the guy in the wig?"

Mike shrugged. "I don't know. Wiley might be more than a killer; perhaps he's a storied figure one hears about, a myth, a symbol."

"They'll always be a Wiley," Judy said grimly. "We breed them here."

"And Judys. You're doomed to an infernal chase."

Mike opened the door and moved inside like a shadow. She sensed, rather than saw, Mike move to her bedroom. Then he was in the hallway, the living room.

He reappeared at the door. "Okay."

She stepped inside and shut the door. She wasn't sure what to say. She hadn't exposed Wiley, and she'd killed Burt. She was supposed to monitor and report. She left Mike in the living room. She felt the heaviness of the tape recorder in her jacket, took it out, and laid it next to the PC. She struggled out of the jacket and draped it over the PC chair.

She realized she was shaking. Bathroom. Mirror, mirror. She looked drawn, harried, black and blue. Her back and legs hurt. There were scrapes under her neck.

She walked slowly into the kitchen, found vodka, and poured an inch into a Mexican art glass. She took it into the living room, let herself down into the sofa, propped her boots on the table, and took a stiff drink. The vodka burned, then made her feel airy. Hive booze, adrenalin, death. She was surprised she was conscious.

Mike stood off to the right of the window, but she could make out his features in reflection. He was a large, tough man with brooding eyebrows, rounded butched hair, rounded butched beard. She interpolated his pockmarks, his too-soft brown eyes.

"I'd better leave," he said, into the window.

"We've been through that. Mike Larew, yo-yo."

Mike turned, grinned, then got somber. He walked over, sat near her, and propped a black tennis shoe on the table. He should have been at ease but wasn't.

"Can you tell me who was in the car?" she said finally.

"No."

He might have meant it. "You don't have to. It was probably Marant Olivier."

Mike shook his head. "It was Marant. So what?"

She felt her mouth purse. "You led me away from Wiley Friday night."

"If it was Wiley. My guess is that it was, and he got a stand-in tonight to avoid direct exposure. Who knows where he is, now? I don't really care."

"Why not?"

"He was a side show, a deadly one. The whole of last week was about smoke, mirrors, and timing. The timing was tonight."

"That makes you on what side?"

Mike frowned, as if he were picking through the events of the last week, then he shook his head. "You see America as an eight hundred-pound gorilla stomping on insurgent movements everywhere. You want me to be on America's side. Is that the right side?"

"America is the right side," she said finally, "but has lousy policies based on fear."

"That's not bad but still contradictory. You were right about most of it," he said. He pointed to the sheet tacked a few feet above the tape recorder. It looked fragile from that perspective, like the last leaf on a bare tree.

269

Judy said, "I know Wiley had two deals, one dope, the other this CIA thing."

Mike leaned into the cushions. "I wasn't sure about the dope part. I am sure about the CIA project, but not about whether Wiley was managing it. We were looking from the outside, and inside people were changing identities like clothes."

"How did you find Wiley, or the faux Wiley? You said you saw him in Tully's."

"I followed one of RM's agents. When he met Wiley, I followed him. I had Wiley, but I didn't know what was going on. He didn't look like a chemist."

"Wiley was supposed to be a chemist?"

"That was the story."

She could tell he was tired, that he may have killed people. He'd told her more but deflected her question about whose side he was on. She did know he was a man, that he had a good heart, that sometimes we do things against our nature.

"Thanks," she said finally. "I suppose you can't tell me anymore."

Mike shrugged. "A fake explosive, an old assassin, a moronic trap were incidental. In the end, it was about a power struggle inside RM."

She thought about what Wiley had done, the winos, the trap. "So Wiley..."

"If he was truly pulling the strings, was either a pawn himself, or playing everyone else. He wasn't in the Labyrinth, so if there was money, he has it. Mike frowned as if were wondering what that meant. "Everyone thinks they're manipulating everyone else."

"What about Wiley? I'll never get him out of my head."

"He was dead a week ago," said Mike. "He dove off the bridge. Remember?"

Judy frowned. "What?"

"That will be their answer."

"You think so?"

"You should know by now that they always do. I wish we could argue more," said Mike. He touched her hair, then drew her close to him.

"Can we sleep with someone we don't know?" she said plaintively.

"You did and don't regret it."

"I'm asking so many questions. Just stay a little longer."

"I will."

She moved over, touched the nearest pockmark with her finger. He was vulnerable; he felt for her, cared. It was a conundrum that we all start out fresh and warm and happy, or at least curious, and we end up fighting, killing, and tearing at each other. She leaned her head on his shoulder. Maybe sleeping with the enemy was a way to erase the hatred.

Harry Mach spent a restless night. Twice he got up. He nervously checked the bank account for Wiley's transfer. No go. When he finally opened his eyes at 5:30, he regarded the crisp sunlight barring his covers, dust rising, for a few seconds before getting out of bed. He threw on his robe and hurried to the dining room table.

Harry stared at his phone. No messages. No message from Studs or Fakir. No money. Something had gone seriously wrong.

Harry surfed to the Chronicle online.

Shooting at the Labyrinth. Worst crime scene in decades, multiple deaths, two people dead in clown masks. One was Bertram "Burt" Wormley...the other, unnamed, was obviously Wiley Brooks. No women. He guessed Judy Ferris got out intact.

Tough luck, Burt. You would have been better off puffing joints, throwing back lite beers, and regaling buds with your fantasies.

Harry sighed. Whither his Trifecta? All his precautions, all his documents, and all his planning. Fakir, Studs, multiple overseas accounts. He had the dope money. He supposed that was a victory. Trifecta lite.

He felt incomplete. It wasn't just the torpedoed deal, and it wasn't just the money. He'd tasted the risk he'd been seeking. It was the adrenalin surge. It beat everything he was doing. It beat making ten million bucks in the market. It beat everything hands down. It felt incredible. It felt like the biggest orgasm he'd ever had. He had to do it again, but he wasn't sure how. Studs?

Harry walked dispiritedly into the living room.

"Hi, Harry."

Harry's heart lodged in his spine. Harry knew the voice. He stared at the tall, muscular figure with cascading red hair outlined in the living room window. "Wiley."

"You played an excellent game. There were a few loose ends, such as

Fakir and Studs, but you don't have to worry about them."

"Fakir? Studs? What..."

Wiley strode up to him. "You're a player, Harry. We're going to work well together."

Harry stared at Wiley. "Together?"

Wiley put his hand around his shoulder and propelled him towards the dining room. "First, let's straighten out these bank accounts."

San Francisco was having a summer day of clean, hot weather, and the tourists who knew about the two summers which sandwiched the usual one, were enjoying a real vacation without hordes of their compatriots. Some probably walked out on the hook of Aquatic Park and turned and videotaped the city, perhaps a sunset, perhaps a cacophonous swirl of gulls fighting over a starfish or a crab thrown on the pavement by fishermen. Some would likely shake their heads at the pirate gulls and have passing thoughts about nature and congratulate themselves on being Homo sapiens, a civilized species.

Judy Ferris, that day, watched for a few minutes not a gull, but a hawk, a red-tailed hawk most likely, spiraling higher and higher on a noonday thermal as if it were going to cycle through the biosphere into the thin regions of space. Finally the hawk became an eyelash and winked out, leaving a gold disk glued to the blue sky.

Judy had just crossed the California Central Valley and was starting to climb the Sierras east of Sacramento. Sometimes she sang, but mostly she was silent, shrouded in thought. Often, she thought of the future, of the remote cabin in the Desolation Wilderness, of her own ultimate spiritual destination. Then sometimes she thought of that night at the Hive.

Whenever she did that, she thought of Mike Larew.

She was awake most of his last night. They made love, not like the first night, which was full of the awkwardness of passion, but slowly, surely. Then, while he slept, she tried to weld into her mind the bed sheet peaks, the intimate hollow between his neck and shoulder, the fluid roughness of his black beard and hair, the position of pockmarks, a large one towards his jaw line, smaller ones washing across his cheek.

She drifted off but awoke when he got up. She watched him dress

272

with his quick, sure hands and saw a scar, which she had seen but not remarked, on his back. He tried to be stealthy, but nude, she caught him at the door.

It was drafty, dark. His body bulked over her. She could barely see his face. She held his jacket with her fingers. "You have to leave."

Mike pulled her close, and she leaned against him. They stayed like that for a few moments in front of the closed door, as if that were his answer. It meant that yes he had to go, but didn't want to. She needed more. "Why?"

"Responsibilities," he said. "Europe."

"Come back, if you can," she said, leaning into him, looking in his face.

"We'll see." His eyes were tired. He kissed her. "Go away, let things settle down."

"If you were with me—"

"Not this time." He opened the door. She felt a rush of cold air and shivered. He scanned the street, dipped his head, and kissed her quickly. And was gone.

She turned and walked slowly to the bedroom, got in bed, and pulled the covers over her head, as if she were hiding. She knew she couldn't sleep, but did. When she awoke, her magician was gone, like the first night. The snapshot views of the bay, the rustling curtains, her succulents. Three nights weren't enough.

Bathroom. The mirror, rimmed with pressed flowers and porcine Columbian women showed her a bruised Judy Ferris. The right side was yellowing with darker hints of hematomas. The green eyes weren't astute or probing. She wasn't resigned, just tired.

She made coffee, lit a cigarette, stared briefly out the living room window, then walked between the kitchen and the patio and the living room, remembering last night, all they'd said in the last week, all they'd done, how he was special.

Finally, she got serious. She was in trouble, serious trouble. Police, fire trucks, wounded or dead people on the floor of the Labyrinth, Burt lying in a rusty bin of broken, jagged glass. Mike watching a cab scoot off into the night. Partly, she hoped Mike was right about everything being covered up, but wasn't she trying to expose cover-ups?

She turned on the radio. The report was about shootings, death, and violence at the Hive, a SoMa disco. It was likely, according to the police, a drug deal gone wrong. Last night, she felt Corbett Avenue, her apartment, had become strange and alien. That day, facing police, lawyers—jail?—she was reassured by its ordinariness. She took her phone and coffee to the patio, gritted her teeth, and punched out Valentine's number. After being passed around, he came on the line.

Judy said, "I was at the Hive last night."

"In the thick of it. Why were you there?"

"Do you want me to come in?"

"You'd confuse things. We have fifty eyewitnesses with contradictory stories already. What were you doing there?"

She told him she'd heard about Wiley being at the Hive.

"You're seeing this guy everywhere. As far as I know, he wasn't there. I've got six dead inside and outside the Hive, one in a red wig, one in a bin full of glass, a couple bikers, and an Algerian drug dealer. It's a fucking mess. The Hive is one of our worst crime scenes."

She wasn't going to insist about Burt. "Remember the homeless who died?"

"Winos? Come on. Two of them were lifestyle deaths; the third died in a drug deal."

"Drugs, drugs, drugs. The universal explanation."

"If it ain't there, lady, it ain't there."

"Thanks, Bernie."

She threw the phone on the table. No complicity, no crime. No body, no nothing. She should have felt a sense of relief, but her story was left hanging in the wind, like the scrap of paper over her PC. How could she write a story at all? She'd have to leave out what she'd done, what Mike had done, Wiley Brooks.

She mooned around her apartment most of the morning and had too many mugs of coffee and way beyond her allotment of cigarettes. Finally, she called Joan Kelly, a reporter at the Examiner. She gave Joan her eyewitness account of what happened at the Labyrinth, leaving out several important moments, such as her rooftop fight with Burt and Mike Larew. Joan said they'd pretty it up and use it in the afternoon edition.

Despite her injuries and the residual trauma of last night, Judy felt momentum. Judy called Myra. They had already crossed and re-crossed the line of what Myra was willing to give her. No, Wiley wasn't involved.

But there might have been an aborted exchange.

What about Harry? She felt she should find out for closure, but she didn't. Burt was dead, and Wiley was dead or sipping mai tais on some beach.

Her story had huge holes in it but late in the afternoon, she tore the Wiley sheet down, sat in front of the PC, and tapped it out. El Salvador, fear, a CIA hoax, Potato, Sugar, Scab—our peasants in an undeclared war. The motive might be personal, but she could still be a witness.

She roughed out and plugged in details from Myra, Mike, and Harry Mach. She flipped on her tape recorder and listened to her recounting of what happened at the Hive. She thumbed Harry's copy of Wiley's address book. Wiley rooked backers in a drug deal. Wiley disappeared. Wiley killed winos in a brainless CIA plot to trap an assassin. She hinted Wiley was at the Hive and had escaped, once again. She wasn't even sure it was lie. They told big ones; all she could do was speculate. She left out Mike Larew, phantom, the tall man, the short woman.

There were loose ends. So what? Loose ends were cinched up in novels, not life. She had loose ends, but she'd cauterized a few when she typed out her punch line about the need for a rigorous and independent civilian oversight of the CIA, of changes in policy, of closing the School of the Americas. That was her quixotic conclusion, but the real punch line was implicit. It was about American arrogance, or was it human fear and arrogance?

She put the final touches on her story and sent it off to editors at the New York Times and Washington Post and also sent a query to Esquire. If they didn't take it, it didn't matter. She was upbeat and full of life, a lot more full of life than a week ago.

That night she was sitting alone, getting moody, sipping a Bloody Mary and watching the lights of the East Bay flickering like fireflies, when she realized she had to get away. Mike had said as much as he rushed out of her life. She thought about going to Napa; she had paid for October. But Bob and Khris had decided to go back, and she needed quiet time.

She rented a cabin in the Sierras near Tahoe, which she'd used before. The next day she bought supplies at the local fruit and vege market, made up her backpack, and had the Mazda oiled and greased. Before she knew it, she was tracking away from the fog down Corbett's winding hills and not much later winding through the East Bay hills and the sunny Central Valley.

As she steered through the barren, brown Sierra foothills down a narrow road, which would soon wind through Sierra forests, she thought about last week. She'd lost security, but she'd found a Judy Ferris she could live with.

The rest was gravy.

www.ingramcontent.com/pod-product-compliance
Lightning Source LLC
Chambersburg PA
CBHW031610240626
47153CB00002B/698